The Green Man's Foe

The Green Man's Foe

Juliet E. McKenna

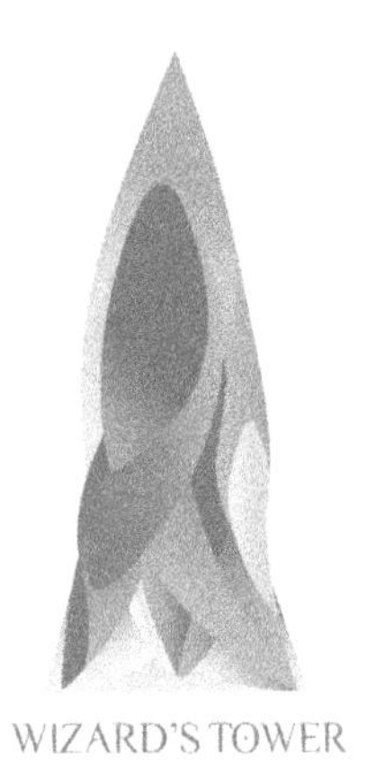

Wizard's Tower Press

Trowbridge, England

The Green Man's Foe

First edition, published in the UK August 2019
by Wizard's Tower Press

Hardcover ISBN: 978-1-908039-87-3

Cover illustration and design by Ben Baldwin
Editing by Toby Selwyn
Design by Cheryl Morgan

http://wizardstowerpress.com/
http://www.julietemckenna.com/

Contents

This story is for everyone who has read and enjoyed *The Green Man's Heir*, and shared their enthusiasm so effectively that the book has become such a success. How could I not write you wonderful people a sequel?

With apologies to Garth

Chapter One

I was standing on neatly mown grass, looking at an imposing old house with a circular sweep of gravel driveway in front of it. Two square towers with battlemented tops stood at either end of the building, framing the frontage of five pointed gables. Three were set back while two jutted forward to give the rooms on all three floors deep bay windows. The golden stone mullions and diamond-leaded panes looked to be in good repair, even in this twilight. Glancing up at the roof, I searched for signs of trouble. No immediate cause for concern. None of the mossy stone slates were missing, as far as I could see. There was no hint of the ridge line sagging, and the clusters of octagonal chimneys were standing solidly upright.

I'm a carpenter and joiner. I've worked on enough projects restoring old buildings that force of habit makes me check things like that, even in a dream. I knew I was dreaming because the Green Man was standing beside me. I could see him out of the corner of my eye, indistinct in the gathering gloom and staring up at the house like me.

I turned towards him, but in that instant, I found myself inside the house. I had no sense of moving, but I knew that was where I was without any need for explanation. This was a dream, after all. I was standing at the foot of a medical bed with steel side rails and a panel of buttons for different functions. Such modern apparatus looked incongruous in this oak-panelled room with its ornate plasterwork ceiling.

There was no sign of the Green Man, but an old, old man lay bald and skeletal beneath the drape of a cellular blanket, its corners tucked with hospital precision. His eyes were closed, and his gaunt face was waxy against the white pillows at the raised head of the bed.

It stood in the centre of the room. On one side of a high, broad fireplace behind it, a Japanese lacquer cabinet bore a tray of vials and syringes. On the other, a bookcase's shelves held rolls of cotton wool, a box of purple latex gloves and a half-used packet of incontinence pants.

Out beyond the half-open door, a soft voice spoke to someone I couldn't see. 'He is asking for you.'

If the Green Man had broken into my dreams to show me this sad scene, he must have had a reason. I looked for clues. Over by the window, I saw a battered mahogany sofa with balding olive velvet upholstery. A length of scarlet knitting was wrapped around the needles thrust into their ball of wool.

'I think so.' The voice outside the door was regretful. I realised whoever was speaking was on the phone.

Heavy brocade curtains and a tasselled pelmet framed a luminous evening sky. Through the window, the closest trees were black against the dusky blue. There was nothing to help me there.

The phone call ended and the opening door whispered across the worn carpet. The old man's eyes opened as a young blonde woman walked to the bedside. She was his nurse. That much was clear from her uniform tunic.

'Do you need anything?'

'No, thank you.'

Since it was obvious neither of them could see me, I followed the old man's gaze, wondering what he was looking at so intently. It was a wren, perched on a hazel sprig in the plasterwork ceiling. Close by the bird, I saw a face formed out of oak foliage. The shadowed eyes were lit with the merest glimmer of emerald light. I looked back at the bed as the old man coughed.

'Do you think they understand?' he demanded.

'I'm sure they do,' the nurse assured him.

I wasn't convinced, and it didn't look as if the old man was either. A crease deepened between his sparse brows.

'The house and the woods must be kept together.' Phlegm rattled in his throat.

The nurse raised his head with a gentle hand. 'They'll be here soon.' She reached for a cup with an angled straw.

'They must understand—' The old man struggled to swallow a sip of whatever was in the cup. He looked over towards three silver-framed black-and-white photographs of uniformed youths on the windowsill. Their corners were crossed with faded black ribbon. 'Thank God the boys have been spared the horrors that took my brothers. But make sure that they read my notebooks.'

'I will,' the nurse said as she laid him gently down.

The old man's eyes drifted back to the moulded twigs and leaves of the ceiling. 'Do you suppose they'll know me, when we meet again?'

'Let's hope so.' As her patient's eyes closed, the nurse returned to the sofa and switched on a lamp standing on a low table. She picked up her knitting, and her needles clicked placidly.

I watched the shallow rise and fall of the old man's chest, and wondered how much time he had left. I supposed something like this must be all in a day's work for the nurse. Though it looked like he'd lived out his full span, and then some more. This could hardly be called an untimely death.

'Nanny always knitted in the evenings.' A faint smile tugged at his withered mouth, though his eyes were still closed. 'Socks, mostly.'

A tawny owl's clipped call echoed in the woods outside the window, sharp with the urgency of the hunt. The nurse was startled into an involuntary shiver that made me jump, even though I wasn't really there.

She looked past the bed to the dark hollow of the cavernous fireplace. A brass clock stood silent on the shadowed mantel, its ornate hands motionless. I could have sworn I'd heard it ticking earlier.

The old man's breath rattled in his chest. She went to him immediately.

'She bequeathed the house to me because I understood. I knew what she had done.' His words shook with an echo of old anger. 'But I didn't know how to put it right. I should have tried harder, but now—'

Just as I was hoping he'd say something to explain why I was there, his voice failed between entreaty and regret.

The nurse slid her stethoscope under his well-worn striped pyjamas. His eyes opened at the touch of the metal on his fleshless breastbone.

'What have you seen?'

'Nothing—' She broke off as he glared at her.

'What have you heard?'

'Old houses make strange noises.' She glanced up at the ceiling. 'I thought I heard footsteps once or twice. I even went upstairs to look.' She managed a brittle laugh. 'There was only the usual dust and cobwebs. It must have been some trick of the wind in the chimneys.'

'At dusk and dawn?' His faded eyes fixed upon hers. 'What have you dreamed?'

She looked at the mantelpiece. 'Clocks. Chimes. It doesn't mean anything though. My gran had a silver carriage clock—'

'You're safe inside.' The old man's voice was the merest thread. 'The woods and the flowing waters are the boundaries. Tell the boys—'

Car tyres crunched on the gravel outside the window.

'They're here.' The nurse hurried out of the room.

The lamp on the low table over by the window flickered, as though a moth had got trapped between the bulb and the green silk shade. Out in the hallway, a heavy door opened and men's voices echoed through the dark house, taut with distress. Far away in the woods, an owl's fluting call sounded. Another answered, more reflective.

The old man's breathing grew harsher and hoarser. He drew a deep, rattling breath. Suddenly, his eyes widened. He stared straight at me, just as if he could see me. His mouth opened as if he were about to say something. Too late. He had no time left to take another breath.

I woke up, surrounded by peaceful silence. I was in my own bed, with the morning sunlight and familiar birdsong filtering through the linen curtains.

Chapter Two

I got up, had some breakfast and got ready for work. There was no point in hanging around. I had no doubt that the Green Man had something that he wanted me to do, but until he made that a damn sight clearer, I had plenty of other stuff to get on with.

Besides, the last thing I wanted to do was sit there remembering that old man's deathbed as I drank my coffee. I still felt unsettled, and I couldn't help remembering his eyes searching my face as he stared up at me in his last moments. Dreams where I see the Green Man don't fade when I wake up.

I got up from the table and put my mug and plate in the sink. Grabbing my jacket from the back of the chair, I checked the pockets for my wallet, phone and keys, and headed out.

My commute to work is short and pleasant. The old estate cottage I've been doing up at weekends and in the evenings is less than a half-hour walk from my workshop in what used to be Blithehurst Manor's old dairy. I supply the gift shop and garden centre that tempt visitors to part with some more of their disposable income after visiting the historic house. The garden centre does a good trade selling hurdles, pergolas, rustic arches and some wooden furniture, while the shop stocks my lathe-turned bowls, plates, candlesticks, egg cups and the like, along with carvings of animals and birds that I work on when I have some spare time.

It keeps me nicely busy, pays the bills with some beer money left over, and there's far less heavy lifting than I've been used to, when I've been working on building sites. After moving from place to place every six months or so for the past four or five years, I was beginning to enjoy the sensation of yes, putting down a few roots.

I use my Land Rover and take the narrow estate road when it's pissing with rain, but there wasn't a cloud in the pale blue spring sky this morning. So I took the path to the dairy yard through the woods. With any luck, walking through the trees would help me shake off that dream, for the moment at least. I've spent my life with a far closer connection to the greenwood than most. That's what happens when your mother is a dryad.

I lengthened my stride and resolutely assessed the hazel thickets now coming into leaf on either side of the path. Fifty years and more ago, these trees had been coppiced, supplying the estate with wood for all sorts of purposes. The plan when I'd moved here seven months ago was that I'd bring the woodland back into productive use. These days, a countryside business like the Blithehurst Estate needs to make all the money it can from its own resources, to end up on the right side of profit and loss.

On the other hand, as I walked, I couldn't help remembering that these particular woods were where I'd learned a whole lot more about the unseen world that I'd been born into, after my near-immortal mother and human father fell in love. A lot of very scary things.

I'd always known there were darker creatures that only people like me with wildwood blood can see, along with the delights like the rainbow sprites that love to dance with butterflies. There are stinking scavengers like boggarts, and slinking shadows like black shucks. But I hadn't imagined anything as terrifying as the wyrm that had so nearly devastated Blithehurst.

It was a mild morning, but I shivered at those memories. The wyrm was the reason the Green Man had brought me here, and I wondered uneasily what he had in mind for me now. I looked through the trees for a glimpse of Blithehurst's dryads, wondering if one of the resident trio might know something useful. Perhaps they had felt the Green Man's presence here last night. There was no sign of any of them though.

I was still trying to decide if that was a good thing or not when I reached the cluster of single-storey, brick-built outbuildings that make up the dairy yard. I'd originally come to Blithehurst hoping to learn more about dryads, since the only one I'd ever met was my mum. I'd soon learned that all those warning proverbs and folk tales about being careful what you wish for were right.

Ageless spirits of wood and water may take on human form, but their priorities are their own, and they take little account of mortal concerns. Anyone without some bond of blood, or another reason to secure their goodwill, should tread very carefully indeed and remember those fairy tale warnings about dealings with the supernatural.

Sineya, the youngest, is approachable, and friendly enough, bearing in mind that young for a dryad means she's at least a couple of hundred years old, even if she looks like a woman in her twenties.

Her mother, Asca, could pass for an elegant forty-something, and she had looked much the same when a sculptor carved a marble likeness of her for one of the ornamental temples in Blithehurst Manor's gardens, back in the 1730s. She is determined to do whatever it takes to keep the estate intact, and to safeguard the woodlands that she has cherished for hundreds of years.

The oldest dryad, Frai, looks like one of those sharp-eyed grannies with a talent for withering sarcasm, rather than one who offers comforting hugs. I've no idea how ancient she might actually be, but I had quickly discovered she was utterly ruthless when it came to protecting her trees.

Walking into the cobbled dairy yard, I saw something that drove all such thoughts out of my head. A gleaming new Audi with metallic-red paint was parked outside my workshop. As I approached, the driver got out and waved with a friendly smile. He wore a grey suit in sharp contrast to my combat trousers, Blithehurst Manor staff sweatshirt and leather jacket.

'Daniel, good to see you.'

'Ben.' I offered him my hand and we shook, by way of a greeting somewhere between friends and business acquaintances. 'What brings you here?'

Benjamin Beauchene – pronounced 'Beechen' – is an architect who lives in London, even if Blithehurst Manor is his ancestral family home, and he has shares in the trust that now preserves the property for future generations. Not that the dryads were convinced that the humans who couldn't see them could be trusted to look after their domain.

'I'm looking for a favour,' he said with a frank grin. 'Shall we head up to the restaurant for a coffee?' He gestured towards the repurposed stable buildings that stood at the top of the shallow slope by the main road.

I checked my watch. It wasn't even nine in the morning. I wondered what this favour might be, to get him here so early. 'They'll still be setting up before opening to the public. If you don't mind instant, I can do that here.'

'Fine by me,' he said obligingly.

I found the heavy key and unlocked the door. 'How are things with you?'

I didn't look at him as I asked, to give him the chance to ignore the question if he wanted to. How do you ask someone how they are coping, less than a year after their brother died? Not that Ben knew what had really happened. His sister Eleanor is the only one of the Beauchene family who can see the dryads like me. So she's the only one who knows the gruesome truth about last summer.

'I'm fine,' he said a little stiffly. 'I stayed with Mum and Dad last night. They're... doing okay.'

I heard the bleep of the central locking as he pressed his key fob.

'Good to know.' I pushed the door open and stepped aside to usher him in. 'I'll get the kettle on.'

Ben went ahead of me into the workshop. He had to duck his head under the low lintel. Like me, he's over six foot tall, thanks to the dryad blood that Asca's son had brought into the Beauchene family line. Ben's skinnier than me though, and Eleanor always said he was born to wear Italian suits. I'm built like the proverbial brick shithouse.

He cleared his throat. 'This looks different.'

'Got everything I need.' I crossed the battered tiled floor to the deep, old-fashioned sink in the corner. 'Take a seat.'

One of the first things I'd done was fit cupboards and a worktop along this wall. After I'd scraped the flaking white-wash off the walls and given the whole place a new coat of paint. After the estate's preferred electrical contractor and I had worked out how to get a new mains supply installed, and we'd ripped out and replaced the potentially lethal 1930s wiring.

I filled the kettle and switched it on. There were mugs on the draining board, and jars of coffee and sugar by the microwave. 'White, no sugar, isn't it?'

As I glanced over my shoulder, I saw Ben was sitting at the old oak table I'd found in the manor's cellars and brought over here, along with a selection of mismatched chairs. He was opening a briefcase that he'd taken out of the car.

He looked up and smiled. 'That's right.'

I still had most of a pint of milk in the fridge. I made two coffees and carried them over to the table. 'What's this favour, then?'

Ben pushed his briefcase down the table and opened up a folder with the logo of the firm he worked for on the front. He took out a photo. 'This is Brightwell House.'

I managed not to spill the coffees as I recognised the place from my dream. The Green Man wasn't wasting any time.

'Okay.' I put the mugs down carefully.

'Built in 1605, on the site of an earlier house,' Ben said briskly. 'Owned by the Sutton family ever since, until they died out in the 1950s. It was left to Cecil Franklin, who was some sort of cousin or nephew of the last owner. He never had children of his own, so his brother's grandsons inherited it when he died last year.'

So I guessed that's who the Green Man had shown me on his deathbed. I picked up the photo and studied it. 'What are they going to do with the place?'

'Turn it into a hotel. The Franklins, our clients, already run a pheasant shoot in the woods that belong to the house. So that's where we came in. You can see it's got great potential.' Ben took a handful of architect's drawings out of the folder.

I recognised plumbing plans and wiring diagrams. 'Where is it?'

'Just outside Bourton under Ashes, in the Cotswolds. A real tourist hotspot.' Ben managed not to sound too envious.

Blithehurst is just inside Staffordshire, close by the Derbyshire border. Eleanor had told me how often visitors told her they were so glad they'd finally decided to stop and explore the area. They'd always thought how lovely the local countryside was as they drove through it on the way to somewhere else, like the Peak District or the Yorkshire Dales, or the Cotswolds, if they were heading south.

'So that's, what, about two and a half hours' drive from here?'

Ben nodded. 'Maybe three, depending on the traffic around Birmingham.'

Less than an hour from the little nature reserve where my parents live, on the Oxfordshire-Warwickshire border. My dad used to volunteer there, and that's how he'd met my mum. He's been the resident warden since he retired from his factory job.

'So there's woodwork needs doing?' The panelling I'd seen in my dream had looked in good enough repair. 'There must be carpenters closer than me.'

'There's more to it than that.' Ben offered me a disarming smile. The dryad blood in the Beauchene family may have thinned in the last seven generations since Asca's son was born, but they still have more than their fair share of charm.

I'm only one generation away from the greenwood. I'm immune. 'I thought there might be.'

'We need a project manager.' Ben picked up his mug and took a swallow. 'Someone to live on-site, keep an eye on things, liaise with the local tradesmen.'

He was telling the truth. Dryads don't lie, and they can always tell when they're being lied to. My mother's blood means I generally get an inkling when someone's lying to me. Ben wasn't telling the whole truth though.

'Go on,' I prompted.

He leaned back in his chair and spread his hands in honest exasperation. 'We've employed two people so far, and they've both walked off the job. The Franklins wanted to recruit someone who would be managing the hotel when it opens and get them in right at the start of the project. That way, they'd know the place inside out from day one, and we'd get the benefit of their hotel-management experience as everything was being set up.'

'That idea hasn't worked out?' I wondered if that was the Green Man's doing. I still had no idea why he wanted me in the Cotswolds.

Ben grimaced. 'It seems hotel managers are used to being with lots of people. Being on their own in a big empty house in the depths of the country freaks them out. Our second choice only lasted a night before she was on the train back to London.'

'So you're looking for someone who's used to living alone, miles from anywhere?' I grinned at him.

'And someone who knows his way around old buildings and woodwork.' He leaned forward, his elbows on the table. 'Someone who won't take any crap from suppliers or be given the runaround by workmen on-site.'

I acknowledged that with a nod. Since I'd come to Blithehurst, I'd helped out with renovations on a couple of the properties the family trust owned and rented out. Ben knew all about that.

'Three-month contract.' He hesitated. 'Six at the most. Good money.'

A year ago, I'd have snatched the job out of his hand, no question. Now I raised a hand to stop him. 'I work for Eleanor,' I pointed out. 'The tourist season's already started, and after Easter, business here will really take off.' And that was the weekend after next.

'Haven't you spent the whole winter making stock for the shop?' Ben gestured at the other half of the wide, airy room.

My tools were racked on the pegboard that I'd fitted to the opposite wall. There was a place for everything, and everything was in its place, the way my dad had taught me. Below that was the long, grooved wooden shelf, where long ago dairy maids had left shallow pans of milk for skimming cream and making cheese. I'd turned it into a work bench with a couple of vices and a solidly fixed table saw at one end and my safety goggles and other personal protective gear at the other. The second-hand lathe that I'd tracked down in Derby stood close by, ready for use.

In between, plastic crates were stacked high with the things I'd made over the cold, wet months. I'd happily worked long days in here, warmly snug thanks to a wood-burning stove that I'd salvaged from one of the other outbuildings. I wondered if Ben had been trying a few other doors in the yard while he'd been waiting for me to arrive this morning. If he'd been peering through the windows, he'd have seen still more woodwork waiting for buyers.

'We don't know how fast things will sell, or which lines will be the bestsellers.' I drank my coffee. 'We don't want to run out of something if we find there's real demand for it.'

'So you can come back at weekends, or for a few days' leave, to restock.'

There was an edge of desperation in Ben's voice. I have to admit, that did intrigue me.

'Just come down to take a look at the place,' he pleaded. 'We really need to get the project moving, and I honestly can't think of anyone better than you.'

I wondered how much of that urgency was some instinct stirred by his dryad ancestry. Then there was my dream last night to consider. I had learned the hard way that the Green Man didn't like being ignored.

'I'll talk to Eleanor.' I raised a warning hand. 'No promises.'

'Great.' Ben's relief was obvious. He took a pen from an inside pocket and scribbled on the front of the Brightwell folder. 'That's my mobile, and my email. Let me know a good time for you to visit. Later this week, if you can?'

I nodded, still non-committal. There were potential complications I needed to discuss with Eleanor that I couldn't explain to Ben.

'Okay.' He finished his coffee. 'Well, I'll let you get on. Do call me if you've got any questions.' He tapped the folder before reaching down for his briefcase and standing up. 'Any questions at all.'

'I will.' I walked with him to the door. 'Are you heading back to London today?'

'I am.' He already had his car keys in his hand. 'Talk to you soon.'

'Have a good journey.' I stood in the entrance and watched as he drove his expensive red car carefully over the uneven cobbles and out of the yard.

I wasn't the only one watching. Blithehurst's oldest dryad, Frai, was standing over in the corner where the path through the woods arrived between two of the outbuildings. As Ben's car disappeared, she appeared at my side inside the blink of an eye.

When they want to, dryads can appear as mortal women, so convincingly that no one without greenwood blood will ever suspect they're not what they seem. My mum masquer-aded successfully as a human mother from my birth until I left school. Granted, the fact that my dad's cottage was a good mile and a half outside the village helped.

Since there was no one else to see her here, Frai didn't bother to manifest in modern clothing. 'What did the boy want?' she demanded.

The old dryad was wrapped in draped-and-tucked folds like some painting from ancient history. She favoured au-tumn shades, and her eyes, without white or pupil, were the vivid copper of winter beech leaves. The green skin of her exposed arms and her face had the seamed roughness of birch bark and a greyish tinge.

'Just estate business,' I said, off-hand.

Frai looked towards the estate road that Ben had followed as he drove away. 'Has he any intention of taking a wife?' Her tone was acid.

What she really wanted to know was if Ben was likely to father any children any time soon, and she didn't give a toss whether he was married to their mother or not. At the moment, Eleanor was the only Beauchene able to see the dryads. Frai was increasingly desperate to see who might have that two-edged gift in the family's next generation.

Unfortunately for her, Ben was concentrating on his career, and their sister, Sophie, was a solicitor in Manchester doing the same. The other brother, Robert, had been more involved in Blithehurst, managing the estate's farmland, but he was dead. Their father had been forced to set his retirement aside until the family could find a suitable new land agent.

'I've no idea what's going on in his personal life,' I said neutrally.

Frai scowled at me and disappeared.

I reminded myself not to take it personally. What Frai really wanted was for me and Eleanor to have some children together, but that wasn't going to happen. When we first met, I'd found she was someone I could like and respect, and facing last summer's dangers had certainly created a bond between us. Even without that, I reckoned we'd be good friends, but there wasn't a spark of sexual attraction.

Not that romance mattered to Frai. She was simply concerned with keeping Blithehurst in the Beauchene family, ideally with at least a few people who could be intimidated into doing the dryads' bidding. But the days were long gone when supernatural beings could dominate mortals with the simple, unnerving fact of their presence.

Though dryads can still make life very uncomfortable for anyone who crosses them. It had been funny when I was a kid to see the trivial bad luck that had plagued a local dog walker who repeatedly ignored my mother's requests to keep his untrained Jack Russell on a lead on the public footpath running through the nature reserve.

It wasn't so amusing to learn that Frai and Asca had been determined to keep Eleanor on the Blithehurst estate, even though they knew managing the house as a tourist attraction wasn't what she wanted out of life. Every time she tried to leave, her car's electrics died before she was more than a mile away. My presence here was the only reason they'd finally agreed to let her go back to Durham University, to study for the PhD she had her heart set on. Not that having a steady job, paying a token rent and living and working in such a nice place was any hardship for me.

So I needed to talk to Eleanor before I made any decisions about this job offer from Ben. I went back into the workshop and got my jacket. I locked up and walked up to the Blithehurst Manor car park, restaurant, gift shop and garden centre.

As I'd said to Ben, the staff were busy getting ready to open up for the day. I exchanged a few hellos. I'd made a couple of friends here, and was on good terms with everyone else, so I could always find company when I wanted to go out for a beer or a curry. Equally, I had my own space and solitude when I preferred to be on my own, in my cottage in the woods.

I walked through the restaurant and waved to Janice, the manager, who was busy behind the hot-food counter. Like the other sides of the business, the restaurant did a good trade with tourists, as well as drawing in regular local customers who had no interest in visiting the manor house itself. Eleanor's passion might be medieval history, but she was still damn good at running a commercial enterprise. The systems she had set up here kept everything ticking over smoothly between her monthly visits.

'Just checking emails.' There was no chance of a 3G – let alone 4G – mobile phone signal down at my cottage, and running a landline into the woods would cost an arm and a leg, so this was a regular routine for me.

'Right.' Janice nodded with a friendly smile and went back to writing the day's specials on the little chalk boards for each table.

I punched in the code to open the lock on the 'Staff Only' door. Thankfully, the room was empty. I sat at the communal desk, switched on the computer and quickly logged on to the Blithehurst network, but that was only for show. What I really wanted was the phone.

Dryads can see and hear all sorts of things that we mortals can't. After my dad's transistor radio first prompted my mum's curiosity while he worked in the woods, she soon learned how to pick her own choice of listening out of thin air. When mobile phones came along, she quickly worked out how to join in with my regular calls home. Eleanor and I had no idea if Blithehurst's dryads could do the same, and we weren't about to ask and give them ideas. If there was something we needed to keep between us, we discussed it over a landline.

I reached for the phone and rang the house in Durham that Eleanor shared with two other postgraduates. With any luck, I'd catch her before she headed out to the library, or wherever she was working on her thesis today.

'Hello?' a bright, cheerful voice answered.

Emma? Amy? I had kept both women at arm's length ever since they had each made a determined pass at me on a weekend visit. Dryads' sons share their mothers' allure, and that's not always the advantage you might think. In this case, causing trouble between Eleanor and her housemates definitely came under the heading of 'don't shit where you eat', as far as I was concerned.

I played it safe, brief and business-like. 'Is Eleanor there? It's Daniel Mackmain. I need a quick word.'

'Just a moment.' The handset was put down with a muted clunk, and I heard distant voices.

Eleanor picked up a few moments later. 'Hi, Dan. What can I do for you?' She sounded more curious than concerned.

'Have you got time for a chat? I had an interesting visit from Ben this morning.' I explained about the Brightwell House project.

'I can see why he thought of you.' Eleanor sounded mildly irritated all the same.

'There's more.' Keeping an eye on the door in case anyone came in, I quickly told her about my dream.

'Oh.' Eleanor doesn't have my ties to the Green Man, but she's seen him for herself and has some inkling of his power. 'Do you have any idea if...'

She hesitated. Emma or Amy must have been within earshot. I could hear voices outside the staffroom door as well.

'I saw the old lady this morning. She didn't seem to know anything about him visiting me.'

I've never managed to fathom the relationship between dryads and the Green Man. They live out their centuries-long lives alongside the trees they have chosen to care for, enjoying sex, and sometimes longer relationships, with those few humans they decide to trust. He is a freer spirit, travelling from woodland to woodland, as untouchable and unpredictable as the wind. They have dealings with each other from time to time, certainly when it's to their mutual advantage, but only they know what determines some shared interest.

'Right.' Eleanor paused. 'I wonder if this has anything to do with last summer's... trouble.'

The 'trouble' that had killed Robert Beauchene.

'That's what I was wondering.'

I waited until she spoke again.

'You had better go down there and see what you can find out.'

Chapter Three

Next Wednesday, I took the motorway south, then A roads, and finally I had a long, straight run along a ridge of high ground. Old toll houses told me this had once been a coaching road, and I reckoned this route went back long enough to have been part of the Romans' Fosse Way.

Just after eleven, by the Land Rover's dashboard clock, I saw a left-hand fork signposted to Bourton, Aylworth and Ashgrove. That last village was where Ben had told me Brightwell's new owner, Edmund Franklin, lived. As I hit the indicator and followed the road down into the valley, I soon found Bourton under Ashes.

Sheep grazed in fields to either side, overlooked by a handful of industrial units that marked the edge of the town. Sunlight glanced off parked cars, bright against the dark glass walls of two modern office buildings. Brown-tiled roofs appeared, and I passed a yellow-brick school matching a new housing estate on the other side of the road.

The High Street had the same mix of shops as everywhere else in the country. As I slowed for traffic lights in the town centre, though, I saw that what had once been some Victorian factory was now boasting freshly cleaned stonework and new windows with discreet cream blinds. A sign announced that The Old Silk Mill was now luxurious modern apartments. I wondered how much those sold for. More than most locals could afford, most likely. Country retreats for London commuters.

The lights changed, and I glanced at the satnav. I needed to go over the railway bridge and then follow Market Hill down to the river. Passing the railway station, I saw a hospital built with the same robust Victorian confidence as that old mill, though the grounds had long since been surrendered to white buildings striped with blue signs.

The tree-lined street heading down the valley looked much more like the Cotswolds we've all seen on postcards. Though judging by the stacked brass plates, these golden stone houses had long since been turned into offices or dentists' surgeries.

Heading down towards the river was like travelling back in time. The tall Georgian frontages with sash windows gave way to seventeenth and sixteenth-century buildings that had been converted into antique shops and tea rooms and other businesses for the tourist trade. By the time I reached level ground, a long medieval building claimed the middle of the street. The upper floor was raised up on thick stone pillars, making the whole lower storey an open arcade. That had been a market hall in days gone by, whatever it was used for now.

The road divided into two lanes to go around it, and I stopped looking at the architecture to pay attention to the slowly circulating cars and muddy four-wheel-drives vying for parking spaces. Anyone hitting my Land Rover would come off second best, but I really didn't need the hassle of an insurance claim.

Once I was past the market hall, I admired a truly spectacular medieval church overlooking the river. I had plenty of time for that, since I had to wait at another set of lights to cross a narrow, hump-backed bridge that was only wide enough for traffic in one direction at a time. The church was to the right of the bridge, and I could see a broad swathe of playing fields running down to the water over to the left.

So far, so picturesque. Once I was over the bridge and turning right into the lane where the satnav was directing me, I was much less impressed.

I drove past a sprawl of 1930s pebble-dashed, semi-detached houses that curved around a scrubby patch of grass where a breeze-block bus shelter was covered in spray-painted slogans. Unravelling wire fences divided untended gardens. One had a dented Toyota with mismatched wings parked beside a rusted Transit van. Defunct Christmas lights trailed from a gable where blocked guttering had overflowed to stain the wall. On the other side of the lane, allotments running down to the river were a wasteland of tangled brambles dotted with derelict sheds, some of them half burned down.

Not what wealthy guests coming by train and taxi would want to see on their way to a luxury, secluded hotel. Well, that wasn't my problem, and besides, things improved as I followed the curve of the lane.

Daffodils nodded on steep banks below hedges thickening with pale green leaves. I passed a long, low farmhouse with a gravel yard. A russet-painted corrugated-iron barn separated it from a row of four stone cottages at right angles to the road, on the uphill side from the river. Shirts flapped on a washing line in one of the gardens, though there was no sign of life apart from that. Next came a squat little church with a stubby tower. Two aged hawthorns were bright with blossom among the gravestones that surrounded it.

I slowed as I approached two tall holly trees guarding a gateway in the low stone wall opposite the church. According to the satnav, I was here. Turning into the gravelled driveway, I recognised Brightwell House.

A burly man in a dark overcoat was checking his watch beside a blue BMW. That was okay. I wasn't late. I was supposed to be here at half past, and I had time to spare. I parked my Land Rover and got out.

'Edmund Franklin?' I tried to keep the doubt out of my voice, but he didn't look like a farmer to me. Then again, my dad always says you never see a farmer on a bike.

'That's my brother. Something came up. I'm David Franklin.' There was only the barest hint of a local accent in his voice.

I guessed he was in his late forties. A head shorter than me, he was broad shouldered, with the thick neck I generally associate with rugger players. Not a man to get on the wrong side of, on the pitch or in the office, I guessed. Whatever his job might be, that suit and the car didn't come cheap.

'Good to meet you, Daniel.' His handshake was firm. 'Let me show you around. I'll tell you what we want to do here, and you can ask whatever questions you might have. We'll see where that leaves us.'

'Okay.' I followed him up the short flight of steps rising between the two bay windows.

A glazed oak door on the left-hand side mimicked the stonework. Franklin unlocked it to reveal a porch with potted plants clustered on the sills and on dirty plastic crates beneath them. He didn't seem to notice the sour, earthy scent. As he opened an inner door to reveal a flagstoned passage panelled with dark wood, I took a last breath of the crisp, clean air outside and followed.

A warning beep pierced the stillness. Franklin pressed a panel that looked exactly the same as the others. It sprang forward to reveal a hidden cupboard housing a modern alarm-system control box. After entering a code, he walked through one of three arches in an oak screen garlanded with carved leaves. 'The house still has lots of medieval features. This screen is original, and the great hall's pretty much untouched.'

That was one way of putting it. I didn't think this vast room rising through the full height of two storeys had seen a duster or a hoover for decades. There were a couple of battered chairs with splintering cane on a threadbare carpet, and a long case clock stood against the screen. Dull panelling to head height needed a damn good polish, and ominous cracks threaded through the expanse of grimy plaster above it. Smoke stains left dark smudges over a fireplace where some medieval lord could have roasted an ox. I couldn't help thinking how different this was to Blithehurst. That had been a cherished family home for generations, and was still full of life and charm.

'As you see, the house is a hollow square.' Franklin nodded towards tall windows framing the fireplace, matching those in the front wall. 'Our great-uncle Cecil lived here until last summer. He was a hundred and seven years old when he died, can you believe it? He had no children of his own, so the estate came to me and my brother.'

I wondered if Cecil had been a dryad's son. We're as mortal as the next man, but we do tend to be hardy, and very long-lived. I looked at the portraits hanging high up on the discoloured plaster, but they were so dirty I couldn't make out any faces.

'You want to open the house up as a hotel?' I tried not to sound too incredulous.

'You've seen the woodland on your way here?' Franklin walked across the flagstones to a shallow wooden dais at the far end of the hall. 'That's all the Brightwell estate. We run a commercial shoot, so we want to offer the guns a place to stay instead of putting them up in local pubs.'

I supposed that made sense, but how much work would this conversion take? I looked at the seats in the windowed bay at the end of the dais, twin to the one housing the entrance. Tapestry cushions were tufted with horsehair as the stuffing poked out of holes. This place must be overrun with mice.

'You're not anti blood sports?' David Franklin turned, his face hardening. 'If you are, there's not much point us going any further.'

'No,' I said mildly.

My dad has plenty to say about the negative impact on the countryside of rearing birds as brainless as pheasants just for rich people to shoot them, but I reckoned this wasn't the time to discuss that.

Franklin opened a door to reveal a smaller room panelled with lighter wood. The windows on two walls showed we'd reached the end of the house.

'This is the walnut parlour. Aunt Constance's sitting room.' He indicated a black-and-white photograph on a glass-fronted cabinet, showing an elderly woman sitting stiff-backed in an open car. 'She was a Sutton, a cousin of Uncle Cecil's mother. She left the house to him because her only son, Arthur, was killed in the First World War.'

Between her cloche hat and her coat's thick fur collar, the woman's eyes looked as hard as some poisoner's in an Agatha Christie drama. More black-and-white photographs were clustered on the sideboard. Edwardian women stood on the house's front steps in their finest hats. Men with bristling whiskers posed behind heaps of slaughtered pheasants.

I didn't go into the room, for fear of knocking something over. A shabby chintz sofa was flanked by little tables crowded with porcelain figurines. They were thick with dust, and a silver tea service was darkly tarnished.

Franklin scowled. 'This was supposed to be cleared out by now.'

I couldn't let him do all the talking. 'It won't take long.' Not with a couple of skips outside the front door.

He grunted and pointed to a painting above the grey marble fireplace. 'That's Uncle Cecil.'

A young man was sitting on a bench in front of a creeper-clad wall. With unruly fair hair and a long, hollow-eyed face, he looked nothing like David Franklin. He didn't look as if he had dryad blood either, and I can usually tell.

Franklin shut the door and headed for the back of the house. 'There were four brothers on the Franklin side of the family. The two eldest, Albert and Harold, died at Verdun and Amiens, leaving our grandad to inherit Ashgrove. That's on the other side of town, where my brother lives now. Uncle Cecil was something of a late surprise, by all accounts. When Constance finally gave up hope of Arthur coming home, she left Brightwell to him. Grandad and Cecil farmed the Brightwell tillage along with Ashgrove. Ed takes care of that now.'

We passed an imposing staircase that showed me that's what the towers at each end of the house were for. Franklin pushed open a heavy door to reveal a room as large as the great hall, though half the height. I'd lived in smaller flats.

'This is the grand parlour.' He wrinkled his nose. 'The whole place needs a damn good airing.'

He was right, but a gorgeous white marble fireplace relieved the darkness of the room's oak panelling with garlands of leaves and swags of flowers that reflected the intricate plasterwork overhead.

'That ceiling's amazing.' I searched the foliage for any hint of the Green Man's presence. No such luck.

'Georgian.' Franklin headed for a door on the other side of a massive table draped with dust sheets.

Movement on the floor snagged my eye. A mouse? No, it was only a dried flower disturbed by the draft. I stooped down to pick it up. Frail and translucent, the papery bell might once have been blue. I wondered what it was doing there.

Franklin had gone through the door and found a light switch. 'The Suttons used this drawing room as a day nursery, but Uncle Cecil moved a lot of stuff down from the library when the stairs got too much for him. We're going to use them both as dining rooms.' He gestured back towards the grand parlour.

I went over to look into another cluttered room that ran along the back of the house, counterpart to the great hall at the front. Wooden shutters on the windows were closed, so there was no natural light, and the light fittings on the walls only had dim fake-candle bulbs. Not that there was any reason to go in for a closer look.

Ugly modern shelving units leaned against the panelling. They were crammed with books, and all sorts of clutter, while two flaking leather armchairs were heaped with newspapers. Closer to the window, a fountain pen lay across a clotted glass inkwell on a leather-topped kneehole desk. A half-written page tucked into the corner of the blotter made it seem that Uncle Cecil expected to be back at any moment.

Franklin shook his head, his expression unreadable. 'Let's see what you make of upstairs.'

I followed him back out of the parlour and up the grandiose stairs. Reaching a narrow landing, Franklin opened a door to show more heavy furniture swathed in dust sheets. 'These bedrooms haven't been used for years, but they'll clean up well enough.'

We walked along the corridor that ran in a U shape around this floor, with windows overlooking the mossy courtyard at the heart of the house. As Franklin opened successive doors, I saw that the bedrooms had views looking outwards to the gardens and the woods beyond.

Something occurred to me. 'This must be a listed building?'

'Grade two.' Franklin was unconcerned. 'We've been through everything with the planning people. The Suttons did extensive alterations before there were any regulations to stop them, putting in dressing rooms which will be ideal for bathrooms. They had the panelling to work with, so you can't even see the joins. Old Aunt Constance's father, John, had political ambitions, and plans for hosting house parties with the rich and powerful. Luckily he lost all his money before he could ruin the place.

He continued walking. I followed him around the next corner and came face to face with a display case of stuffed birds, where a mangy ferret glared at me with baleful glass eyes. Those could go straight in the skip. I also noted the old-fashioned round light switches. 'What about the wiring?'

'We're getting everything renewed,' Franklin assured me.

Now that we had reached the far side of the building, I saw that a wrought-iron elevator had been installed some time ago in the hollow centre of the plain servants' staircase in this tower. 'Does that work?'

'I don't know that I'd trust it at the moment,' Franklin admitted. 'But we'll get it serviced and updated if necessary.'

He led the way up to the topmost floor and opened one of the doors at the front of the house. 'These were originally the maids' rooms, but they'll be fine for guests when they're done, according to our architect.'

I hoped Ben Beauchene hadn't promised more than he could deliver. I wouldn't want to be in his shoes if David Franklin wasn't happy.

These must have been servants' dormitories back in the house's heyday. I walked past a solitary iron bedstead to look out of the window under the gable. Bourton under Ashes was further away than I had realised. I could only just see the distant rooftops climbing the hill on the far side of the valley. In between, the river twisted, disappearing between bulbous banks of dull green turf to reappear bright in tree-lined hollows. Slicks of recent rain glistened in the water meadows.

What I still couldn't see was any reason why the Green Man wanted me here.

'Come and look at this.' Franklin had gone to open a door on the other side of the stairs.

I did as I was told, and halted on the threshold, genuinely impressed. A vast room took up the entire rear of this top floor, running the full width of the house. There were wide windows on all three sides, with the wall space between them filled with glass-fronted bookcases. Eleanor Beauchene would love to browse that haphazard collection of ancient leather tomes, cloth-bound books and even the tattered paperbacks. A magnificent stone fireplace dominated the inner wall, with heraldic shields carved on either side. The coats of arms were repeated in the patterns of the arched plaster ceiling.

'This was the medieval gallery before John Sutton's grandfather turned it into a library.' Franklin looked around, with an unexpected grin softening his expression. 'We used to play up here when we were kids.'

Above the bookcases, and beneath the moulded plaster wheat sheaves, old-fashioned portraits of prize sheep and pigs alternated with what I guessed were pictures of Brightwell House through the ages. One archaic painting showed a medieval hall isolated in the middle of dense woods. An engraving ornamented with curlicues and flourishes showed the current house surrounded by formal gardens that must be lost beneath the lawns.

I walked slowly along the room, looking out through the unshuttered windows. The views were magnificent, all the way to the countryside far beyond the dark sprawl of the trees that lay beyond the garden's well-tended flowerbeds.

'We'll make this a private lounge, with its own bar, for residents.' Franklin turned around, clearly picturing what he had planned. 'The restaurant downstairs will be open to the public, and we're not only relying on the shoot for trade. We're close enough to Stratford-upon-Avon for people who want to take in some Shakespeare while they're on a country house retreat. American tourists will love that. Then there are the races at Cheltenham, and that's within easy reach. We'll also promote the place as a venue for small, specialist conferences or management strategy meetings during the week. Outside peak season, we'll offer weekend breaks for people looking to get out of London or Birmingham.'

'That's a solid business plan,' I agreed.

Whatever David Franklin did while he was leaving his brother to run the family farm, I reckoned he earned his top-of-the-range BMW and that status-symbol watch.

'Is there anything else you want to see?' He checked the time again. 'There's the kitchen, and the cellar floor, but that's a disaster area at the moment. We've got to rip everything out and start again, fit proper cold stores, pantries, the lot. At least there's plenty of space.'

And plenty of money to invest, by the sound of things. I raised a hand though. 'I'm a carpenter, not a plumber.'

'We've got a specialist firm lined up for the kitchens, and a local firm to fit the bathrooms, and redecorate,' Franklin said. 'What we want from you is a thorough check of all the panelling, the roof timbers, the stairs, anything made of wood, basically. Make sure nothing nasty's lurking where we can't see it. There's plenty of loose moulding that wants fixing, and dents and scrapes to make good.'

'I can do that.' I had already seen that several glass-fronted bookcases needed some skilled attention. 'And you want me to live on-site?'

'Let me show you the housekeeper's flat.' Franklin headed out and down the servants' stairs, and I dutifully followed.

Back on the ground floor, he opened a door in the corner of the house that was diagonally opposite the walnut parlour. Windows in two walls looked out over the gardens. 'The sitting room.'

'Okay.' It seemed clean enough, and at least the small two-seater sofa and coffee table were from the 1980s, not the 1880s. The black-leaded fireplace was Victorian, but it was disfigured by an ugly little electric fire sitting in the grate.

Franklin threw another door opposite to reveal a small bedroom overlooking the central courtyard. 'En-suite's through there.' He pointed to a door on the far side of the single bed, before walking on towards the front of the house. 'Don't worry. There's an old toilet out in the garage for Geoff Kemble's men to use.'

He opened another door just before we got back to the carved wooden screen that separated the great hall from this corridor. 'Here's the kitchen.'

It was small, but I was pleasantly surprised to see modern units and a wall-mounted boiler, along with a washing machine, a fridge and a white-enamelled compact cooker. There wasn't a window, and I realised whatever room had been here originally had been split in two with a new stud-and-plasterboard wall. This half by the corridor was now the kitchen. The other half overlooking the inner courtyard must be the en-suite bathroom that opened off the bedroom.

'We converted the butler's pantry, and put this in for the nurse who lived with Uncle Cecil,' Franklin explained. 'She stayed with him till the end.'

For the first time, he hesitated. 'He died in the house. It's what he wanted. He was born at Brightwell, when his mother was visiting and they got snowed in. If you're afraid of ghosts, there are supposed to be at least two others here.'

I shrugged. 'Doesn't bother me.'

'There are going to be deliveries to sign for, and a lot of different people coming in and out,' he continued briskly.

'We want someone on-site to keep an eye on everything. There's been a spate of local break-ins lately. Thefts from isolated houses, sheds and garages, that sort of thing.'

'I'm guessing there'll be some interest in this project from your neighbours down the lane?' I jerked my head in the direction of the rundown pebble-dashed houses. 'Just having someone in the house should stop anyone getting ideas.'

Certainly seeing someone my size on the premises should give an opportunist thief second thoughts. That went without saying.

'Better safe than sorry.' Franklin checked his watch again. 'Is there anything else you want to know? If not, I could really do with getting back to London before the traffic gets stupid. With the schools on their Easter holidays...'

I didn't envy him that drive. 'I've seen everything I need to, thanks. If I think of anything else, I can always ring Ben Beauchene. Is there anything you want to ask me?'

I braced myself. I had expected this to be rather more of an interview. I definitely expected some extremely awkward questions about the police investigation I'd got mixed up in, back in Derbyshire. David Franklin struck me as a man who'd check any prospective employee's background before considering them for a job.

He surprised me with another smile. 'I work in the City, so I know exactly how far from the truth tabloid-newspaper bullshit can be. You were never charged with anything, and no reporter had more on you than biased assumptions. The police caught the monster responsible, and he's in Broadmoor, isn't he?'

I nodded, though to be strictly accurate, the man the monster had sent mad and used as a tool was locked up. I'd had to destroy the monster myself, and it had done its best to kill me.

David Franklin was still talking. 'Ben vouches for your work, and he says his sister only employs the best. That's a good enough reference for me. That, and we need someone in here as soon as possible, if this hotel is going to open for this year's pheasant shooting in October. We don't have time to piss about.'

'Good to know,' I said, relieved. 'Okay, you get on your way. I'll find a pub for a late lunch before I head back.'

'The Boar's Head in town is always good.' Franklin was all business again. 'Okay. Think it over, talk to the Beauchenes, and let us know your decision as soon as you can.' He gestured towards the door. 'You go on out first and I'll set the alarm and lock up.'

I went out through the plant-crammed porch and sat in the Land Rover, seeing if the satnav could find The Boar's Head. Franklin waved briefly as he headed for his own car and drove away.

I found the pub on the screen. It was close by the market hall, which was apparently the local museum and tourist information office these days. Fingers crossed, I'd be able to park. I would have looked to see if the pub had a website, but I discovered there was no mobile phone signal. Well, I was used to living with that.

Turning the Land Rover around, I drove slowly out between the holly trees. I wasn't sure how much visibility there was along this lane, and I didn't want to lose a headlight to some local doing fifty because they thought Brightwell House was empty.

I could see the road was clear to the right. I was about to check to the left when movement straight ahead caught my eye.

Looking through the windscreen, I saw a man standing motionless in the churchyard. His lank hair brushed the epaulettes of his army-surplus greatcoat, and the olive-drab colour blended into the browns and greens of the yew trees whose branches hung over the lane.

The ground around the graves was a good deal higher than the tarmac. High enough for me to clearly see that the man had his fly open and was taking a piss against the stone retaining wall. He could see that I was watching him, and he didn't give a fuck. Taking his time, he finished, zipped up and sauntered away towards the ancient church.

I was trying to decide if I should go after the dirty bastard, in case he was going to try to break into the little church, when the holly tree by the Land Rover's door rattled furiously in a gust of wind. Startled, I looked around.

The Green Man was standing right there beside my window. He looked as ferocious as I had ever seen him, eyes blazing with emerald rage. Whoever that bloke pissing on someone's grave might be, I realised he was the reason the Green Man wanted me here.

Chapter Four

I was back at Brightwell the Monday following the Easter bank holiday weekend. Eleanor and I had agreed I'd sign a three-month contract, much to Ben Beauchene's relief. This time, as I drove through the gateway, a burly man with thin grey hair and a weather-beaten face appeared through a gap in the beech hedge that ran along the edge of the lawn to my left. Shallow stone-slated roofs beyond indicated what I guessed had once been a stable yard.

'Mr Mackmain, is it?' The man tucked secateurs into a baggy corduroy pocket. He wore two old hand-knitted sweaters, blue wool showing through the holes unravelling in the red one. 'Mr Edmund'll be here any time now.' His accent was thoroughly local.

'Daniel. Call me Dan.' I offered my hand.

He shook it, his calloused palm damp with soil. 'Bill Delly. Gardener.'

'Good to meet you.'

As I spoke, a Range Rover turned in between the holly trees. The driver threw open his door as he hauled on the handbrake. 'Sorry, sorry. I meant to be here ten minutes ago. I tell you, never have kids!'

'Edmund Franklin?' I didn't really need to ask, given the family resemblance to his brother. 'I'm Dan Mackmain.'

'Good to meet you. And I'm Ed, please.' He wore faded jeans and a much-washed rugby shirt beneath a green waxed jacket, and his handshake was as calloused as Bill Delly's. Expensive education was apparent in his voice, like David's. I guessed he was a few years younger than his brother, a bit taller and a bit leaner.

He dug in a coat pocket and produced a bunch of keys bristling with paper tags. 'Nicki, my wife, she's labelled everything. This is the one for the porch.' He freed it from a strand of orange twine. 'Care to do the honours? You'd better get used to the locks. They can be tricky.'

'Thank you.' Despite his warning, I opened the door easily enough, and was pleased to see that the plants had been cleared out of the porch.

Motes of dust sparkled in the sunlight as I opened the inner door, and the alarm made its presence known.

'I'd better get that.' Ed Franklin slid past me to thump the panelling and open the hidden cupboard. 'The alarm code's 1673.' He phrased it like a date.

'The year Mary Anne Sutton was wed,' Bill commented.

'One of Brightwell's resident ghosts.' Unconcerned, Ed punched the buttons. 'Not that Dave or I've ever seen her.' He threw open the closest door, directly opposite the arches in the great hall's screen. 'This is the oak parlour. We've been using it as an office.'

A gate-leg table with two wooden chairs was set beneath the window. A couple of wire filing trays held note pads, builders merchants' catalogues, pencils and biros beside a stack of red and blue plastic folders. An old-fashioned push-button phone stood on an empty mahogany bookcase, its cream wire trailing over to the skirting board.

'The chaps from Kemble and Coates will be starting work on Wednesday, so that gives you a day or so to settle in.' Ed sat, gesturing for me to do the same. 'Let me show you what's happening first.'

I took my jacket off and sat in the other chair, trying to look as if I didn't recognise the room. That wasn't easy. I had seen it in my dream. This was where old Uncle Cecil had died.

Ed Franklin was unfolding an architect's plan. 'We're starting at the top and working down.'

I tried to pay attention to his detailed explanations. That wasn't easy either. I wanted to look up at the plasterwork frieze around the edge of the ceiling, to search for some sign of the Green Man's presence.

'I've told Geoff Kemble to give you a ring tomorrow morning.' Ed nodded towards the outdated phone. 'That's the only landline at the moment,' he added, apologetic, 'and if we try to run an extension off it, as soon as we plug in more than one handset, nothing works. Oh, and there's no telly.'

'That's not a problem.' I rarely watched TV.

'Dave's organising broadband and cable,' he assured me. 'Can't run a hotel on one dodgy phone line.'

I could just hear David Franklin saying that. I'd bet he was working on solving the mobile-reception problem as well.

'Cup of tea?' Bill appeared in the doorway carrying a tin tray with two steaming mugs. Delicate silver tongs balanced incongruously on a crystal dish of sugar lumps.

'Yes, please. Say thanks to your mum for us.' Edmund took the tray and set it on the table. As Bill disappeared, he grinned, dropping three lumps of sugar into one of the mugs. 'You'll be meeting Martha Delly soon enough. She was born in the cottage down the lane where the two of them still live. That whole row belongs to Brightwell, and we'll be using the other cottages for staff housing. Anyway, Martha started working in the house as a maid when she was twelve. She knows endless old stories about this place.'

'That'll be interesting.' I hoped she'd have something to say that could give me a clue about why I was here.

I reached for the other mug. The tea was the colour of London brick, and strong enough to strip paint, with the unmistakable tang of tinned evaporated milk.

Ed didn't seem bothered as he took a good swallow and reached for a bright blue folder. 'The plumbing's the biggest job, so Mark Coates will be doing the pipework first. That means you'll need to take up the floorboards and deal with the panelling.'

I forced myself to concentrate on the practicalities of the job as he went on with his explanations. Finally Ed indicated where the trench for a new waste pipe would be dug, through the stretch of grass on the far side of the other hedge, on the opposite side of the house to the stables.

'They brought the mains services up here when they put the Broad on the sewer,' he explained.

'The what?' I queried.

'You saw those council houses down the lane?' Ed gestured at the diamond-paned window. 'Back in the way back when, this side of the river was the parish of Bourton Abroad, and the town parish was Bourton Within. Uncle Cecil knew all about the history of it. I expect his notebooks are still around somewhere.'

As grief momentarily shadowed his eyes, I remembered my dream. I remembered the dying man insisting that his heirs must read those notes. I had no idea how I was supposed to make that happen.

'Anyway, now those houses are just called the Broad by everyone around here,' Ed went on briskly.

Bill Delly reappeared in the doorway. 'I'll get off now. It's time for my dinner.'

'Hell, is it lunch time already?' Franklin checked a silver pocket watch as the gardener left. 'Sorry, I've got to see a man about the late lambing. Look, have a read through all this once you've unpacked and ring me with any questions.'

He stood up and rummaged through the filing tray to find a sheet neatly printed with different names and numbers. 'This is us, Ashgrove Farm, house and farm office numbers, and that's Dave's home and office in London. Rufus Stanlake is our gamekeeper. He lives at the Home Farm house, back down the lane by the estate cottages.'

'Thanks.' I got to my feet.

'Come for dinner, sometime soon,' Ed invited. 'Better talk to Nicki, though. She keeps the family calendar.'

'I'll ring her.' I followed him to the front door.

He nodded at the panel hiding the alarm box. '1673.'

'Got it,' I assured him.

I watched him get into his Range Rover and drive away. That wasn't the latest shiny new model like his brother's BMW, I noted. I also wondered if David Franklin's habit of checking his watch was prompted by his brother's habitual lateness.

I went down the steps and got my holdall and rucksack out of the Land Rover. I travel light as a rule, and this was only going to be a short stay. Once I'd dumped my stuff on the narrow bed, I went back out and fetched my toolboxes. I put those in that corner sitting room, tucked under a small dining table with angular wooden chairs that had appeared from somewhere to join the two-seater sofa.

It was cold, but I didn't put the electric fire on. I'd rather have a real fire, so I had better remember to check when the chimneys were last swept, if I wanted to get rid of that eyesore. Come to that, I probably should start a list of things I needed to ask.

But there were other things I wanted to do first. Pleased to find keys for the housekeeper's sitting room, and for the bedroom opposite, I locked both doors. If workmen were going to be going in and out of here all day once work started, I didn't want anyone borrowing my tools.

I guessed they'd need to use the housekeeper's kitchen though, if the basement level of the house was the disaster David Franklin had said it was. Opening the cupboards showed me I was probably right. There was a catering tin of instant coffee, a big bag of tea bags and a large box of sugar lumps alongside a dozen supermarket basics mugs. Another cupboard had four dinner plates, four side plates and four bowls on a shelf above a four-pack of baked beans, two tins of corned beef, six eggs, ketchup, salt, pepper and a loaf of sliced white bread. There was butter, bacon and two pints of milk in the fridge. Someone's idea of emergency supplies. I wouldn't starve if I didn't get to a supermarket today.

In that case, I decided to see what I could learn from a walk around outside before I went into the town in search of lunch. I fetched my jacket from the office. This time, I did take my time studying the plaster foliage along the tops of the walls, and found several wrens and squirrels hidden among the twigs. What I didn't find was any sign of the Green Man. I couldn't even see the face that I could swear had been there in the leaves in my dream.

Maybe he'd show himself in the woods. I set the alarm, locked up and went down the stone steps at the front of the house. As I headed for the gap in the hedge, I saw a set of steps running down to what must be the basement kitchen door at the side of the house.

On the far side of the hedge, I found I'd guessed right about the outbuildings. They flanked a cobbled yard and had the double doors of old stables and carriage houses. Small dormer windows in the shallow roofs indicated rooms for grooms to sleep above the horses. I saw three wheelie bins in one corner, one each for garden waste, recycling and landfill rubbish, as well as a smaller bin for food waste. There was a lingering smell of oil, though there was no sign of any vehicles.

A padlocked gate in the boundary wall opened onto the lane. I checked for a key and found one labelled 'garage yard gate', and made a mental note to ask if the Franklins wanted me to park my Land Rover around here instead of on the gravel at the front of the house.

I saw a door with a sign saying 'Gardener – Private', so that must be Bill Delly's domain. There was also a key labelled 'garage toilets', and I found that opened the door closest to the path from the house.

The walls and floor were green-tiled, a plastic crate by the door held an eighteen-pack of bog roll, and there was a strong smell of bleach. Three stalls had old-fashioned lavatories, with wooden seats, high-level tanks and dangling chains. They faced three wash basins on the opposite wall below a high, barred window. I didn't envy those long-ago stable lads coming down here in the middle of a winter night, but I was very pleased to see that this project was going to manage without portable toilets. I hate those things.

There was nothing else to see, so I locked up, walked back and went past the kitchen door to the rear of the house. Borders of mulched black earth framed a shallow grassy terrace. Below that, a broad, flat lawn stretched out to meet flower beds bright with tulips, daffodils and white hyacinths clustered beneath well-pruned shrubs coming into leaf. Bill Delly certainly knew what he was doing.

A weathered iron fence separated the gardens from the woodland beyond. I recalled the black iron fence at Blithehurst. That had been there to keep the dryads, and other, scarier things, well away from the house. Maybe I'd find some answers beyond this barrier here.

I found a gate with squealing hinges and walked over the less rigorously tended grass to the trees. I waited for a moment, to see if anyone, or anything, would appear to see who I was and what I was doing.

Nothing happened, so I decided to see what was on the far side of the house, on the land further down the lane where I hadn't driven so far. I headed for the largest gap between two gnarled oak trees, their branches still bare despite the warm weather. As I walked on, my boots stirred last autumn's leaves, too sodden to crackle, pungent with decay.

It wasn't long before I was making another mental note for that list for the Franklins. They needed to get someone in here to do some serious clearance. For the fourth time, I found that what looked like a path dead-ended in yet another snarl of brambles. Trying a different route, I ended up surrounded by holly bushes. There was a hell of a lot of work to be done if they expected to offer their hotel guests scenic woodland walks.

Backtracking and skirting around, I stepped on a patch of ground that looked no different from the rest. My foot sank to mid-shin in a hidden hollow, and I nearly lost my balance.

'Fucking hell!' I could have broken my sodding leg.

I struggled to pull my boot free without my other foot sliding into the same hole. I realised that I'd stepped into a narrow gully choked with leaf mould. When I did get my foot out, the leather and laces of my boot were black and stinking.

I would probably have sworn some more, but shrill barking cut short any further profanity. Startled, I looked around. Dog walkers? More barking echoed through the trees. Not dogs, I realised, now that the shock of nearly wrecking my ankle was subsiding. Belatedly, I recognised the sound. Muntjac deer.

Still, that made me think of something else as my pounding heart rate slowed. Dog owners keep to public footpaths, by and large. This land was private property, but there was every chance there were rights of way over Brightwell land. Presumably there'd be records of those back at the house, and walkers generally keep paths like that clear. I'd be much better off finding a map before coming out here again.

Of course, I had to get back to the house to find something like that. I decided I'd cut through these woods to the lane and follow that back, rather than try retracing my steps. I had no idea what other hidden gullies might be buried under these dead leaves, and spraining an ankle, or worse, out here didn't bear thinking about. I'd have to make my way back to the house, however badly I got injured, because no one knew I was out here.

Fine, but which way was the bloody lane? I was disconcerted to realise that I'd completely lost my bearings. That was an unwelcome, and unfamiliar, sensation. I'm a dryad's son. I don't get lost in fucking woods. I looked up, but the sky was clouding over, and in any case, these old oak trees were crowded far too close together to give me a clear view of the sun.

I took a moment to get a grip on myself, closed my eyes and took a deep breath. My sense of direction returned, and I began walking in what I fervently hoped was the right way. If it wasn't, well, presumably I'd hit the river, and at least that would give me something to follow, all the way back to those abandoned allotments if necessary.

I wanted to hurry, but I forced myself to go slowly. Picking up a dead branch, I tested the ground ahead of me before I trusted my weight to every next step. I was glad I did when the wood hit rusted metal links. I scraped away the leaves and undergrowth to follow a staked chain to an old trap for foxes or badgers. It was the kind that's been illegal for years, with iron jaws that snap shut to leave a maimed animal dying in slow agony.

At least there was no danger of that now. Decades of rain and frost had blunted its vicious teeth and a hawthorn sapling was growing through it, with the young tree's roots firmly anchoring the bar in the middle. All the same, I was glad I hadn't tripped over the sodding chain, or worse, the metal stake, even if my tetanus shots were up to date.

The insidious smell of rot grew stronger. I saw a fallen silver birch crusted with shell-like fungus. Darker lumps blistered a log smothered by moss while creamy brackets bled rusty streaks down a beech tree's flank. That wasn't what I was smelling, though. This was something far more ominous than the natural woodland processes of decay.

I gagged as a fugitive gust of wind suddenly hit me with a far more rancid odour. As I walked on, increasingly uneasy, I found a clearing around a single barren blackthorn tree. Dead crows were skewered on its spikes. Some were swollen with rot, and a few were visibly crawling with maggots. Feathers and vile stains littered the ground beneath them.

I clamped a hand over my nose and mouth. A gamekeeper's gibbet? I remembered Dad telling me how they used to kill anything that threatened their precious pheasants and hang the corpses on fences or trees, back in the olden days.

In the olden days? How much had things at Brightwell changed since those Edwardian slaughters? So much for modern country sportsmen actually being all for conservation. I wondered if the Franklins knew about this, or if it was – what was his name – Rufus Something's doing?

I'm not squeamish, but there was no way I was going near that disgusting thing. I skirted the clearing, heading away to the left. I walked as quickly as I dared, even though the undergrowth snatched at my boots and branches lashed at my face as I forced a path through the trees.

The edge of the woodland caught me unawares. I stumbled into a strip of field scarred with a track close to the trees where rainwater glinted in narrow wheel ruts. Away to my right, I saw the sparkling waters of the river. The sky had cleared, and the sun was shining again.

Okay. I breathed more easily. Standing with my back to the river, I saw what had to be the lane that went past Brightwell House. It curved around to head away from the water, with an impressive expanse of woodland on the far side and well-kept farmland on this side, beyond the hedge that bounded the field where I was standing.

This field was not well-kept land. The grass was uneven and tussocky, and a dirty cream caravan was squatting where the rutted track coming up from the river met the lane. Green algae stained the caravan's sides, and blankets were nailed up inside to cloak the windows. A dented metal dustbin stood by the padlocked door, its upturned lid weighted with stones. A few paces away, a recent fire had burned a black scar into the ground. I saw scorched, empty tins amid the ashes.

This was something else to ask the Franklins about. Though perhaps it wasn't on their property, I realised. I really did need to find a map of this place. And of course, even if these squatters, or travellers, or whoever they might be, were on Brightwell land, getting this eyesore towed away wasn't going to be particularly quick, legally speaking, or easy, in practical terms. There was no sign that a car had been parked here recently, and thick weeds were tangled around the caravan's flat tyres.

For the moment, I decided this wasn't my problem, and that I'd had enough of exploring. I'd get back to the house, clean my boots and go into Bourton to find a supermarket and stock up for the next few days. I headed up to the lane, turned left and began walking along the tarmac, making sure to keep to the right-hand side of the road so I would be facing any oncoming traffic.

I reckoned I was about halfway back to the holly trees guarding the gate when the sound of motorbike engines shattered the woodland silence. I tried to work out where they were, because the lane was empty. There was a wooden fingerpost a short distance ahead on this side of the road. I couldn't read what it said, but a gap in the trees indicated a route through the woods. That's where those bikes must be coming from.

I stood still as two riders appeared at the junction with the fingerpost. They barely slowed as they turned the corner. Their bikes' engines were roaring as they accelerated towards me. Anonymous behind tinted visors, they swept past me, coming so close that I could have shoved them off their saddles, if I'd been stupid enough to be provoked into trying it.

'Did you get their fucking number plates?' A man appeared by the fingerpost. His heaving chest showed he'd been running, though he wasn't out of breath.

Wiry build, wiry red hair, and wearing clothes for working outdoors, whoever he was, he wasn't the man I'd seen in the churchyard.

He was scowling at me like I'd done something wrong. I wasn't going to react. He had firm hold of a braided leather dog lead, and one of the biggest Golden Retrievers I've ever seen looked at me with agate eyes as unfriendly as its master's. I'd have backed myself in a fight with its owner, since he was five feet ten at most, but I wouldn't want to take on that dog.

'For fuck's sake, did you get their plates?' the man demanded again. 'We can't set the coppers on the pricks if we can't give them the details!'

'I'll remember that for next time.' I began walking again, looking calmly past the rude bastard and away down the lane.

As I drew closer, the Retriever pressed against the man's thigh with a menacing growl. Its dark lips drew back from sizeable teeth.

'Quiet, Bess,' he said sharply, before some belated realisation hit him. 'Oh, fuck. You've come to do the woodwork at Brightwell, haven't you?'

I stopped walking, still keeping my distance from the dog. 'That's right. Dan Mackmain.'

'Shit. Sorry.' The man offered a hand. 'I'm Rufus Stanlake.'

'The gamekeeper.' I took a cautious step forward. Since the dog didn't bite my hand off, I shook his. 'Bloody hell, what's that?'

Now I was close enough, I saw a mangled animal carcass lying at the foot of the fingerpost.

'Roe buck, hit by some fucking car last night.' Regret coloured Stanlake's tone before his voice hardened. 'He was lucky not to get it through his fucking windscreen. Those wankers and their fucking motorbikes scare the animals out of their fucking wits.'

'If I see them again, I will try to get their plates.' That was as much as I was going to offer him.

'Fair enough.' He nodded and turned around, stooping to take hold of the dead deer's least mangled leg. He walked away into the woods, dragging the roadkill behind him.

I told myself firmly that none of this was my problem. Except, as I walked on, I realised that I might well have to deal with the abrasive gamekeeper, if whatever the Green Man wanted me to do took me into those woods. That wasn't an appealing prospect.

I looked from side to side, searching the trees that flanked the lane for any sign of some supernatural presence, for any hint of a reason why I was here, but I still didn't have a clue by the time I arrived at the house.

What I did hear, as I walked up the steps, was the phone ringing inside the office. I hurried to find the key and get inside. As I opened the alarm cupboard and punched in the code, I kept expecting the caller to give up. But the phone was still ringing when I snatched up the receiver.

'Hello? Daniel? It's Nicki Franklin.'

'Hi.' I tried to catch my breath. 'Sorry, I was outside.'

'I guessed you must be.' The friendly voice was amused. 'The sooner David gets a new line installed and some extensions around the place, the better. Anyway, I was ringing to see if you wanted to come over this evening? Rufus needs to talk to Ed about the pheasants, and I was thinking he could give you a lift. It won't be anything fancy, just supper with the kids, but you're very welcome?' She left the question hanging in the air.

I'd been planning on going out to The Boar's Head. When I'd had lunch there on my first visit, I'd found the food was good, the local beers were interesting, and there was a steady phone signal, so I could ring my dad. I'd told him about Brightwell House, and he and Mum were as curious as I was to find out what the Green Man wanted from me.

'Or not, if you fancy a quiet night in,' Nicki continued easily.

'No, I'd love to come over,' I said politely. I might as well meet her sooner rather than later, and it wouldn't hurt to know a bit more about the gamekeeper.

'Great. I'll tell Rufus to call for you around six. It won't be a late night,' Nicki added. 'School for the kids tomorrow.'

'Right.' I nodded.

'Till later then.' She ended the call.

Okay, I'd better get moving, if I was going to get to the shops and get a bit more settled in by then. I looked down at my feet. And I had better clean my filthy boots.

Chapter Five

My Land Rover's nowhere near new, but it's been well treated and well maintained. The battered blue Defender that pulled up outside Brightwell at ten to six looked as if it had been bought second-hand in a war zone.

I'd been waiting in the office, studying the plans for the plumbing and hoping that the Green Man might make his presence known. No such luck. I put down the plans and went to set the alarm, and the warning beep followed me out until I locked the front door.

'Thanks for giving me a lift,' I said as I opened the passenger door.

Rufus Stanlake just grunted. Maybe he took a while to get to know people. I could relate to that. On the other hand, maybe he was just a surly git.

The Defender's floor was thick with mud, and black gaffer tape mended several splits in the creased seat. At least the seat was clean, which was a relief as I was wearing my good jeans and a decent shirt. I noticed Stanlake was looking fairly presentable as well.

He started the engine and snapped on the headlights, though it was nowhere near dusk. As we started moving, I realised the dog, Bess, was right behind me. The Retriever huffed noisily through the wire mesh that separated us, sniffing at the back of my neck. Out of the corner of my eye, I saw Stanlake's lip curl with amusement.

I bit down on a sharp comment and checked my mobile instead. It would be worth knowing how far I'd have to walk to get a decent phone signal. Stanlake could say something to me if he wanted a conversation.

We passed the cottages and the farmhouse where Stanlake lived. As we rounded the bend, I suddenly got a phone connection. Just then, Stanlake changed gear with a shove and accelerated. We were approaching the depressing houses of the Broad, and I saw a gang of teenage lads kicking a football around on the lane, using the graffiti-covered bus shelter for a goal.

Rufus didn't slow down. The boys scattered onto the rutted grass or into the abandoned allotments. One of them kicked the football hard, unerring, and it slammed into the back of the Defender. Bess retaliated with deafening barking.

As Stanlake drove on, I used the wing mirror on my side to see the teenagers reclaim the lane. They were making obscene gestures and doubtless swearing at us with meaningless bravado, though I couldn't hear anything over the furious dog.

I raised my voice. 'Are any of those the idiots who go riding those bikes in the woods?'

'Bess, quiet!'

The dog subsided.

I waited for an answer.

'I don't think so,' he finally said as we reached the traffic lights at the bridge.

I waited for something more. The lights changed and we crossed the river.

'I'm keeping an eye on those little bastards regardless,' Stanlake went on ominously as we drove past the market hall. 'The ones from the Broad. Make sure you always set the alarm, and lock your Landy.'

'I will.' I also decided I'd keep on parking at the front of the house, until I was told different. I didn't like the idea of leaving my vehicle out of sight in the stable yard.

Since Stanlake didn't have anything else to say, I looked out of the window to see what Bourton under Ashes might have to offer. As he took a side road running past the secondary school, I was pleased to spot an Indian takeaway and a Thai. Civilisation.

We left the town and drove for another ten minutes before turning off at a sign that said 'Ashgrove Farm. Private Road.' A hundred yards down a gravelled lane, I saw a substantial farmhouse, far more elegant than Brightwell's Home Farm, with a collection of barns and workshops beyond it.

Rufus yanked on the handbrake as we pulled up between Ed Franklin's Range Rover and a compact blue hatchback. A dark-haired girl of eleven or so came running out of the farmhouse, wearing wellies beneath her school-uniform skirt.

'Bessie! Bessie!'

'Hannah.' Stanlake opened his door. 'Ed and Nicki's youngest.'

With the dog's enthusiastic barking deafening me again, I was thankful to get out of the Defender.

'Come on, Bessie, come and see your mummy.' Hannah opened the back door and the Retriever jumped down to fawn around her. 'That's all right, isn't it, Rufus?'

As the gamekeeper shrugged, the girl looked at me, bright-eyed. 'You're Dan. Hello, I'm Hannah.'

'Hello,' I said cautiously. I've never had much to do with kids.

'See you later. Come on, Bessie.' With a perfunctory wave, the girl ran off, the dog frisking at her side.

I followed Rufus towards the house. He didn't volunteer any more information about the Franklin family. He also didn't knock before pushing open the back door to reveal a tiled lobby. Discarded boots jostled dog bowls beneath a deep stone sink, and Rufus sat on a bench beneath pegs hung with waterproofs and anoraks.

A woman opened an inner door. 'Come on in. Good to meet you, Daniel. You don't need to take your boots off unless they're really muddy.'

'Thanks.' I recognised Nicki Franklin's voice from the phone. She was about the same age as her husband, and her dark hair was threaded with silver. She wore it cut short, as practical as her black trousers and green sweater.

'Is Ed in the office?' Rufus looked up from unlacing his own filthy boots.

'He is, and you tell him dinner's nearly ready,' Nicki warned. 'Dan, come on through.'

Once Rufus vacated the bench, I sat down to take off my boots. Following him through the door, I found that the sizeable kitchen was straight out of some Sunday newspaper's magazine, with lime-washed cabinets, a quarry-tiled floor and an eight-burner steel cooker. Though it wouldn't be ready for a photo shoot until the piles of letters, newspapers and other clutter were cleared off the dresser. Hessian shopping bags had been tossed into a corner by the two-door fridge-freezer, and half-built Lego robots were spread across the pine table.

'You can pour us each a glass of that.' Nicki nodded towards a bottle of red wine standing beside a corkscrew. 'Sit down. I've only got to mash the spuds.'

As she drained an enormous pan into the sink, I opened the wine with the corkscrew I found ready and waiting.

Nicki set the pan down and cut a hefty chunk of butter from an earthenware dish. 'So, did Rufus say more than ten words on the drive over?' She nodded towards the door he'd disappeared through into the hall. 'Not counting the swearing?'

'Hard to say.' I poured wine into two glasses and took a sip. Not expensive by what I'd come to learn were Beauchene standards, when Eleanor and I combined our monthly business meetings with going out for a steak. It wasn't a supermarket special offer either, though.

'Don't let his manner put you off.' Nicki began mashing the potatoes. 'He's not too bad when you get to know him.'

I nodded, non-committal. 'Has he worked at Brightwell long?'

'Since he left Marlborough.' The potatoes were rapidly yielding. Nicki Franklin was solidly built. 'His eldest brother was in the same class as Ed. That's how we know the family.'

'Right.' I nodded again.

'As you've gathered,' Nicki continued drily, 'Rufus isn't really a people person.'

I took another sip of wine. 'He certainly doesn't get on with the local teenagers.'

'The ones from the Broad?' Nicki crossed to the door on the other side of the kitchen to shout up the stairs. 'Josh, come and lay the table!'

She went to fetch plates from the dishwasher. 'They're just bored most of the time. That's what causes the mischief. There's nothing for teenagers to do around here if they haven't got any money, and there are barely any buses to take them further afield.'

She put the plates down. 'Thirty years ago the Silk Mill was still making ribbons that sold all over the world. Twenty years ago, there was still the meat-processing plant and a couple of other middling-size factories. Now there's nothing to offer a practical job with some training for sixteen-year-old school leavers without much by way of qualifications. Once upon a time, a lot of them would have gone to work on the farms, but that life's long gone, and our true-blue Tory MP would rather drum up support for restoring his constituents' human rights to hunt foxes instead of fighting for grants to tackle rural poverty.'

'Practising your council election speech again?' Ed Franklin came in from the hall. Rufus was close behind him.

'Something like that,' Nicki said. 'Get the serving bowls out, please. Rufus, did you remember those receipts?'

The gamekeeper nodded. 'I put them in the office.'

'Dan, sorry, I should have said this morning.' Opening a high cupboard, Ed looked around at me. 'Nicki'll sort you out with a petty cash box before you go. Give her your receipts and she'll put everything through the books.'

'I'm Brightwell's accountant.' Nicki took a patterned bowl from Ed. 'And Ashgrove's and for a couple of other farms and businesses. Don't let this domestic goddess stuff fool you.' She opened the oven, releasing an appetising smell. 'Ed, get Josh down here. Rufus, take those plates through, please, and the glasses.'

As Rufus obediently picked up the crockery, a teenage boy came down the stairs and loitered in the doorway to the hall. He was maybe sixteen years old, with bristles amid his inevitable spots, and unmistakably a Franklin.

'Can I take my dinner upstairs? I want to finish my level and my team won't—'

'After you've eaten with the rest of us.' Nicki silenced him with a raised hand. 'As long as your homework's done. Get the knives and forks out, please, and don't forget the serving spoons.'

Jaw jutting mutinously, the lad crossed to the cutlery drawer in the dresser.

'This is Dan, who's come to manage the Brightwell conversion for us,' Ed told the boy.

'Hello,' Josh muttered as he found mustard, salt and pepper on the shelf of the dresser.

'Nice to meet you.' I had no idea what else to say.

'Hi, I'm Natasha.' Slender and leggy, a girl who I guessed was a sixth-former drifted in through the open door to the hall. 'What's for tea, Mum?' She had her mother's dark hair with her father's height.

'Pork and pears.' Nicki drained another saucepan into the sink amid a cloud of steam. 'Help set the table, please.'

'Looks like it's done.' Natasha leaned against a cupboard. 'Mum, Iz Oxway says her mum's dating someone.'

'That's no one's business but Jude's, and Isobel should know better than to gossip.' Nicki poured carrots and peas into the second serving dish. 'Go and put out all the heat-proof mats, then give Hannah a shout, and tell her to wash her hands after playing with the dogs.'

'That really was shit, what happened to Mr Oxway.' Josh scowled as he returned to find a bottle of ketchup in a kitchen cupboard.

'It was,' Nicki said crisply, 'but you'd show more respect if you could say so without swearing. Take these through, Tash.'

'Yes, but it was.' Natasha picked up the vegetable dish, somehow managing to convey an air of doing her mother a favour as she followed her father, who was carrying the potatoes.

'What are we talking about?' Hannah appeared in the hall, her face lively with curiosity.

'Mr Oxway.' Josh pushed past her. 'Weren't you listening in assembly?'

'Behave, the pair of you. Simon Oxway was an English teacher at the secondary school, killed in a car accident three years ago this week,' Nicki explained to me as she took a wide glass dish out of the oven. 'They've just announced an essay competition in his memory, with a prize at speech day.

Right, we're ready to eat. Bring the wine, please, Dan. Josh, find the apple juice.'

'He was in a head-on with a tree. Swerved to avoid someone, according to the skid marks. That's what the police said, anyway. Probably some tosser of a drunk driver who'd already lost his licence.' Out in the hall, Stanlake rested his hands on Josh's shoulders to stop him getting in his mother's way. 'They should string up the c—clowns.'

I noted that the gamekeeper cleaned up his language as well as his appearance around Nicki Franklin and her children. I picked up the wine bottle and followed everyone through to a comfortable dining room. Nicki was already dishing up pork chops slowly cooked with pears and garlic. It smelled wonderful.

There was one empty chair left, and it was opposite Natasha. The last thing I needed was the Franklin's older daughter getting a crush on me, so I looked past her to the bookcase against the wall. There were multiple titles by Andrew Taylor, Val McDermid and Michael Connelly. Someone in the Franklin household was keen on crime novels.

'If you see something you'd like to borrow, just say.' Nicki passed me a generous plate. 'I don't imagine you'll find anything recent or readable at Brightwell. Help yourself to veg.'

'Thanks.' I avoided Natasha's gaze as I took some mashed potato. Nicki Franklin wasn't going to see me showing any interest in her daughter.

'Judith Oxway runs the bookshop by the church. Shayler's,' Nicki went on. 'New and second-hand, well worth a look if you're passing.'

'Or you'll meet her when she comes to catalogue the books at Brightwell,' added Ed. 'We're not going to sell them, necessarily, but we should know what's there, at the very least for the insurance.'

Natasha took that as her cue. 'Dad, Isobel was saying—'

'Tash, if your mother doesn't want to hear it, what makes you think that I do?' Ed asked with faint exasperation.

As Natasha scowled at her plate, I saw Hannah grinning at her sister's embarrassment. She saw me glance at her and stared back, unabashed. 'Is this Grumpy or Greedy for tea, Mum?' she asked innocently.

'Fussy, though I don't know why you ask.' Nicki shot a warning look at her youngest.

I knew exactly what Hannah wanted. To see how the visitor might react to eating meat that had once had a name. Maybe the Green Man had nothing to do with those hotel-management types from London leaving.

'Whatever this pig was called, it's very tasty.' I continued eating. Being taunted by an eleven-year-old was nothing compared to some of the tricks that get played on newcomers to building sites.

Conversation about the children's schoolwork went back and forth across the table, with what seemed like a fair amount of rivalry between Hannah and Natasha. Josh ate in silence.

I concentrated on my meal. I have no idea how brothers and sisters are supposed to work. I'm an only child, and so was my dad, and he was nearly fifty when I was born. The last of my mother's sisters moved away from our woods some time during the Napoleonic Wars, so I've never had aunts or uncles or cousins either.

I've never missed what I never knew, and since meeting Eleanor, I'd come to appreciate how much simpler that had made my life. I can't keep track of all the various Beauchenes on their sprawling family tree, and I've never had Eleanor's problems, when she's had to explain away the things she's been doing to keep the dryads happy. My family is just me, Mum and Dad. We get on fine with each other, and we have no secrets. At least, no important ones.

'I'm doing biology, maths, statistics and chemistry,' Natasha told me, though I had only asked her to pass the pepper. 'I'm going to the Royal Agricultural College in Cirencester to study rural land management.' She seemed confident that getting the required grades posed no problem.

'Did you go to university, Dan?' Nicki asked casually, though I could tell she was interested in knowing more about me.

I supposed that wasn't so unreasonable if she was going to invite me into her home. I swallowed my mouthful and nodded. 'Glasgow, to study earth sciences, but I only did a year.' I shrugged. 'It just wasn't for me.'

Across the table, Natasha looked unimpressed, and I had no problem with that, if it made me less attractive in her eyes. Josh looked up from his plate with unexpected interest, but before he could say anything, Hannah spoke up.

'Josh can't make up his mind what he wants to do.' Her innocent air didn't fool anyone.

Beside her, Josh went red and glowered. Before he could retaliate, Rufus Stanlake chipped in.

'Have you seen Dave's new car, Ed? It looks like a real stump-puller to me.'

Ed seized on this new topic of conversation, and Josh joined in, looking a lot happier to be discussing torque and horsepower and the merits of two-door versus four-door models.

My opinion of Stanlake went up a few notches, and I joined in on his side when Ed and Josh argued in favour of Range Rovers over Land Rovers. Out of the corner of my eye, I could see Natasha looking increasingly bored, and that was also fine with me.

Once everyone had finished eating, Hannah was told to clear the plates and load the dishwasher. Nicki countered her protests with the unarguable fact that the other two had laid the table. Natasha sauntered out towards the kitchen with a serving dish in each hand, and Josh followed, muttering about homework, though I soon heard faint noises of alien mayhem from somewhere overhead.

'Coffee?' Ed got up from his seat at the head of the table.

'I'm fine.' Stanlake looked at me. 'But if you want some?'

I took the hint. 'I'm happy to head back if you've got things to do. Thanks very much for dinner,' I said to the Franklins as everyone stood up.

'I'll fetch you that cash box and a receipt book.' Nicki went out into the hall.

Stanlake followed, whistling, and as I went after him, three dogs appeared from what I guessed was the living room.

'Let's get you two fed.' Ed Franklin patted the older of the resident Retrievers, and the dogs followed him into the kitchen.

By the time Stanlake and I had got our boots on, Nicki had returned with the promised cash box, its key in the lock with a dangling plastic tag.

'There's a hundred quid float in there, and the book,' she said as she handed it over. 'Excuse me, I need to see to the kids.'

'Okay, thanks.'

'Ready to go?' Stanlake asked from the back door.

'Fine with me. Thanks again,' I said to Ed Franklin as I passed him in the boot room.

'See you soon.' He sketched a wave with the dog-food spoon.

A security light snapped on as we went outside to the Defender. Stanlake opened the back, and Bess jumped in. We drove back to Brightwell without either of us feeling the need to say anything.

Some teenagers were still hanging around by the bus shelter as we drove past the Broad houses. It was hard to tell how many of them there were in the dusk, as the closest street light wasn't working. I could see the pinprick flare of cigarettes in the gloom, and I wondered what they were smoking. Whatever it was, all I could smell was warm dog. At least no one threw anything at us as we drove past.

As we approached the farmhouse, I realised Stanlake wasn't slowing down. 'You can stop at home,' I told him. 'I'll walk the rest of the way.'

'Okay.' He braked and changed gear, swerving smoothly onto the gravel beside the russet barn.

'Thanks for the lift,' I said as I got out.

'See you around.' He went to let the dog out of the back.

The two of them headed for the farmhouse door without a backward glance, so I began walking along the lane. There was no street lighting, and the windows of all but the closest cottage at the end of the row were dark.

I felt a breeze on the back of my neck and my instincts stirred. Not fear, not even apprehension, but some sort of heightened awareness. Something, or someone, was telling me I needed to stay alert. I crossed the lane as quietly as I could and walked along the grassy verge by the Brightwell wall, to avoid any sound of my boots on the tarmac.

A silent owl flew overhead as a cat padded out of the cottage gardens, slinking across the lane like a grey-and-white shadow. It brushed against my legs, head questing upward for a scratch behind the ears. Once I had obliged, it went about its night's hunting.

By the time I drew level with the church, my eyes were fully accustomed to the darkness, and as a dryad's son, my night vision is better than anyone else's I've ever known. I halted as I saw movement in the churchyard.

A lean figure was walking slowly between the graves. He traced the time-worn writing of one memorial with a forefinger before going a little further on and sinking to his knees. It had to be that man who'd stirred the Green Man's anger. I had no doubt of that.

I couldn't see what he was doing though, so I fixed the place in my mind as best I could. I'd come back in the daylight and see if I could work out what the bastard was up to.

He got up and strode away, towards the church. I walked a bit further along the lane until I was standing by the closest holly tree, hidden in its dark shadow. Now that unexpected instinct was telling me to wait.

The man soon reappeared, coming down the churchyard path to the lych-gate. Far more modern than the church, though at least a hundred years old, it had a pointed roof raised on four pillars. Inside the gates opening onto the lane, the pillars supported stone ledges for coffins, one on either side of the path as the dead halted here on their last journey to be buried.

The man in the greatcoat jumped over the wall instead of using the gate. He'd gone widdershins around the church, I realised: counter-clockwise. All the folklore I'd ever read said that was either bad luck or something done with malicious intent.

I stood motionless, tightening my grip on the cashbox. I couldn't see how he could fail to see me. Well, if he wanted to make anything of it, I was ready.

Either he didn't see me, or he ignored me again. He went striding away down the lane with his long coat flapping around heavy, noisy boots. I followed, cautious and silent, sticking to the grassy verge.

He passed the fingerpost without slowing and carried on to the bend in the lane. As he turned down the rutted track that led to the river, I crossed the tarmac as quietly as I could and stopped beneath an oak tree, where I had a good view of that shabby caravan.

I'd guessed right. I watched him find some keys and unlock the padlock. He opened the door and went inside. The door closed, and a few minutes later, faint yellow light showed around the edge of the blanket that shrouded the window.

I waited and watched for a little longer, but the bastard didn't reappear. As I walked slowly back to the house, I checked behind me after every third or fourth step. By the time I reached the holly trees, I was satisfied I was alone.

Quickly unlocking the door, I went in and unset the alarm before going back to lock up again. Going in to the office, I turned on the light and put the cash box underneath a heap of paint catalogues in one of the wire filing trays. I'd need to find somewhere more secure for that tomorrow. Then I found some paper and made a list of things to do first thing in the morning.

Find out more about the alarm. I wanted to know if there were motion sensors in the house or if the system was linked to the doors and windows. If that was the case, I could set it when I was in here on my own, and good luck to anyone trying to break in.

Go and see if I could work out what the sneaky bastard had been doing in the churchyard.

Ask Ed Franklin what he knew about that field by the bend in the lane, and how he planned to get rid of that caravan.

Then I made myself a mug of tea, read my book for an hour or so and went to bed. I expected to have a restless first night in an unfamiliar place, but I slept well, and without any dreams.

Chapter Six

I did forget to draw the bedroom curtains though. I realised that when the early light woke me. That wasn't a problem. I got up, washed and dressed, and had some toast while I thought about what to do about those things on the list I'd made last night. It was too early to ring the Franklins, I decided. Nicki would be getting her three kids to school.

I could go and see what there was to see in the churchyard though.

Before I could head out, I heard someone knocking at the front door. Going into the porch, I saw an elderly lady on the steps outside. She wore a faded blue raincoat and her white hair was being teased by the breeze.

I opened the door. 'Mrs Delly?'

'Best call me Martha, my duck. Everyone does.' The old woman's voice was as richly rural as her son's, and she couldn't have been more than five feet tall. I towered over her.

Unbidden, she walked in through the porch, leaning on the stick she'd been using to bang on the door. 'You ent from London, my Bill says.'

'No, Warwickshire,' I said amiably.

I was far more likely to learn something useful from an old woman who'd lived here all her life than I was from someone as aggressively uncommunicative as Rufus Stanlake. If the price of that was answering personal questions, I'd have to put up with that. I wasn't particularly surprised at her nosiness. I had grown up in a countryside community where everyone knows everyone else's business. Or at least, they like to think they do.

Martha peered up at me. 'You went over to Ashgrove yesterday. They're keeping well, Mr Edmund's family?'

'Yes, very well.' As far as I could tell, anyway.

'Nichola Berrow as was, Mrs Franklin.' Martha nodded, apparently satisfied. 'Not a local lass. Malvern way, that's where her family farms.'

That distinction of less than fifty miles was clearly important. I knew friends of my dad with the same attitude. Local to them means being born within ten miles at most.

'You ent busy this morning then?' It was barely a question.

'Not really. The builders start work tomorrow.' As I had no doubt she already knew. 'What do you think of all this then? A hotel will make things a lot busier around here.'

'Good thing too.' The old lady clearly meant it. 'It'll be nice to have some neighbours again, especially if they're young folk. Might get the church opened up some more, especially if the Diocese thinks there's donations to be had from the visitors. Most weeks it's only me and my Bill at matins.'

'Right.' I hoped she didn't expect me to go with them. I couldn't think when I'd last set foot in a church.

'Mr David showed you round?' Martha looked at me more intently. 'You seen the sewing room?'

I tried to recall the house plan. 'I don't think so.'

The old woman scowled. 'Then you better had, my duck. Tis off the walnut parlour. You'll need the key.'

'Okay.' By the time I had fetched the tagged bundle from the filing tray in the oak parlour office, Martha was already halfway through the great hall. The carpet and battered cane chairs had gone, along with the filthy portraits, leaving only the long case clock against the oak screen.

I caught up as the old woman opened the walnut parlour door. I was relieved to see that the shabby furniture and dusty ornaments had been cleared out of here too.

'Sewing room's through here.' Martha used her stick to outline an inner door skilfully hidden in the panelling.

Without someone to show me, I could have gone in and out of there ten times without realising where it was. I found a slender key with the right label though, and Martha showed me the keyhole hidden behind a bit of moulding that swung aside. I turned the key carefully in the stiff lock.

As I pictured the plan of the house, I realised this room was tucked right underneath the grand south stair. Though there was nothing left to explain why it was called a sewing room. I'd half expected dusty old needlework boxes or some ancient treadle sewing machine.

Two upright chairs flanked a plain oak table in front of the fireplace, which must have shared a flue with the walnut parlour on the other side of the wall. A roll-top mahogany desk stood against the wall to my left, opposite the narrow window. Photographs were clustered on top of that, and I recognised them from my first visit, tucked out of harm's way in here.

Martha went in and used her stick to point at Old Aunt Constance's forbidding photograph. 'Mrs Constance's father was Sir John Sutton. She married her cousin, and he was a Sutton as well. Change the name but not the letter, marry for worse and not for better. So they say, anyway. I don't know about marrying and not changing your name at all, but he broke his neck out hunting when Arthur was still a boy.'

I glanced at the photo and reckoned the woman had good reason to look bitter, if her husband and son had both died.

'Sir John lost all his money. He had grand plans until then. He was going to build an east wing when he inherit-ed, and a west wing where the stables is. But in 1900 he got a letter, and him not long widowed,' she added with some relish, 'saying some Spanish gentleman living in Charlbury had made himself a tidy fortune but he'd gone back to Spain on family business. He'd been thrown in prison on account of some trouble he'd been caught up in as a boy. That's why he'd come to England in the first place.'

'What happened?' I could see she was enjoying telling the story, and maybe the house's history would give me some clue about why I was here.

'So this letter said, the Spanish man had feared something of the sort might happen, so he buried his fortune in sovereigns out in Charlbury woods,' Martha said with a glint in her eye. 'He wanted Sir John to send money to bring his darling daughter safe to England. If Sir John would stand as her guardian, she'd show him where the fortune was buried.'

I couldn't help laughing. 'It sounds like some con off the Internet.'

'I wouldn't know about that. My Bill deals with them computers for me. But that letter was a pack of lies,' Martha said crisply. 'Only Sir John was sure that the girl would marry him and all them sovereigns would be his. No fool like an old fool. More letters strung him along while he sent money for steamer fare and train tickets and all sorts. But once they had the name of his bank, they went running up bills in his name all over London and Paris.'

She shook her head with a snort. 'He should of asked himself how anyone living in Charlbury could make a fortune. Come to that, he should have asked if anyone in Charlbury had ever heard of this Spanish fellow. And where's the sense in burying sovereigns instead of keeping them in the bank? When he went to the police, they said fools had been falling for letters like that since the Armada.'

'I can believe it.' I'd once worked on a small housing development where the site office was plagued by bogus invoices. One of the older electricians remembered his dad getting telexes in the sixties asking for help getting money out of Nigeria during the Biafran War. There really is nothing new under the sun.

'Only stayed out of the bankruptcy courts by the skin of his teeth. He died of the shame, so folk reckoned.' Martha looked around the room. 'Mrs Constance was left all on her own, apart from her Franklin cousins.'

She pointed towards more photographs. 'That's Albert, Harold, Edward and Cecil, and Mrs Constance's Arthur.'

I recognised the first three from my dream of the old man's death bed. Martha shook her head and turned away to glower at whatever was hung on the fireplace wall behind me. I turned around to see and took a step back, startled.

The picture above the mantelpiece was truly bizarre. A pre-Raphaelite maiden in a flowing white dress cowered in the midst of an ominous forest. She was shrinking away from a massively brawny man with masses of hair and a bushy beard. Bare-chested and barefoot, he wore some sort of ragged leggings and brandished a staff. He also seemed to have antlers, though in this dim light, it was hard to tell if they were his own or were some sort of crown.

'What's this?' I moved closer for a better look.

'Something painted by one of them scoundrels who took her for every penny they could, what with her grieving over Arthur.'

I couldn't tell if Martha's scorn was directed at Constance Sutton or whoever had painted this picture. I saw something else lying on the mantelshelf beneath it. A heart-shaped piece of wood was skewered by a pencil, with two dull black candlesticks on either side still showing traces of red wax. 'And what's this?'

'Mrs Constance's planchette.' Martha gave me an unfathomable look as I turned my head. 'You never seen one?'

'No.' I shrugged. 'What's it for?'

'Spirit writing.' Martha walked to the window and looked out at the copper beech hedge. 'Messages from the Other Side.'

I waited to see what else she might say.

'Lots of folk took up spiritualism after the first war, trying to talk to their dead.' The old woman shook her head, more pitying than condemning. 'Mrs Constance, she had mediums visit, all dangling beads and daft scarves. They'd go on about sensing vibrations and holding seances with the housemaids. My mother and her sisters were working here then. They used to come home scared silly, so my grampy said. One of them set the missis to eating her meals with an empty place set at the table for poor Arthur. She said his spirit needed something to come home to.'

Her withered lips pursed with disapproval. 'Then there was the one who called himself a magician. His hangers-on came to stay, and there was talk of drugs and all sorts of trouble, but Mrs Constance wouldn't hear a word against him. Then a girl died and they all ran away from the scandal. At least that happened before they took the last of her money. Else they'd have bled her dry.'

'Poor woman.' Though it sounded as if gullibility had been a Sutton family trait.

Unless something else had been going on here. I took another look at the melodramatic picture, and recalled the tangled legends of horned hunters in the wildwood. Though I still had no clue what that might mean, or any idea why this house's sad history had prompted the Green Man to bring me here.

'She lived here alone after that, till the day she died,' Martha went on, her faded eyes distant. 'It was all Mr Cecil could do to keep the house and the land together when he inherited, but he swore he'd never sell.'

'The Franklins should be able to keep the place in the family if they make a success of this hotel.'

Martha nodded readily enough. 'Mr Cecil always said new blood would turn the house's luck.'

I remembered the dying man saying something about luck in my dream. Before I could ask what she thought he meant by that, Martha was scowling out of the window again.

The old woman shook her head. 'They shouldn't never have left Mr Cecil all alone, not till the funeral was done. Nor shut up the house before he was buried.' Her voice faltered. 'I said I'd sit with him and do the needful, till he was called home, but no one listens to me.'

I realised she was looking towards the little church, on the other side of the lane. 'Where is he buried?' Though I guessed the answer before she told me.

'Over yonder, in St Diuma's churchyard.'

I remembered my list from last night. 'Will you show me?'

The old woman looked at me, her eyes narrowed. She took so long to reply that I got worried she was about to ask me some question that I couldn't possibly answer without sounding insane.

Instead she made up her mind and gave me a sharp nod. 'I can do that.'

She left the hidden room walking quickly, stick or no stick. I locked the door and made sure the moulding hid the keyhole before I followed. Martha was already halfway down the outside steps before I'd set the alarm and locked the front door.

The spring sun was warm enough outside, though there was a fresh breeze that cut through my sweatshirt.

'So who was St Diuma?' I asked as I caught the old woman up. I'd never come across a church with that name before. Though to be fair, I don't pay much attention to churches.

'He came here to spread the gospel after the Romans left.' Martha shot me a sideways glance. 'They was already trying to build a church down by the bridge, so the story goes. Only the walls kept falling down and their tools were always breaking. They said it was the devil's work, but they weren't going to give up, so they asked the bishop to send a priest to help them. The morning of the day Diuma arrived, they found everything had been moved way up here, set down by the standing stone that marked the path to the river. So the saint told them to lay down the old stone for an altar and build their church over that. As soon as they started work, the trouble stopped. So when he died, they named the church for him by way of thanks. He's buried over Charlbury way, so they say.'

'That's quite a story.' And I was ready to believe it, though I wasn't about to blame any devils.

I wondered who or what had really been wrecking the church builders' plans, and why. It could be naiads resenting interference around their river, or dryads objecting to having their trees felled. What would be really useful was finding that one of them was still around here.

We crossed the lane to the lych-gate, and I saw the notice explaining that there was a service at 8 a.m. on Sunday mornings. For the rest of the time, St Diuma's was kept locked, and anyone interested in seeing the church's pre-Reformation wall paintings was invited to contact the rectory office at St Michael and All Angels, Bourton under Ashes. I guessed that must be the big church near the market hall.

I let Martha set the pace through the churchyard while I looked for signs of anything amiss. It was good to know the church was secure, but that bastard from the caravan had been up to something around here.

Martha paused beside a gravestone, and I saw it commemorated Gilbert Norton, who had died in 1947, aged fifty-four.

'Never the same when he come back from the first war, my dad. He was gassed. Died of pewmonia when I was six years old. Left my mum with the seven of us to clothe and feed. But Mrs Constance wouldn't see any of us go into the workhouse, even if they was calling it something different by then. Let us stay on in our cottage rent-free, she did, and helped me and my brothers and sisters find jobs as soon as we were done with school.'

She waved a hand in the direction of the bridge over the river. 'The workhouse was over in the Broad, till they closed it once and for all after the second war. They turned it into the fever hospital. They built them houses after it burned down.'

Ed Franklin was certainly right about Martha being a fount of local history. I hoped it wasn't all this depressing.

She walked a little further on and paused beside a far more recent grave scarring the grass. There was no headstone, just a rosemary bush marking its foot. There were also clear signs that something, or someone, had been digging into the mounded earth.

Martha stabbed her stick angrily into the damp path. 'He's been up here again, that sly beggar. Took some dirt, the filthy wretch, and stole a sprig of my rosemary. How's Mr Cecil supposed to rest easy?'

'Do you mean the man from the caravan?' Not that I had much doubt.

'He wants watching, that one,' Martha growled. 'I keeps telling Rufus. Won't no one else do it but us.'

She poked at the disturbed earth, and the end of her stick hit something with a dull thunk. 'What's that?'

I hunkered down and brushed the dark soil aside. 'A bottle.'

It was a flat glass bottle that had once held whisky or vodka, now without a label. I pulled it out of the ground and was very glad to find that the top was screwed on tight. Whatever the murky liquid in it was now, there was no way I was going to open it.

'You empty that out somewhere up street, right across the river in the town,' Martha said wrathfully. 'You smash it, and you chuck away every last bit of glass, well away from here. You promise me that!'

'Okay.' I had no idea what this was about, but whatever that bastard was up to, I knew the Green Man had brought me here to stop him.

There was a moment's silence, broken only by the birds singing in the hawthorns.

'Will you do something else for me?' Martha demanded abruptly.

I stood up. 'If I can.'

'You won't ask all sorts of fool questions?' She looked up at me, belligerent.

'Not as long as you don't ask me to do something stupid or dangerous.' I wondered where this was going.

The old woman surprised me with a wicked grin. 'Can't say fairer than that. Right, you go down to the bins where Rufus puts out his recycling and find me a couple of jars. Ones with good, tight lids to them, mind.'

She was already heading back towards the lane. 'I'll wait for you here, and then I'll show you the spring in the woods. The bright well itself.'

'Okay.' I still had no idea where this was going, but my instincts told me to go along with it. I looked at the foul bottle I was holding. 'What shall I do with this?'

We'd reached the lych-gate by now. Martha sat on one of the ledges and pointed to the cobwebbed space under the one opposite. 'You leave that in there for now.'

'Right.' I crouched low and shoved the revolting thing as far back as I could, well out of sight. Whatever it was, the longer it was before the bastard realised it was gone from the grave, the better.

'I'll be as quick as I can.' Though I had no idea what I'd say to Rufus Stanlake if he found me going through his bins.

Thankfully there was no sign of him as I walked quickly down the lane and found the farmhouse recycling bin beside the russet barn. I found a couple of glass jars that told me Stanlake had a taste for Chinese stir-fry sauces. They were exactly the right size to fit into the big pocket of my combat trousers.

Martha was on her feet as soon as she saw me coming back. She pulled the lych-gate closed, and we began walking along the lane. I wasn't surprised when we reached the fingerpost and she turned to take the path through the trees.

I kept my ears open for any sounds of motorbikes, ready to pick the old woman up to get her out of harm's way if needs be. Thankfully all I could hear were the peaceful sounds of spring in the woods. More than that, in some way I couldn't define, the atmosphere here was distinctly different to the undergrowth-choked trees on the other side of the lane, on the land running down to the river. The air felt clearer, cleaner, somehow, and not only because there was no hint of rotting birds impaled on a blackthorn.

'Are we going far?' We were walking up a broad, grassy ride that was smooth enough underfoot, but I'd done the maths after seeing that gravestone and I knew Martha was pushing eighty years old.

'A tidy step,' she admitted with a slight smile.

'Okay.' I let her set the pace. If it came to it, I could always carry her back, even if that meant risking a smack from her stick.

Martha was content to walk in silence as we headed into the woodland. I glanced from side to side, hoping for some glimpse of a dryad, or maybe the Green Man. All I saw was pussy-willow softening spindly twigs and primroses bright amid rosettes of wrinkled leaves.

'Shit!' I took a startled step backwards as a hen pheasant erupted from a clump of dogwood, noisily rattling its wings.

Crows cawed a rebuke, high among the trees.

'You best get used to that around here.' Martha was amused. 'And watch your step. Rufus don't like anyone disturbing his birds. You want to look out for deer as well.'

'Muntjac?' I remembered the barking I'd heard.

Martha nodded. 'Little nuisances. My Bill, he gives them what-for if he sees them round his roses. Roe deer too, but they don't come near the gardens. Mr Cecil said this was a hunting forest since before the Conquest,' she remarked. 'All part of the Wychwood.'

I remembered that picture in the hidden sewing room, and wondered if that had been inspired by the local wildlife or by something more eerie.

We walked on. I heard a familiar cry overhead and looked up to see the angular silhouette of a red kite cut across the blue ribbon of sky.

'This way.' Martha left the grassy track for a path scarcely wide enough for a muntjac.

She was skinny enough to ignore the clawing gorse. I wasn't, and was soon regretting not getting my leather jacket before coming out here. My sweatshirt was no protection against the vicious prickles.

Ahead of me, Martha simply pressed on. Any stray fronds of gorse slid over her raincoat with a faint rasp. The path turned this way and that, but we were heading steadily north-west.

Martha skirted a stand of young silver birch trees, and I guessed we had arrived. A small lake stretched out ahead of us. Around the margins, alder trees were heavy with catkins, while clumps of reedy plants spread up from the shallows. I was surprised not to see any ducks on the water though.

'What now?' I reached down to take the jars out of my trouser pocket.

'Not here,' Martha said sharply. 'We needs to go round to the spring proper. This water's no good, and you better watch your step.'

As she set off around the edge of the water, leaning precariously on her walking stick, I saw what she meant. The turf squelched underfoot, and with the water lapping around those alder thickets, I couldn't tell where the solid ground ended and the lake proper began.

I followed her, watching my step. It was impossible to tell how deep the water was, and I certainly didn't want to fall in. I can swim, thanks to compulsory lessons at school, even if I hated them. If I'm ever on a ship that sinks, I won't drown, at least not quickly. Swimming for pleasure, though, that's a contradiction in terms as far as I'm concerned.

Still, I really wanted to know what the old woman meant about the water here being no good. Without a friendly local naiad or dryad to ask, I could only think of seeing what my greenwood blood might tell me. Keeping a wary eye on Martha's back, I paused and went down on one knee, so I could stick a hand into the shallows.

I got a shock. It really felt like a physical jolt, like sticking a nine-volt battery on my tongue. That had been a fad back at school, when I was fifteen or sixteen. Boys would dare each other to lick a PP3, with the added uncertainty of not knowing if the battery on offer had been passed from pocket to pocket for days or was fresh out of the packaging.

This shock was much, much stronger, and it came with a shiver of dread that chilled me far more than the fresh spring breeze. There was something very wrong with this lake.

I stood up and hurried after the old woman.

Chapter Seven

We made our way around the lake without incident and reached a grassy hillock bare of trees. About halfway up the slope, stones the size of my fist ringed a shallow hollow filled with water. A stream spilled over the lower edge and ran away to the lake, sparkling in the sunlight. A bright well, indeed.

Martha grunted with satisfaction. 'You can fill them jars now.'

Trying to share her confidence, I knelt and did that. I braced for some unpleasant sensation when my fingers touched the water, but nothing happened. So I submerged my hand to the wrist as I filled the jars. If there was a naiad anywhere in the area, one who had anything to do with these waters, I hoped she'd get some sense of my presence, and of my mother's blood. I hoped she'd be as curious as the naiad I'd met before, back in Derbyshire.

Martha had taken a few steps away from the water and was poking at the base of a low bush with long fronds of paired leaves. I didn't recognise it.

'Cut a bit of this liquorice root.' Delving in her raincoat pocket, she tossed over a venerable horn-sided clasp knife to land on the grass beside me. 'A finger for each jar.'

Once I'd screwed their lids on tight, I opened the knife carefully. The hinge was stiff, and the blade was lethally sharp and illegally long. I knelt by the bush and scraped away the soft earth to uncover long brown-and-yellow roots. Digging underneath one with the knife blade, I cut free a piece as long as my hand.

'And I put this in the jars of water?'

'When we get back,' Martha said with satisfaction. 'Along of some sugar, a pinch of salt and a sprig of mint. We'll bury one under the myrtle bush by the kitchen door and put the other one by Mr Cecil's grave.'

I wondered what that sly bastard from the caravan would make of that. I also really wanted to find out what my mum would have to say. Was this just superstition, or could it possibly be something more? 'What will that do?'

'Keep ill will from the house.' Martha waved a finger at me. 'Because Brightwell don't have a master no more, nor yet a mistress. There's them'll take advantage of that.'

'Fair enough.' I stood up and put everything in my pockets.

'I'll have my knife back.' Martha held out her hand.

I handed it over, and wondered if Bill Delly knew she was carrying it around. I couldn't see it being much use to her, given how difficult it was to open.

'That'll do for now,' Martha said enigmatically. 'We'd best get back before my Bill starts fretting. He don't always have time for my walk of a morning, and he do fuss if I goes out on my own.'

'Okay.' I hoped the old woman realised I wasn't going to be available to come out here with her once the work on the house started. On the other hand, I was as uneasy as Bill must be at the thought of her wandering these woods on her own. More so than Bill, most likely, given what I'd sensed in the lake.

I watched the wind ruffle the surface of the dark water as we took the path back around the edge. There was nothing to see, but I felt the skin on the back of my neck prickling with unease when I was forced to turn my back on the lake and follow the narrow path back to the broad, grassy track.

We hadn't walked far towards Brightwell before Rufus Stanlake's battered Defender appeared, driving up the grassy ride. He pulled up and wound his window down as we approached.

'Bill was wondering where you got to.'

'No call for him to be wasting your time,' Martha said tartly.

'I was coming up to the pens anyway.' Rufus grinned at the old woman. 'Been up to the spring to work some of your witchcraft?'

'You know there ent no witches round here.' Martha waved a dismissive hand. 'Not since Doris Ditchfield died.'

'When was that?' I asked.

'Candlemas, 1963.' Martha's lips thinned with remembered dislike. 'The bad winter did for her, and not before time.'

'Oh.' I'd been expecting some date back in the 1600s.

'Do you want a lift back?' Rufus's gaze switched to me, faintly challenging. 'Martha can sit in the front, but you'll have to go in with Bess.'

'Mr Edmund don't pay you to drive me around,' Martha told him. 'We'll walk.'

'Fair enough.' He turned the key, and the Defender's engine echoed loudly along the ride.

'Just a moment.' I raised a hand. 'That caravan, on the corner of the lane where that scrubby field runs down to the river. What do you know about it?'

'Turned up mid-January.' The gamekeeper's face hardened. 'Along with a mouthy bastard who keeps wandering around the woods. When I tell him to stick to the paths or sod off, he gives me a load of bollocks about his right to roam. I reckon he's after a smack in the mouth, so he can play the victim for the coppers.'

No wonder Bill didn't want his mother going out on her own. 'Can't you get him moved on?'

'Not unless he does something the cops can have him for, or until we can work out who owns that piece of land.' Rufus was clearly exasperated. 'Brightwell demesne only runs up to the track along the trees. That's been a footpath for centuries. According to their maps and deeds, Auster's Farm's boundary is the hedgerow on the far side of that stretch of grass. Bastard in the caravan says that piece in between is common land and he's entitled to camp there. He says he's a gypsy.'

'He's no Romany,' Martha said with contempt. 'That's unlucky land, and the travelling folk know it, for all that it used to be a lamp acre.'

'Lamp acre?' I didn't know that term.

'The rent for that field was used to buy lamp oil for the church. Not that that necessarily means the church ever actually owned it. There's nothing in the Land Registry to help us.' Rufus shrugged. 'David's got some consultant looking into the original enclosure records, and whatever else she can find at the county archive. As soon as we know the situation, we can get started on moving the sod on.'

'Unless he trips up first.' Martha clearly relished that prospect.

'How do you mean?' I prompted.

'I told you. It's unlucky land. That path as runs down to the water.' Martha gestured towards the distant river. 'There was a bridge there long since, but just wooden planks, no rail or nothing else to it. A lad fell in and drowned, coming back from drinking to Queen Victoria's jubilee in the town. His girl tried to pull him out but she died along with him. They took down the bridge after that. The crowner insisted at the inquest. Romany folk never used that land again.'

'The girl's ghost flags down drivers on the lane.' Rufus grinned at me. 'Dripping wet and begging for help. If anyone stops and opens a car door for her, she vanishes. Watch yourself.'

'Better men than you have seen her, Rufus Stanlake,' Martha said.

'Whatever you say.' The gamekeeper revved his engine and looked at me. 'If you ever see that bastard sneaking around the house, give me a call. With two of us to go to the cops, we can get him warned off Brightwell land at very least. Who knows what else they might find if they go knocking on his door.'

He didn't wait for me to answer before he drove away.

Martha smiled at me with a glint in her eye. 'Don't you worry. The poor lass ent been seen these past ten years. Now, let's you and me get back, and have a cup of tea before we see to the basement door and Mr Cecil's grave.'

Once again, I let her set the pace. Even though we were walking downhill, she was flagging by the time we got back to Brightwell House. I offered her my arm at the bottom of the steps, and she accepted the support without comment as we made our way slowly up to the front door.

'You sit down and get your breath.' I ushered her into the oak parlour office and went to put the kettle on. While it boiled, I took the jars of water and the liquorice root out of my pocket and went through the cupboards. 'I've got sugar and salt,' I called out. 'Where will I find some mint?'

'There's—' Martha's voice broke. She coughed and tried again. 'There's a bed of herbs along the side of the house.'

I took her a mug of tea. 'Right. You stay here, and I'll go and get some mint.'

She looked up at me, her expression speculative, and once again, I thought she was going to challenge me. I still didn't have a good answer if she asked why I was going along with all this. She reached for the mug and drank some tea instead.

I found the herbs where she'd said they would be, kept neat and tidy like everything else in Bill's domain. I pinched off a couple of sprigs of mint and went back into the house. Martha was in the housekeeper's kitchen. She had already put salt and sugar into the jars and found a knife to cut the liquorice root in two. I handed over the mint and she added that to the... talismans? Potions? I had no idea. So I drank my own tea.

'All done,' she said with satisfaction, screwing the lids on the jars. 'Come on, my duck.'

Either having some tea and a sit-down or just getting her own way had given her a second wind. I followed her out of the house and around to the basement door at the side.

The myrtle bush was at the end of the herb bed, overhanging the small flagstoned area outside the old kitchen entrance. I went down the steps. That put ground level for the herbs at waist height for me, so I could easily bury the jar without bending double. Martha stayed up on the path, looking down at me with smug contentment.

As I scooped out a handful of earth, I paused when I caught a familiar and unwelcome scent. I took a cautious breath and had to swallow a surge of revulsion. Someone had come down these steps and taken a piss. I looked down to see old leaves and windblown dirt, and a metal grating over a drain. That was obviously there to stop this entrance filling up with water every time it rained.

It could have been anyone. Maybe it had been someone working for whoever the Franklins had hired to clear out the old furniture and ornaments. Someone who didn't know there were loos by the garages, or who couldn't be arsed to walk that far. They'd seen this handy grating, and the steps down to the door made using it like a urinal fairly discreet. Maybe some curious passer-by had stopped for a cheeky snoop around the old house and its gardens and had been caught short.

It could have been anyone, but I didn't think so. It was that dirty bastard from the caravan, I was sure of it. Did he have some compulsion to go around pissing to mark his territory, like some animal? Sod that. He had no claim on this house, or the churchyard, and I'd welcome the chance to explain that to him.

'What you waiting for?' Martha said impatiently.

'Right.' I dug out more earth and shoved the jar deep in among the myrtle bush's roots. 'Let's lock up and get this done.' Now I knew that bastard was sneaking around so close to the house, I wasn't going to leave any of the doors open, not even for a few moments to cross the lane to the churchyard.

Since there was already a hole in the earth over Uncle Cecil's grave, where we'd dug out the bottle that had started this, burying the second jar was quick and easy.

'You get rid of that nastiness we found here,' Martha said as I got to my feet. 'I'll be getting along home.'

'Wait a moment and I can give you a lift.' I brushed the soil off my hands. 'I'm going into Bourton.'

'Go on with you. I ent so feeble.' Martha waved that idea away with a sweep of her stick.

'Okay.' I didn't see any point in arguing the toss.

We walked down to the lych-gate, and I retrieved the flat bottle from underneath the stone bench. Now I got another look at it, I could see there were twigs and leaves in the murky liquid, as well as some other shit, literally or metaphorically. I sure as shit wasn't going to open it, and I'd be damn careful not to drop it before I could get rid of it.

'I'll be seeing you soon.' Martha set off up the lane. I couldn't say she had a spring in her step, but she wasn't leaning on her stick so much.

I headed back to the house and left the foul bottle outside the front door as I went inside and got my jacket. I set the alarm when I locked up this time. Since I didn't want that bottle sliding around in the footwell, I stuck it in the passenger door pocket, wedged securely with some rag. By the time I'd done that, Martha was standing in her garden gate by the end cottage when I drove past. She gave me a wave and turned to go indoors.

There was no sign of Rufus or his Defender around the farmhouse. As I drove on, I wondered about stopping as soon as I got a phone signal close to the Broad. I really wanted to talk to my mum and dad after this morning's excursion.

Now that I was getting some clues about why the Green Man had brought me here, I was realising how badly I missed having someone like-minded to discuss all this with, and to help me work out what to do next. When Blithehurst had been threatened, Eleanor and I were allies. Before that, I'd had Kalei, the naiad, to tell me what I needed to know, even if the price of that had been doing what she wanted. I had no one here.

As I rounded the bend, I saw a handful of teenagers hanging around the bus shelter. Not waiting for a bus though. There was no sign of a timetable or an actual stop. Whatever route this had once been had fallen victim to council cuts.

Parking up within sight of bored kids bunking off school would be asking for trouble. I drove on, turned the corner, crossed the river and found an empty space in the shadow of the market hall to call home. Unfortunately, Dad's phone went to voicemail, and if I wasn't talking to him, I had no way of contacting my mum. I'd have to wait and try again later, using the Brightwell landline. The Franklins couldn't object to that, if I had no way of using my own phone for personal calls from the house.

Meantime, I could at least get rid of that sodding bottle, over here on the far side of the river, like Martha wanted. I wondered what that was about. Perhaps Eleanor would know. I might ring her later as well.

I got out of the Landy, got the bottle out of the passenger door pocket and looked around for a bin. No matter what Martha had said, I wasn't going to empty it or smash it and risk getting whatever was in it on me. A refuse lorry would do that very effectively, and dump the bits in the local landfill.

There was a black metal council rubbish bin over by the gate to the massive church. That would do. I crossed the road and dumped the bottle. As it hit the bottom of the bin with a dull thud, I was more relieved to be rid of it than I expected.

Since I was here, I read the church noticeboard. This was indeed St Michael and All Angels, where building had started in 1220 when the town got its market charter from King Henry III. Local wool merchants paid for it, and work finally finished about two hundred years later, apparently. I hoped the builders at Brightwell were a bit quicker about things than their forefathers.

Looking around, I saw that the church overlooked a side street leading away from the main road, where the graveyard wall faced a row of shops with mismatched frontages. Dellow's had windows bright with gold and silver jewellery, while The Wool Shop's offered a rainbow array of sweaters.

Shayler's was beyond that, a taller, three-storey building with an open door between two rounded bay windows. I remembered what Nicki Franklin had said about a local bookseller coming to catalogue the house's library. A chalk board on the narrow pavement outside offered 'Books, New and Second-hand', as well as coffee and free Wi-Fi. That was definitely worth checking out. I'd need to check my email sometime soon, and I couldn't do that at Brightwell. I could get a coffee and introduce myself, and come back with my laptop later in the week. I headed towards the entrance.

The right-hand bay window held a shelf unit displaying the latest bestsellers and several glossy coffee-table books about the Cotswolds. On the other side of the door, romance paperbacks were spread across a swathe of cherry-red velvet draped over a table. That meant passers-by could see in to the tables and chairs and the coffee shop counter inviting them inside.

The solid wooden street door opened into a small glass-walled porch. I could see there had been a wide entrance hall inside when this was still a house. That would have run back to a flight of stairs about halfway along before carrying on to what was probably a kitchen door at the back. There would have been doors on either side, opening into sizeable rooms. When the building had been converted, the interior walls had been removed, nearly as far back as the foot of the stairs. That left a wide, U-shaped shop floor, with the load-bearing walls up above safely supported by steel universal beams. A wide counter had been installed to block access to what remained of the hall. The stairs and the kitchen door both had 'Private – No Admittance' signs regardless.

An old-fashioned bell jangled as I pushed open the inner door. The right-hand half of the shop had the new books. Paperbacks were shelved along the walls while two tables offered a judicious selection of the latest hardbacks. The other side had what looked like a good range of second-hand stock surrounding the coffee shop tables and chairs.

There was one space on the wall that wasn't shelving. That had a community noticeboard thick with flyers beneath a placard advertising *The North Cotswold Mercury*. There was no one reading them at the moment. There was no one else in the shop.

The woman sitting behind the counter looked up, hit a key on her laptop and waited for me to finish looking around. When I turned back at her, she smiled. 'Hello.'

I walked over and offered her my hand, business-like. 'Mrs Oxway?' I reckoned that was a safe guess. She looked about the same age as Nicki Franklin, which made sense if their daughters were at school together. 'I'm Dan Mackmain. I'm working for the Franklins over at Brightwell House.'

Her smile widened. 'Good to meet you, and yes, I'm Judith Oxway. Everyone calls me Jude.'

'Let me know when you want to come and sort out the books, and I'll keep the workmen out of your way.'

She nodded. 'It'll be interesting to see what's tucked away there.'

The door to the rear opened and another woman appeared, carrying a cardboard box. 'Where do you want this, Jude?'

'What is it?' Jude turned to see.

The contrast between the women was striking. The newcomer had long brown hair, as straight as Jude's black hair was curly. She had striking red highlights where Jude Oxway had natural grey. Jude wore jeans and a comfortable sweater, while the newcomer wore smart trousers, a blouse and jacket, as well as jewellery and enough make-up for a magazine cover. I guessed she was a few years older than me.

She dumped the box on the counter, and her bracelets rattled as she tore open the top. 'Tarot cards? Honestly, Judy. Are these for those halfwits hanging round with that creep doing his fortune-telling under the market hall?'

'Each to their own,' Jude said placidly. 'Petra, this is Dan Mackmain. He's working for Ed over at Brightwell.'

'Oh, hello.' She looked at me with sudden interest. 'Petra Oxway. I work for the local paper, when I'm not stacking bookshelves. I imagine there's an awful lot to do?'

'It's early days, but it's all very well planned.'

'I'd like to do a feature on the conversion,' she offered with an inviting smile. 'I'd bring a photographer, do a proper spread.'

'Talk to Ed Franklin,' I suggested. 'If it's okay with him, it's okay with me.'

Petra grinned. 'We can give you very good coverage locally, and when you're ready to take bookings, I'd like to approach the London papers, maybe interest them in a colour supplement piece.'

'I'm only here for the building work,' I pointed out. 'That's something for the Franklins to decide.'

Petra nodded. 'I'll give David a ring.'

'Coffee?' Jude asked me.

'Please.' I nodded.

'Latte? Cappuccino?'

'Just ordinary filter's fine, thanks.'

'Take a seat.' She headed for the coffee counter, with its glass-fronted display of cakes and sandwiches and the gleaming steel espresso machine.

As I walked towards a table, I saw that the second-hand shelves had a local history section. I stopped to see if anything looked likely to offer me any clues about what was amiss at Brightwell.

Petra Oxway appeared beside me. 'Looking for anything in particular?'

I shrugged. 'Just curious about the history of the house.'

'Have you seen any of Brightwell's resident ghosts?' Petra grinned.

I shook my head. 'Not yet. What's supposed to go bump in the night?'

'Everard Sutton's been winding the clocks since the 1850s, or so they say.' Petra turned to lean against the shelves, so she was facing me, her hazel eyes bright. 'And of course there's the tragic Mary Anne.'

Whose wedding was commemorated in Brightwell's alarm code, I remembered. 'What happened to her?'

'You haven't already heard about her from Martha Delly? Well, she was the cousin of Mountjoy Sutton, who was a prize bastard, figuratively if not literally.' Petra had clearly told this tale a good few times.

'In 1673, Mountjoy was about to be thrown into prison for debt unless he could come up with some cash. Mary Anne was heiress to her mother's money, so Mountjoy went up to London and kidnapped her. They got back to Brightwell at midnight, and he sent his thugs to wake up the vicar. He married her in St Diuma's in the Broad, with one of his pistols on the bride and the other on the priest. His henchmen were the witnesses. You can still see where they signed their names with an *X* in the register.'

'That can't have been legal,' I protested.

'No, but by the time Mary Anne's father arrived, she and Mountjoy had been locked in his bedroom for two days.' Petra grimaced. 'So it was a done deal, so to speak.'

'What happened after that?' I wondered if there were any stories about the house that weren't miserable and depressing.

'Mountjoy kept her locked up at Brightwell while he spent her money on clearing his debts. Since any child of the marriage would inherit another fortune from Mary Anne's father, he set out to get her pregnant as soon as possible. He was all ready to invite the king to visit Brightwell once he thought she was going to give him an heir, so he had the

Brightbrook dammed to make an ornamental lake. He had the gardens dug up and drew up plans for fountains and pavilions. Only, Mary Anne miscarried and went into a fatal decline. The story goes that she cursed him and his whole family on her deathbed, and Mountjoy was dead within the year.' Petra shrugged. 'Anything from the plague to the pox could have actually carried him off, of course.'

'Serves him right.' I wanted to know more about this business with the lake, but couldn't think how best to ask.

'The house and apparently the curse both went to his brother. The legend goes the family's been unlucky ever since. Poor Mary Anne supposedly walks around, wringing her hands and weeping, whenever a Sutton is about to die.'

Petra broke off as her phone rang. Finding it in an inside pocket, she frowned at the screen. 'Sorry, let me deal with this.' She answered the call and walked towards the front of the shop. 'Hi, Shaun.'

'Your coffee.' Jude came over with a tray holding a cafetière, a mug and milk, and a plate of unsolicited gingernuts. 'Sugar's on the tables.'

The bell rang as the shop door opened. 'Judith, you rang about my order?' A middle-aged lady in a black coat looked our way, expectant.

I took the tray. 'Thanks.'

'You're welcome.' Jude nodded and headed for her customer. 'It came in this morning, Mrs Barnes.'

I took a seat, poured myself some coffee, and saw the Wi-Fi pass code on the top of the menu card in a plastic holder on the table. I got out my own phone and logged on to check the news headlines, more for something to do than any desire to see how much was going wrong elsewhere in the world.

Jude escorted her customer into the other half of the shop, and Petra was still on the phone by the window. The bell over the door jangled a few minutes later, and I looked up to see a long-legged teenage girl wearing skinny black trousers and a droopy cardigan over a T-shirt, carrying a school bag.

'Great, see you soon.' Petra quickly put her phone away. 'Nessie, hold the fort. I've got to go out.'

The girl didn't look thrilled. 'I've only got my lunch hour.'

'Please?' Petra begged, though more for show than anything else. 'I've got a lead about these break-ins.'

'I can't be late back to school,' the girl insisted.

'I'll be back before you have to go, I promise.' Petra hurried over to me, offering a business card. 'What's your number?'

'Do you have the Brightwell one? There's no reception out there.' Besides, I'm very choosy about who gets my number. I took her card though.

Petra grinned. 'If I haven't got it, I can get it. We'll talk soon.'

She left without a backward glance. That left the teenager looking at me. She dumped her bag behind the counter and came over. I could see she was curious.

'Can I get you anything else?'

'Just the bill, please.' I smiled at her, friendly but not too friendly. 'Are you Tasha Franklin's friend? I thought she said your name was Isobel?'

She gave an exaggerated sigh. 'Auntie Petra thinks she's so funny. She says Nessie's short for Is-a-bell-necessary-on-a-bicycle.'

It didn't seem particularly funny to me, but I supposed it's the sort of thing that family can get away with. Like I said, I don't understand relatives.

'You must be Daniel, who's working over at Brightwell?' She didn't have much doubt about that. I wondered what Tasha had said about me.

For the moment, I nodded, by way of an answer. 'For a couple of months.'

Isobel smiled politely. 'Let me get your bill.'

As she did that, a middle-aged couple looking for a drink and a sit-down appeared, and she went to take their order. I paid for my coffee at the counter and left Jude Oxway using her laptop to look up the latest in a series of kids' books for an apologetic but impatient customer.

Walking back to the main street where I had parked, I saw a small gathering in the shadows underneath the market hall. When I got closer, I saw it was a group of teenagers. I couldn't tell if any of them were from the Broad, though something about one caught my attention.

I unlocked the Land Rover and got into the driver's seat, apparently ignoring the teenagers. Once I was inside the vehicle, I could take a closer look at them without it being so obvious. At least I hoped it wasn't. I had seen someone I knew, at least a little. Josh Franklin was sitting on the broad base of one of the pillars on the far side, in his school uniform. He was smoking a cigarette.

I turned the ignition and drove away. It wasn't my place to interfere in young Josh's life. He was presumably out of school on his lunch break, like Isobel Oxway. I didn't imagine his parents wanted him smoking, but there are worse ways to rebel.

All the same, something about seeing him there made me uneasy. I might mention it to Rufus Stanlake, I decided, as I drove over the bridge. He seemed to know Josh well enough to have a quiet word, if there really was some cause for concern. If Ed or Nicki needed to be involved, that would come far better from someone with close ties to the family.

Chapter Eight

I parked in front of the house when I got back to Brightwell. Instead of going straight in, I walked around the outside, checking for any signs that someone, anyone, had been here while I was out. There was nothing that I could see.

So I went through the hedge to the garage yard and used the bunch of keys to open up doors until I found a store-room with a couple of battered black buckets, an old shovel and a yard broom. I'd already spotted an outside tap. Sweeping up the leaves and dirt from the sunken entrance to the basement kitchen, I shovelled them into one bucket. Then I filled the other one from the garage yard tap and poured the water down the steps. I did that three times and then used the yard broom to scour the flagstones, until I had forced the last of the water down the drain. Now all that I could smell was the freshness of cold water on limestone.

As I worked, I thought about everything I'd learned today. I knew a hell of a lot more about the house and its history now, but I still couldn't see how any of that might tie up with whatever was wrong with the lake, or whatever was wrong with the woods on this side of the lane, come to that.

Because there was definitely something unfriendly out there as well. I had no idea where Bill Delly kept his compost heap, and besides, I didn't feel like adding that bucket of dead, dirty leaves to it. I walked across the lawn and through the gate in the iron fence, looking for a hollow among the closest trees where I could empty the bucket.

As I did so, I felt a chill swirling around me, like a cold breeze. No leaves were stirring though, not on the ground or in the branches above my head. This wasn't like the Green Man's warning breath on the back of my neck either. This was something old and dank and hostile.

I retreated to the lawn and made sure the gate in the fence was secured. I wanted cold iron between me and whatever was out there. I also really wanted to talk to my mum and dad, but I was starting to think that conversation needed more than a phone call. I'd go home at the weekend, I decided, and we could discuss everything I'd learned so far. Then I'd ring Eleanor Beauchene and see what she might have to say.

I put everything back in the garage store and went into the house, locking the front door behind me. After having corned beef sandwiches for lunch, I did ring Nicki Franklin.

'It's a quick question about the alarm,' I explained. 'Is it only hooked up to the doors and windows, or are there motion sensors in the house anywhere?'

'Hang on, let me save what I'm working on.'

There was a short pause, and the sound of computer keys at the other end of the line.

'Okay, I've double-checked,' Nicki said a moment later. 'It's just the doors and windows, and the fire alarm's part of the same system, linked to the security company's office, so they can call out the emergency services if needs be. Oh, and I've had you added to the list of key holders, okay?'

'That's all I needed to know, thanks.' So I could set the alarm while I was inside. Good. I'd do that when I went to bed.

'Okay then, call me if there's anything else. Bye.'

'Bye.' I barely said it before Nicki rang off. She was clearly a busy woman.

Of course, that's when I realised I had wanted to ask if there was any news about who owned that land where the sneaky bastard's caravan was squatting. On the other hand, I remembered Rufus saying David Franklin was dealing with the consultant investigating that, so there was no reason to suppose Nicki would know. More than that, after meeting

David Franklin, I had every reason to think he'd be in touch as soon as he had a cast-iron plan for getting rid of the intruder.

I looked around the oak parlour and wondered what to do with the rest of the day, at least until it was a reasonable time to see what one of Bourton's curry houses had to offer. The cash box caught my eye. That needed to go somewhere secure before the place was full of workmen tomorrow. I had no reason to think any of them would be dishonest, of course. Equally, better safe than sorry. A hundred quid might not be much money to the Franklins, but I'd be uneasy until the box was under lock and key.

I walked through the great hall, through the lobby at the foot of the grand staircase, and went through the grand parlour to the drawing room that Great-Uncle Cecil had filled with his books. I'd bet this had been called the great or grand drawing room as well, most likely.

Nothing had been touched since I had been in here last time. I didn't envy Jude Oxway the task of clearing away the clutter randomly shoved on the shelves before she could even start sorting out the books. Well, that was something I could usefully do with the next couple of hours.

I opened the shutters on the tall windows to let in some daylight, and looked at the stacks of newspapers. They were copies of *The North Cotswold Mercury*, and the most recent was about five years old. I couldn't imagine the Franklins would want to keep them, though I would check. There was a second door that opened into the corridor by the housekeeper's sitting room door, so I carried the piles through to the oak parlour office and dumped them in a corner. There's always a use for old newspapers on a renovation job.

Now that the armchairs were empty, I began filling them again with the stuff I found randomly shoved in between and on top of the books on the shelves. There were letters in brown and white envelopes, neatly slit open, as well as leaflets, brochures, folded pages torn from newspapers and magazines, three pairs of glasses in dusty cases, a corkscrew, a hip flask and several tins that might have held ancient boiled sweets or something else entirely. I didn't open anything, putting the junk on one chair and the paperwork on the other. It was probably mostly rubbish, but that wasn't my call. Someone, a Franklin, would have to go through it all and decide. Nicki, most likely.

As I went, I looked through the books for any local histories that might offer some insights into whatever was going on here, through old myths and legends. I found a couple of possibilities, including a collection of ghost stories by Petra Oxway: a thin green paperback with a stark black woodcut of St Diuma's church on the cover. I took her card out of my pocket and stuck it in the book. Maybe I could see if she knew anything useful, if she persuaded the Franklins to let her do that feature.

When I'd gone through the shelves, I sat down at the kneehole desk. That's what I'd really come in here for. If I could find the keys to those drawers, it would be a damn sight more useful in the oak parlour office than that gateleg table. I couldn't move it by myself, but it would be easy enough with someone from Kemble and Coates to help me. The table could come in here, to give Jude Oxway a place to put her laptop.

I pulled the top right-hand drawer handle. It slid open easily enough, and there wasn't much inside: some ancient pencils, a letter knife like a miniature sword that could probably qualify as an offensive weapon and a couple of small keys on a rusted split ring. I tried one in the drawer lock. It fitted. So did the other one. Excellent.

The next drawer down had a couple of local, large-scale Ordnance Survey maps. Those would definitely come in useful. As I took them out, I found a stack of yellowed envelopes and a sheaf of headed notepaper held together with a dark blue ribbon. Brightwell House, Bourton under Ashes, Gloucestershire. That had obviously been enough of an address for letters to get here, back in the days when phone numbers still only had four digits, like the one included below the neat printing.

The bottom drawer was twice the depth of the top two, and when I pulled the handle, I found it was locked. When I opened it, I discovered it was packed with black-bound notebooks secured with elastic bands. Most of those had perished into useless, sticky tendrils long ago. Whatever these notebooks were, they had been here a while.

I looked at the drawer for a long moment. These must be the notes the dying man had wanted David and Ed Franklin to read. I knew that for a certainty, but I had no way of explaining why. No reasons to offer that would make any kind of sense.

I wondered if there might be something written in one that would make for a plausible excuse for mentioning it. Though even as I picked up the closest, I couldn't see myself handing it to Ed Franklin. What was I supposed to say to him? 'I know I'm only here to do some woodwork, and sign for deliveries, but here's something interesting I found when I went snooping through your dead relative's desk.'

I opened the notebook carefully, as my hands were grimy with dust. It was signed and dated inside the front cover.

Cecil Franklin, Brightwell Manor, 1992.

I flipped through a few pages. Some long-dead schoolmaster had evidently drilled young Cecil in that old-fashioned copperplate handwriting that looks so elegant at first glance but is sodding difficult to read.

The Golden Bough.

Hesiod.

Thoreau. Walden.

Virgil. Eclogues.

A Shropshire Lad.

I turned a few more pages. It seemed Uncle Cecil had been copying out quotations, each one neatly attributed. I recognised some of the names, though that was about all I could have said about them. These particular excerpts were about woods and forests.

The next notebook was about lakes and rivers, though here the ink was faded, and the pages had turned yellow-edged. The date inside the front cover was August 1947. Whatever Uncle Cecil had been doing, he'd been doing it for decades.

In 2003 he'd taken to sketching, though not very well. A shadowy, horned figure, reminiscent of that weird picture in Aunt Constance's sewing room, was on the page facing a bleakly resonant poem of warfare in the trenches of World War One.

The next notebook was full of lists. A long series of flowers and herbs was bracketed together under the heading 'august amulet'. One page was reserved for names: Dion Fortune, Moina Mathers, Margaret Murray.

That first name rang a faint bell, but I couldn't even remember if they were a man or a woman, and I couldn't look any of them up without Internet access. Though that reminded me that I'd been planning on seeing what I could find out about horned men in folklore. Sod it. If I'd found all this earlier, I could have taken my laptop into Bourton and used the bookshop Wi-Fi. Now that would have to wait.

Flicking through to the end of this particular notebook, I found a series of curious headings, one to a page. The Hunter, the Witness, the Helper, the Sage and the Chatelaine. The Wanderer, the Dispossessed, the Dupe and the Despoiler. Successive names had been crossed out, leaving only one at the end beneath each title.

I was startled to see that Rufus Stanlake was the final name in the sequence under the Hunter. Martha ended a much shorter list for the Witness, while the faded ink suggested that Cecil had identified himself as the Sage a long while ago.

Constance Sutton had been displaced as the Chatelaine by Ivy Martlet, only for that name to be crossed out in turn, with none following on. Meanwhile, Constance had replaced her father as the Dupe, and that was the final name in a list that began with Mountjoy Sutton.

I guessed Martha Delly could tell me who Ivy Martlet had been, once I came up with a remotely plausible explanation for how I'd come across the name. Nothing sprang to mind.

Meantime, these notebooks needed to go somewhere safe, at least until I found some way to decide if there was any way I could make any sense of them. The Green Man had brought me here for a reason, and he'd shown me the old man's concerns as he lay dying. These notes had been part of that.

So these little black books needed to go somewhere else. If I moved this desk into the oak parlour, the last thing I wanted was Ed Franklin finding them, deciding this was some sort of bizarre family history project and binning the lot.

I thought for a moment. The sewing room seemed like a good place. No one was going to find it if they didn't know it was there, and I could keep the door locked. I reckoned it was even possible the Franklins had forgotten about it, at least for the moment.

After Martha had shown it to me, I'd found the room on the renovation plans, but turning it into a business facility with computers and printers for guests was way, way down on the list of things to be done. David hadn't shown it to me on our tour, and whoever Ed had sent to clear the house's remaining furniture and those dirty portraits from the great hall hadn't taken that roll-top desk or the picture of the horned man.

I could let the Franklins know I'd put Uncle Cecil's papers in here for safekeeping once I'd worked out what these lists and quotations meant. If I could work it out. I began stacking the notebooks on top of the blotter. I could use that to carry them out of here. After I'd removed the top few layers, I found a folded piece of paper slipped between the books and the inside of the drawer. It was old, coarse, and tattered at the edges.

I pulled carefully and it came free easily enough. Pushing the dried-up inkwell aside, I unfolded it. Fine, pale dust clung to my dirty fingertips, and I wiped it away on my trousers. Fully open and spread out on the desk, the sheet was the size of an old-fashioned broadsheet newspaper.

I contemplated a tracery of faded black ink criss-crossed in turn with heavy pencil lines and different marks in different colours. What on earth was this? Well, whatever it was, it had something to do with the house.

BRIGHTWELL

That had been written and overwritten in the centre, where the creases were beginning to tear the paper. The word was shadowed with older echoes and surrounded by other names. I recognised *The Lamp Acre* but had no clue what *The Straw Piece* might be. Another question for Martha Delly. Right, because that would be so easy to drop into casual conversation.

I looked across the room at the cheap, modern shelving, searching for something that had caught my eye earlier. Spotting it, I got up and fetched an old framed map of the Brightwell estate, propped precariously on top of a bookcase and leaning against the panelling. When I laid it on the desk and compared it to the sheet of paper, it looked like

Uncle Cecil had copied out the names that the long-dead map-maker had noted for the manor's fields and copses.

He hadn't been drawing any kind of map though.

THE FLOW OF THE LUCK

Blue lines swept through and around those words.

OBSTRUCTION

Red-ink asterisks were sprinkled here, there and everywhere.

STAGNATION

Dotted green lines seemed the most recent additions. Some enclosed larger areas, while others cut tight spirals.

I had absolutely no idea what any of it might mean. I simply had a strong feeling that it was important. So strong that I looked around the room for some sign of the Green Man's presence. I didn't see anything, but my certainty didn't fade.

Until I could work out how important this stuff might be, I needed to keep it safe. Anyone else looking at these notes and this diagram was just going to think that old-fashioned, private education had given Uncle Cecil a better class of senile delusion. I remembered the old man on his deathbed though. He'd had his wits about him until the very end.

I folded the sheet of paper back up and put it on top of the notebooks before getting another stack out of the drawer. Using the desk blotter like a tray, I carried everything from the bottom drawer carefully into the walnut parlour. I put the blotter on the floor and went to fetch the house keys. Once I'd opened up the sewing room, I tried to lift the roll-top of the desk in there, but that was locked and so were the drawers. There was no sign of a key anywhere on top of the desk, or on the mantelpiece.

I went back and checked the remaining empty drawers of the kneehole desk, but they were empty apart from the bottom one, which held a battered tin box. Inside, I found blunted colouring pencils, yellow bone dominos studded with brass and creased playing cards advertising cigarette brands I'd never heard of. There were also a few toy grenadiers, with red jackets and black bearskins chipped to reveal grey lead beneath their paint.

So the Franklins would have to get a furniture specialist or a locksmith in if they wanted to find out what might be inside the sewing room desk. I put the tin box back where I'd found it and looked at the maps still lying on the leather desk top. Since the old framed one of the estate might help decipher Uncle Cecil's notebooks, I took that through to the sewing room too, and stacked everything on the table in there.

Once I'd locked the door, I fetched the Ordnance Survey maps and headed back to the oak parlour office. I could spread them out on the table there in much better light, once I'd washed my hands.

As I came out of the kitchen into the entrance hall, movement outside on the steps by the front door snagged my eye. Keeping close to the panelling, I moved quickly and quietly towards the porch, to see who was out there. Sod it; I realised my phone was in my jacket pocket in the office. I thought about going to get it. A photo of that bastard from the caravan trespassing might interest the police.

No need. It was Hannah Franklin. She was trying to peer into the house through the front window. I took a pace forward so she could see me. Startled, she recoiled. I shoved the maps in my hand into a pocket and hurried into the porch. I unlocked the door and went outside, afraid that she'd fallen backwards down the steps.

If she had, she'd picked herself up, unhurt. Wearing trainers, jeans and a fleece, she was hurrying towards her bike, which was laid on the gravel beside my Land Rover.

'Hannah!'

She stopped and reluctantly turned to face me.

'What are you doing here?' I tried not to make that sound like an accusation. I don't think I succeeded.

She shrugged with unconvincing unconcern. 'I'm out for a bike ride.'

'All the way from Ashgrove, right through Bourton and over the river?' I came down the steps. 'Through the Broad, with those fu—halfwits always hanging around the bus shelter? What does your mum say about that?'

She shrugged again, and dodged that question too. 'I like to cycle.'

'You should train for the Tour de France.' I went to lean against the Land Rover. 'Who were you looking for inside the house?'

She opened wide, would-be-innocent eyes. 'No one. Okay, I'll go—'

She went to pick up her bike, but I was closer and quicker. I grabbed the handlebar and lifted it away, right out of her reach.

'Okay. Let's put this in the back of the Land Rover, and I'll give you a ride home.'

'There's no need. I'll be fine.' This time she tried for little-girl charm.

'No,' I said, uncompromising. 'Either I take you home, or I ring your mum and ask her to fetch you.'

'No! Please!' That was the first honest thing she had said to me.

'Then tell me what's going on.' I waited for her to reply. I could see her trying to find an answer. 'I'm not going to be responsible for letting you go home on your own, through rush-hour traffic on a pushbike.'

'I won't be on my own,' she said brightly. 'I came to find Josh. He'll be at Rufus's. You don't need to worry.'

'How stupid do you think I am?' I retorted. 'You had to come past the farmhouse to get here. Josh isn't there either, is he? Now, how about you tell me what's really going on? Or I ring your parents.'

Hannah blushed red and her eyes filled with tears. She wasn't faking that.

'I don't know where he is. He had a horrible row with Dad and got sent to his room. But I saw him going out, and I thought – he keeps hanging out with that bunch of losers—'

I let go of the bike. 'That lot from the Broad?'

Hannah nodded, the colour in her cheeks fading. 'I heard him on his phone. They were talking about meeting up at the Hoar Stone. Then I thought he might have come here. He always liked coming to see Uncle Cecil. But if he isn't... I don't want to get him into trouble, but—'

'You don't want him getting himself into trouble, either. Okay, where's this – what did you call it?'

'The Hoar Stone. It's in the woods.'

That settled it. There was absolutely no way I was letting her go off on her own, with fuck knows who or what loose out there among those trees.

She looked at me warily. 'What are you going to do?'

'I can go and see if I can find him. If I can, I'll take you both home, and no one needs to know anything about this.'

'Why would you do that?' She was more surprised than suspicious.

I surprised her some more with a grin. 'I did a few stupid things as a kid that my dad still doesn't know about.'

Though I'd had the Green Man watching out for me, instead of a little sister. He'd appeared more than once to warn me off getting sucked into something potentially dangerous as well as idiotic.

I remembered the OS maps in my pocket, and spread the most recent one out on the Land Rover's bonnet. 'So where am I looking for him?'

Hannah came to stand beside me. She put an unerring finger on Brightwell House. 'We're here. It's this way.'

She traced a route through the woods that I recognised as the broad, grassy ride I'd walked with Martha this morning. Instead of turning right towards the lake, her fingertip headed left, along a path that curved back through the trees that stretched out behind St Diuma's, the cottages and the farmhouse.

'Okay.' I saw the dot and Gothic writing that indicated a standing stone. 'You can wait inside the house, and I'm locking the door.'

Hannah shook her head. 'I'm coming with you.'

'Not a chance.' I folded up the map. 'You do as I say, or we don't do this at all. Your call. Are you staying here, or am I ringing your parents?'

Hannah reddened again. 'Oh, all right,' she said crossly.

'Okay then.' I handed her the maps and picked up her bike. 'Come on. There are biscuits and stuff if you're hungry.'

I ushered her up the steps. As soon as she went through into the entrance hall, I put her pushbike in the porch and locked the outer door. Heading for the holly trees, I turned left instead of right, though, and broke into a jog. I'd said I wouldn't tell Hannah's parents. I hadn't said I wouldn't tell anyone else.

I wasn't going into those woods alone if I could help it. The daylight was starting to fade, and I had no idea how many of those teenagers might be out there. I'm big, and strong, but that only gets you so far in a fight, especially if you get surrounded. I'd learned that lesson the hard way, getting the shit kicked out of me as a teenager doing one of those stupid things I'd mentioned to Hannah. Though I wouldn't have much choice if Rufus Stanlake wasn't at home.

Thankfully I found the door to the russet-painted barn open, and the gamekeeper was a little way inside, working on a Harley Davidson. Bess was lying down close by. As I approached, the dog looked up at me, curious.

Stanlake turned his head. Seeing me, he stood up, and for some reason decided to get his retaliation in first. 'It's not bikes I have a problem with. It's where and how those fuckwits are riding them through the woods.'

'Sounds fair.' I hadn't actually been going to say anything. 'We have a different problem. One that needs sorting out now.'

I explained the situation quickly.

'Fuck,' Stanlake said tersely.

'It'll be best if he sees a familiar face, don't you reckon?'

'Right.' Stanlake nodded, wiping oil off his hands with a rag. 'We don't want him just legging it.'

I could see he was thinking things through. I waited.

'There are two ways to the Hoar Stone from here,' he began.

'Hannah showed me the one off the path that leads up from the fingerpost,' I told him, 'on an OS map.'

'We call them lights around here, those wide rides.' Stanlake thought for a moment longer. 'Okay, you go that way. Me and Bess will take the public footpath up from the Broad. Whichever way he goes, he'll meet one of us.'

'What about the rest of them?'

Stanlake scowled. 'Fuck 'em. For now, anyway. We need to get Josh home, and Hannah.'

'Will you...?' I hesitated.

'Give him a bollocking? You can count on it. Tell Ed and Nicki?' Rufus grimaced. 'I'd rather not. They're already worried sick about him.'

'Okay.'

I stepped back as Rufus came out of the barn door and locked it.

'Right then, I'll see you there. Don't do anything till you hear Bess, and don't get fucking lost,' he warned as he headed for the farmhouse. Bess padded silently along beside him.

I headed the other way, staying alert for any sign of someone else out and about. The last thing I needed was Martha or Bill Delly flagging me down for a chat. I passed their cottage without that happening, but I stayed watchful. There was also the question of where that sly bastard from the caravan might be. Last but by no means least, I'd have given a lot for a glimpse of the Green Man as I reached the fingerpost and turned to take the broad path through the woods.

Chapter Nine

I found the turn off the main route through the woods, or the light, as Rufus had called it. I could see why now. With the dusk beginning to thicken, it was far darker underneath the trees than it was out on the wide stretch of grass. Thankfully, finding my way through the trees wasn't a problem, with my night vision. This path was also a good bit wider than the one Martha had taken to the lake, so I could follow it without brushing against gorse or saplings, making a noise to let anyone know I was coming.

That did mean I nearly stumbled over a couple lying on a coat, entwined beneath an elder tree. He had his hand up her top, with the dark cloth rucked up around his wrist. The pale twist of her unfastened bra twitched against her naked ribs as she pressed herself to him, her hand inside the unzipped front of his trousers.

I took a hasty step backwards, wondering how I was going to get past them without some uproar that would alert whoever else was in these woods. The lad wasn't Josh Franklin, to my heartfelt relief. Dragging him out of there with his cock hanging out of his trousers really wasn't something I wanted to do.

The couple were groping each other with increasing urgency. I took another step backwards as the lad suddenly got up to kneel and strip off the girl's jeans and pale knickers. She twisted and heaved herself up to help him, until her clothes were hanging off one ankle. He forced his own trousers and underpants down, and shadows dappled his fleshy buttocks as he thrust into her, his grunts matching her gasps.

They certainly weren't paying any attention to me now. I got past them as quickly, and as quietly, as I could. The path twisted and turned, and I followed it through a cluster of oak trees thick with mistletoe. Finding the standing stone well before I expected it, I nearly stumbled into the clearing I'd seen on the map.

It wasn't an inviting place. Brambles encroached on last summer's bracken lying beaten to the ground, slimy and brown. The standing stone was a massive, ominous presence over on the far side. It didn't look to have been shaped by tools, however primitive. It was simply an irregular slab of limestone looming out of the fading light, with water stains trickling dark down its lichen-spotted sides.

A group of people were sitting on some fallen logs about halfway between me and the stone, towards the right-hand side of the clearing. Not just teenagers. I could see that bastard from the caravan, as well as three girls and two lads. One of the boys was Josh Franklin. As I watched, one of the girls passed him a bottle. He took a long drink. They were smoking weed as well. I could smell it on the air.

The sooner Rufus arrived, and we got Josh out of here, the better. No fifteen-year-old needs drink, drugs and some stinking rash he can't tell his parents about. That couple fucking under the elder tree certainly hadn't been bothered about condoms.

I listened for any sound of Stanlake's dog barking. Instead I heard motorbike engines revving erratically through the trees. Two bikes appeared on the far side of the stone, and I guessed that's where the path from the Broad arrived. I wondered where Rufus had got to.

One bike had a single rider, helmetless and wearing a leather jacket hanging open over his faded T-shirt. He spun his back wheel around, buckled boots digging into the tangled grass.

The other lad had the sense to wear a helmet, and so did the girl riding pillion behind him. She got off the bike and took it off, shaking out long blonde hair. Either her black jeans had been painted on or she'd been poured into them, but she looked unbothered by the roll of flesh above her studded belt. The boy on the other bike was more interested in her admittedly impressive tits, thrust forward on display thanks to a top with a plunging neckline beneath her short denim jacket.

'What's this place then?' she demanded petulantly. 'Where are we going to sit? This is well rank, Nathan, and I'm cold.'

She lifted one foot to examine the mud on her high-heeled boots.

The lad who'd brought her here was trying to find a solid footing for his bike's stand. 'You've never been hassled here, Ryan?'

'Never,' the other bike rider said confidently.

I looked forward to making that change. Meantime, with everyone's attention on the new arrivals, I made my way silently through the trees around the edge of the clearing. I wanted to get behind the log where Josh was sitting. If needs be, I'd step in, grab his sweatshirt and drag him out of there by the scruff of his neck.

'It's the Hoar Stone.' A rangy boy with a straggly, sandy beard got up from the fallen trees and walked towards the monolith. Red and black cords were braided into ragtag epaulettes on his army-surplus jacket.

'Prehistoric. Five thousand years old.' A girl following him took a bite of an oozing kebab.

'They used to chain witches to it,' one of her friends said, 'and burn them.'

The third nodded mute agreement, sitting beside Josh. I wondered how he told them apart, all three of them favouring pale make-up, purplish lipstick and heavy eyeliner. Not goths though; I've seen enough of those to know the difference. This trio wore army-surplus coats over khaki trousers, like the boy who'd stood up. Josh didn't, I noticed. I hoped that was a sign he wasn't in too deep with this clique. This cult?

The newcomer wasn't going to be left out when it came to sharing local horror stories. 'This is where they found that dead Yank, isn't it? In the war, with his throat cut.'

The blonde looked unimpressed. 'Ryan? You got the cider?'

I made a mental note of these names, to tell Rufus later. I also wondered yet again where the fuck he'd got to.

'Here you go.' The boy in the leather jacket swung over a tattered canvas knapsack to the other bike rider.

The bearded youth held out a hand. 'Give us a beer.'

'Give us a fag for it, you wanker,' Ryan in the leather jacket retorted amiably.

The blonde girl was making her way over towards the vacant log, looking around. I could see sharp intelligence in her eyes.

Nathan dug a silver-labelled bottle out of the knapsack and took it over to her. 'There you go, Tiff.'

'Ta.' Grudging, she sat down on the log. 'Where's Leanne then? And Tyler.'

The girl eating the kebab gave up on it and tossed the remnants into the shadows. She giggled. 'Worshipping, most likely.'

The girl sitting beside Josh stiffened. 'Leanne's going with Tyler now?' Her voice was shrill, halfway between anger and jealousy.

The blonde, who I guessed was called Tiffany, looked around the group with distaste. 'You're telling me Tyler's Leanne's boyfriend?'

The taller of the other two girls tossed long hair. 'We don't have *boyfriends*.' She mocked the very idea. 'We've reclaimed our sexuality, ent we, Soph? We takes what we wants, when we wants it.'

'Fuckin'ell!' Ryan adjusted the crotch of his jeans.

'Like I said, we never get hassled here,' the boy with the beard said confidently.

'Don't think you're getting a shag in the woods, Nathan Ditchfield.' Tiffany shot her ride here a warning glare.

The bastard from the caravan had been sitting quietly still on his log all through this. Now he stood up, his back to me. I was grateful for that. The longer I went unseen, the better, certainly while I was here on my own.

'If you're cold, Tiffany, we'll light a fire.'

She looked at him dubiously. She was definitely a bright girl. 'Who the fuck are you then?'

The other girls protested at her rudeness. The bastard silenced them with an upraised hand.

'You can call me Aiden.'

An Irish name, but there wasn't a trace of an Irish accent in his voice, and I have a pretty good ear for such things.

'Hi.' Nathan sat down beside Tiffany and slid his arm casually around her shoulders.

Aiden, or whatever his real name was, held out a hand to Tiffany. 'Blessed be.'

She'd learned some manners from somewhere. She raised her own hand to shake his, but he suddenly stooped as he took it and turned her palm upwards to kiss it.

'Fuck off!' She pulled her hand back, startled.

'Hey!' Nathan wanted to protest, but couldn't work out what to say.

'Let's have a fire.' Aiden the bastard turned away, but not before I glimpsed his slyly satisfied smile.

'Blessed be.' Sophie and the other girl hurried towards him.

'Blessings to you.' He took Sophie's hand first, then the other girl's, brushing a kiss in the palm of each. 'Now, find some firewood, all of you.'

As the girls and the lad with the beard hurried off to do as they were told, I braced myself. As soon as one of them wandered over here, I'd be discovered. That wasn't going to be good. My best option was heading straight back for the light and flattening what was his name, Tyler, if I had to.

For the moment, I stayed and watched. Aiden was walking over towards the far side of the stone, heading for an elder thicket. 'If we're lighting a fire here, we use witch wood for protection.'

Twitching his coat back, he took a long knife from its scabbard on his belt. The bone handle gleamed beneath twisted cords of black and red. That really wasn't good.

'Wicked,' Ryan breathed.

Awestruck, Nathan left Tiffany sitting alone and went over to stare at the narrow blade. 'The feds'll fucking have you if they catch you carrying that.'

Yes, they would, and I'd do my damnedest to make sure that they did.

'They'll never see it.' Apparently that notion amused Aiden.

He cut a thin branch from the elder tree and walked to the standing stone. Snapping off the leafy twigs, he piled them beneath one flank. He stripped away the bark from the branch with the knife and scraped the wood into a froth of shavings. He might not be a Romany, or any sort of genuine Irish Traveller, but the bastard had learned some decent woodcraft from somewhere.

'Here.' Nathan offered a plastic lighter.

'We don't pollute the flame.' Aiden knelt down and took a metal matchbox from his pocket.

'Sorry.' Mystified, Nathan stepped back.

Aiden struck a match. Lighting the kindling stick, he thrust it among the leafy twigs and strips of bark.

'Here.' The girls hurried up with more wood to feed the flames.

I could only hope the ground was too damp for a fire to run out of control.

Closer at hand, Tiffany shifted on her log and turned to the thin-faced girl sitting beside Josh. 'Bring any smokes, Jade?'

Jade made her wait a few moments before reaching into a pocket and then opening her hand to reveal four fat roll-ups.

'Sweet.' Tiffany took one, flicked a plastic lighter and sucked hard, making the ember flare.

'D'you want a drink?' Jade took a bottle out of an inside pocket. A flat whisky bottle, like the one buried in Uncle Cecil's grave. With the firelight behind it, I could see it was half full of clear liquid. Leafy sprigs stirred dull sediment in the bottom. That's what Josh had been drinking.

Tiffany made no move to take it. 'What's that then?'

'Let's have it,' Sophie said eagerly.

'Ever seen someone's aura, Tiff?' Jade handed the bottle over and lit a joint for herself. 'It'll help.'

Aiden walked over and took it from her, drawing the smoke deep into his lungs.

'Hey,' Tiffany said to him, 'what exactly are we smoking?'

'It's Dutch skunk, Moroccan resin and a few things to enhance our sixth and seventh senses.' Aiden took another drag and offered the joint to Josh.

To my relief, he hunched his shoulders, hands between his knees as he stared at the ground. 'I don't do drugs.'

Aiden plucked a shred of tobacco from his tongue with long, stained fingers, and handed the joint back to Jade. 'That's your right. You can't follow the path unless you're prepared to pay the price.'

He turned to Tiffany. 'How about you? Are you ready to give me a token of your trust?'

'Fuck off.' But she didn't sound as certain as I expected.

Nathan came over and took the joint out of her hand. 'What's the token?'

Aiden smiled at Tiffany. 'A strand of your hair.'

'No one's cutting my hair,' she said firmly. 'My mum'd go mental.'

Aiden shook his head. 'I wouldn't violate your beautiful hair with metal.'

'Don't you know nothing about spiritual harmony, Tiff?' Sophie's superior tone stumbled.

Even at this distance, I could see her pupils were dilated. Whatever was in that bottle was nothing good. It was long past time this little gathering was broken up, as far as I was concerned. Where the hell was Rufus?

'What are you talking about?' Nathan was staring at Aiden, fascinated.

He turned to the boy. 'Will you let me pluck nine hairs from your head? As a gift, freely given?'

Nathan laughed. He'd barely smoked any of whatever that shit was, but he looked completely stoned. 'All right then.'

His swiftness taking the boy unawares, Aiden ripped a thin lock from his head.

'Fuck!' Nathan scrubbed at his scalp with a grimy hand. 'That hurt, you arsehole!'

Aiden looked at him unblinking. 'A real man can stand a little pain in return for something worthwhile.'

'It fucking better be,' Nathan said, suddenly belligerent.

'Try some of this.' Sophie pressed the whisky bottle to his lips.

Nathan took a swallow and his eyes widened.

'Want me to kiss it better?' Sophie took the bottle from his unresisting hand and locked her lips on his.

'I've had enough of this bollocks.' Tiffany stood up. 'Nathan, I want to go home.'

'What?' He pushed Sophie away.

The tall girl looked at Tiffany as she drank some more from the bottle, triumph burning through the haze clouding her eyes.

'Better do what the missis says, Nate.' Ryan pressed a mocking thumb to his forehead.

'Fuck off, Ryan. Nathan, you can do what you like. I'm going home.' Tiffany strode purposefully across the clearing, heading for the path that led back to the Broad.

'Oh fuck, Tiff!' Nathan took a few steps after her.

'You can't let her walk home alone,' Aiden said. 'She's your responsibility.'

'Yeah, right.' Nathan squared his shoulders. 'But—'

'You're welcome to join us again,' Aiden assured him. 'Ryan vouches for you.'

'Right. Okay.' Nathan hurried to retrieve his motorbike. 'Tiffany! Fucking wait!'

Then a whole lot of things happened at once. I heard Bess barking on the far side of the clearing. I couldn't see into the shadows behind the stone, with that fire between me and the darkness, but the teenagers who were closer could. They turned to Aiden, anxious.

He was already striding away, not towards either path but heading down the length of the clearing into the shadows. I had to let him go. These stupid kids were between me and the bastard, and could only get in my way. Getting Josh Franklin out of there was my priority.

Ryan and Nathan still had some of their wits about them, despite the weed. They both grabbed their bikes, swung a leg over the saddles and kicked the engines into life. Tiffany came running out of the shadows behind the stone and scrambled onto Nathan's pillion.

'Aiden!' one of the girls shrieked, but the bastard was nowhere to be seen. The rest looked at each other, panicked, as the two bikes and their riders disappeared down the path I'd followed to get here.

Rufus Stanlake appeared on the far side of the clearing. Bess was at his side, growling ferociously, hackles raised. Her bared teeth gleamed like ivory in the firelight. I rubbed my eyes. For a moment, Rufus looked as if he had stag's horns, like that fantastical figure in Constance Sutton's peculiar picture.

Before I could decide whether it was a trick of the light or something more meaningful, Jade sprang to her feet. She held out her hand. 'Come on!'

Josh stood up and took a pace forward. I stepped out of the shadows, scowling as nastily as I know how. That and my size have saved me from a few fights, though I didn't think the straggly bearded boy was going to present much of a challenge, if he was stupid or stoned enough to think he could take me.

He was looking directly towards me, but he didn't react. Neither did the girl, Jade, even when I stepped up close behind Josh, reaching for his shoulder. Even though I was looking straight at her, and the firelight was filling the clearing.

I grabbed a fistful of Josh's sweatshirt. He was going nowhere without my say-so. The instant I touched him, the girl screamed. The bearded boy yelped with shock, and they both staggered backwards. Now they were definitely looking at me, startled and fearful.

Josh twisted in my grip to see who had got hold of him. Mouth open, he looked on the verge of tears. When he realised I was his captor, I saw guilty relief in his eyes as well as recognition. Good. I'd much rather he came with me willingly.

The others were scattering into the darkness. Rufus made no move to stop them, more concerned with stamping out the fire that was licking up the side of the standing stone. He was swearing, foully and repetitively. As far as I could see, he didn't have horns.

Somewhere out in the woods, I heard someone being violently sick. Incoherent yells suggested someone had tripped over the two who'd been shagging under the elder tree. I didn't care.

'Come on.' I urged Josh forward, gently enough, though without letting go of his sweatshirt.

Bess came to meet us, tail wagging and ears pricked. She jumped up, putting her front paws on Josh's chest and rubbing her head against him. As the Retriever whined with concern, I felt Josh sag in my grip. I let him sink to his knees, wrapping his arms around the dog and burying his face in her thickly furred neck.

'Okay then.' Rufus finished killing the last remnants of the fire and walked towards us. Without the flames, the shadows rushed in to surround us, and I felt an ominous chill. Rufus took a torch out of a pocket and snapped it on. The darkness receded.

'What took you so long?' I demanded.

'What the fuck?' He stared at me, genuinely taken aback. 'I got here before you did!'

I opened my mouth, recalled how the teenagers hadn't seen me, changed my mind about arguing the point and asked my most urgent question. 'What now? Do we go to the police? I heard a few names, and that sly bastard's carrying a blade as long as my hand, as well as feeding these idiots fuck knows what drugs.'

I wasn't at all keen on coming to the police's attention again, even to just make a statement, but I was even less keen on letting Aiden, or whatever his real name was, carry on doing whatever he was up to with those idiot kids.

Rufus scowled, though his hostility wasn't directed at me. 'I'd rather get Josh straight home.'

Kneeling between us with the dog now resting her chin on his shoulder, the lad stiffened. He didn't look up though.

'I'd rather keep him out of this entirely,' Rufus went on. 'If what you're saying's true—' he raised a quick hand '—and I believe you, don't get me wrong, then we can catch them some other time. Get photos for the cops.'

I nodded, for Rufus's benefit. 'As long as Josh keeps right out of it from now on, right away from them all.'

We both looked down at the boy. He still didn't look up. I glanced at Rufus, who grimaced.

'You head back to the house and tell Hannah everything's fine,' he suggested. 'Me and Josh will go the other way, and drive round to you to pick her up.'

'Okay.' That should give them some time to talk without anyone else listening. I only hoped Rufus could talk some sense into him. Well, he had more chance than me, surely.

'Do you want a torch?' Rufus offered me the one in his hand.

I shook my head. 'I'll be fine.'

He looked surprised, but shrugged. 'See you back there then.'

He turned around and headed off. At his whistle, the dog sprang after him. Josh scrambled to his feet and hurried after them, not looking back at me.

I waited a few moments for my eyes to adjust to the twilight now that the torch was gone. Then I made sure that no trace of the fire was still smouldering. I kept a wary eye out while I did that, and crossed the clearing back to the path to the light, still alert. Those young idiots could still be stumbling around the woods, out of their skulls, and I had no idea where that bastard Aiden might be lurking.

Listening, and looking, I followed the path. I soon realised something very odd. It seemed to take a whole lot longer than it had before, when I'd been going in the other direction. That normally works the other way round, with getting back feeling quicker than going somewhere for the first time.

At least I didn't see or hear any sign of anyone else, either in the trees or when I got back to the light. Better able to see where I was putting my feet, I broke into a jog. Even so, I'd barely reached the holly trees at the house entrance when I saw the Defender's headlights coming towards me down the lane. By the time I was unlocking the front door, Rufus had pulled up by my Land Rover.

'Hannah!' I called as I put her bike out onto the steps. 'It's okay. We found him. Rufus is going to give you a lift home.'

The door to the housekeeper's sitting room opened, spilling light into the entrance hall as I found a light switch by the oak screen.

Hannah appeared, indignant. 'Why did you tell Rufus? I didn't—'

'Don't,' I advised her. 'Not to me, not to Rufus, not to Josh. You did the right thing here, and we can all be grateful for that. For the moment though, keep your mouth shut.'

She looked at me, startled. That probably wasn't the best way to talk to an eleven-year-old, I thought belatedly. I braced myself for some sort of outburst, maybe even tears.

Instead, Hannah just walked past me, not making eye contact. 'Thank you,' she said in a small voice.

That made me feel a bit less of a bully. 'You're welcome.'

I stood in the doorway and watched Rufus putting Hannah's bike in the back of the Defender. Bess rushed up to greet the girl, and Hannah climbed into the back with the dog.

As they drove off, I locked the door and set the alarm. I wasn't going to leave the house unattended tonight, so trying a local curry would have to wait. I ate beans on toast for my tea, and then went to bed to read the last few chapters of a decent thriller.

I set the alarm on my phone. I had to be up for work in the morning. Kemble and Coates were coming.

Chapter Ten

The workmen were due at eight o'clock, so I set my alarm for seven. I was woken up by determined knocking on the front door not long after six. I dragged on some clothes, grabbed the keys and went to see what the hell was going on.

Stanlake was outside, on the steps. I went to unlock the door, stopped just in time, went back to unset the alarm, and then unlocked the door.

'Come in.' I headed for the kitchen and put the kettle on. 'Coffee?'

Rufus followed me, with Bess padding obediently at his heels. 'I'm fine.' He didn't wait for me to ask what he was playing at, getting me out of bed so early. 'How about you and me go and see that prick in the caravan?'

I spooned sugar and coffee into a mug and got the milk out of the fridge. 'To do what?'

'To tell him to sling his hook. Tell him we know what he's up to, selling weed to kids. If he doesn't want to discuss that with the cops, he can fuck off out of here.'

'I thought you didn't want to involve the police?' I waited for the kettle to boil and poured hot water into the mug. 'That's what you said last night.'

'He doesn't know that, does he?' Rufus grinned, and I was reminded of seeing his dog snarling.

At the moment, Bess was looking hopefully around the kitchen with soulful brown eyes. When I opened a cupboard and got out some biscuits, I had her undivided attention.

'What if he calls our bluff? What if he threatens to drop Josh Franklin in the shit if the police come to talk to him?'

'Then we say he's lying.' Rufus wasn't deterred. 'You, me and Josh, we were all round at mine last night, having a few beers – not Josh, obviously. Just talking about Brightwell and stuff. Josh will say what I tell him to.' He had absolutely no doubt of that. 'What's the bastard going to do? Insist on telling the cops he was getting a whole load of kids stoned in the woods?'

I didn't suppose any of them would admit they'd been there, even if they could remember last night. I drank some coffee. 'What are you going to do?'

'Throw a scare into the prick.' Rufus grinned again. 'This early, he won't know if it's the police putting his door in or us. That might be enough to run him off, without any more trouble.'

I doubted it. I ate a biscuit.

'Come on,' Rufus urged. 'It'll be better if there's two of us.'

Better, I noted, but not essential. Rufus was going to do this, with or without me. I could leave him to it. That way, I'd stay out of trouble.

On the other hand, I wouldn't mind getting a closer look at this Aiden. I wanted to know if he was some ordinary, human predator, or something worse. That meant I needed to see his eyes. If he wasn't human, my greenwood blood meant I would see that as soon as he blinked. With any luck, the colour of whatever sheen I saw would give me, or more likely my mum, some hint of what he really was.

'Okay then.' I held up a biscuit. 'Can Bess have this?'

'Just this once.' Rufus meant it.

I tossed the digestive, and the dog snapped it out of the air. Tail wagging, she followed Rufus to the front door. As I came out onto the steps, I saw him getting a crowbar out of the Defender.

'You promise me you won't use that on him,' I said sharply, 'or you're going on your own.'

Stanlake looked at me, considering his response.

'I mean it.' I didn't move. 'A few years back, I got a suspended sentence and community service for breaking a badger baiter's arm. I'm not getting into any more trouble like that.'

That gave him something to think about. Rufus pursed his lips. 'Okay then.'

We walked along the lane. The sun had barely risen, and mist was still hanging around between the hedges.

'What did Josh have to say for himself last night?' I asked because it didn't look like Rufus was going to tell me.

'Not a lot.' He was exasperated, but not unsympathetic. 'Jade Taysel invited him. He said he doesn't know why he went along with them. It was just something to do. He won't do it again, he promised me that much.'

He shook his head. 'He doesn't know what to do with himself, if he's not playing computer games. He knows what his parents want for their kids, and that's fine for Tasha, because that's what she wants for herself, and she's good at exams. But Josh isn't a great one for school. He's not stupid, but I can't see him at university, and neither can he. The problem is, he may know what he doesn't want out of life, but he has no fucking clue what he does want.'

'We've all been there,' I said with feeling.

We slowed by unspoken agreement as we approached the bend. As we rounded the edge of the trees, we couldn't see as far as the river, with the mist coming up off the water.

There was no sign of life in the caravan. As we drew closer, I could see that the padlock was secure on the door. I looked at the fire pit and tried to decide how old those ashes were.

'He didn't come back here last night then.' Rufus was annoyed. 'I did come down to see, after I'd dropped the kids back at Ashgrove, but there was no sign of him.'

I was about to ask if he'd seen Ed or Nicki, but he was already ripping the padlock hasp off the door frame. Once he had the door open, he looked at me.

'What's he going to do? Report a burglary? Bess, stay, guard.'

The dog took up an alert stance as Rufus stepped up and went into the caravan.

I followed. 'Try not to touch anything.'

Rufus was already ripping down the blanket that covered the nearest window. 'What a pig sty.'

I couldn't argue with that. The daylight showed us discarded clothes on the dirty carpet, empty beer cans and takeaway containers spotted with mould. Half-consumed scented candles were stuck in empty jam jars on the surfaces of the filthy kitchenette. The lingering, sickly reek of the candles couldn't mask the fact that the whole place smelled musty and damp.

'See if you can find anything that might have his name on.' Rufus had moved down to the end of the caravan where a built-in sofa that converted to a bed was a tangle of unwashed sheets. 'Dave Franklin should be able to find out something if we can get a full ID.'

He tore another blanket away from the window, and began using the crowbar to lift sheets and shirts and toss them aside.

I tugged down the cuff of my sweatshirt sleeve to cover my hand as I started opening cupboards. I was less concerned with leaving fingerprints than touching something foul. I'd just noticed two used condoms discarded in a foil food tray in the sink.

'What exactly does he do, David Franklin?' I found four flat bottles of vodka, unopened and garishly labelled with a double-headed eagle. I guessed what was in them was as Russian as me.

'Something with sales data.' Rufus was sweeping newspapers and what looked like tourist information leaflets off the shelf unit beside the bed. 'Analysing the stuff companies get off loyalty cards. He got into IT right from university, set up his own company. He's done very well.'

I opened another cupboard to find a mundane selection of packets and tins. 'I'd be surprised if this charmer has any store cards.'

Still, if we could find out his real name, Eleanor Beauchene might be able to check it against credit reference agencies and whatever else running a business like Blithehurst gave her access to.

Rufus hooked the cushions off the sofa bed and used the crowbar to lift the lid of the storage space that revealed. 'Found his stash,' he said with satisfaction. 'Let's burn this shit.'

I wasn't about to argue as he made for the open door with two substantial bags of weed.

'Matches.' I tossed him a box that I found sitting between two candle jars. 'Don't stand downwind.'

Plates and glasses. A few saucepans, and some cutlery. There was only one cupboard left to open, at the very top of the kitchenette unit. The door was hinged at the top, with a horizontal handle to lift it up. I nearly didn't bother, until I saw a strip of transparent tape that had been carefully stuck along the very edge of the door.

I looked around, and saw a roll of tape on the floor with the stuff Rufus had swept off the shelves. I went and grabbed that, then came back to peel the seal carefully off the edge of the door. I screwed the tape into a ball and shoved it into a pocket. If Aiden wanted to know if anyone had looked in his cupboard, then I wanted him to stay ignorant.

I lifted the door and saw a row of books. Old books. Some were cloth-bound, with titles in French: *Le Petit Albert* and *Agrippa Le Noir*. Others had black leather covers with the gold-lettered titles long since worn away. Nine books. I counted quickly, and wished I had something to write on, to make a note of their titles. Then I could go across the river to Shayler's and see what I could find out, either from the Internet or from Jude Oxway.

There were two candles on either side, acting as bookends. Each one was as thick as my forearm, and deep, blood red. They definitely weren't scented crap from some gift shop for tourists in Bourton.

I hesitated, then reached up to take out one of the black leather books. Opening it, I saw a name written inside the front cover. Not Aiden anything, but Mungo Peploe, written in cramped and faded ink. Its title was *The Long Secreted Friend*, which made no more sense to me than the ones in French.

As I put the book back, about to take a look at the next one, I realised there was something right at the back of the cupboard. Shifting the books and candles aside, I saw the long, bone-handled knife that the bastard had been wearing on his belt last night. So he had come back here, at least briefly.

I was going to take a closer look at it, maybe take it away altogether, when I had second thoughts. As long as he didn't find me and Rufus here, Aiden wouldn't know who for certain who had trashed his place. As long as he found his secret cupboard still sealed, he could tell himself he'd lost his stash to someone who didn't like having a drug dealer around, or someone who didn't like having a rival in their town.

If he thought someone had been looking at his books, when he realised someone had taken his knife, he was sure to go looking for whoever that could be. Those idiot kids he was grooming for whatever the fuck he was up to, that would be where he'd start. Josh Franklin was one of them, and one who wasn't fully under the bastard's thrall. I didn't know what might happen, and I decided I didn't want to find out.

I put everything back the way I had found it, and began carefully stretching out a new length of tape to seal the cupboard door.

'Dan,' Rufus called, from outside the caravan door.

'Just a moment.'

He didn't sound too urgent, and the dog wasn't barking. I concentrated on making a neat job of the tape.

'Dan!'

Okay, now he meant it. That was fine. I was finished. I tossed the roll of tape into the heap on the floor and stepped down out of the door. Rufus was kicking dirt over the smouldering, feathery ashes of the burned weed. The breeze carrying the morning mist away was taking the last of the pungent smoke with it.

Bess was standing looking attentively at the lane, ears pricked. Rufus gestured in that direction.

'A car just went past. Whoever it was might decide to be a good citizen and ring the cops about the smoke. We don't want to be here if a patrol car comes to take a look.'

'We don't,' I agreed.

'Find anything useful?' Rufus glanced at me as we made our way back towards the lane.

'Nothing to identify him.' A new thought struck me as I recalled stumbling out of these trees on my first day here. 'Do you have much work to do in the woods on this side of the lane, running down to the river?'

'No, we keep the birds on the higher ground. The drainage round here is fucked, thanks to Mountjoy Sutton. Why do you ask?' He was curious.

'That bastard might be ready for a fight, when he comes back and finds his door open. Probably best if you steer clear.'

'I can take him.' Rufus had no doubt of that.

'If he's carrying a knife? You could still end up with stitches.'

'Seeing him done by the cops for that would get rid of him once and for all.' But Rufus sounded a lot less inclined to fight.

We walked back along the lane, and I wondered when I should tell him about that dead tree with the rotting birds. Clearly, that had nothing to do with the gamekeeper. It must be part of whatever weird shit this Aiden was up to. I still had no idea what that might be.

Until I did, I decided, I didn't want to alert him to the fact that someone was on to him, so telling Rufus about that carrion tree had better wait. The gamekeeper would want to get rid of the foul thing, and I couldn't blame him. I certainly had no good reason to try and talk him out of it.

This was getting frustrating. I needed to talk to my mum. I needed to talk to Eleanor. There was no chance of doing that just now. As we approached Brightwell, a trio of Transit vans appeared. The first driver gave us a cheery toot on his horn and a wave as he turned in between the holly trees. The logo on the van's side told me Kemble and Coates had arrived, though it was only half seven.

'I'll let you get on.' Rufus went on his way.

I walked down the gravel as eight workmen got out of the vans, ranging from a white-haired man with an unmistakable air of being in charge to a couple of apprentices who were looking up at the house, wide-eyed.

'Geoff Kemble.' Fifty-something, and solid in paint-flecked overalls, the older man offered me his hand as I reached the group. 'Everyone calls me Gaffer.'

'Good to meet you.' I shook. 'Dan Mackmain.'

He glanced towards the lane. 'Been stretching your legs with Rufus Stanlake?'

That struck me as an odd thing to say, and I let him see that. 'Just while he was out walking the dog.'

Geoff Kemble cleared his throat. 'Right, let's get started then. We've got a skip coming first thing, so we'll need the garage yard gate unlocked.'

I nodded. 'I'll open up the house and go and do that.'

The gang of men followed me up the steps. I shut off the alarm as they came into the house, and pointed at doors on the opposite sides of the hallway.

'Kitchen's in there, with tea, coffee and biscuits.' I'd better remember to claim for the biscuits I'd bought through petty cash. 'That's what we're using for an office.' I indicated the oak parlour door. 'There are loos in the garage yard.'

'We know our way around,' Geoff assured me amiably.

'Okay then.' I matched his friendly tone. 'I'll get that gate unlocked.'

'We'll get unloaded.' Geoff had what looked like a referee's whistle on a lanyard around his neck. It was startlingly loud when he blew it to get the apprentices' attention. They'd wandered into the great hall and were staring up at the ceiling. 'Davey, get a brew on.'

By the time I got back from opening up the garage yard and unlocking the old stable washroom, young Davey had a row of steaming mugs lined up on the draining board. He was opening the cupboards, and as I came into the kitchen, I saw him taking out a jar of jam. Two slices of bread were already in the toaster.

'The Franklins are providing tea, coffee and biscuits,' I said mildly. 'Ask me before you help yourself to anything else, please.'

'Sorry.' He looked at me, uncertain what to do.

I could see he hadn't thought this through. 'Go ahead, if you need some breakfast. Don't make a habit of it though.'

'Daniel!' Geoff stuck his head through the door. 'We need the basement door open.'

'Right.' I followed him out of the house and around to the side entrance. I was happy to see the steps were as clean and piss-free as I had left them.

David Franklin had been right when he called the original kitchen floor a disaster area. The kitchen itself was dank and dispiriting, with one obstinate tap dripping into a stained stone sink. The wooden work surfaces were warped, splintered and spotted with mouse droppings. Charmless white tiles on the walls were cracked and smudged with damp. The high windows were filthy and tightly barred, so the only light came from a single fluorescent strip on the ceiling. I guessed that attempt at modernisation had been installed around the same time that the original cast-iron range had been ripped out of the fireplace alcove and replaced with an enamelled cooker with an eye-level grill. Whatever else had once been in here was long since gone.

Geoff looked around with bright-eyed anticipation. 'We'll refit this whole level with a proper kitchen and cold stores, preparation space, pantries, the lot. There's the old dairy on the other side of the courtyard, a game larder and wine cellars, so there's plenty of space for everything David Franklin wants.'

I nodded. 'Let me know when you take these ceilings down. I can take a good look at these beams before you put up new plasterboard. That'll save me taking up the floorboards up top.'

'Good idea. Plaster and lath can hide a lot of mischief,' he said with feeling. 'I don't know if Ed said, but he agreed we could leave our tools and that down here overnight.'

'That's fine,' I said. 'I always set the alarm when I lock up for the evening.'

He headed for one of the two interior doors. 'We'll use the old servants' hall. We won't need to do anything in there until we do the decorating.'

'Right.' As I followed him, I remembered Ed Franklin showing me the plans and saying this was going to be the staff break room. It was hard to imagine that at the moment, looking at the flaking ceiling, the grimy walls and the remnants of birds' nests that had fallen all the way down the chimney to land in the fireplace's rusted grate.

The servants' stair arrived here, and Geoff headed upwards. I saw a door in the opposite wall, with a key in the lock. I opened it to find myself out in the courtyard at the heart of the house. Looking up, I could see the windows and the inner face of the roof. Underfoot, mossy cobbles sloped gently towards the front far corner, where I could see a drain. That had doubtless been well used in days of old when the kitchen's and dairy's messy jobs were done out here. Ancient lead guttering and downpipes carried the rainwater off the roof down to keep the drain flushed clear.

There were doors in the other three sides of the courtyard, and when I walked over to check them, I found two dark, dank cellars and a room with a massive iron boiler that must have been installed a hundred or more years ago. Replacing that was another job for a firm of specialists, I recalled from Ed Franklin's plans. They weren't even going to try testing it, in case it blew up and took half the house down.

The doors were all unlocked. It was obvious that the Franklins hadn't bothered finding the old keys or fitting new locks, and wouldn't be doing so before these renovations were finished, which made sense, I supposed. As far as they were concerned, the only way to get into the courtyard would be by flying.

The problem was, I knew there were creatures out there that could do just that without any problem. I really needed to get a good look at that bastard Aiden's eyes, to get a better idea of what I was dealing with here.

For the moment, though, I had a job I was being paid for. I went upstairs and found young Davey finishing his toast.

'Come on, you can help me move some furniture.'

Once we'd carried the gate-leg table into Uncle Cecil's reading room and carefully manhandled the heavy kneehole desk out to the oak parlour, I went and made myself some toast.

Then I fetched my tools and got to work.

Chapter Eleven

I didn't have too much time to worry about Aiden Whoever-he-was for the rest of the day, or for the rest of the week. Geoff Kemble was presumably working to a price instead of being paid a day rate, so he wasn't hanging around on this job. He wanted the pipework done as far as first fix as soon as possible, so the bathroom fittings could be brought in.

So I was kept busy taking up floorboards and carefully lifting panelling away from the walls, while the Kemble and Coates team stripped out old lead pipework and installed gleaming copper. A local scrap dealer took away anything made of metal, and the skip in the garage yard was soon filled with junk from the basement level and the bedrooms.

In between helping Geoff Kemble's blokes, I started a survey of the interior woodwork, beginning with the long gallery bookcases. There was plenty of work to be done there, replacing pieces of inlay and moulding that had come loose. It was time-consuming and fiddly rather than difficult. As I went, I looked at the books in hopes of finding out more about Brightwell House's history. I didn't learn much more than I already knew though.

I didn't see any trace of trespassers when I walked around the house, outbuildings and gardens first thing every morning, and again each night before I set the alarm and locked up. I made sure to find time during each day's lunch break to go over to the supermarket in Bourton and restock the kitchen with milk and biscuits, as well as getting something for my evening meal. That way the house was never left unattended, though it meant I still hadn't had that curry.

There was a bit of excitement halfway through Friday afternoon. I heard Mark Coates coming back up the stairs and expected him to bring me a cup of tea. He was working in the old staff bathroom, which was going to be turned into a bar area to serve the residents' lounge that was planned for the long gallery. He was about my age and had been married for three years, with a toddler, and another kid on the way. We'd got talking about different jobs we'd worked on, as I helped him strip out the flimsy partitions and load three claw-footed, chipped enamelled baths into the rattling lift. We'd agreed that we'd take turns to save each other the walk downstairs and all the way back up whenever Geoff's whistle signalled a tea break.

Mark halted in the gallery doorway. He wasn't carrying any mugs. 'Come and see what Davey found in the beer cellar.'

'Okay.' I decided I could do with stretching my legs, after a long session kneeling and bending down to mend the bottom of a bookcase's glazed door. I also wanted a cup of tea.

In the entrance hall, Davey was relishing his moment as the centre of attention, instead of being the one at everyone else's beck and call. He was the youngest of the Coates contingent, some sort of cousin to Mark.

He grinned as he held out two bulbous brown glass bottles, unlabelled and lumpily sealed with wax. 'Got a corkscrew?'

'I wouldn't,' Graham Kemble said quickly. He was one of Geoff's many nephews. 'Those are witch bottles.'

'What?' Davey gaped.

'Where did you find them?' I asked.

'By the end door in the beer cellar. There's a little room off to the side, goes right under the bay window.' Davey gestured into the great hall.

I pictured what had once been the beer cellar running nearly the full width of the house, underneath the great hall. A sturdy wall divided it from the wine cellar under the walnut parlour. Refitted, the wine cellar would retain its original function, while the beer cellar was being converted into storerooms for the hotel's necessities. I only recalled seeing a single door in there, leading into the wine cellar, apart from the ones to the basement kitchen and out to the courtyard.

'There's a hidden room?' Any job has its unforeseen occurrences, but Brightwell House had more than its fair share of secrets.

'We didn't even know it was there till we took off the old render. Someone skimmed right over the door.' Graham stepped forward to take the bottles.

Davey was happy to relinquish them. 'What's in a witch bottle then?'

'Piss and pins.' Graham grinned at him. 'Not something you want to drink.'

'Fuckin'ell.' Davey looked repelled.

'You watch your mouth, my lad.' Geoff had come out of the oak parlour to see what was going on. 'Or I'll wash it out with soap and tell your mum why I done it.'

'Sorry, Grandad – I mean, Gaffer.' Davey blushed furiously.

Graham carefully shook one of the bottles. 'I can't feel anything inside this one.'

'Where'd you learn about witch bottles?' I'd read enough folklore to come across them, but Graham only ever talked about horse racing and cricket. He'd been sorry to learn I wasn't going to be here long enough to try an innings with the local club. I was a bit surprised to realise I was too. I'd been a useful bowler at school, and could generally do a bit with a bat.

'What's it supposed to do?' Davey asked.

Graham answered him first. 'All the pins give the witch such pains in her... in her innards, that she has to stop casting her spells or die. The ones without pins in, they're to keep ghosts from walking.'

He glanced at me. 'My dad was a roofer. He came across a few of these in old houses. Came across all sorts of things when he was stripping back thatch. Any number of old shoes up the rafters, and no one ever knows why.'

'There's more of 'em,' volunteered Davey.

'They'll need to be moved, Gaffer.' Graham looked at Geoff.

'Without breaking them,' he said with distaste, 'and catching who knows what.'

We waited while he thought for a moment.

'Best stick them in a box out in one of the garages. Nicki Franklin can decide what to do with them. Right,' he said briskly. 'Let me have a look at this space you've found and we'll see what we can do with it.'

That sent everyone back to work, or in my case, across the hall and into the kitchen, to put the kettle on.

Mark came with me, putting tea bags in a couple of mugs. 'Got any plans for the weekend?'

'Probably visiting my mum and dad, up Warwickshire way.' I'd been thinking about doing that since Wednesday. Now I was definitely going home to see what advice they could offer me.

He nodded, getting milk out of the fridge. 'Depending when you get back, there's usually a few of us in The Whittle and Dub of a Sunday evening. Join us for a pint, if you want.'

'Where's that?' I hadn't heard of that particular pub.

Mark gestured away down the lane. 'Just follow the road round. It's on the first crossroads you come to. Good beer, good food.'

'Okay then.' I finished making my tea. 'Ready to get back to it?'

We went back upstairs and worked steadily until we heard the gaffer's whistle. I came downstairs to find Geoff sat at the desk in the oak parlour, checking that he had everyone's time sheets.

'All done.' He tapped the paper into a neat stack and got up. His smile showed his satisfaction with the job's progress so far. 'See you on Monday.'

'See you then.' I walked with him to the front door, and stood in the porch to watch the works vans drive off.

I locked the door, went downstairs to the kitchen and headed outside, locking that door behind me before walking through to the garage yard to lock up the washroom and the gate to the lane. Coming back to the house, I went into the oak parlour and found Nicki Franklin's list of phone numbers. I used the crackling landline to call the Home Farm.

After a few rings, Rufus answered. 'Hello?'

I wasn't interested in small talk either. 'Are you going to be around this weekend? I want to visit my parents, and I'll probably stay over Saturday night. I'll leave everything locked up, but can you do a walk-round with Bess in the evening and the next morning?'

Rufus didn't reply. I was beginning to wonder if we'd been cut off when the line crackled again and he spoke, brusque. 'I'm going out tonight, but I can be around tomorrow.'

I wondered where he was going, but he didn't say, so I didn't ask. I had a more important question.

'Have you been down to the Lamp Acre at all?'

'I have.' Even over the bad connection, Rufus sounded annoyed. 'He's back in that caravan. Fucker's riveted a new lock fitting onto the door, and covered up the windows again.'

I supposed it was too much to hope that the creep had decided to leave. 'Let's hope David Franklin's consultant comes up with something to get rid of him soon.'

'What if she doesn't?' Rufus challenged me.

I had no answer for that. 'I'll head off tomorrow lunchtime, and be back Sunday afternoon.'

'Fine.' Rufus hung up.

'Okay then,' I said to the empty room.

Checking the phone list again, I rang Nicki Franklin and told her my plans. 'I wanted to let you know I'll be away. I've told Rufus, and he's going to keep an eye out.'

'That's fine, and I'm sure Bill Delly will be in and out. Okay, thanks for keeping me up to date, and have a nice time with your family. Bye now.'

'Bye.'

She sounded so unconcerned that for a moment I was shocked. Then I realised the Franklins had no reason to be worried. They had no idea what that creep was doing with the local kids out in their woods, and absolutely no idea that there was something nasty lurking in Brightwell's little lake.

I could tell Nicki about this Aiden screwing up those teenagers with drink and drugs, and encouraging them to screw around. Only I couldn't see how to do that without risking involving Josh. From what I'd already seen of tensions in that family, that was the last thing the boy needed – or his parents, come to that. I was far enough from my own teenage rebellions to understand both sides now.

As for the rest of it, there was nothing I could say to the Franklins that would make any kind of sense. Not to people who had no idea that there were more things in the woods and waters than most normal folk ever dreamed of. There wasn't much more I could say to someone who wouldn't think I was mad, like Eleanor Beauchene. I still had no idea what was hidden under those dark waters.

I only hoped Mum had some idea, as well as some answers to my other questions. I rang Dad's number.

'Hello,' he answered, almost as curt as Rufus.

'Hi, it's me. This is the Brightwell House number.'

'Oh, right.' He laughed. 'I wondered if you were going to tell me my car had been in an accident, or I had a virus on my computer. So how are you getting on?'

'Very well.' I brought him up to date with the project's progress.

'And what about everything else?'

I knew what he was asking.

'I was thinking I'd come home tomorrow and tell you about it then. Tell both of you.'

'Oh?' Now he was even more curious.

'I know why the Green Man wanted me here,' I said. 'Beyond that, it's all very odd.'

'How odd? How dangerous?'

He might have forgiven me for not telling him about the risks I had run last summer, but I could tell he hadn't forgotten.

'I don't know,' I said honestly. 'Until I have some idea what's in the lake. I'm hoping Mum might have some suggestions.'

'What will you do then?'

'See if Eleanor's got any ideas?'

Dad grunted. 'I suppose so. Okay, what time should we expect you?'

'Early afternoon.' I had the usual boring weekend things to do, like laundry and tidying up.

We said our goodbyes, and I walked through the house, to make sure no tools needed putting away and nothing else needed tidying up. There was nothing that needed my attention, so I walked around the house and the gardens, making sure there was no sign of anything amiss.

I paused at the gate in the iron fence, tempted to go out into the woods. I could take another look at that revolting tree and see if that bastard was still sticking dead birds on the thorns. Except that would tell me nothing useful, not yet anyway. Tripping over him in the woods risked a confrontation over what had happened to the caravan. While I still wanted to get a good look at his eyes, things could turn ugly if he had those teenagers with him.

I went back into the house, locked up again, set the alarm and spent the evening in the housekeeper's sitting room, watching of the next disc of a spy thriller box set on my laptop. I went to bed expecting to sleep as soundly as I usually do.

I didn't. I woke up several times in the night, sure I'd heard a clock chime. Only, I couldn't have, because the only one in the house was the long case clock in the great hall, and that was still waiting for an expert to come and see if it could ever be got running again.

In between, I had that sensation of not quite knowing if you're awake or asleep. I kept hearing footsteps, but when I dragged myself up, reaching for my phone to use the torch, I realised the house was as dark and silent as it always had been.

I hadn't set an alarm, since I was sure I'd wake up at a reasonable hour. After such a bad night, I didn't, so I started Saturday having overslept and still knackered regardless, which struck me as hardly fair. It's a good thing it wasn't a working day, as I did my chores in a filthy mood.

I went to The Boar's Head for lunch. My temper improved after eating something that wasn't a reheated ready meal and a couple of pints of beer, even if they were alcohol-free. I was also pleased to see no sign of those teenagers hanging around under the market hall.

The weather was fine, and my spirits rose as I drove north and east towards the village where my parents live. I stuck to the back roads, ignoring the satnav's plaintive requests for me to do a U-turn where possible, to get me back on the fastest route. That kept me driving through well-kept farmland and plenty of trees, and it really refreshed me. I hadn't realised how oppressive the atmosphere in the Brightwell woods was until I got away.

I took the turn before the village that took me past the old chapel and its little cemetery. Just beyond the junction that would take me back to the village or further away, I reached the five-barred gate that was the entrance to the wildlife reserve.

I followed the single-width track that led to my dad's house carefully. There are always visitors at weekends, and it doesn't occur to some of them that there might be traffic coming the other way.

There were a couple of cars parked by the visitor centre on the opposite side of the track, and I could see dog walkers heading away down the closest footpath. I pulled up outside what had been a woodsman's cottage when this stretch of ancient trees had been owned by some distant landlord only interested in profiting from them.

My dad had done some research. That family's fortunes had foundered after the Second World War. Their London house was bombed, and their stately home down in Surrey had been sold off and turned into a boarding school when they owed two lots of death duties inside nine years. The rest of their land had been sold off piecemeal, and this particular bit had passed from owner to owner who hadn't really known what to do with it, until a local wildlife charity bought it in the 1960s.

I hadn't thought about it till now, but Brightwell House had been lucky not to suffer a similar fate.

Dad had heard me arrive, and opened the front door. As I gave him a hug, I was pleased to see he was looking fit and well. I hadn't been here since Christmas, after all, and though I didn't like to think about it, he was seventy-six, even if most people assumed he was still in his sixties.

'Good trip?'

I nodded. 'Nothing much on the road.'

He turned to go back into the house. 'I'll get the kettle on.'

Mum was sitting at the kitchen table, in the guise of a middle-aged woman with greying hair, wearing a comfortable jumper and a long, flowing skirt. It's how she looked when there were people about, or she stayed invisible. Outside opening hours, once my dad had locked the entrance gate, she reverted to her preferred manifestation, and was as graceful and beautiful as a nymph off a Greek vase.

She got up and gave me a hug. I hugged her back tight, and felt tension that I hadn't been aware of flow out of me.

After a few moments she held me at arm's length. 'You're somewhere unhappy, aren't you?'

I hadn't thought about it in those terms, but as soon as she said it, I realised she was right. She wasn't talking about me being miserable either. 'The Brightwell woods are unhappy, certainly. The house is a bit different.'

'I made a cake.' Dad put it on the table and filled the teapot. 'Okay, let's hear all about it.'

He and I went through several mugs of tea, and half the fruitcake, as I told them about my eventful week, with the three of us sitting around the kitchen table. After I told them about my broken night, we sat looking at each other for a long moment. My first question was obvious.

'So, Mum, are there really such things as ghosts?' I couldn't quite believe I was asking that, and I wasn't at all sure I wanted to know the answer.

She nodded, unbothered. 'If that's what you want to call them. Humans sometimes linger in the ethereal plane after their bodies have died. Some fade away quickly, once and for all. Some come and go and come back again. I don't know why.'

'You never said.' Dad was astonished.

She looked at him, mildly surprised. 'You never asked.'

He knew better than to argue that point. 'Are there any ghosts around here?'

Mum thought about that for a moment. 'There was a woodcutter killed by a falling tree, not long after the railway was laid.'

She glowered at that memory. Dryads hold grudges when it comes to lines of iron rails being laid across the landscape.

'He left a young family,' she went on, 'and was desperate to see his family grown. But I haven't seen him since well before Daniel was born.' She smiled at me.

No wonder she hadn't mentioned it. For all that their lives span centuries, dryads live day to day, in the here and now. Unless the topic came up, Mum would have no reason to discuss ghosts or anything else.

When something did come up for discussion, I reminded myself, a dryad would always tell the truth, but any human needed to listen very carefully, in case they weren't getting all of the truth. That wasn't necessarily out of malice, but a dryad's view of what a mortal needed to know would always be seen through a dryad's eyes.

'What about this business with old bottles and local witchcraft? Is there really any such thing as magic?'

'There is...' Mum hesitated. 'Barter, sometimes. Bargains can be made. Perhaps that's what this is.'

She paused again, and frowned. Her eyes turned solidly leaf green as she sought for the right words. 'We can extend our reach, to encompass those who are irrevocably bound to the physical plane by time and space...'

'Like when you take us from place to place?' Dad prompted.

He and I exchanged a glance. We had both experienced the unnerving, not to say nauseating, sensation of being swept along by a dryad's power, helpless as a leaf on the wind. When a naiad carried me through Derbyshire's underground rivers, I'd been utterly terrified that I was going to drown.

'It's more than that. You know that we can beguile or daunt, reveal or conceal, as we see fit. We can... lend?' Mum shook her head. 'No, that's not right. Share? However you want to phrase it, we can grant such abilities to ordinary people, at least for a while. In return for some recompense, of course.'

Dad sat up straight in his chair. 'Is that why it seemed as if no one could see Dan until he grabbed hold of Josh? Is that why he reached the standing stone so much faster than Rufus?'

Dryads can step aside from the normal flow of time, and take humans with them. That's where those stories have come from down the ages, of someone spending a night in Faerie and coming home to find out a hundred years have passed. Dad accidentally lost a week once, before he realised what could happen and explained the problem to Mum.

'The Green Man could be lending you a hand. You're doing his bidding, after all,' Dad pointed out.

'We haven't made any sort of bargain,' I objected.

'He wanted you there, and you went. You didn't have to do that.'

Yes, of course I could have refused, if I wanted his furious presence in my dreams every night. As for him giving me temporary superpowers, I wasn't convinced. For a start, that wasn't much use if I had no idea how to go unnoticed if I wanted to. Though I could well believe that he had hidden me in the woods, as well as got me to the clearing before Rufus.

I looked at Mum. 'Well?'

'I don't know,' she said helplessly. 'Perhaps. Or perhaps he's simply extending his protection over you. We know he's done that before.'

That seemed far more likely to me.

'What about these bottles, and the herbs and stuff?' Dad changed the subject. 'How do they fit in with magic and making deals?'

'I've no idea.' Mum looked a little exasperated. 'I've never needed to resort to such bargains with your folk to get something I want.'

I recalled why I hadn't got through the first episode of the last supernatural TV series I'd watched. The first eldritch being that the trio tracking the monster had encountered had an encyclopaedic knowledge of every other uncanny creature. I found that as believable as expecting a volunteer guide who knew the history of Blithehurst to tell me about some remote castle tucked away in Wales. Then the trio had immediate access to all sorts of books and even databases holding any information they might need. That's when I put the DVD box in the pile to go back to the charity shop.

I set that aside. Thinking about books made me recall the other things Aiden had hidden in his sealed cupboard. If magic, for want of a better word, was a reality, maybe there was more to this situation than super-strength weed and bottles of vodka.

'This man could well have some unnatural influence over these kids. If so, where's he getting that from? Could the source be whatever's in the lake?'

'A naiad?' Mum glowered. 'That wouldn't surprise me.'

Someday I really would have to ask her why she disliked naiads so much. Not today.

'No, it's not.' I was certain of that. 'This is something different.'

'You're so certain, after meeting one naiad?' she challenged me.

'What else *could* it be?' Dad sought to move the conversation forward.

Mum's eyes flashed to solid green again, but she answered him. 'I suppose it could be a nix,' she said unwillingly.

'I don't imagine that's good news, if it is.' I knew that was only one name for those dangerous things living at the bottom of deep water.

Nix, necker, knucker. The creatures seemed to have as many names as they had shapes they could change into, from snakes to fish to swimming men. What they had in common, from the folk tales I remembered, was a taste for drowning their victims.

'This Aiden,' Dad said warily. 'He couldn't be the nix himself?'

That was an even nastier thought. I considered it for a moment.

'I don't think so. He's not luring them to the lake, and he has no problem handling metal or dealing with fire.' Though I realised I shouldn't discount the possibility until I got a good look at his eyes.

'So what do you do about a nix?' Dad wondered.

'You leave them well alone,' Mum said swiftly. 'The Green Man wanted you to rid the place of this despoiler of children. Nothing more. Drive him off and have done with it.'

'Brightwell will certainly be better off without him around.' I nodded, though with a sideways glance at Dad. 'I'll see if Eleanor Beauchene has ever turned up anything interesting about nixes, though.'

'It does sound as if the place would be better off without it,' he said grimly.

'Let's hope we can find a way to get rid of it as well.' I got up, put the kettle on again and changed the subject. 'So what's the latest news around here?'

Dad brought me up to date with local goings-on. Mum and I went out for a walk through the nature reserve, and she showed me the latest things to delight her out there. When I came back to the house as dusk fell, energised by spring's vigour surging through my veins, I realised how drained the woods around Brightwell made me feel.

Dad and I cooked a roast chicken dinner. Mum joined us, not to eat but simply to enjoy spending the evening with us. Dryads can and do eat ordinary food, although they have no particular need for it. Mum got quite interested in watching me and Dad cooking as I grew up and we experimented with recipes. She was particularly curious about anything with herbs and spices from far afield, and would often sample those meals. Thai food intrigued her.

I spent the night in my old room, and slept like a log. On Sunday morning, I cooked a full English breakfast for Dad and myself, and then he and I went out for a walk. I told him about the renovations at Brightwell, and we discussed the practicalities of instituting separate paths for dog walkers and mountain bikers around the nature reserve. Mostly they got on fine, but there were a few inconsiderate regulars on either side who caused or made complaints.

We went to the pub in the village for a sandwich lunch, and then I headed back to the Cotswolds. My good mood lasted all through the journey, right up until I pulled up in front of Brightwell House and saw Aiden and his gang of acolytes crowded on the top of the steps, peering through the windows and trying the door.

Chapter Twelve

I accelerated hard. At the last moment, I threw the Land Rover into a sideways skid and came to a halt right across the bottom of the steps. The Landy wasn't long enough to block their escape entirely, but not knowing what I was going to do kept them frozen in place.

As I killed the engine and opened the driver's door, one of the three boys in the group seized his chance. He jumped down the steps to slip through the gap between the bonnet and the bay window at the dais end of the great hall. Heavy-set, he still had an impressive turn of speed. He ran as fast as he could towards the lane, slipping on the loose gravel my skid had thrown up.

I let him go as I reached for my mobile phone. Luckily I'd had it plugged in to charge as I drove back. Standing with the vehicle between me and the rest of them, I used the phone's camera to take photographs of them all.

The man in the great coat, Aiden, made it very clear that this didn't intimidate him. He stood on the top step, with his shoulders back and his hands in his pockets, as he stared down at me. I met his challenge by taking my time to take another set of photos, this time zooming in. That meant I got a good look at his eyes, in particular as he blinked. There was no hint of anything in his gaze to indicate that he was a nix or anything else uncanny. Whatever he might be up to here, the bastard was solely and wholly human.

I recognised three of the girls from the clearing by the standing stone, and guessed the fourth one had been half of the couple I'd nearly tripped over when they were screwing in the woods. Since the straggly bearded boy was still there, the one who'd legged it was presumably the other outdoor sex fan. The last of the gang, cowering behind the rest as they looked to Aiden for guidance, was Josh Franklin. I did my best not to show that I recognised him. Hopefully my scowl included them all.

'Right.' I raised my voice, cold and forceful. 'This is private property, and you are trespassing. Get out of here now, and don't come back. If I see any of you anywhere around the house or gardens again, I will ring the police, and I'll let them have these photos. I hear there have been some break-ins locally. I'm sure they'll be interested.'

Josh looked as if he was about to pass out, and the skinny boy looked seriously worried. The girls were watching Aiden. He gazed down at me, disdainful. I wondered if he was going to call my bluff, by dragging Josh forward and claiming they were here by invitation.

Instead, he waved a hand, as if I was expected to do whatever he said. 'Move your vehicle.'

I stayed where I was. 'There's plenty of room to get past.'

He stared at me for a long moment. I stared back, as intimidating as I knew how. A breeze rattled the holly trees behind me.

Aiden drew a deep breath and turned to look at his hangers-on. 'We've seen all we need to here.'

He strolled down the steps, ignoring me completely. I kept my gaze on him, and kept well beyond arm's reach. I hadn't forgotten he'd had that knife in the woods. A whole lot of other things could be hidden underneath that coat.

As he went past the Land Rover and made his way, unhurried, towards the lane, the teenagers scurried after him. They snatched glances at me as they passed. I silently challenged the boy with the straggly beard by taking a half-step forward. I was pleased to see him flinch and walk faster. The girls seemed apprehensive, not making eye contact with me. Apart from the thin-faced one called Jade, who looked at me with sly defiance.

Josh Franklin didn't look my way at all. His shoulders were hunched and he stared at the ground as he followed the others. I was tempted to call the boy back, but changed my mind at the last moment. If Aiden didn't know I recognised him, the bastard couldn't use that as leverage over Josh. Plus, that coin had two sides. I might get some useful information if I could persuade Josh to talk to me. I could only hope he wasn't in too deep just yet. He still wasn't wearing the same army-surplus gear as the rest of them, which should surely be a positive sign.

I watched them go out into the lane and turn left. So they were heading back to the Broad council houses, or maybe going on over the bridge and into Bourton. That was a relief. Whether they were hanging around in that bus shelter or underneath the market hall, there'd be people around to see them. Whatever they were going to do, Josh would surely be less at risk than he might be in that foul caravan.

First things first. I walked through to the garage yard and checked that the doors and windows were secure. Then I examined the front door and the basement kitchen entrance for any signs of an attempt to force them open. Finally, I walked around the house, checking for anything amiss with any of the windows.

Nothing looked to have been tampered with, but there was a cluster of footprints in the flowerbed underneath Uncle Cecil's reading room window. The sill was so high up that even I couldn't see into the house, but I reckoned the skinny lad could have done that, if the broad-shouldered boy had given him a boost.

There were no more footprints on the far side of the house, but the springy grass wouldn't have shown them anyway. I paused all the same as I reached the narrow window at the base of the square turret. The matching one on the kitchen side shed light into the servants' stairwell, but now I knew this was the sewing room window. I thought about that for a moment. Nicki Franklin had told me all the windows and doors were alarmed, but if the sewing room was so easily overlooked, maybe the security company hadn't realised it was there.

That was easily tested. I went onwards, back around to the front of the house. After moving the Land Rover to its usual parking spot, I went inside, unset the alarm and made sure the front door was firmly shut before punching in the alarm code again. I walked through the silent house to unlock the sewing room door, and let myself in. Ignoring the weird painting over the fireplace, I went over to the window and opened it.

The security company had done a thorough job. The sound was ear-splitting. My head was ringing by the time I got back to the entrance hall and put in the code to silence the racket. I had barely a moment of blissful quiet before the phone in the oak parlour rang. It was the security company.

'Good afternoon. We've had an alert at this property.'

'Yes, sorry, that was me. I opened a window when the alarm was still on.'

'Can you confirm your identity please?'

I gave the polite lady my details while sorting through the paperwork in one of the filing trays with one hand, to find the security company handbook with the additional code I needed to give them.

'Thank you, Mr Mackmain. That's all confirmed. Have a good evening.'

'Thank you, and sorry for the trouble.'

'No trouble,' the polite lady assured me. 'Goodbye.'

I'd barely put down the phone when I heard a vehicle outside. I walked to the front window to see it was Rufus Stanlake's Defender. He and Bess were already getting out. They reached the front door as I opened it.

'I heard the alarm.' As usual, Rufus didn't do small talk.

'That was me.' It was good to know the sound had reached as far as the Home Farm house.

'Oh, okay. Well, at least we know you're back.' Rufus turned to go.

'Hang on a minute.' I explained who I'd found here when I arrived.

'That cocky prick!' Rufus was furious. 'In broad daylight?'

'I reckon he's been watching the house.' I'd been giving that some thought. 'He's realised I do a walk-round mornings and evenings, and guessed you'd do the same. Time to vary the pattern, I reckon.'

Rufus acknowledged that with a nod. 'But you say Josh was still with them? Fuck,' he said with heartfelt dismay.

'Can you let me have his mobile number? I want to try having a word with him. Maybe I can scare him straight, if he's too pig-headed to listen to you.' I hoped Rufus didn't think I was criticising his efforts the other night. It wasn't as if I could explain that I was afraid the boy was under the influence of some unpleasant magic.

He was much more concerned about Josh. 'Let me have your phone.'

I handed it over, and Rufus quickly put in the boy's number.

'Can you hang on here?' I asked. 'So I can go down the road and get a signal?'

'What are you going to say to him?' Rufus looked torn between wanting to protect the boy and really wanting to see some sense shaken into him.

'That he can talk to me or I talk to his parents,' I said simply.

Rufus raked his fingers through his wiry hair. 'I suppose so.'

He didn't look keen, but I guessed he liked the alternatives even less.

'Get the kettle on.' I left him and Bess in the hallway and drove quickly up the lane. It wasn't far, but taking the Landy was quicker than walking, and I didn't want to encounter Aiden and his acolytes on my own.

Driving with one hand on the wheel and holding my phone, I pulled up as soon as I saw that I had a signal. Thankfully that was out of sight of the Broad's houses.

Josh's phone went straight to voicemail, which was no great surprise given the reception around here. Well, he'd get the message as soon as he got a signal. That would have to do. On second thoughts, I sent the same ultimatum as a text message. Just to underline the point.

Doing a three-point turn in the Land Rover between the high banks of the narrow lane was a mistake. I'd have been better off reversing. After a fair amount of frustration and going back and forward through the gears, I managed it and drove back.

Rufus was outside the house. He'd got an old spade out of the back of the Defender and was tidying up the mess I'd made of the gravel.

'That saves me a job. Cheers.' I locked up the Landy. 'Cup of tea?'

He shook his head. 'Things to do.'

He didn't explain. I waited as he put the spade and the dog in the Defender, and waved as he drove off. I went inside and found that the kettle was full, and recently boiled.

I left a teabag brewing in a mug and, not for the first time, thought about buying a teapot the next time I was in the supermarket. I hate making tea in mugs. Apart from anything else, it's wasteful. You can get at least a mug and a half out of each teabag by using a pot. More, if you top it up with hot water. Only, then I'd have two teapots when I went back to Blithehurst. Unless I bought it on the petty cash and left it here at the end of the job.

I debated with myself as I walked through the ground floor of the house and closed all the shutters. That would stop anyone peering in and getting any bright ideas. It wasn't as if Kemble and Coates were working in any of these rooms yet. If anyone asked, I'd say I thought I'd seen prowlers, and that David Franklin had warned me about these local break-ins.

Josh can't have been very far away, wherever he was when his phone picked up a signal. He was standing outside on the steps when I got back to the entrance hall. I unlocked the door and let him in. 'Tea?'

He stood on the threshold and looked at me with abject misery.

I looked back at him, unemotional. 'Is anyone dead or pregnant?'

'What?' That shocked him out of his silence. 'No!'

I'd have to tell my dad that blunt question had worked as well on Josh as it had on me as a teenager, when I'd wanted someone, anyone, to get me out of a mess but had no idea how to ask for help.

'Okay then. Anything else can be fixed. Come in and tell me what's going on.' I gestured towards the oak parlour, and as he went in, I fetched my mug of tea and a packet of biscuits.

I put the biscuits on the desk between us. 'Help yourself.'

He ate several chocolate digestives. I looked around the room as if I were unconcerned. As a matter of fact, I was trying to see if there was any sign of the Green Man's presence in the plaster foliage frieze. No such luck.

The silence lengthened. I was going to have to make Josh talk to me.

'I thought you told Rufus you were going to stay away from those other kids.' I tried to make that more an observation than an accusation.

Josh cowered in his seat all the same. 'I was going to. I wanted to – but – only—' Anguish strangled him into incoherence.

I waited.

'Jade Taysel – I know her from school – she's been sending me pictures – you know, photos – sexts?' He looked at me, hollow-eyed with apprehension.

I fought to keep my face impassive, though I thought I could guess what was coming next. 'And?'

'I sent her – I sent her – just once – just one...' His face twisted as he began crying, wracked with anger and betrayal, as well as a fair amount of fear.

I got up and left him to it, walking through to the housekeeper's kitchen to get a roll of paper towels out of a cupboard. I wasn't sure I could hide my exasperation, and that wouldn't help. How could he have been so stupid?

Come to that, I've never understood people taking sex photos of themselves. What was the point, if you had the person you loved there with you, warm and willing? And in this day and age, unless you were with someone you trusted absolutely, and forever, there was always going to be some risk. I'd only ever been asked once, by a girl who wanted to take photos of us in bed. I'd said no, and that was the end of that casual fling. At least that meant when the tabloid press had been wondering if I was a killer, no one had those pictures to sell.

I took a deep breath, went back into the oak parlour and put the paper towels next to the biscuits. Josh's sobs were subsiding, and a few minutes later, he tore off a ragged length to scrub tears and snot from his face. He looked up at me, blotched and spotty and desperate.

'Let me guess,' I said, as calmly as I could. 'She said if you didn't do what she wanted, she'd send the photo all round the school.'

'She sent it to Aiden.' For the first time, Josh was angry. 'He said if I didn't help him, he'd send it to my parents.'

'Then he'd be in a shitload of trouble with the police,' I said bluntly. 'He'd go to prison for sharing child pornography.' I knew that much from some radio programme or other.

'Really?' Josh had clearly been so distraught he hadn't thought this through. 'But my mum, and my dad—'

'Oh, you'd be in a shitload of trouble with them.' I had no doubt of that. 'Like I was with my dad when I ditched university. We had a hell of a row and barely spoke for months, but we got over it. Your mum and dad would get over this. Do you honestly think they'd let some bastard do something like this to you?'

'Aiden says – he says he can do what he likes, and no one can say different.' Josh was looking apprehensive again. 'He says he's got protection. That's why no one's been able to tell him to move his caravan on. He says they won't be able to—'

'Really?' I said, sceptical. 'Well, I've only met your uncle David once, but I'd back him any day of the week against some squatter who has to blackmail kids to get what he wants.'

'Maybe.' Josh was clearly torn between wanting his formidable uncle as an ally and having David Franklin know what he'd done.

'Of course,' I said, as casually as I could, 'if we knew what he wanted, this Aiden, if we could make it clear that he wasn't going to get it, then there'd be no point in him doing anything with that photo. All that would get him is that shitload of trouble with the police. Then all this bollocks goes away.'

Now Josh looked hopeful for the first time.

'Why was he trying to get into the house?' I prompted.

Josh bit his lip. 'He says – he says there are things in here that belong to him. That belonged to his great-grandfather. Constance Sutton stole them from him – his great-grandfather, I mean. Aiden says he was a magician. Not card tricks and bollocks like that, but real magic. Aiden can do magic too. That's what Jade says anyway. That's why he can do what he wants and no one can touch him. He says he wants what's his.'

I did my very best to look as if I didn't believe a single word of this. 'Then why hasn't he gone to see your mum and dad, or your uncle David, and told them about these things he says are his? That's what anyone honest would do, wouldn't they? If he could prove his story?'

'He says they wouldn't believe him.' Josh was turning sullen. 'He said once they realised what they had, they'd want the stuff for themselves. These things are really valuable.'

'But he hasn't told you what he's looking for. Doesn't that strike you as odd?'

'He says he can't trust me, not until I prove myself—' He broke off, looking guilty.

'Until you get him inside the house,' I guessed.

Josh's ugly blush told me I was right.

'Have you got a key?'

'No.' But Josh wasn't telling me the whole truth.

'Can you get one?'

'Maybe.' He squirmed in his chair.

'Does Aiden know that?'

'I haven't said,' Josh replied, defensive, before capitulating. 'He told me to find out where my mum keeps the spares though.'

'Do you know the alarm code? Have you told him what it is?'

'No.'

That was another half-truth. I guessed that Josh did know the code, but had told Aiden that he didn't. The bastard wouldn't need magical powers to tell him the boy was lying. I imagined he'd be confident he could get it out of Josh when he needed to.

'Anything else?' I wanted to bring the conversation to a close.

Josh looked defeated. 'No. Not that I can think of.'

'Come on then.' I stood up and took my jacket off the back of the chair. 'I'll give you a lift home.'

'My mum—'

'I'll drop you at the end of the lane.' I looked down at him, knowing full well he'd find that intimidating. 'And you stay home until we get this sorted out.'

I hoped he wasn't going to ask how I was going to do that, but he had other things on his mind.

'Please,' he said suddenly. 'Don't tell anyone about today, or about... about...'

'I won't tell anyone who doesn't absolutely need to know, to help us get rid of this bastard,' I promised him. 'No one who we can't trust, both of us. Now, tomorrow you go to school, and you come home and you don't go out. You stay away from Jade and whoever else is in this little gang, and if they threaten you, you tell them you'll go straight to your teachers and tell them about the weed and the drinking in the woods. How much trouble will they be in then? Tell them you don't care if you get in trouble as well.'

'Okay.' Josh stood up. He looked unconvinced, and I couldn't see him standing up to anyone. But I could see him avoiding Aiden's acolytes as much as he could.

'Come on,' I said again. 'I don't want to be away from here for too long.'

It was taking a risk, but it was still daylight, and I reckoned Aiden would be too wary to come back for today, at least.

So I drove Josh to Ashgrove and came straight back. There was no sign of anything amiss when I looked around the house and the garage yard. I went straight into the oak parlour to ring Eleanor Beauchene up in Durham.

'Can you talk?' I asked as soon as she picked up the phone. 'Really talk?'

'Give me a minute.' A few minutes later, I heard a door close. 'Okay, what's wrong?'

By the time I'd told her everything, we'd taken a break for me to make more tea, as my throat was dry, and for Eleanor to fetch some paper and a pen to make some notes.

'Wow,' she said as I concluded.

'Right.' I waited for her to say something else.

'So do we think this Aiden is somehow descended from this magician Martha Delly was talking about? The one who was mixed up in some scandal?'

'That would explain why he left in a hurry and left something valuable behind.'

'So who was he?' Eleanor was thinking aloud as much as talking to me. 'Can you find out?'

'I can ask around.' But I had another idea in the meantime. 'Can you get online? Let's look up those books I saw in the caravan.'

'Okay, give me a minute.'

I waited, hearing assorted noises, until the faint patter of keys told me Eleanor had got her laptop ready.

'Go ahead.' The distance in her voice told me she'd put my call on speaker.

'*Le Petit Albert*, *Agrippa Le Noir* and *The Long Secreted Friend*.' I waited, listening to soft keystrokes.

'Well,' Eleanor said a short while later, 'those are books for people who deal with the occult. Grimoires. The sorts of books that used to get burned, and probably got people burned. Collectable, in the right circles, for the right editions. What was the name you saw written in one?'

'Mungo Peploe.' I spelled the surname for her. I heard her mutter something, exasperated. 'I didn't catch that?'

'Google thinks I want to look for Mungo People instead.' Eleanor hit a key with some force. 'But even so, there's nothing about him online. Let's try Aiden Peploe.'

I waited.

'Nothing,' Eleanor said a moment later.

'He may not have the same surname,' I pointed out, 'or may not even be a relative. Perhaps he heard some story about something valuable being left here and came to see what he could find.'

'What do you think he's after?'

'I suppose it could be that weird picture, or the spirit-writing thing, the planchette.' I wasn't convinced though. 'Or it could be something else entirely, hidden where no one knows about it. I'll have to keep my eyes open while the renovations are going on.'

'This business about him being protected,' Eleanor said thoughtfully. 'Do you think he's doing the sort of magic your mother told you about? Could he have made some sort of bargain with whatever's in the lake?'

'It's got to be possible, surely?' It seemed likely to me. 'And isn't it safest to assume so?'

'Then he's not some innocent dupe in whatever's going on, is he?' Eleanor's voice sounded more distant than the call being on speaker phone could account for.

I knew she was thinking about Robert, her brother. He'd had no idea that he'd been sucked into an ethereal monster's scheming, and that had got him killed.

I'd been thinking about that too. However hard ethereal creatures might be to fight, once they're dead, their uncanny nature means all traces of them can be swept away, at least as long as we have ethereal allies by our side. At Blithehurst, that had been the dryads, and Kalei the naiad. Here, I'd have to rely on the Green Man.

A human enemy was a whole different challenge. Whatever arcane powers he might be in league with, whatever I did to get rid of him would have to stay within the law. Or at the very least, I'd better not get found out breaking any laws, because fighting eldritch evil wasn't going to be a defence I could rely on in court.

'We need to deal with whatever's in the lake first.' I hadn't only been thinking about the best way to make tea while I'd been walking around the house. 'If he hasn't got that power to call on, he's much less of a threat.'

'True.' Eleanor picked up her phone again, turning the speaker off. 'So how do we get rid of a nix? How do we find out if it even is a nix?'

'Where's a friendly naiad when you need some help?' I said lightly.

Not that Kalei was particularly friendly, and the help that she'd given us had been strictly on her own terms, but Eleanor knew what I meant.

She sighed. 'I'll get down to Blithehurst as soon as I can. Maybe one of our three friends there will know something useful. And I'll see what I can turn up in the academic library catalogues, or the journals online. You never know.'

'I'll find out what local history around here has to offer. I'll give you a call as soon as I have anything useful.'

'Same here,' Eleanor assured me.

We said our goodbyes. As I put the phone down, I heard an engine outside. It was Rufus. He got out of the Defender and walked round to the passenger door. I watched him get a six pack of beer and a brown paper takeaway bag out of the footwell.

'Curry,' he said as I opened the door. 'If you tell me what Josh had to say for himself.'

'Come in.' I stepped back to let Bess past me. 'If you promise not to go straight round and beat the living shit out of that prick in the caravan.'

Chapter Thirteen

We ate the very good takeaway in the housekeeper's sitting room. I told Rufus that Aiden had been trying to get into the house, most likely to steal anything that wasn't nailed down. I didn't mention magicians or stolen occult property or anything else that could lead a conversation down potentially awkward paths. I did tell him about the sexting though, to explain that Josh wasn't going along with this willingly. I also couldn't think how else to dissuade Rufus from going straight to Ed and Nicki Franklin. I stressed that I had promised Josh I'd only tell people we could trust, and who needed to know.

Rufus was calmer about that than I expected. 'I had an ex who tried that revenge porn crap with me once.'

Then he looked as if he hadn't meant to say that, and since I definitely didn't want to know any more, I was glad when he changed the subject.

'Do you reckon this bastard's got anything to do with the other break-ins around here recently?'

'I've been wondering that.' If the nix could lend Aiden and his acolytes some concealment, that would come in very handy for thieving. 'If he is, and if we could find out enough to put the cops onto him, maybe they could take care of him good and proper, and Josh would stay out of things completely.'

And if the police did pick Aiden up for questioning, I'd ring in a confidential tip suggesting that they check his phone for obscene images. I'd bet he had a lot more on there than Josh's idiotic dick pic.

Rufus drank the last of his beer, thoughtful. 'There was nothing in that caravan to interest the cops though. I wonder if he's got another place tucked away somewhere.'

'That's got to be a possibility,' I agreed.

'I'll ask around, discreetly.' Rufus stood up. 'Right, work tomorrow.'

Bess had been sleeping in front of the empty fireplace. She looked up, ears pricked. As Rufus headed for the front door, she got up and followed him, tail wagging placidly. I wondered what she had seen in the woods, and wished we had some way to ask her. If you've ever wondered why dogs bark and cats hiss at apparently nothing at all, and why there are places where horses refuse to go, it's because animals can see ethereal and uncanny creatures.

I locked up behind Rufus and went to bed. Clearing the remains of the curry could wait until the morning. I wasn't going to risk an encounter outside in the dark while I was here on my own. That meant I was rinsing out the recycling when the Kembles and the Coateses arrived the next day.

'Had a bit of a session last night?' Mark glanced at the six empty beer cans as he made himself a coffee.

'Rufus brought round a takeaway.'

'You're mates, then, are you?' He sounded a little surprised.

'We get on okay.' I shrugged. 'We were talking about that squatter, in that caravan down the lane. We've both seen him sneaking around here, and I don't trust him as far as I could throw him. I wouldn't leave your vans unlocked, even during the day.'

'Right.' Mark saw the sense in that. 'I'll tell the others.'

'Have you ever seen him across the river, in Bourton?' I asked casually.

Mark shook his head. 'I don't think I've ever seen him at all.'

I wondered if that was because the creep was just careful, or whether there was some other reason.

'I'll get my tools and we'll make a start.' Mark added more milk, to make his coffee cool enough to drink. 'Let's see if we can work out where that old wiring on the top floor goes, shall we? We've got to get that sorted before we can start work on the power showers.'

As he went downstairs to get his tools, I heard him telling the others to keep an eye out for trespassers. When I took the recycling through to the bins in the garage yard, I met Geoff Kemble and brought him up to date. The more eyes on Aiden, the better.

'He stinks of weed,' I said bluntly. 'I can't prove it, but I think he's selling drugs to those kids who hang around the bus shelter in the Broad.'

'If he comes near our Davey, he'll regret it,' Geoff growled.

The house's light switches and sockets had been installed and updated at various times by different electricians. Mostly they hadn't bothered stripping out the old wires, and there were junction boxes and spurs in some very odd places. Sorting out the rats' nest that left us with kept me and Mark busy for the rest of the morning, given we were continually having to check that we were pulling the right fuses from the antiquated box in the basement. When we heard the gaffer's whistle for lunchtime, I went and fetched my laptop from the housekeeper's sitting room and told Geoff I was heading out for lunch.

As I parked by the market hall, I saw the huddle of teenagers sitting amid the pillars again, though there was no sign of Aiden. They looked sullenly at me. I stared back, and used my phone to take a photo of the lad who'd run off the day before. He didn't like that. He stood up and walked towards me, his face threatening.

'Tyler, isn't it?' I said with a smile. 'I wouldn't try anything, genius, not to mess with me or my car. There's CCTV all around here.'

He had already stopped coming, shocked to realise that I knew his name, as well as deterred by the reminder about security cameras.

I took my backpack out of the Land Rover and looked at the teenagers as I locked up, just to make the point. Then I turned my back on them and headed for Shayler's. As well as getting some lunch, I wanted to go online and see what I could find out about those occult books for myself. That meant using a proper keyboard. Doing anything like that on a phone touchscreen is an exercise in frustration when you've got hands as big as mine.

I found quite a few things to read as I ate my sandwich and drank my coffee, though I wasn't at all sure what to make of what I was learning, by the time I finished. I'd met a few people who called themselves Wiccans, or pagans, on the craft show and living history circuit, where I'd made extra money selling wood carvings before I'd settled down at Blithehurst. They'd seemed like any other group of people to me. There were some I wouldn't trust to pour water out of a boot with the instructions written on the sole. There were others I wouldn't hesitate to ask if they'd look after my full cash box, when I left my table to get something from the Landy, or to go for a slash.

I'd vaguely registered that the ones who were serious about it reckoned they could access arcane powers for support and guidance, through rituals and things like Tarot cards, but I'd never asked much about that. I'd never had my cards read either. Why would I, when I already knew the world was full of things that most people couldn't see? Why would I risk a conversation that might see me let something slip about my mother's nature, when I spent my life keeping that secret. Now I was thinking it could have been useful to find out how their beliefs overlapped with my reality. Hindsight's a real pain in the arse.

I wondered if I could find out anything else useful. I typed a couple of words and then stopped, not sure what to add.

'Can I get you anything else?' Petra Oxway came over. She looked at the laptop screen, as she'd clearly intended to do all along. 'Mungo Peploe? Martha's been telling you her stories, has she? She doesn't know the half of it.'

'And you do?' I tried to make that more of an invitation than a challenge.

Petra's smile widened. 'Tell you what, why don't I tell you about it over dinner? And you can tell me how the work at Brightwell's going, so we can work out when to do the feature? Nicki Franklin's okayed it, but I don't have time to sit down right now.'

She waved a hand around the busy shop, and there was no denying that. Every chair and table was taken.

I wasn't keen. 'How about I come back later? When you're not so busy.'

Petra looked thoughtfully at me, her lips pursed. 'I did google you, obviously, Daniel. So I know you got monstered by the tabloids last year. I can see why you don't trust the press. But that's not how I work, and this is good publicity for the Franklins, as well as good for me. I don't need to even mention your name.'

Her tone was matter-of-fact, and I couldn't argue with anything she said.

'How about the Whittle and Dub?' she persisted. 'Do you know it?'

'I can find it,' I assured her.

She shook her head. 'I'll pick you up. Six-thirty?'

'Okay.' I saw a couple looking for a table, and packed my laptop away. 'I'll see you then.'

On the way back, I stopped off at the Home Farmhouse, to let Rufus know I'd be out that evening. He wasn't in, so I pushed a note through the door. Bill Delly was out working in his own garden, so I asked him to pass the message on as well. Then Mark Coates and I carried on unravelling the old servants' dormitories' wiring.

I knocked off at six and grabbed a quick shower and a shave. As I came out into the hall with my hair still damp, I met Geoff Kemble, who was finishing off something in the oak parlour.

He took in my not-work clothes. 'Going out?'

'Do you know Petra Oxway, who works for the local paper?' I realised I'd better check with the gaffer before I agreed to anything that might interfere with his men's work. 'She wants to talk about doing a story on the conversion. Is that okay with you?'

'If it's okay with the Franklins,' he said agreeably. 'As long as she gets my vans into a photo.'

As he chuckled, I heard voices outside. Walking with Geoff to the porch, I saw Petra had arrived, driving a Mini. She was chatting to the last of the Kembles and Coateses, who were about to leave. Geoff passed her on the steps, and they stopped to exchange a few words.

I noticed that she was wearing a nice dress under her coat, and smart shoes, and wondered belatedly if she thought this was a date. Oh well, I'd just have to keep things business-like.

'Is that your Land Rover?' she called up to me. 'Shall we take that instead of my car? I can show you where to go.'

'Fine with me.' I was all in favour of not having to fold myself in half to get into a car that small. 'Let me get my jacket.'

I locked up and we got into the Landy.

'Turn right, out of the gate,' Petra told me as she fastened her seat belt. 'Then left at the fingerpost.'

'Up the light?' I wanted to make sure I understood her.

'It's fine,' she assured me. 'It's a public right of way, even if it's not tarmacked, and we'll cut off the corner of the lane. The lights were used as roads for centuries, until highwaymen started hiding out in the woods and robbing travellers.'

Petra settled herself on the seat. 'This wasn't the "Give us your money and we'll leave you alone" type of highway robbery. There were beatings and rapes, even a couple of murders, so people started taking the long way round. The authorities did put up a gibbet at the crossroads, to show they were catching the felons and hanging them, but that didn't particularly help. People found the sight of a rotting corpse wrapped in chains a bit off-putting.'

'I can imagine.' I drove out between the holly trees. 'We can go that way if you're sure.'

Not driving past the caravan suited me. That way Aiden wouldn't know I'd gone out. I didn't like the idea of him knowing the house would be empty.

'I did a feature on green lanes a while back. Rabid ramblers in green wellies and waxed jackets versus the four-by-four brigade.' Petra smiled. 'Once a highway, always a highway, apparently.'

The Land Rover had no trouble going off-road, and I drove carefully to avoid tearing up the grass or frightening any wildlife. We passed the path to the Hoar Stone and reached a crossroads in the middle of the woods.

Petra pointed in each direction. 'We've just come up Brightwell Light, and that's Eyford Light going north. Slaughter Light heads east, while Naunton Light goes west.'

'And we're going...?'

'West,' she confirmed, 'and left at the end.'

When we reached the tarmacked main road again, I took my time at the junction. There was a fair amount of traffic, and the visibility wasn't great. Wilting bunches of flowers tied to a road sign opposite suggested someone had come to grief here.

Checking left, I caught sight of Petra's expression and was startled to see tears in her eyes. 'Are you okay?'

'What? Sorry.' She sniffed and blinked. 'Yes, I'm fine. It's – that's where Simon crashed. Some of the kids from the school must have come up here with flowers again. I thought they'd stopped doing that.' A hint of annoyance sharpened her voice. 'And before you ask, he was following the main road, not taking the shortcut through the woods.'

I guessed speculation about who was to blame for the crash was a sore point. Satisfied it was safe, I pulled out. 'So what's a whittle?' I asked, hoping to change the subject. 'What's a dub, come to that?'

'Anywhere but here, they'd be called a whistle and a drum.' Petra swiftly regained her composure.

It wasn't far to the pub, at another crossroads, like Mark Coates had said. There was plenty of parking, accessed by a broad sweep of gravel. With no oncoming traffic, I was able to pull smoothly across into a vacant space. There was indeed a whistle and a drum on the sign, as well as a swinging plaque advertising 'Bed and Breakfast' and a restaurant.

'David Franklin will need to hire a good chef if he's going to give Jack Logan a run for his money,' Petra observed as we went through the door.

'Right.' I nodded, although that had nothing to do with me.

Inside, I saw there was a definite theme to the pub, though thankfully it wasn't overwhelming. Horse racing memorabilia like old posters advertising point-to-point meetings were interspersed with photos of a victorious jockey surrounded by cheering crowds. It was the same jockey in all the pictures, and the same slightly built man, greyer and more weathered, was standing behind the bar.

Seeing Petra, he came out to greet us. 'Sweetheart! Grand to see you, as always. Are you wanting to eat?'

However long he'd lived around here, his Irish accent was undimmed.

'We are. A table for two, if you please.' Petra turned to introduce me. 'This is Dan Mackmain. He's project manager for the Franklins at Brightwell. Dan, meet Jack Logan, who won just about all the racing cups worth winning.'

'In my glory days, till I stopped bouncing back from the falls. So I bought this place, and a wreck it was then, so I know what a job you've got on. Best of luck to you.'

He offered me his hand, and as we shook, I waited for him to say something about how tall I was, since I was well over a foot bigger than him. He didn't. He was more interested in Brightwell, or he knew from his own experience how tedious remarks about your height get.

'I hear you're planning to open this autumn? It takes a broad field to make a horse race, so I'm happy enough. A bit of competition for the restaurant trade will keep that one's mind on his job.' Logan jerked his greying head towards the pub's kitchen door. 'And it'll be good to have somewhere close to recommend, when someone stops by and finds we're already fully booked. Assuming you'll return the favour, of course. As for losing the guns for the Franklins' shoots, to be honest, I won't be sorry to see the back of their mud and their dogs. We won't lose by it. We get more passing trade than we can handle alongside our regular bookings.'

Before I could explain I was only here for the renovations, he turned to lead us towards the windows overlooking the car park. 'Let's find you a table.'

Once we were seated and he'd lit the candle in a glass vase on the table, he went off to fetch us some menus. Petra leaned forward, her voice low enough to be discreet.

'Jack Logan's definitely what the Irish call "cute". This place was notorious years ago, for drug dealing and underage drinking. When the police eventually raided it, the magistrates revoked all the licences and the owners went to prison. Logan bought it for a knock-down price at auction. It was falling down round his ears, but he brought half his family over from Ireland to help rebuild it. He got investors through his racing contacts, and the place hasn't looked back.'

'Is there much trouble around here with drugs?'

'It comes and goes.' Petra's attention sharpened. 'Why do you ask?'

'You know that squatter in the caravan?' I gestured in the general direction of the river. 'He stinks of weed, and I've seen him hanging around the kids from the Broad. I wouldn't be surprised if he's dealing, or worse.'

'Worse?'

'I've seen him snooping around Brightwell, and around the church. Weren't you saying something to your niece about break-ins locally, that first day we met?'

Petra looked thoughtful. 'When did he turn up? It would be interesting to see how that timing ties up with these latest burglaries.'

'Rufus can tell you.' I took out my phone and found a picture that didn't have Josh in it. I held it up so she could see. 'This is what he looks like, though no one knows much about him.'

The more eyes on Aiden, the better, I reckoned. Plus, a journalist might dig up something unrelated to the Franklins to stick a spoke in his wheel.

Petra studied the photo for a moment. 'Can you email that to me? Use the Wi-Fi, the code's on the specials board over there.'

'Sorry,' I said with genuine regret. 'I don't do email on my phone. The keyboard on the screen is too damn small. I'll do it from my laptop later.'

I thought she was going to say something else, but Logan came back with our menus. I put my phone away.

Me updating Petra on the work at Brightwell saw us through our starters, and when the main course arrived we were both more interested in eating than talking. The service was quick and the food was great. I had smoked trout with bread and butter, followed by a venison steak. What wasn't home-made was local produce, according to the menu.

When Logan brought over the dessert menu, I opted for crème caramel, and Petra had coffee. She smiled at me as she stirred sugar into her cup.

'Okay, you've sung for your supper. What did you want to know about Mungo Peploe? Why do you want to know about him, come to that?'

'I saw his name in an old book.' I shrugged.

'At Brightwell? That doesn't surprise me. Okay, how much do you know about Constance Sutton getting into spiritualism and the occult after the First World War?'

'That she was trying to contact her dead son, and there was some sort of scandal? That's all Martha Delly said.'

'That's not the half of it.' Petra grinned, clearly assuming I found this local history as fascinating as she obviously did.

'Most of the mediums who Constance Sutton contacted came and went and took her money, and if they were fakes, they didn't do much harm. Mungo Peploe was different. He called himself a ceremonial magician, and claimed to be a priest of the Ancient Oriental Temple of the Dawn.'

Petra broke off. 'Have you ever heard of Aleister Crowley?'

The name rang a faint bell, but I couldn't have said why. 'No.'

'Look him up when you get a chance. Peploe claimed to be working in the same tradition as Crowley, but said he knew even more powerful rituals. There's no proof that he ever even met Crowley, but when the scandal broke, the press were drooling about Peploe's debauched practices. If what Crowley got up to is any guide, that means Mungo favoured rites using drugs and sex supposedly in the service of dark magic.'

She took a sip of her coffee. 'Once Mungo got his feet firmly under Constance Sutton's table, he filled the house with his cronies and got her to invite her spiritualist friends back. One weekend all the servants were told to go home. No one was to come back until they were sent for. Only one of the grooms, Martha Delly's father, in fact, went to see to the horses on the Sunday morning. He said at the time that he hadn't been intending to go anywhere near the house. He only wanted to make sure the horses had enough hay, or whatever, and water. He said Mrs Constance surely couldn't have intended for the poor dumb beasts to go hungry and thirsty. When he got to the stable yard, though, he heard the screaming.'

She paused to drink more coffee, and to see how I was taking this. It was no effort for me to look startled. Satisfied, Petra went on.

'Gilbert Norton knocked on the kitchen door and a girl answered, in utter hysterics. Her name was Emily Southwark, and she was supposedly the handmaiden to one of the spiritualist ladies, Elspeth de Rippe. She'd just found her mistress dead in one of the cellars, beaten to a bloody pulp. Who knows what else had been done to her. The coroner's report had some heavy hints, but refused to go into details, to spare the family.' Petra's grimace as she took another sip from her cup had nothing to do with the coffee.

'The police must have been called,' I prompted.

'Eventually,' Petra said, waspish. 'At first, Gilbert fetched Mr Leigh, the estate manager who lived in the Home Farm house. When Leigh knocked on the front door, one of Peploe's hangers-on admitted that someone was indisposed, and agreed that Leigh should fetch the doctor. Peploe tried to make out that the medium, Elspeth de Rippe, had fallen down the stairs, but the doctor could see that was a lie straight away. He sent Leigh to Bourton to get the constable, and eventually an inspector came all the way from Gloucester.'

She shook her head. 'Of course, by then, so much time had passed, and there was nothing much by way of forensics back in those days. The police couldn't make any sense of it. No one could say when Elspeth had last been seen on the Saturday night. It turned out that everyone had been drunk or drugged or both, in order to perform some ritual, which is why they'd sent the servants away. God knows what they'd been getting up to. Emily Southwark said she'd found de Rippe in the inner cellar when she went searching for her in the morning. Apparently there was a separate store off the main cellar.'

'Right.' I realised this was the room where the door had been rendered over, and where Davey Coates had found those witch bottles. Maybe they weren't so ancient after all.

'Only the girl swore that the door had been locked with the key on the inside,' Petra went on. 'She had to get two of the men in the house party to help her break it down, and they confirmed that. Peploe still tried to brazen it out. He said that proved it couldn't have been any of the other guests who killed her. He said no one could be held responsible if de Rippe had lost control of some spirit she'd summoned up from the Other Side.'

'I take it the police weren't convinced?'

Petra nodded. 'The inspector decided de Rippe must have fought off her attacker and locked herself in the cellar to be safe, only to die of her injuries. So he told Peploe and the rest that they couldn't go anywhere. He left men guarding the house to make sure everyone stayed put, and said he'd be back the next morning after he'd reported back to the chief constable.'

'What happened?' I could see from Petra's face that this story wasn't over.

'One of Peploe's young acolytes went mad in the middle of the night. Raving and smashing up his room, screaming that the devil had come to take his soul, that the devil had made him do it. The rest of them swore on a stack of bibles, quite literally, that they tried to calm him down, to lock him up for his own protection, and to send for the doctor. Somehow, though, he got away from them, and got past the police. He ran out into the woods and no one could find him in the dark. The police found him the next day. He'd hanged himself from the old gibbet at the crossroads in the lights. Some reports say he'd tried to cut his own hand off. That suicide, with or without the self-mutilation, was seen as admission of guilt, and the file on de Rippe was closed.'

'Did they have any idea why the acolyte went psychotic?' I wondered what had really happened.

Petra shrugged. 'It came out at the inquest that he'd been invalided home with shell shock after going all through the

First World War in the trenches. Post-traumatic stress disorder.'

An obvious, tidy solution, to anyone who didn't know better. 'What happened then?'

'Everyone was sent home, once the police had finished questioning them. Even without arrests or a trial, the papers latched on to the scandal. Constance Sutton became a recluse from the shame of it. The disgrace seems to have finished off Mungo Peploe's career. There are a few reports of him in London over the next few years, but no one else in spiritualist circles wanted anything to do with him. A year or so before the Second World War he was convicted of some sort of cheque fraud, and died in prison a few months later.'

So he'd lived long enough to possibly father a child, in or out of wedlock, or to tell someone this story of lost treasures hidden at Brightwell. I decided against telling Petra any of that.

'All told, it's not a story David Franklin will be putting in Brightwell's publicity. I expect someone will dig it up for a feature though, especially if the hotel opens around Halloween.' Unconcerned, Petra sat back from the table as our bill arrived. 'I had a glass of wine, but you had a pudding, so shall we just split this fifty-fifty? Plus a decent tip?'

'Fine by me.' I got out my wallet and matched the notes and coins that Petra put on the plate with the bill.

Even on a Monday night, the place was getting busy now. Jack Logan waved a brief goodbye from behind the bar as I waited for Petra to come back from the loo, and we walked out into the car park. I drove down the road, and decided against taking the shortcut through the woods now that it was getting dark. That did mean driving on to take the lane that curved past the Lamp Acre to head for Brightwell. I saw slivers of faint light outlining the windows and wondered what the bastard was up to. I wondered if Petra might turn up something that actually linked him to Mungo Peploe.

Arriving back, I pulled the Land Rover up beside Petra's Mini. 'That was a really nice meal.'

I expected her to say something equally inconsequential and open the door to get out. Instead, she undid her seat belt and leaned across to kiss me. Really kiss me, using her hand to turn my face towards her. She teased my lips with her tongue.

Caught unawares, I responded, before reluctantly pulling away. 'Look, I'm flattered, believe me, but I'm only here for a couple of months—'

Petra laughed. 'And in the last six months, I've applied for jobs in London, Manchester and Edinburgh. With any luck, I'll be out of here before you are. I'm not looking for some happily ever after, so how about you get over yourself and we have a bit of fun? Off the record, guaranteed.'

She kissed me again, and this time she took my hand and cupped it around her breast. That was undeniably pleasant. Since splitting up with my last serious girlfriend, my sex life had consisted of quiet nights in with a box of tissues and my imagination.

'Come on, you know you want to.' Petra had no doubt of that.

There wasn't much point me denying it, with her fingers tracing my erection through the fabric of my jeans. 'I haven't got any condoms.'

'I have.' She picked up her handbag from by her feet and got out of the Land Rover.

I watched her start walking up the steps. What the hell. Since we each knew where we stood, I might as well go with the flow.

Once we were inside she watched me unset the alarm. I turned to see a question on her face.

'The bedroom's through there.' I pointed to the door.

She laughed as I followed her in. 'A single bed? Oh, well, I'm sure we'll manage.'

She was already unbuttoning the front of her wraparound dress. Seeing her transparent rose-pink lingerie, I guessed she'd always intended to end this evening with some recreational sex. I wasn't sure what I thought about that, but my cock was doing more thinking than my brain by now.

She stepped close to help me take off my shirt. I did my best to keep kissing her as I kicked off my trainers and got out of my jeans. Without her high-heeled shoes, Petra had to stretch up to kiss me. 'You really are very tall.'

'Not when I'm lying down.' I sank backwards onto the bed and drew her down with me.

She straddled me and we began to move together. She leaned forward to kiss me, and then withdrew so I could suck her nipples through the gossamer bra.

I felt her softness sliding against me. I had an erection like a steel rod. A few moments later, Petra drew a deep, satisfied breath, and got off the bed. Finding her handbag, she tossed me a condom, and stripped off her underwear as I got ready for her to come back to me. This time, she slid onto my cock, slow and teasing. I kept my eyes on hers, seeing the laughter in her gaze. Two could play at that game. I began rolling her nipples between finger and thumb. Now that we were joined, I felt her warm flesh drawing me deeper inside her.

Petra laughed. She began riding me faster and with more purpose. I took a long, deep breath. This wasn't the best position for me, as a rule. In the circumstances, that was a good thing. Self-restraint was going to be a challenge.

I drew her forward, and licked and kissed her tits as her long hair brushed my face. I didn't relent as I felt the rising tension in her body. With my hands on her sides, I pushed her down onto my cock. Her thighs gripped my hips, and I barely felt the shudder of her orgasm before I lost control completely. There was no time for me to change position. No room for me to move in the way my body was urgently demanding. I made do as best I could. Now Petra followed my lead, to draw out the moment as long as possible.

As we slowed to a halt, she lay on my chest. Her hair tickled my nose and I blew the stray wisp away. We lay there, quietly comfortable, for a little while. I wondered how long it might be before I was ready to go again. I had a fair amount of celibacy to make up for.

Then I wondered if Petra would have been quite so ready to get into my bed without the allure of my mother's blood. I tried to convince myself that really didn't matter, since she was so clearly only after a mutually satisfactory fuck.

A few minutes later, Petra got up. 'Bathroom?'

'Through there.' I sat up and found a tissue for the condom.

When she came back, she picked her knickers up off the floor and stepped into them. Evidently we were done, for now.

'You're welcome to stay the night.' I offered more out of politeness than expectation.

'Share a three-foot bed with a man who's nearly as wide?' Petra laughed as she put her bra back on. 'Neither of us would get any sleep. Besides,' she added, 'I'm not doing the walk of shame past Gaffer Kemble and his minions tomorrow morning.'

'Fair enough.' I sat up and found my own clothes. 'Well, thank you for a very pleasant evening.'

'Maybe we'll do it again sometime,' Petra said lightly.

I took the gleam in her eye as a promising sign as we both got dressed. I walked her to the front door, trying to decide if I wanted a cup of tea or if I was going to go back to bed and sleep.

Petra kissed me briskly. 'Don't forget to email me that photo.'

It took me a moment to realise what she was talking about. 'Okay.'

She got into her Mini and was circling around when another set of headlights turned in through the entrance. As the Mini pulled away, I saw it was Rufus in the Defender. My first thought was to wonder what had happened now. Then I wondered if I needed to say anything about Petra being here.

Rufus wasn't interested. I don't think he'd even registered passing her car. He raised his voice to call up to me, standing beside his open driver's door. 'Martha Delly's been taken bad. I need to get her up to the hospital, her and Bill. I'm not waiting for an ambulance.'

I started down the steps. 'What can I do?'

'Take Bess.' Rufus snapped his fingers and the dog jumped out of the Defender. 'Fuck knows how long we're going to be, and I don't want to leave her shut in on her own.'

'Okay.' I was going to ask more questions, but as soon as his gesture sent Bess to my side, Rufus got back into the vehicle and drove away.

I looked down at the dog. She looked hopefully up at me. We went back into the house.

Chapter Fourteen

So much for my hopes of getting a good night's sleep. I tried to get Bess to settle in the housekeeper's sitting room, but she was having none of that. She was determined to lie in the porch with her head on her paws, looking at the front door.

Until I went to bed, that is. She came and scratched at the bedroom door until I opened it. As soon as I did that, she was satisfied, and went back to the porch. I went back to bed, only to hear the dog's claws clicking on the floorboards as she approached. I opened the door again and looked thoughtfully at her. This time, I left the door ajar. Bess went back to the porch.

I hate sleeping with an open door. Restless all night, I half-woke to hear the dog heavy-footed on the stairs, and out in the corridor, several times. By first light, I was ready to give up and get up. As I walked out to head for the kitchen, Bess came trotting out of the great hall, her feathered tail wagging.

'I suppose you want some breakfast?' I put down a cereal bowl of water and searched the cupboards as the Retriever lapped thirstily.

A tin of corned beef and some crumbled rich tea biscuits were the closest I could come to dog food. Bess ate it readily enough though, and if Rufus didn't approve, he should have thought about that and left me something to give her.

I made myself some tea and toast, and tried ringing the Home Farm house. There was no answer. I came out of the oak parlour to find Bess standing in the porch. She looked at me, expectant, her tail held high.

I checked the time. We still had ages before the Kembles and Coateses would arrive. I got my jacket and the keys and unlocked the door. As I did so, I realised I hadn't set the alarm last night. Well, I was pretty sure Bess would have barked fit to shatter the windows if anyone had been slinking around. I set the alarm before I went outside regardless.

Bess raced for the holly trees, and squatted for a pee on the rough grass on the left-hand side of the entrance. Then she stood between the stone pillars, looking at me, her ears pricked.

'Wait there,' I said sternly. 'Stay!'

Whether I was saying the right thing or not, the dog got the message. We walked up the lane to the cottages and Rufus's house with her frolicking around me. There was no sign of the Defender by the barn though, and no answer when I knocked on the door.

I didn't bother trying the Dellys' cottage. Even if nothing much was wrong, the hospital had probably kept Martha in overnight, to be on the safe side. I certainly hoped nothing much was wrong, but either way, I wouldn't find out until Rufus or Bill got back.

'Come on, dog.' I began walking.

After a moment's reluctance, Bess followed me, her tail drooping. Then, as we approached the lych-gate into the churchyard, she raced past me and stood over something in the long grass of the verge, barking loud enough to startle sparrows out of the hedges.

'All right, that's enough.' I went to see what she had found.

A crushed mess of dark red flesh and bone was surrounded by a scatter of dark feathers. I could pick out two twisted feet and a dull grey beak amid the blood and blackness. A dead crow. Okay, I'd seen a cat around here, which I assumed belonged to the Dellys, and Rufus had said there were foxes locally. One or the other could have caught a crow and eaten it here in the shelter of the churchyard gateway.

Even so, I felt a chill that had nothing to do with the early morning. I remembered that foul tree in the boggy stretch of the woods running down to the river. I still hadn't told Rufus about that. I looked at the dead bird again. Had Aiden killed the crow and left it here as part of... What?

'Come on, Bess, leave it.' I wasn't going to find any answers here. I'd have to see what Eleanor could find out about occult ideas about killing birds, when I told her about Mungo Peploe. Until then, I'd watch my back.

As we reached Brightwell's entrance, the dog's ears pricked and she barked, looking back towards the Broad. A minute or so later, I heard the distinctive note of the Defender's engine. We waited outside the house by the steps until Rufus arrived. Bess rushed up to greet him as soon as he stepped out of the vehicle.

'Martha's got to stay in hospital,' he said without preamble. 'Chest infection. Bill and I were there most of the night, until they could take her to a ward. We've come back to get a few hours' sleep while they're doing tests and stuff.'

'How poorly is she?' I asked with some trepidation.

'They'll know more when the antibiotics kick in. Bill's been telling her to go to the doctor since she woke up wheezing on Saturday. She's had that cough since the middle of last week.' Rufus looked down and fondled Bess's ears. The dog pressed her muzzle up against his thigh. 'Of course, she reckons that all she needs is a bottle of water from that spring of hers. She says she's been drinking it all her life.'

His voice was flat with implicit challenge, but I wasn't sure who I was supposed to agree with, or about what, if it came to that.

'It'll probably make her worse to be fretting that she can't have it,' I said cautiously. 'Get it right from the spring, stick a water purification tablet in it, and I don't suppose it could do any harm. If someone could get it to her without the nurses seeing it.'

I'd guessed right. Rufus's expression lightened.

'It might even do her some good. What do they call it? A placebo?'

'I could go up there,' I said quickly. 'At lunchtime, anyway, if you're not taking Bill back to see her before then.'

'That would be good.' Rufus yawned. 'I've got to see to the birds, and do a few other things.'

'Not a problem,' I assured him.

He left, and I went to the Land Rover to fetch the emergency bottle of water I keep in there. The plastic ring sealing the top was intact, so it would be sterile enough once I'd emptied it out. I put it on the sitting room table, before getting my toolbox and heading up to the long gallery and the work on the bookcases that I had planned. Whatever else was going on, there was still work to be done.

Everyone was used to me heading out at lunchtime, so no one gave me a second glance as I got into the Land Rover and drove away. I turned right and drove to the fingerpost before heading up the light towards the crossroads in the centre of the woods. Checking that Ordnance Survey map had shown me a much better path to the spring, even if Martha's route was more direct.

In the daylight I saw there was another fingerpost at the crossroads, indicating the different directions that Petra had told me about. Parking and locking the Land Rover, I looked around as I tucked the plastic water bottle inside my jacket. There was nothing to see, in the woods or along the broad, grassy tracks.

As I set off along the light that led out of the woods to the road to the pub, I thought about what I might do if Petra offered me another quickie. Sex with her might not count as crapping on my own doorstep while I was working here, but it came pretty close.

Add to that, I prefer emotional connections with girls I take to bed. Unfortunately, I've learned the hard way that true intimacy is impossible when you're keeping a secret like mine. Was keeping my sex life purely physical going to have to be the answer? For the next couple of months, maybe. Longer term, that prospect was as unappealing as ever.

Not that Petra was looking for the long term, I reminded myself, and if she offered me a second invitation, turning her down would hardly be polite. On the other hand, I'd stopped shagging girls who were only drawn to me by my greenwood blood a few years ago, because I didn't want to be that sort of prick. I still didn't.

I took the path off to the right that should lead me to the spring. As the trees closed around me, I walked more slowly, alert for some reason that I couldn't have explained. Getting closer to the edge of the lake, I saw sunlight glinting on the surface. The birch saplings around me thinned as the ground sloped upwards towards the spring. Before I reached the edge of the trees, I stopped. There was someone kneeling on the turf by the bubbling waters.

Someone with very sharp ears, apparently. I'd been moving as quietly as I knew how, and for me in any sort of woods, that's pretty much silently. This woman had heard me though. She stood up and turned around, scanning the lake and then the trees to both sides. Then she stopped and looked expectantly in my direction.

I stepped out from among the birches. 'Good morning.'

'More like good afternoon.' She was studying me without any attempt to hide it.

I returned the favour. I guessed she was about my age, average height and build, and she had the palest blonde hair I had ever seen. For a moment, I wondered if she was an albino, but as I got closer I saw that she had penetrating blue eyes. She was sensibly dressed for a walk in the woods, with a weatherproof jacket, heavy cotton trousers and lightweight hiking boots.

I was trying to decide what to say next when she took the initiative.

'Are you Daniel?'

'I am.' I was surprised. 'And you are...?'

'Finele Wicken, freshwater ecologist.'

That explained her interest in the spring, though I wasn't sure I'd heard her name right. 'Is it okay if I call you Finlay?'

'Fi-ne-le.' She spaced the three syllables out. 'Like Fionnula, only different. Call me Fin. It's easier.'

'I'm Dan. You're doing some work for the Franklins?'

I was surprised that no one had mentioned it to me, but then I realised there was no reason they should. I guessed Rufus must have known she was coming, but he'd had other things on his mind this morning.

She shook her head. 'Sineya Beauchene suggested I visit you.'

It took a minute for my brain to catch up with my ears. Whoever this woman was, she knew the Blithehurst dryads. What on earth did that make her?

'How did you get here?' I did my best to sound as if I was just making conversation.

'Train and taxi.' She took a mobile phone out of her pocket and grimaced. 'Any chance of a lift back to the station, or at least as far as somewhere I can get a signal?'

So she definitely wasn't a dryad, or a naiad, come to that, if getting so close to so much metal didn't bother her.

'And what's your interest here?'

She looked up from her phone, and I realised she was having some fun at my expense by keeping me guessing about her. 'The same as yours.'

I wasn't interested in playing games. I nodded at her phone. 'Sineya didn't ring you on that. What's going on?'

She put the phone away. 'I actually spoke to Eleanor Beauchene last night. She went to see Sineya yesterday, to see if she knew anyone who could help you work out what's in this lake. Sineya told her to look me up online. She did, and I got on a train this morning. I'm based near Bristol.'

'What's your area of expertise, exactly?' I was surprised that Eleanor hadn't rung me.

Fin grinned. 'It's probably easiest if I show you.'

Before I could say anything else, something unexpected dazzled me. It was like sunlight reflected off rippling water, only about ten times as bright, and anyway, I wasn't even looking at the lake. I blinked and rubbed my eyes, and when I was able to focus again, I realised Finele had vanished. A sizeable swan was standing by the spring, looking at me with unnerving intensity.

I took a step back as the bird spread its wings. Turning, it took a few ungainly steps down the grassy slope, its broad wings beating strongly. A few more paces and it launched into flight. Now cutting elegantly through the air, the white bird swept low across the surface of the lake.

Something moved beneath it. I could see a swift darkness mirror the swan's flight, but this wasn't the bird's shadow. The water bulged, as though something barely submerged was swimming after the swan. The bird flew faster. Whatever was chasing it accelerated. The swan wheeled around, with its great wings clapping against the air. The thing in the water was caught unawares. As it threw itself into a tight turn, flinging out an arc of spray, I saw a sinuous shape reach up. A bony, distorted hand snatched at the swan's feet.

The bird was already soaring far beyond the creature's reach. It – she – flew back down the length of the lake. Using its wings to brake as it approached, it – she – spread webbed black feet and landed on the turf with an inelegant, stumbling run. I was about to laugh when I was painfully dazzled again. I turned away, swearing under my breath. When I looked back, wiping tears from my eyes, Finele was standing there. She was breathing heavily, as if she'd been running. Other than that, she looked exactly the same as she had when we first met.

'You can turn into a swan.' Before the words were out of my mouth, I realised that was a blindingly stupid thing to say.

'Well spotted. It's a family thing.'

She was smiling, but clearly it wasn't something she was about to discuss. Fortunately, I had an obvious change of subject to hand.

'So what is that creature in the lake?'

'Eleanor Beauchene was right. It's a nix.' She had no doubt about that, as she turned to stare at the water. 'No wonder there are no water fowl here.'

'I'd noticed that.' I decided not to point out that my mum had been the first one to suggest the problem here might be a nix.

'Have you noticed the lack of everything else that you and I might see?' She glanced at me. 'No sprites, no hobs or sylphs, nothing, not even boggarts.'

I couldn't say that I had thought about that. Fortunately Fin was staring at the lake again.

'What do you know about nixes?' she demanded.

'Next to nothing.' I felt that was my safest answer. 'Apart from they like to drown people, and they're shapeshifters.'

'There's a lot more to them than that,' she said with feeling. 'But they're not shapeshifters like dryads or naiads. They can't pass for human so well that they can mingle with us, unnoticed. A nix is limited to the shapes it uses to lure victims into its waters.'

That was a relief, and the thought of an ally with directly relevant experience was even more welcome. 'You've dealt with one before?'

'Not me, but I know about them.' She shook her head. 'It's a family thing. I'm from Cambridgeshire originally, and they were a blight throughout the fens for centuries.'

A cold wind blew across the surface of the water, and she shivered. 'Let's get out of here.'

'Okay.' As I turned, I felt the weight of the water bottle inside my jacket. 'Sorry, hang on a moment.'

I took out the bottle and offered it to her. 'Are you thirsty?'

'No thanks.'

I uncapped it and drank about half, careful not to touch the bottle's neck with my mouth. Then I poured the rest away. Kneeling by the spring, I refilled it.

Fin watched me, in between glancing warily at the lake. 'What's that for?'

'There's an old woman who lives locally.' I explained Martha's request. 'Do you think it's safe for her to drink this?'

'Oh yes. The Franklins could probably bottle it and sell it if they wanted to.' Fin had no doubt of that. 'But you say she was taken ill unexpectedly? Within the past few days?'

'I think so.' I stood up and put the top on the bottle.

'Then this nix has quite a reach.' Fin was thinking aloud, at least as much as she was talking to me. 'That's not good.'

'It can do that?' I didn't like that idea in the least. 'Make people sick?'

'If it's strong enough. A nix is...' She searched for the right word. 'Malign. It doesn't drown people for the fun of it, or even just to eat them. It thrives on their terror, their pain, and on the fear and misery of the people who come searching for a lost loved one.'

'And it's willing to make some sort of bargain with someone who gives it what it likes?'

'What are you talking about?'

'Let's get away from the water.' I had no idea if the nix could hear us, but there was no point in taking chances. 'This way.'

As I led Fin back to the Land Rover, I told her what I'd learned from Petra Oxway about Mungo Peploe, and explained that I hadn't had a chance to tell Eleanor yet.

'And I've been hearing about other local deaths ever since I got here, as well as rumours of local witches.'

I told her about Mary Anne and Mountjoy Sutton, and then Martha's story of the drowned Romany couple, as well as the tragedies that had beset Aunt Constance and the mystery of Simon Oxway's car crash.

'Could a nix do all that? Or am I imagining things?'

'A nix could be involved, if it was powerful enough.' Fin was looking increasingly concerned. 'And the more misery it causes, the stronger it will become.'

'It must have had plenty of misery to feed on, when the local workhouse was close by.' I outlined the history of the Broad as we approached the Land Rover.

Fin's thoughts had already moved on. 'You say this Mountjoy Sutton created the lake, that he was the one who first dammed the brook?'

'That's right.' Something else occurred to me. Belief in witchcraft had flourished under the Stuarts, at least according to Mrs Roberts, my English teacher, when we'd done

Macbeth at school. 'Do you suppose that bastard was the first one to make a bargain with the nix, looking for some way out of his debts?'

Fin nodded. 'That's entirely possible. Of course, trusting the treacherous thing was his first mistake.'

'When his plans went wrong, the nix had still more misery to enjoy.'

There's a reason why so many folk tales warn against making any kind of deal with supernatural creatures. They're only ever really interested in a good outcome for themselves.

'Have you any idea what's happened to the local drainage, where the stream leaves the lake?' Fin looked at me across the Land Rover's bonnet.

Not a question I was expecting, but at least I had the answer. 'According to the local gamekeeper, it's wrecked.'

'Show me.' Fin opened the passenger door and got in.

I realised I'd probably better show her something else as well, if we were heading for the woods by the river. 'Is it only *people's* fear that a nix can feed on? What about animals?'

'They feel terror, and that's enough for a nix.' She looked at me dubiously.

I started the engine. 'Did Eleanor tell you about the man we think might be in league with the nix now?'

Fin nodded. 'Aiden something, possibly this Mungo Peploe's great-grandson.'

'I think he's killing birds for the nix.' As I drove carefully down the light to the lane, I explained about the foul blackthorn tree and the dead crow I'd found that morning.

Fin didn't say anything, and we continued in silence to the Lamp Acre. I drove a short distance down the track and stopped. 'Wait here.'

There was no sign of life at the caravan, but I went and hammered on the door all the same. I stood and listened intently, but there wasn't a hint of movement inside. I walked back to the Land Rover.

'If he's in there, he's hiding.'

'We'll be okay.' Fin grinned briefly as she got out. 'Don't you know a swan can break a man's arm with a blow from its wing?'

'Really?' I made doubly sure the Land Rover was locked.

'No idea. I've never tried, but I'm willing to give it a go.'

Her good mood didn't last long as we made our way into the woods. I became aware of the same oppressive silence that I'd noticed before. Now it felt all the more ominous.

'Watch your step.' I found a fallen branch and started probing the ground. 'There are hidden gullies around here.'

'I can tell.' Fin crouched down and ran her fingers through the dead leaves. A moment later, she snatched her hand back and sprang up.

'What is it?' I remembered the unwelcome sensation when I had first put my hand in the lake.

'The nix.' She swallowed, as if she were trying not to throw up. 'I think it's trying to find a way to reach the river.'

'What happens if it does?' I couldn't imagine that would be good.

Fin looked grim. 'I'd need to check some maps to be sure of the watershed, to work out where this river goes, but my guess is the nix would head for the nearest city, somewhere it could find more misery to feed on. Who knows what it might do after that.'

I guessed it would find plenty of unhappiness to savour these days. 'With Aiden tagging along, ready to do whatever he could to cause more strife in return for whatever power the nix is offering him.'

Fin nodded, now looking nauseous. 'Let's get out of here.'

I wasn't sorry not to see that horrible tree again, but it still had to be dealt with. 'What do you think I should do about the blackthorn?'

'Leave it, for the time being,' she said slowly. 'It's probably best not to start anything that will alert this Aiden until we have some idea of how to finish it.'

'Then let's get out of here.' I retraced my steps, and breathed the fresher air gratefully once we reached the track along the edge of the trees. 'Do you think we can finish it? The nix, I mean. Destroy it somehow?'

'I think we need to try, don't you? If the nix gets loose, and it has a willing human accomplice, even if the fool has no idea what he's really dealing with—' She stopped dead as we turned for the Land Rover. 'Hang on. There's been these centuries of local death and misery, but the Franklins' Uncle Cecil lived to be over a hundred years old. How on earth did he manage that?'

That was a very good question. 'I think he was doing something, but I've no idea what. I can show you his note-books, and there's some sort of bizarre diagram, but I warn you, I couldn't make sense of any of it.'

'Let's focus on what we do know.' Fin checked her watch. 'I'd really appreciate a lift back to the station. I need to get home and make some calls.'

I wondered why she didn't save on rail fares by flying from place to place, but decided not to ask. 'Have you got the Brightwell number, so you can ring me if you need to?'

Fin nodded. 'Eleanor gave it to me.'

We drove past the house, through the Broad and over the bridge. As soon as we had a signal, Finele got out her phone and started checking maps. I noticed her switch to the satellite view and zoom in, and wondered if that's what the countryside looked like to a swan flying over it. That was something else I wasn't going to ask until I got to know her a good deal better. If I got to know her better.

'How do you know Sineya?' I asked as we drove past the market hall. Just like anyone else asking about a mutual acquaintance.

'I visited Blithehurst the year before last.' Fin scrolled down her screen. 'She could see me for what I was, and I could see her, of course.'

'I'm surprised she never mentioned you.' Though I could imagine the dryad's reply if Eleanor or I ever raised the subject. We'd never asked. I decided that was going to change.

'Why?' Finele looked up from her phone. 'What makes you so special?'

'Sorry?' From her tone I realised I'd dropped a bollock somehow.

'What did you expect her to say? "Oh, by the way, and not that it's any of your business, but I happen to know a swan maiden. Would you like to know how to find her?" How would you feel if she casually told me your secret, in case I'd ever been curious about meeting a dryad's son? Before this business with the nix, I mean.'

'Sorry.' I raised a hand from the driving wheel to signal surrender, and gave up trying to make conversation. I had been going to ask if Fin knew Kalei or any other naiads who knew how to fight a nix, but that could wait for another time.

After I dropped Finele at the train station, I went back down the hill and parked by the market hall. Leaving the bottle of spring water in the Landy, I went to get a sandwich and a coffee at Shayler's. After talking to Finele, I'd remembered that I still hadn't looked up horned hunters online. So much for me telling the Franklins that I wouldn't be bothered by the lack of Internet access at Brightwell.

I'd rather have had my laptop, but I managed to do some research on my phone. Not for the first time, I found an array of myths and associated theories about the origins of such folklore. Some overlapped and some contradicted others. I didn't find any suggestion of men who could turn into stags, so I decided I didn't have to try finding a way to drop that question into casual conversation with Rufus. Though I'd be asking Sineya what she knew.

I'd be interested to know what Finele made of Rufus. I'd have to see if I could introduce them, assuming she came back here again, hopefully with some idea how to get rid of the nix.

Thinking about Fin, I looked up swan maiden myths. At least those were mostly consistent and straightforward. The stories mainly warned mortal men against thinking they could get the better of such women in the long run, even if they controlled them short-term. Duly noted, not that I had any intention of telling Finele Wicken what to do.

I wondered what was the best way to phrase another search, to see what sort of online profile Fin had. A freshwater ecologist must have some sort of professional web presence. With any luck I might get some idea of what she actually did.

'How are you getting on?' Jude Oxway startled me.

I switched off my phone. 'Fine, thanks. The renovations are going very well.'

'Good to know. Can you let Geoff Kemble know that I'll be coming over tomorrow, to make a start on cataloguing the books? Petra's going to cover the shop for a few days, so I can get an idea of how long a job it's going to be.'

Jude gave no indication that she had any idea that her sister-in-law and I were anything more than passing acquaintances. That was a relief.

I nodded. 'Of course.'

Since I'd finished my coffee, I got up to go. I still had to drop off that bottle of spring water with Rufus, I remembered. Smuggling it into the hospital was up to him or Bill.

When I got back to Brightwell, I decided, I'd make sure to be working wherever Jude started sorting through the books, whether that was in the long gallery library or Uncle Cecil's reading room. That way I could make casual conversation about whatever she might find by way of local history or folklore.

If the old man really had found some arcane way to frustrate the nix, we might find something to help us get rid of it completely in one of his books.

Chapter Fifteen

I was in the hallway when Jude Oxway arrived the next morning. A couple of technicians had come to take a look at the rattling old lift, and we were discussing possible alterations to the servants' staircase to accommodate a more modern installation. Though Jude wasn't the first person to arrive.

'What's she doing here?' the gaffer demanded as he came in through the porch. 'That Taysel girl. I don't want her sort anywhere around our Davey, or our Jack.'

I went to see who he was talking about, and saw the girl from the woods, the one who had made Josh Franklin's life such a misery. She was hanging around between the holly trees.

'I'll get rid of her.' I put down my laser measure and nodded to the lift guys. 'Give me a minute.'

Jade backed warily away as I walked down to the entrance, but clearly she wasn't about to leave. I noted she wasn't wearing the little cult's army-surplus gear today, just jeans and a faded red sweatshirt with some sort of slogan half worn away. Knotted bracelets of multicoloured thread ringed her scrawny wrists.

'I come about the job,' she said defiantly. 'Seen the card up in Shayler's window.'

I had no idea what she was talking about, but that didn't matter. 'There's nothing for you here.'

'You want cleaning done. I can do that,' she persisted. 'I done pub work last year up the Whittle. When can I start? Tomorrow? I already left school.'

She took a hasty step closer as a car shot past the entrance, heading away from the Broad. In the daylight her hair was implausibly black, and her eyes were hollow beneath clumsily applied make-up. Her pupils were dark and dreamy despite the bright sun, and I could smell something sickly and alcoholic hanging around her, on her breath or in her sweat.

'Go away and sleep off whatever you've been taking,' I said, repelled.

To my astonishment, she stepped closer to stare up at me, unafraid despite my size.

'You better give me a job. You'll regret it if you don't.'

'How?' I challenged her.

She smiled, now sly. 'Else I go to the police. Say you raped me. You and Rufus Stanlake. Both of you, led me on and then fucked me, taking turns.'

'No one's going to believe that.' It might have been funny, if the threat wasn't so revolting, and if the girl wasn't so pathetic.

'They will, when I tells it.' She was unnervingly certain of that. 'I'll say you let Josh Franklin watch an' all.'

I wondered if this was her idea, or if Aiden had put her up to it. If Aiden had done a web search on me, he'd be right to guess the last thing I wanted was more police attention. I had no idea about Rufus, but I reckoned there was a fair chance his abrasive personality had got him into some sort of trouble before now.

If Aiden could get Jade inside the house, that had to be a step towards finding whatever he thought was hidden here. If not, the police would have to investigate her allegations, however flimsy her story might be. They'd have no choice. Getting me and Rufus tangled up in something like that would leave Bill Delly as the last man standing. There wouldn't be anyone else to keep watch on the house at night. If Bill was visiting Martha at the hospital, there'd be no one here. No one to hear the alarm, assuming Aiden didn't already have the code to switch it off.

None of that was going to happen.

'Let's see what the police have to say about attempted blackmail.' I took my phone out of my pocket, glad I'd been using it to get a photo of an awkwardly placed joint on the stairs.

I called up the number pad and dialled 999. Putting the phone to my ear, I nodded. 'Police, please.'

'You're fucking about. There ent no signal here.' But Jade's voice was shrill with uncertainty.

'Brightwell House, Bourton under Ashes,' I said to the non-existent police officer answering my fictitious call. I nodded at the girl. 'Check your own phone.'

I don't know if she was always so suggestible, or if I could thank whatever shit Aiden was shoving into her, but she reached into her pocket. As soon as she looked down at the screen, I slipped my own phone away and snatched hers out of her dirty hands.

She was caught completely off her guard. 'You prick! Give it back!'

Jade tried to grab my arm with one hand, reaching for her phone with the other. I stepped away so she couldn't touch me, raising the phone high above her head.

'Give it, you bastard!' Her distress was genuine. 'That's mine!'

I looked at the screen. Locked. Fuck it. 'What's your passcode?'

'Not telling you!' She made another grab for the phone.

I warded her off with my free hand, and to my relief, she backed off. I knew we must have an audience of Kembles and Coateses, so I really didn't want to lay a finger on her. They couldn't see me scowl at her though, looking as threatening as I knew how.

'Tell me or I smash the fucking thing. Either way's fine with me.' I meant it.

'No!' she wailed. 'Two six nine seven.'

'Good move. Now, shut up and you might get this back.' I backed away, still keeping half an eye on the girl, and unlocked the screen. Thankfully the main icons were the same as the ones on my phone, and her messages were immediately accessible.

'Either you tell me where to find that photo Josh Franklin sent you or I delete everything here. Reset to factory settings. Is that what you want?'

She stared at me, at a loss. However she'd imagined the morning would go, she hadn't expected this. 'What?'

I repeated myself. 'Or I could take your phone to the police and explain how you blackmailed him. He's underage, so that's a shitload of trouble for you.'

She was in no fit state to work out if I was telling the truth or not. 'It was the week before last.'

I scrolled back through the messages and found Josh Franklin's number. There were a whole load of texts and attachments. I quickly deleted the lot without looking any closer, and deleted him from her contacts as well. 'Did you back up that photo anywhere? On a computer?'

'What? How? I ent got a laptop.' Her bitter reply had the ring of truth.

In other circumstances, I could have felt sorry for her. I held out the phone, only to lift it out of her reach at the last minute. 'I give this back, and you go away, and you stay away. You stay away from Josh Franklin. If you don't there'll be trouble.'

She looked at me, sullen. 'Yeah, okay, whatever.'

'Convince me.' I scrolled through her contacts. Finding an entry for Aiden, I memorised the number. I had no idea what use it might be, and there wasn't a surname for him, but any information might be worth having.

'I promise, all right? Please, let me have my phone,' Jade begged.

I handed it back reluctantly. From what I'd seen in films, I guessed some technical expert could retrieve those deleted messages, but I didn't reckon Jade was an IT genius, and I had to hope that Aiden wasn't either.

'Now get lost, and I don't want to see you around here again.'

She clutched her phone with both hands, as though it was truly precious to her, and retreated towards the entrance. I stood there, watching her go. At the last moment, she spun back around to spit at me.

'You'll be sorry, you prick. I understand more'n you know. I got friends cleverer'n you an' all. I'm learning the magic of this place, and you don't belong here.'

That might have been more impressive if she hadn't had to dodge out of the way as an ageing Ford Fiesta slowed to turn into the entrance. I could see Jude Oxway was driving. I stepped out of her way myself, and when I looked back at the holly trees Jade was gone.

I walked back towards the house, where Jude was waiting by her car. 'What did Jade Taysel want?'

'A job. Apparently you've been advertising?' That came out harsher than I'd intended.

Jude stiffened. 'I'm sorry. Should I have spoken to you first?'

I raised my hands. 'Sorry, I didn't mean to snap. Only she got quite aggressive when I told her there was no work for her here.'

'That doesn't surprise me.' Jude shook her head as she went around to the back of her car and opened the boot. She sounded more sad than angry though.

'Can I carry anything for you?' I offered.

'Oh, yes, please.' Jude took a laptop case out and a cloth bag with a ring-binder in it. 'That crate, please.'

I lifted out a plastic box with a hand-held vacuum cleaner in it, along with an assortment of dusters and other cloths. 'Where do you want to start? There are books in the library in the gallery, and in the drawing room.'

Jude nodded. 'Nicki said. Let's see what's downstairs first.'

We headed up the steps. Geoff Kemble met us in the hall.

'What did she want? I hope you told her to sling her hook?'

'Go ahead. It's the door at the end, on the right.' I stopped to let Jude go past me and down the corridor before answering him. 'She was asking about work. I told her we didn't need anyone.'

Geoff grunted. 'No one needs her sort. No better than she ought to be, her or her mother.'

Satisfied, he headed up the stairs. I looked around for the lift technicians, and then heard them talking to Mark Coates upstairs. Deciding they could wait for a moment longer, I headed for the drawing room.

Jude was surveying the packed shelves in the dim electric light. 'I wonder how many of these have ISBNs to help me out.'

Since I couldn't answer that, I opened the shutters to let in the daylight. 'Do you need an extension cord for your laptop, or anything else?'

'I brought one with me.' Jude was fitting a brush attachment to the little vacuum cleaner. I was interested to see that she'd put a square of muslin over the nozzle first.

I gestured towards the leather chair where I'd left the oddments from the shelves. 'One of the Franklins will need to go through that lot. It's probably mostly junk, but there might be something someone wants as a keepsake.'

'Wait a moment,' Jude said as I turned to go. 'Close that door for a minute, will you?'

I shut the door to the corridor and waited to see what she wanted to say.

'I heard Geoff Kemble just now.' She shook her head. 'You shouldn't listen to everything he says about the Taysels.'

'You think I should give her a job?'

'God, no,' Jude said with feeling. 'I made that mistake. I thought she could help out behind the coffee counter last summer. That was before I realised she can barely read or write. Then I went out to the bank last thing one Friday, and came back to find the place full of her mates. She'd been giving them bags of crisps and cans of Coke. None of it paid for, but I honestly don't think she thought she was stealing, and I don't even think it was her idea. But I couldn't be having that.'

'Of course not.' I wondered why she was telling me this.

'The thing is, she's one of those kids who's never really had a chance. You should know that. Simon did all he could, but there are some problems that are so deep-rooted that it would take more time and money to make a difference than our councillors are ever going to spare.'

She carried on talking as she unpacked the plastic crate and set up her laptop. I recalled Nicki Franklin saying Isobel Oxway liked to gossip. I reckoned I knew where the girl had picked up that habit. Still, I stayed where I was, on the off-chance I might learn something useful.

'The Taysels are one of the old water meadow families. You've seen that playing field over the river, across the road from St Michael's? That used to be a warren of terraced stone cottages until they were bulldozed after the war. It needed doing,' Jude assured me. 'The whole place was a slum that flooded every wet winter. That's where the Taysels lived, along with the Hillyards and the Ditchfields, mostly. Most of them were farm labourers and the like. They tended to marry each other, since decent folk like the Coateses and the Kembles, who had good jobs in the ribbon mills or on the railway, wanted nothing to do with them.' Her sarcasm was withering.

'When the water meadows were cleared, the families were rehoused. Some went to live in the Broad and some went to the new terraces up by the hospital. Most have done perfectly well for themselves, but those particular families still have Granny Taysel's legacy to deal with, and that's what's given Jade such problems.'

I recognised my cue. 'How do you mean?'

'Granny Taysel lived in St Michael's Meadows around the early 1900s. Despite walking with two sticks all her life, she married and had twenty-odd children, who mostly married Ditchfields and Hillyards. Their children have often ended up marrying cousins to some degree. Only, the reason Granny Taysel walked with two sticks was she suffered from congenital hip dysplasia. It keeps coming through in her descendants, the girls especially, in those three families.'

Jude sighed. 'Some are more badly affected than others. Jade's mother's been on crutches since her pregnancy, and whoever her father was, he's never shown any interest. So Jade's been left to skip school and do pretty much whatever she likes while her mum scrapes along on benefits. I don't suppose her own future holds anything better, but you see, it's not all her fault.'

'Okay.' I could certainly see why the wretched girl was such easy prey for someone like Aiden. That didn't make her, or him, any less of a threat. 'Right, if you've got everything you need, I'll let you get on.'

I went upstairs to find the lift technicians, and found they needed access to the roof space. Coming back down to the oak parlour to check the house plans, I discovered we needed to go up through a hatch in a lumber room that was at the other end of the long gallery. That was accessed through another well-concealed door in the panelling that faced the grand staircase as it arrived on this top floor. At least that meant I could check the roof timbers while we were up there. I was pleased to find the joists and rafters were in good order, and made a few notes about where to start when I came to fitting out the lumber room to serve as the hotel linen store.

By the time the gaffer blew his whistle for lunch, the lift guys had all the measurements and information they needed to write their report advising David Franklin what the options were. I walked them out to their van and watched them drive away. I was wondering how best to casually enquire if Jude Oxway had found anything interesting in the drawing room books when the Franklins' Range Rover pulled in through the entrance. Nicki was driving.

'Oh good,' she said as she got out. 'I was hoping I'd catch you. How are you doing for petty cash?'

'It's mostly going on milk and biscuits.' Though the cash box didn't need replenishing just yet.

'I'll take the receipts while I'm here.' Nicki walked with me up the steps, looking around as she came into the entrance hall. 'How's everything going?'

'Very well. Do you want to speak to Geoff Kemble?' I halted by the oak screen. The gaffer and other senior Kembles and Coateses favoured the seats in the deep bay window by the dais when they stopped to eat their sandwiches.

'No, that's fine, as long as you haven't got any concerns.' Nicki waved at the men. 'Don't let me interrupt your lunch,' she called out with a smile.

I opened the oak parlour door, and closed it behind Nicki as she followed me in. 'There is something you should know about.' Something I didn't think Geoff Kemble and the rest of them needed to hear.

Doing my best to stay matter-of-fact, I told her about Jade Taysel's visit that morning, and the girl's ugly threats. If anything came of that encounter, I wanted Nicki as a witness. She would be able to swear that she knew about Jade's attempt to blackmail me for a job well before the girl went to the police. I didn't mention Josh, obviously, but I warned Nicki that Rufus might be dragged into any mess Jade tried to stir up.

To my utter bemusement, Nicki laughed. She clapped a hand to her mouth immediately, horribly embarrassed. 'I'm so sorry. It's not funny, of course it isn't. It's just—' She glanced at the door.

I waited for an explanation.

'There's no way Rufus would be involved in something like that,' she said quietly. 'He's gay, and anyone who knows him well enough can vouch for that. Please keep it to yourself though. He doesn't like people knowing his private business, not around here. Bourton isn't the most enlightened place of the world. It's not a problem for you, is it?'

A combative note in her voice told me that if it was, I'd have a problem with her.

'Not as far as I'm concerned.' I hoped she could see that I meant it.

I could hardly explain that the love of my father's life is an ageless, near-immortal tree spirit. On that basis alone, I've never felt I have any right to pass judgement on who anyone else might choose to sleep with. That's their business, not mine.

Two things did occur to me. I saw a couple of comments from Mark Coates and Geoff Kemble in a new light, and reckoned Rufus's secret wasn't as secret as he thought it might be. I also wondered if his abrasive manner was his way of keeping people at a distance, in case they got curious about his love life. There are downsides to living in small, close-knit communities.

'That's okay then.' Nicki looked relieved.

I wasn't so certain that the police would discount accusations of rape on that basis alone. There's such a thing as being bisexual, as I'd discovered at university. A basketball player who I knew had a girlfriend surprised me by making a pass after a game. I wasn't offended, and I explained I simply wasn't interested, and that had been that.

Since that was absolutely not a conversation I was going to have with Nicki Franklin, I got the cash box out of the locked desk drawer. 'I think I've got everything accounted for.'

She was more than willing to change the subject. 'Let's have a look.'

We were sorting through receipts when there was a knock on the door. 'Nicki?'

It was Jude. I went to let her in.

'I'm not interrupting, am I?' She looked from me to Nicki.

'Not at all.' I waved that away. 'I'll leave you to it.'

'No, wait, I want to talk to you both. I was coming to ring you, Nicki, when I saw your car.'

She didn't sound concerned. She looked more excited than anything else, so I wondered what she wanted.

Jude turned to me. 'When you've been working up in the long gallery, have you noticed any books with these titles?'

She handed me a neat, handwritten list.

The Book of Black Magic and Pacts. The Long Secreted Friend. The Grand Grimoire.

Le Petit Albert. Le Livre Noir. Cyprien Mago ante Conversionem.

'No.' I shook my head, because that much was true, even if I did recognise a few of those titles from the books in that sealed cupboard in Aiden's caravan.

Nicki held out her hand, and I passed the list over. She read it and looked at Jude. 'What are they?'

Jude ran a hand through her unruly hair. 'I'll have to check online, when I get back to the shop, but if Cecil owned these books, depending on the state of them and how old they are, they could be worth an awful lot of money.'

Nicki's forehead creased. 'I don't understand. If they're here, they must have belonged to him.'

'Sorry, I'm not explaining myself very well.' Jude took a moment to gather her thoughts. 'Cecil clearly had a great deal of interest in the occult. Quite a few of the books I've found so far dealing with spiritualism and ritual magic are pretty valuable in themselves, certainly to the right collector or a specialist dealer.'

'I had no idea.' Nicki was mystified as she put the piece of paper down. 'I mean, I know the stories about Constance Sutton trying to contact her dead son, but I had no idea Cecil followed in her footsteps.' She looked disapproving.

'I don't think he took it that far, but he was certainly curious.' Jude perched on the edge of the desk. 'I've found slips of paper in a lot of his occult books that are clearly cross-referencing passages and ceremonies from one to another, and a lot of those notes mention those other books as well, the ones I've listed there. The ones that I haven't found yet. I can't see how he could be doing that if he didn't have them to hand.'

'How unexpected.' Nicki still looked bemused. 'It's a good thing we didn't take that second-hand dealer's offer to clear the shelves for a price.'

'Very,' Jude said firmly. 'I'll know more when I can get online, but if you do find any of those books, Dan, please make sure you put them somewhere safe.'

'I will.' Not only to protect the Franklins' interests. I guessed this must be what Aiden was after.

Though that was potentially awkward. If he really was Mungo Peploe's great-grandson, and if these books had belonged to the magician, didn't he have a legitimate claim to them? Perhaps, but those were two big ifs, and I could think of another one. If he could prove who he was, and that those books should be his, why didn't he just knock on the Franklins' front door and explain what he wanted?

'Is that everything?' Nicki looked at us both.

Jude nodded, then held up her hand. 'There are some oddments that Ed and David should go through, in case there's anything they want.'

'I'll get them.' I picked up a cardboard box from the corner of the room, one I'd used for some shopping at the supermarket.

By the time I returned with Uncle Cecil's clutter, Jude and Nicki were outside, chatting by the Range Rover.

'Thanks, Dan.' Nicki opened the rear door so I could put the box on the seat.

'No problem. Okay, I'd better be getting back to work.' I went back into the house and into the study, where I picked up that list of arcane titles before going upstairs to start searching the long gallery in between working on restoring the bookcases.

Chapter Sixteen

The phone in the office startled me out of a deep sleep early the next morning. I scrambled out of bed and hurried down the corridor. My heart was pounding as I snatched up the old-fashioned receiver. 'Yes?'

The line crackled. 'Hello? Is that Dan? It's Fin Wicken.'

'Oh, hello. How—?'

She spoke before I could work out how to ask what I could do for her. I still wasn't fully awake.

'Can you meet me at that crossroads in the woods at noon? By the fingerpost where you were parked the other day?'

'Okay.' I couldn't see any reason why not, even half asleep.

'Great. See you then.' Fin rang off before I could ask what this was about.

Since I was up, I thought about ringing Eleanor, to let her know Fin was coming back, before she headed for the university library. As soon as I'd had the house to myself last night, I'd called to tell her what Jude Oxway had said about those potentially valuable books. We'd also shared our astonishment at discovering that swan maiden myths had a basis in fact, and speculated about a few other folk tales.

I tried ringing Eleanor's mobile, but it went straight to voicemail. I thought about ringing Rufus, to ask about Martha Delly, but he'd said he'd let me know if there was any news when I'd dropped off the bottle of spring water. I could only hope that modern medicine, and being beyond the nix's reach, would see her on the mend.

So I got ready for work. Frustratingly, I couldn't carry on searching the long gallery bookshelves, since Geoff Kemble needed my skills on the bedroom floor today. Now that the pipes to get water to the new en-suite bathrooms were installed, we needed to get the waste sorted out. I spent the morning taking up floorboards and helping work out the best ways to get new connections through to the existing drainage.

I had my phone in my pocket, and I kept an eye on the time as I worked. At a quarter to twelve, I began putting my tools away. 'Sorry, I've got somewhere to be.'

At the other end of the floorboard we'd just taken up, Conrad Kemble looked at me, dubious. 'Have you told the gaffer?'

I was tempted to point out that I didn't actually work for Geoff, but that risked sounding unfriendly. 'I'll let him know on my way out.'

That was easy enough, since the gaffer was on the ground floor, working out where the waste pipe from the housekeeper's kitchen sink went down to the basement level.

'I've got to go out for a bit.' I smiled as I said it, but kept moving towards the sitting room, to make it clear I wasn't asking for permission.

Geoff didn't look overly pleased as I came back from putting my toolbox inside the sitting room door. 'What's that, then? This errand you've got to run?'

'I'll be back as soon as I can.' As I went down the steps, I tried to think of some convincing excuse. Something that wouldn't arouse suspicion or even just nosiness.

As I got into the Land Rover, I put that out of my mind and wondered what Fin wanted me for. Driving up Brightwell Light, I kept a look out for Rufus's Defender. I'd need another excuse if we met him in the woods. This could be a problem. I'm not good at making up stories, and I've never been a convincing liar. I mostly rely on a silent scowl to stop people asking questions.

When I arrived at the crossroads, though, the only person I could see was Finele Wicken. She was sitting on the grass, leaning against the fingerpost, and wearing the same clothes as last time. As I parked and walked over, she looked up, shielding her eyes with a hand.

'Have you any idea what an utter pain it is, finding a route that a dryad can use to get around Birmingham?'

'Er, no.' That wasn't a conversation I'd ever expected to have.

'Hello, Daniel.' The air shimmered like heat haze as Sineya appeared and immediately shifted from a vision of ethereal beauty to her usual physical manifestation of a lithe and leggy twenty-something with long red hair. Her clothes were identical to Finele's.

She was the last person I expected to see. I'd also never expected to see a dryad looking quite so knackered. Come to that, Fin looked exhausted as well.

'Are you okay?' I looked at her and then at Sineya.

'You people – your father's people – have cut down so much woodland,' the dryad said crossly. 'I never thought we would get here, even with Finele showing me the way.'

I guessed that meant she'd flown here as a swan, but catching her expression out of the corner of my eye, I decided not to ask.

'I'm very glad to see you.' I hoped that would prompt Sineya to explain what she was doing here.

The dryad grinned, tired as she was. 'You'll have some grovelling to do when you get back to Blithehurst. Grandmother isn't pleased.'

So I could look forward to another bollocking from Frai. Lovely.

Fin stood up, brushing the damp from her trousers. 'I asked if she could come and talk to these trees.'

'Okay.' I wanted to ask what that had to do with defeating the nix, but that could wait.

Sineya looked along the lights, back and forth in all four directions. Her eyes shone bright green, without white or pupil. I was startled to see she was on the verge of tears.

'They are so lonely, the trees here. They were abandoned when the nix came. The dryads who lived here couldn't stand to stay, not after he killed the naiad who tended the spring. The trees are still grieving, for the naiad and the dryads alike.' She scowled, sniffed, and wiped her eyes with the back of a hand. 'The nix relishes their sorrow.'

'There was a naiad here, as well as the dryads, once upon a time?' I asked the next obvious question. 'Have you been able to contact Kalei? Does she know what happened here?'

The naiad only ever did what suited her own purposes, but I reckoned there was a decent chance that would include taking revenge for one of her own.

Sineya nodded. 'I got a message to her, but she's going to find it even harder than I did to work out a route to get here.'

Fin was moving on. 'We need to see that blackthorn tree you told me about.'

I looked at Sineya. 'It's across the lane, away towards the river. Shall I meet you at the corner of the road?'

As the dryad nodded, I glanced at Fin. 'Do you want a lift, or...?'

Her grin told me she knew I was asking if she was going to fly. 'I've had more than enough exercise already today, so thanks, a lift would be great.'

Sineya walked up to the closest tree and then into it, as easily as someone going through a door. I saw Fin's eyes widen.

'My mum does that. You get used to it.' I was tempted to add it was a family thing, but didn't. It wasn't as if I could do anything like that, after all.

We headed down to the Lamp Acre, and I drove further down the track this time. As we passed the caravan, there was once again no sign of life. I was more and more convinced that Aiden must have another bolthole somewhere.

'Sod it.' I realised I still hadn't emailed that photo to Petra Oxway.

'What is it?' Fin sat up straight, looking startled.

'Nothing. I mean, it is something, obviously.' As we parked, I got out my phone and showed her the picture. 'This is the bastard we think is in league with the nix.'

She looked around. 'Did you see him?'

'No, I've just remembered I meant to send this to someone, a local reporter.'

'Why?' Fin looked wary.

I could understand why she kept her distance from professional snoopers. 'He's selling drugs and delusions to the local teenagers. If she can nail him for that, dealing with the police could keep him out of our hair while we deal with the nix. I'm not about to trust her with anything else,' I added. 'Though she is the sister of the man who died in that car crash I told you about.'

'Okay.' Fin still had reservations, and I couldn't blame her for that.

'There's Sineya.' I saw the dryad at the edge of the trees.

I kept my phone in my hand as we went over, and held it out to show her the picture. 'This is the man who seems to be working with the nix.'

'We will make him regret that.' Sineya's eyes were blazing again, this time with fury. 'These trees are terrified. He has made this a place of death and corruption. If he can kill them, or still them once and for all, he can reach the river. The trees have been doing their best to stop him, and they try to keep innocents away, but he has too many ways to lure them here.'

I wasn't sure if she meant the nix or Aiden, but I guessed that didn't matter. They were in this together, and I was glad to think that I had the dryad as an ally against them now.

Fin looked at me. 'Where's this tree?'

'Let's see if we can find it. It's vile,' I warned.

Seeing and smelling it had nearly made me throw up. I could only imagine it would be a whole lot worse for them both. Sineya would feel whatever cruelty had been inflicted on the blackthorn, and I guessed Fin must share some sort of kinship with the dead birds.

We walked into the woodland, as close as I could recall to the point where I'd staggered out onto the track. I looked around for anything I might remember. To my surprise, I found I knew exactly where I was, the way I always did in woods. I had been expecting to be wandering around until the stink of rotting flesh drew me to the blackthorn. Now I realised that these trees wanted to be rid of the disgusting thing as soon as possible. They were opening our way to the clearing.

It wasn't far. Fin recoiled, and went even paler than her hair, which I wouldn't have thought was possible. She turned her back. 'I'm sorry. I can't—'

The tree was as ghastly as I remembered. More. Worse. There were fresh feathered corpses skewered on the branches. On the stained leaves carpeting the ground below, heaps of writhing maggots feasted on ones that had rotted enough to succumb to gravity. Flies buzzed around us, and the stench made me gag.

Sineya flashed into her ethereal state, but she was no winsome woodland nymph. Green radiance like I'd never seen before swirled around us. Sineya's hair and flowing gown snapped and fluttered as if she were caught in a gale, though the air around me stayed fetid and heavy. No, as if she were summoning the gale. The trees around the clearing thrashed and writhed. I heard the crack and thud of dead branches falling to the ground. The dryad looked like a wrathful goddess from some terrifying fairy tale.

'Burn it!'

I wasn't sure if she'd spoken or driven the words straight into my brain. I wasn't at all sure what to do. I'd assumed all dryads would disapprove of fire as thoroughly as my mum did. Anyone ignoring the portable barbecue signs at home soon found their picnic ruined beyond repair. Not that that was remotely relevant here and now. Shock was scattering my wits.

'Burn it!' Sineya rounded on me.

I took a hasty step backwards, raising my hands like someone facing a gun. I'd rather have faced a gun. 'I can do that, but we have to do it right.'

'What do you mean?' Sineya's fury made my head ring as she strode towards me.

I stumbled backwards. 'Wait.'

'Please.' Finele added her voice to mine.

The angry creaking in the trees overhead slowed, and the eerie light around Sineya faded away. She didn't look the least bit calmer though. 'Fire is the only way to be rid of this abomination,' she said with clipped savagery.

'I'm sure it is,' I said cautiously, 'but we can't set it alight without some sort of plan. The smoke will draw attention from anyone driving along the lane, for a start.' And I had to get back to work soon, though I decided not to mention that just yet. Also, I wasn't carrying any matches.

'This isn't Blithehurst, where Eleanor's the boss and able to cover for us. There's a gamekeeper who looks after these woods, and he answers to the Franklins,' I pointed out. 'We have to let him know what's going on, as far as he needs to know, at the very least.'

'He's right,' Fin said to Sineya. She gestured towards me. 'If we get into trouble now, if Dan loses this job, we won't be able to take on the nix without a lot more trouble.'

Sineya shivered into her physical manifestation, though her eyes were still livid green. 'What do you suggest?'

'We come back when I've finished work – I'm sorry,' I protested as they both looked at me, disbelieving. 'If we want to avoid making anyone suspicious, everything needs to go on as normal. So I go back to work, but I'll ring the gamekeeper and ask him to meet us here later. When he sees this tree, I'm sure he'll agree to burn it, especially when we tell him that bastard in the caravan must be responsible. That's got to be the quickest way to get rid of it.'

'If he doesn't agree, you must light the fire.' Sineya was adamant.

'Agreed.' I wasn't keen, but I would do it. I looked at Finele. 'What do you say?'

She nodded. 'That sounds like a plan. What time do you finish work?'

'About six. What do you want to do in the meantime?' I realised I didn't want to leave her anywhere in the woods as long as we had no idea where Aiden might be. 'You could come back to the house?' I tried to think of some explanation I could offer for her presence.

But Fin was shaking her head. 'Can you give me a lift into town? I need to find a bed for the night, and buy a toothbrush.'

'Oh.' I hadn't thought about that. I should have guessed she wasn't going to find a comfy riverbank and tuck her head under one wing.

Fin was still ashen-faced, but she managed a grin. 'There's a limit to what we can bring with us, but luckily plastic is light.' She patted the front of her coat where an inside pocket must be. 'Is there a decent B&B close?'

'There's The Boar's Head in Bourton, or the Whittle and Dub on this side of the river. That's closer.'

'Closer's best.' Fin looked at Sineya. 'What are you going to do?'

'Reassure these trees.' Inside three paces she went translucent, then transparent, and then vanished.

Fin and I shared a look of mutual understanding, and equally, incomprehension.

'Let's go.' I gestured towards the Lamp Acre.

We walked through the trees, and I saw Fin's face regain some colour. I was trying to find a way to offer some sympathy about the dead birds when we reached the track running down to the river. What I saw drove that thought right out of my head.

Aiden, the young thug called Tyler and the bearded lad whose name I still didn't know were standing around the Land Rover. They were peering in through the windows.

'Hey!' As I shouted, the three of them looked in our direction.

Tyler sneered at me, openly challenging, as he tried the passenger door handle.

I had my keys in my hand. They'd add a decent weight to my fist if I punched the little shit.

Aiden said something. We were too far away to hear it, but the boys retreated towards the caravan. Aiden waited a little longer and then turned his back on us to stroll away.

'So that's our friend,' Fin said quietly as we got into the Land Rover.

'And his minions. That's another reason to have Rufus, the gamekeeper, with us when we torch that fucking tree. They're bound to notice, and come to see what's going on. The more potential witnesses, the less likely I think they are to start any trouble.'

I drove carefully along the track. As we drew level with the caravan, I glanced at the three of them standing around the open door. One of the girls was in the doorway, not Jade but one of the others. She was wearing some sort of shiny purple sleeveless tunic. That was all she was wearing, at least I think it was. It was long enough to cover her backside, but her legs and feet were bare. I could see the bruises mottling her thighs and arms, and hated to think what might be going on in there.

Fin was silent, deep in thought, as we drove along the lane. She drew a breath as we reached the river. 'That Aiden won't be the only one who notices when we burn that tree. The nix will feel it too. What do we do if it turns up?'

I halted at the lights. 'How do we kill a nix?'

'Beat it to a pulp, apparently.' Fin exhaled, apprehension hissing through her teeth. 'I gather you've done something of the sort before?'

'Not subtle, but it gets the job done.' I wondered how much Eleanor or Sineya had told her about last summer's battles at Blithehurst. Then I wondered what tools I had to hand that would make a suitable weapon. It hadn't occurred to me to pack the Victorian fake halberd that I'd used on the wyrm.

'What do we say to the gamekeeper if the nix turns up while he's there?' Fin wondered.

'I have no idea,' I admitted as the lights changed and we drove over the bridge. 'I suppose we'll just have to see how he reacts. I mean, if it's right in front of him... and anyway, there may be something about Rufus, something in his blood.' I hesitated. 'This is going to sound really odd.'

'Really?' Fin said sardonically. 'Odd? To me?'

'Fair point,' I acknowledged. 'Okay. A couple of times, when I've looked at him, it's seemed as if he has antlers, like a deer, just for a second. Does that mean anything to you?'

'Sorry, no. Not beyond the obvious myths about Herne and Cernunnos and such, but I've no idea how they relate to people like us.' She was as mystified as me.

I drove past the market hall and headed for the High Street. 'The shops you want are up here, but the parking's a pain, so if it's okay with you, I'll wait for you back down there, at the bottom of the hill.'

'No need to wait, and you can drop me off anywhere here. I'll get a taxi to – what did you call it? The B&B place?'

'The Whittle and Dub. It's a pub that does rooms.' I wondered what their prices were. The meal I'd had with Petra hadn't been extortionate, but it hadn't exactly been cheap, either. It wasn't as if there was anywhere we could submit our expenses for this.

'I'll hop out here.' Fin unclicked her seat belt as I slowed for a light-controlled crossing. 'I'll ring you at six. We'll go and see the gamekeeper together.'

She slipped out of the Land Rover before I could say anything, and headed for a chemist's. I drove on till I found a place to turn around and headed back.

I parked up by the market hall, to grab a quick lunch in the closest cafe on the other side of the street. I didn't want to go to Shayler's and risk getting into a conversation with Petra. I did use the cafe's Wi-Fi to set up email on my phone and send her that photo of Aiden. And yes, doing that was exactly as much of a pain in the arse as I expected it to be.

Thinking about it, I sent a couple more of the photos, making sure that none of them included Josh. Then I sent the one I'd taken of the lad called Tyler, by the market hall.

My message was brief:

These are the kids hanging around with this conman. If you know any of their names, I'd be interested.

Then I sent a text to Josh:

I've dealt with Jade. No more pictures.

He sent the briefest possible reply:

K

I guessed that was that, so I drove back to Brightwell and spent the rest of the day laying white polyethylene waste pipes with the Kembles and the Coateses. We were packing up when the phone in the oak parlour rang. It was six o'clock exactly.

Chapter Seventeen

It was Finele on the phone. 'Can you pick me up at the Whittle and Dub? Then we can go to see this gamekeeper.'

'Okay. I'll be about ten or fifteen minutes. I've got to wait for everyone to leave before I can lock up.'

'Right.' Fin understood the realities of my life, which made a nice change to dealing with dryads. 'See you soon.'

I put down the phone and picked it up again immediately to ring the Home Farm house. There was no point in taking Fin over there if Rufus wasn't in. If he wasn't, we'd have to balance the risks of burning that foul tree without him against leaving the nix to continue drawing strength from it.

To my relief, he answered after a couple of rings. 'Stanlake.'

'Are you in for the next half hour or so? I need to see you.'

'I'll be here.'

'See you in a bit.'

As Rufus rang off, I was grateful for his lack of interest in casual conversation. I also hoped that Fin had some good ideas about how to explain what we wanted to do, because I hadn't come up with anything that sounded remotely convincing to me.

While I was waiting for the gaffer and his blokes to finish clearing up and leave, I went through to the garage yard and unlocked the door with the sign saying 'Gardener – Private'. I hadn't been in here till now, not wanting to tread on Bill Delly's toes, but now I was looking for whatever I could use against the nix, as well as thinking about the practicalities of my second venture into woodland arson to foil some monster.

Whatever this storeroom had originally been used for, now it held a collection of gardening tools and equipment that ranged from museum pieces to a modern, petrol-driven grass strimmer and a heavier-weight brush cutter with a three-sided blade. I wondered what that might do to a nix, but decided against taking it. There was the risk of me getting injured myself trying to use it in any sort of fight. Then there was the possibility the thing would get wrecked, leading to a need for awkward explanations and a fraudulent insurance claim.

I did put the plastic can of petrol that I found over by the door though, and pocketed a box of Bill Delly's matches. With a bit more time, I'd have jellied some fuel, as that's much more useful if you need to get a fire going outdoors. I couldn't have done something like that this afternoon though, not without having to explain myself to the gaffer.

Looking at the hoes and mattocks and other edged tools neatly racked on the walls, I considered borrowing an entrenching tool. On second thoughts, I decided I'd prefer something with a bit more reach. Over in the far corner, I spotted a long-handled shovel, the sort that most people associate with gravediggers. That would do nicely. Like all Bill's tools, it was scrupulously clean, and I found it had a keen edge.

I left it where it was for the moment, along with the petrol, to avoid awkward questions from Geoff Kemble. Heading back to the house, I found Davey Coates was the last one out of the basement, as usual. I waved the vans off and went down the steps to lock up. Coming back up the servants' stair, I set the alarm, locked the front door and went to get the shovel and petrol. I took the route through the woods to get to the Whittle and Dub. Once again, the less Aiden knew about what I was doing, the better for us all.

My phone got a signal fifty metres past the flowers where Simon Oxway had died, and I rang Fin as soon as I pulled into the car park. 'I'm here.'

'I'm on my way out.'

As she rang off, my phone told me I had a new email. I nearly didn't bother checking, but when I saw it was from Petra Oxway, I hit the screen. Her message was short and to the point:

Jade Taysel. Sophie Asthall. Courtney Hawling. Leanne Foxhill. Tyler Campden. Oliver Summerhill. All known to social services and/or the police.

Apart from Jade, I still wasn't going to be able to tell which girl was which, but at least I could put a name to the lad with the straggly beard now.

Thanks.

As I hit send, Fin appeared in the pub doorway.

'What are we going to say to Rufus?' I asked as she secured her seatbelt.

'Just follow my lead,' she said confidently.

'Where's Sineya?' The dryad could hardly come with us in the Land Rover.

'She'll see us there.'

I thought she meant the dryad would meet us out in the woods, but when we pulled onto the gravel by the red-painted barn, Sineya materialised as soon as I opened my door. There was a fierce set to her jaw.

'This way?' Fin looked at me for confirmation as she walked towards the side door of the house.

'That's right.' I followed and waited to see what she was going to do.

Rufus answered the door when Fin knocked and was momentarily taken aback to see a stranger, until he realised she was with me. He glanced from her to me and back again. 'Yes?'

Before either of us could answer, Bess appeared in the doorway. She saw Sineya and immediately slipped past Rufus. A deft twist of her head evaded his grab for her collar.

'Who's a good dog then?' Sineya cooed with delight and dropped to one knee. Bess rubbed her head against the dryad's shoulder, ecstatic. As Sineya hugged her, the dog flopped onto her side and rolled over to wave all four paws in the air. Sineya obliged by rubbing the Retriever's exposed belly. 'What a lovely girl you are!'

She looked up at Rufus, smiling with all of the charm that a dryad can summon, and that's a lot. 'I do love dogs.'

'Bess certainly likes you.' Rufus was amused as well as surprised. What he wasn't was the least bit interested in Sineya, even though her coat was unzipped to show a sweatshirt clinging to seductive curves, and in her kneeling position her jeans were stretched enticingly taut over her gorgeous backside.

If the situation hadn't been so serious, I could have laughed as I saw Sineya realise that he was a man she wouldn't be able to lead by the cock. Her eyes flickered to Fin, who immediately reached into an inside pocket.

All things considered, I wasn't sorry we weren't relying on dryad wiles. I'd rather have Rufus's full attention on what we were doing, instead of him being distracted by calculating his chances of getting into Sineya's knickers.

'Hello.' Fin held out her hand, and I saw she was offering him a business card.

I guessed this must be Plan B.

'Finele Wicken. I'm a friend of Dan's. He was telling me about Brightwell, and since I was in the area, I stopped by. I wanted to take a look at this ornamental lake with my intern.'

She sounded so convincing that anyone would have thought she'd known me for years. Clearly swan maidens had none of my problems with spinning a yarn.

Fin gestured at Sineya. 'Seeing what happens to these old water features can be very useful for students. Dan told me there are issues with the drainage between the lane and the river. I take it you realise the culverts have collapsed?'

Rufus still looked a bit bemused at this unexpected encounter on his doorstep, but nodded. 'The ones under the roadway are fine, but as soon as you get into the undergrowth, whatever the original plan was, the tree roots have wrecked it.'

I saw Sineya's smile of satisfaction out of the corner of my eye, as she carried on fussing over Bess. I guessed that was something the trees had done to frustrate the nix.

Fin nodded. 'We went to take a look. Incidentally, I'll be happy to talk to the Franklins about a quote for sorting it out. Only we found something very unexpected.'

She grimaced, and then looked at me. Following her lead was easy enough, since I only had to tell the truth.

'Our friend in the caravan has been making himself some sort of gibbet.' I let Rufus see my revulsion. 'Killing birds and skewering them on a blackthorn.'

He stared at me. 'The fucker.'

I nodded my heartfelt agreement. 'As far as I'm concerned, the best thing to do is torch it, but I thought you should see it first.'

'And take some photos,' Fin added, 'in case you need some evidence. I can make a statement, if anything comes to court.'

'Right. Good.' Rufus's eyes gleamed at the prospect of finally getting something on our enemy.

'See you down there?' I suggested.

'Let me get my jacket.' He turned away, heading back into the house.

Sineya vanished, leaving Bess bereft. The dog scrambled to her feet, whining and looking around in all directions.

'Quick.' I headed for the Land Rover and could only hope Rufus didn't notice I only had one passenger as I pulled away.

'Put your foot down.' Fin was clearly thinking the same as she looked back over her shoulder. 'We need to turn down that track before he does.'

I got to the corner of the lane just ahead of Rufus. As we pulled up, the Defender surprised me by pulling straight past us, stopping a good few metres closer to the caravan. I realised I didn't have to worry about Rufus wondering where Sineya might be. As he got out, his attention was fixed on Aiden and the two lads who were so in thrall to him. They were sitting on old plastic beer crates around a small fire flickering on the burned scar on the ground by the metal bin.

I went around to the back of the Land Rover and got the petrol and shovel out. With the vehicle between me and the caravan, Aiden couldn't see what I was doing, even if he wasn't warily watching Rufus.

'Shall I carry that?' Sineya appeared beside me and reached for the plastic fuel container.

I let her take it. I held on to the shovel. Fin came around the Land Rover to join us.

'I'm leaving the dog.' Rufus raised his voice to not far short of a shout, to make absolutely sure that the three sitting by the caravan heard him. 'If you come anywhere close, I'll hear her barking. If you touch either of these vehicles, the police will be the least of your problems. Got it?'

Hearing the threat in his voice, I was convinced. So were the teenagers, going by the uncertain way they looked at Aiden. He simply stared back at the gamekeeper, expressionless.

'Come on.' I gestured with the shovel as Rufus looked around. 'It's this way.'

The trees shivered around us as we walked through the woods to the vile clearing. I hoped Rufus would simply think it was a breeze. I knew for certain it was something more, though I couldn't tell if the trees were responding to Sineya or if the Green Man was somewhere close. Either way, the mood in the wood felt different, and I guessed we had the dryad to thank for that.

The blackthorn was as revolting as it had been the first two times I'd seen it. Fin still couldn't look directly at it. As Sineya turned away, I could see her eyes flickering from a human gaze to vivid dryad green as she fought to keep her own fury in check. The only thing in our favour was the breeze carrying the stink away from us.

Rufus stared at the obscenity in disbelief. 'Mother fucker.'

'So do we burn it?' I stuck the shovel in the ground and got out my phone. 'Once we've got the evidence?' I began taking photos.

'Too fucking right!' Now Rufus was angry. 'Mother fucker!'

'Dan.' There was a warning note in Fin's voice.

I lowered my phone and turned to see her looking back along the path we'd taken to get here. Following her line of sight, I saw movement among the trees. I put my phone in my pocket and took hold of the shovel's handle.

'We can see you, you know. No point in hiding like little bitches.'

Rufus's scornful challenge was too much for the lad with the pathetic beard. He strode forward to claim the path.

'You told us to keep away from your piece-of-shit car, so we came for a walk, didn't we?' He squared his shoulders with a cocky thrust of his chin at Rufus.

'Are you responsible for this?' Rufus gestured towards the foul tree.

'What if we are?' The stocky lad, Tyler, came to stand a few paces behind his mate. He didn't look so defiant, but I got the distinct impression that he was quicker-witted. He was also looking repellently satisfied as he glanced at the blackthorn.

I took a sidestep to get a clearer view of Aiden, who was hanging back some distance away. As soon as he saw me looking at him, his face went blank again. Too late. I'd seen his irritation with his underlings. This venture into the woods to follow us hadn't been his idea.

Fin moved to get a clear view down the path. 'I'd need to double-check with the Wildlife and Countryside Act to see exactly how many offences have been committed here, but if you did do any of this, you're in all sorts of trouble.'

Her tone was matter-of-fact as she took several photos of the boys, not making any attempt to conceal what she was doing. They didn't like that. The skinny one looked uncertain, but the stocky one scowled, belligerent. He took a couple of steps forward and shoved the skinny lad in the small of the back to drive him on ahead.

'Tyler Campden and Oliver Summerhill,' I said loudly as I took a firm hold of the shovel handle and calculated how fast I'd need to move to get in front of Fin before they could reach her. 'You do realise we know exactly who you are?'

Neither of them liked that. They both stopped, looking apprehensive. I looked at Aiden and saw him smirking. He didn't think we knew his name.

I was tempted to see if I could wipe that smug smile off his face by calling him Aiden Peploe. Almost as quickly, I decided that was taking too much of a risk. If we were wrong, he'd see our ignorance as some sort of victory. If we were right, we'd gain nothing meaningful, and we might well lose by it. Mentioning that name would let Aiden know that we had some idea of what had really brought him here. Worse, the only person who could have told us he was after some supposed inheritance was Josh Franklin. That definitely risked these pricks tracking him down to take some revenge.

I opted for something else, remembering a couple of building sites I had worked on where the foreman had been forced to take steps to drive off some local louts.

'This is the second time you've trespassed on Brightwell land, and we've got good reason to think you're up to no good.' I focused on the boys. 'If we see you anywhere around here a third time, we'll take these photos and make statements and a formal complaint to the police. We've got an independent witness now.' I gestured at Fin. 'You can see if you can talk your way out of a caution, or a Community Protection Notice, but I wouldn't bet on it.'

'You think you're so bold and wicked? You think this is anything to boast about, inflicting pain and terror on weak and helpless birds?' Sineya was standing beside Fin now. 'These maggots and the worms in the dirt are worth more than any of you. At least they are doing what comes naturally, not trying to hide their weakness behind wanton cruelty.'

Her utter contempt was chilling. I don't only mean her tone was cold. I felt my scrotum shrivel up as if I'd just jumped into cold water. I knew that dryads could seduce a man with a word if they chose to, but I'd had no idea they could lash out with such lacerating scorn. I felt gutted, and I have some immunity to the greenwood's influence. As the teenagers stumbled backwards, they looked as if she'd threatened to cut off their balls with a rusty knife and they had absolutely believed her.

Not Aiden though. I was still keeping a close eye on him. He went pale and his jaw slackened as he looked at Sineya. I didn't see any particular recognition, so I guessed he didn't know exactly what she was. But he'd clearly come into contact with some similar power, so he knew it when he felt it again.

He spun around and strode away down the path. The boys stumbled after him. Rufus took a step to follow, then stopped himself. I wondered about the effect of Sineya's words on him, but couldn't think of a way to ask. Then we heard Bess's muffled barking.

'Go,' I said quickly to Rufus. 'We can take care of this.'

Rufus looked at me. 'Can you do that without setting fire to the whole fucking wood?'

'Yes.' I held up the shovel. 'I brought this to clear the ground to make sure the flames can't spread.' Which was true, if not the whole truth.

'Okay then.' He headed away, up the path.

'Let's get this done.' I didn't want to leave Rufus facing those pricks alone for any longer than I absolutely had to.

I used the shovel to dig a shallow trench around the blackthorn as quickly as I could, getting as close to the rotting birds as I could stand. Even with the unnatural breeze to help me out, the stink made me gag, and I was very glad I hadn't eaten anything since lunch.

Coming full circle, I handed the shovel to Fin. 'Look out for the nix when I get this alight.' Something born of water could probably tackle most fires.

'I will know if it's coming.' Sineya handed me the plastic petrol can.

I'd heaped up the leaf mould and earth around the outer edge of the trench, to add to the fire break. That left a carpet of dead leaves under the tree. The past week had been mostly free of rain, so the top layer was fairly dry. Still, setting an effective fire is nowhere as easy as it looks in the movies. I looked around for some dry, dead wood, and saw a couple of fallen branches.

I glanced at Sineya. 'Is it all right if I use these?'

She nodded. 'The trees want this abomination gone.'

I broke the branches into shorter lengths with a boot, and gathered up some lighter twigs and dead undergrowth. Taking a deep breath and holding it, I picked my way through the maggots to pile fuel at the base of the blackthorn. Then I headed back to get the petrol, and to take another, fresher breath.

Going back to the tree, I unscrewed the cap on the petrol, reminding myself that I would need to get that refilled, to keep Bill Delly happy. I also had to make sure not to give myself flash burns that would need explaining away.

Pouring the petrol carefully on the dead wood and around the base of the tree took longer than I could hold my breath. I was forced to give up, taking the shallowest breaths I could. At least the reek of petrol overwhelmed most of the other stench. When I'd emptied the can, I screwed the cap securely back on and went to put it down well away from the tree.

'Anything?' I asked Fin.

She was still looking down the path. 'Nothing.'

Sineya was nowhere to be seen, so I carried on. As I went back across the trench, I got the matches out of my pocket. They didn't come from whatever Hollywood factory makes those matches that can be dropped from a height into a puddle of petrol without going out. I used one to light a twiggy branch the length of my forearm that had been smothered by honeysuckle.

Once it was well alight, I stopped as far from the tree as I dared and tossed the burning branch at the base of the blackthorn. Now I was holding my breath in hope that I'd been working fast enough to get this done before too much of the petrol vapour evaporated.

The honeysuckle twigs smouldered for a moment, and then the dead branches caught fire. Flames licked up the blackthorn's trunk. The dead leaves flared up around the tree, sweeping towards me. I retreated hastily, nearly slipping on the banked earth and leaf mould as I stepped over the trench. Now the ground inside the circle was well alight. I braced myself for the stink of burning feathers and worse, but it never came.

'Bloody hell,' Fin said faintly as she came to stand beside me.

The breeze was swirling around inside the trench. Flames taller than me were consuming the blackthorn and its vile burden. There was no smoke to speak of. The fire was burning too ferociously for that. Standing as close as we were, we should have felt the heat scorching our faces, but I could barely feel any warmth. Looking around, I could see that the dancing leaves on the closest trees were still fresh and green, when they should have been seared and shrivelled.

Sineya appeared on my other side. 'The nix is angry. This hurts it, though it shows no sign of leaving the lake.'

I tried to decide how much of that was good news, and how much was bad. Destroying the tree uninterrupted was a plus, but we needed to lure the nix out if we were going to kill it.

'Thanks for this.' I gestured towards the unnatural fire.

'It's none of my doing.' She watched the tree burn with satisfaction all the same.

Fin leaned forward to look past me to the dryad. 'Then whose is it?'

Sineya glanced at her, surprised that she needed to ask. 'The Hunter, of course.'

'Who's he?' I could do with every possible ally against the nix.

'The Hunter.' Sineya stared at us both, mildly exasperated. 'He rides the storm, so wildfire comes within his purview.'

So much for asking a dryad a direct question and hoping to get a straight answer.

'But who is he?' Fin persisted. 'What does he look like?'

Green veiled Sineya's eyes. 'If he's not revealed himself to you, he must have his reasons.'

I tried a different approach. 'What's his interest here?'

The dryad looked at me as if that was the stupidest question she'd ever heard. 'Your friend, the dog's master, is under his protection.'

'Rufus?' I suddenly remembered Uncle Cecil's notes. 'What does that mean?'

'You would know that more than me, since the Green Man claims you for his own.' Sineya shrugged.

'So Rufus isn't wholly human.' Fin looked down the path. 'He's... What?'

The dryad waved that nonsense away. 'He's mortal, and human, through and through. That has nothing to do with this.'

I was trying to find another question to ask, one that might actually get us some answers, when a sharp cracking interrupted us. I turned to see the blackthorn's trunk split from its crown to its roots. The remnants of the tree's branches collapsed into a smouldering heap. I couldn't have made a neater job of destroying it if I'd brought pruning shears and a saw to turn it into a bonfire.

'Can we—?' I turned to ask Sineya if it was safe to leave it, but she had vanished again.

'Dryads may not lie,' Fin observed, 'but they're damn good at avoiding questions they don't want to answer.'

'Tell me about it,' I said with feeling.

'What now?' she asked.

'Give me that.' I held out my hand for the shovel.

I walked across the trench and began digging again, close to the tree this time. Whoever or whatever the Hunter might be, I wasn't leaving here until I'd turned over enough dark, damp earth to smother the embers of the burned black-thorn.

I worked fast. Even if Rufus had some arcane protection, I wanted to know what had set Bess barking.

Chapter Eighteen

By the time Finele and I got back to the Lamp Acre, Rufus was in his Defender with the engine running. I could see Bess in the back. The caravan was locked up tight.

Rufus leaned out of the driver's window to call out to us. If he wondered where Sineya was, he didn't say so.

'Those girls had shown up. That must be what started Bess barking. When I got here, the bastard rounded them up, and off they went. What have you done about the tree?'

'Torched it. Buried the embers.' I held up the dirt-covered shovel, and the plastic petrol can that I'd initially forgotten, so I'd had to run back and fetch it.

I expected Rufus to express some surprise at how fast we had followed him here, but he had his mind on other things.

'I want to know where the fuckers have gone. I'm going to have a drive round the lights, maybe check by the Hoar Stone. You should get back to the house.' He didn't wait for an answer, hauling on the steering wheel to turn the vehicle and drive off.

I watched him go. At least I wasn't quite so concerned about him being out in the woods on his own, now that I knew he had his own guardian watching over him.

'Do you want to see the house?' I looked at Fin. 'Or shall I take you back to the Whittle and Dub?'

I was assuming that Sineya could take care of herself.

Fin thought for a moment. 'I'd probably better get back to my room and download these photos, for a start. Can you let me have the pictures you were talking about?'

'You're serious about going to the police?' I found my keys and put the shovel and petrol can in the back.

'I think we need to consider it, don't you? If we're going to fight the nix, we need to keep these idiot kids well out of the woods.'

That made sense. 'I'll talk to Rufus about the best way to approach the Franklins about it. They'd need to sign off on whatever we do.'

And Rufus and I would need to work out how to keep Josh out of trouble with the cops, if we possibly could. I wondered how doable that was likely to be as I got into the Land Rover's driving seat.

'Remind him to give them my business card.' Fin got into the passenger side.

'You really want to quote for sorting out the drainage here?' I started the engine.

'Once we've got rid of the nix. That lake will be a whole lot healthier if we can get a through-flow from the spring to shift some of the silt. It could be a prime wildlife habitat.' She looked thoughtful. 'If we can get rid of the nix.'

'We're going to have to lure it out somehow.' I turned right at the end of the track to take the lane towards the pub. 'Any ideas?'

'Not at the moment,' she said, rather defensively.

'Me neither,' I assured her. 'I can see if there's anything useful in Brightwell's library, or Uncle Cecil's notes. Do you want to ring Eleanor Beauchene, or shall I? She might have turned up something by now.'

'Could you talk to her? There are some other calls I can make.'

I wanted to ask her about that, but Fin was staring out of the window as we drove past the Brightwell woods. She sat quiet, deep in thought, all the way to the Whittle and Dub. I half expected her to get out and go on her way without saying anything to me.

Instead, she shook off her preoccupation. 'Do you want to come in? We could get some food.'

That was a potentially good idea. I raised my forearm and sniffed my sweatshirt sleeve, and was relieved to find the material barely smelled of petrol. 'Okay.'

We opted for bar food rather than a table and the restaurant menu. The burger and chips I had was every bit as good as my last meal here. Fin had a prawn salad, and I wondered if she ate red meat at all, because swans didn't as far as I could recall. My dad would know, but I decided I'd need to know Fin a bit better before asking if she minded me telling him about her.

In the middle of a busy pub, we couldn't discuss what really concerned us, so we talked about books and films. Fin turned out to be far more up to date about movies than me, and I read a lot more than she did, so we swapped some recommendations.

As we finished eating, she gave me her email address, and I used the pub's Wi-Fi to send her those pictures of Aiden and his minions skulking around the house. Then Fin went up to her room, and I headed off to find a petrol station and refill Bill Delly's plastic can.

When I got back to Brightwell, there was no sign of Aiden or his minions. I put the petrol back where I'd found it and cleaned the long-handled shovel to Bill's high standards, before putting that in its place as well.

Inside the house, I set the alarm and made a mug of tea. Taking that into the oak parlour, I decided to ring Rufus first. I got straight to the point.

'Did you see them anywhere?'

'No sign anywhere along the lights, or at the stone, but there are public footpaths through the trees. They could have been somewhere out of sight.'

'Finele, my friend, thinks we should go to the police. Get them properly warned off. We should have enough evidence now.'

'Really?' Rufus's tone was guarded.

'It's something to think about.' I let him hear my own reservations. 'Maybe talk to Nicki and Ed? Without landing Josh in the shit.'

'Maybe.' He still wasn't convinced.

I changed the subject. 'Have you heard from Bill Delly? Any idea how Martha's getting on?'

'She's much better.' His voice brightened. 'She should be home in a day or so.'

'Good to know.' Though I'd prefer to think the old woman was out of the nix's reach. I wondered how much we had weakened the creature by burning that tree, and if we could possibly be rid of it before Martha came back.

'See you.' Rufus rang off, catching me by surprise.

Since I had the phone in my hand, I pressed the buttons to ring Eleanor's mobile.

She answered at once. 'Daniel? How are you? How are you getting on?'

I had questions of my own. 'Where are you? Did you know Sineya was coming here?'

'I do now,' Eleanor said ruefully. 'I'm at Blithehurst for a few days, and Frai is absolutely furious. She's blaming both of us.'

I winced at the thought of the old dryad's wrath. 'How about Asca?'

'Angry with all three of us. I think she's just hiding it better.' Eleanor sighed and moved briskly on. 'So tell me what's happened.'

I told her what we'd done to the vile tree, and what Sineya had said about Rufus, and about the mysterious Hunter's presence in these woods.

'He's something to do with the Wild Hunt, do you mean?'

'I have no idea. She wasn't exactly forthcoming. Her main concern is the trees.'

'The Wild Hunt are associated with storms in some legends, so there could be some link between lightning strikes and his control over fire.' Eleanor was thinking aloud.

'Maybe. At the moment I know he's opposed to the nix, and that's good enough for me.' I wanted to concentrate on the matter in hand. 'We still need to know how to get the nix out of the lake, if we're ever going to get rid of it.'

'I'll keep looking.' Eleanor sighed.

'Me too. I'll talk to you soon.'

'I'll be in touch if I find something useful. Bye.'

'Bye.' I stood there for a moment. Eleanor had said 'if', not 'when', and it didn't sound as if her research was getting very far.

I walked through to the drawing room where Jude had been working steadily for the last two days. Books were stacked on the table by her crate of cleaning materials, and on the leather chairs that now stood by the window. Here and there, other books had been put back on the shelves at right angles, resting on their front edges rather than standing upright, so that they stuck out as markers. She clearly had some system in hand.

Deciding not to risk disturbing anything, I walked on through to the walnut parlour and unlocked the sewing room. Uncle Cecil's notebooks were still stacked on the table. I switched on the light and sat down to start going through them. I might not be a Franklin, but I had some idea about what was amiss here. The Green Man had sent me to witness the old man's dying regret that he hadn't been able to put things right.

Some while later, not having found anything useful, I paused and looked at the painting over the fireplace. I wasn't quite so ready to dismiss it as some amateur fantasy now. Of course, the scene might still be pure invention, and actually, I hoped it was, seeing that girl cowering away from such menace. All the same, I wondered if the antlered figure was anywhere near an accurate representation of the Hunter. If so, I wouldn't want to meet him in a dark wood. Mind you, the prospect of Aiden encountering him definitely appealed.

I went back to the notebooks, but as the evening wore on, I got more and more overloaded with references and quotations and lists. I couldn't tell what might be significant, or if Uncle Cecil had just jotted something down because he liked it. His terse comments here and there might be legible with some effort, but they were incomprehensible. Sorting the notebooks into date order didn't turn up any coherent pattern, and separating them by theme didn't get me any further.

I went through the stack dealing with rivers and lakes a second time, and confirmed a total absence of instructions on killing a nix. All I found were enough scraps of myth and folklore to convince me Finele was right when she said these things were a blight on wherever they lived.

Looking at the picture over the fireplace, I wondered how much worse things might have been here without Uncle Cecil and whoever else, or whatever else, working to confine the nix to its lake. I remembered that Martha Delly had said the old workhouse in the Broad had burned down. If the Hunter had some power over fire, I wondered if he'd had a hand in that, to deprive the nix of the misery it loved.

I leaned back and stretched my arms over my head to ease my stiff shoulders. The central heating engineers were coming tomorrow, a different firm. Gaffer didn't like any Kembles or Coateses dealing with gas, what with the certification and insurance that demanded. Regardless, all the old, bulky cast-iron radiators were going to be stripped out and replaced with modern, much more efficient replicas, along with a new, energy-efficient boiler to serve the whole house. I'd need to be on hand to help, and to see where the woodwork needed making good. So I shut the sewing room up, took a shower and went to bed.

The sound of sobbing woke me up. At least, that was my first thought, until I realised the phone in the oak parlour was ringing. Sitting up, I reached for my mobile, and saw it was twenty to midnight. What the fuck was the emergency?

There had to be some emergency, for anyone to be ringing me so late. Using the torch on my phone, I went out into the corridor. Since I sleep in pyjama shorts, I soon regretted not stopping to grab some clothes. It was sodding freezing. I hurried to answer the phone.

'Daniel?'

'Yes?' I didn't immediately recognise the voice. Male, but not Rufus. Too young to be Ed or David Franklin.

'It's Josh.' He was speaking quietly, but there was no concealing his anxiety.

'What's the matter?'

'Jade texted me.' He could barely get the words out. 'She says everyone's going for a midnight swim in Brightwell lake.'

'Where are you?' I demanded. I couldn't hide my anger.

'At home,' he shot back. 'I'm not an idiot. But she says Nathan Ditchfield's going with them.'

'And?' I stood there, barefoot and shivering.

'Nate's a wanker, but he doesn't deserve to get dragged into Jade's weird shit. Moonlight swimming is a fucking stupid idea. Especially if they're doing drugs and drinking that stuff she was passing around last time. Somebody could drown.' His voice cracked with stress.

'You're right.' More than the night air chilled me. Sineya had said that we'd hurt the nix. If it could drag one of those idiot kids down to the lake bed, that would surely make up for whatever we'd done. 'Thanks. I'll get out there with Rufus and we'll put a stop to any nonsense. You can stay out of it.'

'Right. Thanks. Bye.' Josh's relief was heartfelt as he ended the call.

I stood there for a moment, wondering about ringing Fin. She must have gone to bed by now, and going out again so late would surely cause comment at the pub. Then there was the time it would take for me to go and get her, unless she was prepared to fly to the lake.

The biggest problem was I couldn't think how to explain why I'd involved her to Rufus, and I wanted Rufus with me if we were going up against Aiden, Oliver and Tyler again. If we found ourselves going up against the nix, so be it. Rufus would just have to cope, and I hoped having him there meant the Hunter would lend us a hand.

I rang the Home Farm house, and got a sodding answerphone. I left a message, short and to the point. Then I went and got dressed, swearing under my breath all the way. Making very sure I set the alarm and locked up, I drove along the lane and turned up Brightwell Light.

There was a full moon, but I wasn't about to try following Martha Delly's path to the lake on my own at night. I drove to the crossroads and turned right, driving on to park by the well-trodden route to the spring. As I got out, I looked around for any sign of Sineya, or the Green Man. I'd have even welcomed a glimpse of the Hunter. Nothing.

I looked around the trees again. 'If you're going to do anything to help me, now would be the time.'

I wasn't entirely sure who I was asking, but it didn't matter, because there was no response. I set off down the path. As I drew closer to the water, I heard voices, and walked on more slowly, cautiously. Reaching the edge of the silver birches, I saw there were people on the grassy slope beneath the spring. No one was in the water yet, not as far as I could tell. I decided I could wait to see if Rufus turned up, for a little while at least. Maybe while I was waiting, I'd have some idea about stopping these idiot kids ending up as a nix's midnight snack.

I stopped and laid a hand on the nearest sapling's trunk. If Sineya was anywhere around here, I hoped she might sense my presence. If the Green Man was looking this way, I hoped he might hide me from sight again.

The first girl I recognised was Jade. She was closest to me, hanging back as the other girls and Oliver built what was presumably going to be a fire. She was wearing some sort of black lace dress. It was ragged around the hem, where I guessed gorse had caught at it on her way through the woods. I couldn't understand why she wasn't freezing, dressed in so little, even though the night air was warmer than I had expected.

I watched Aiden walk over to her. Jade was gazing at the waiting bonfire. The pair of them were close enough for me to hear their conversation, so I really hoped the Green Man was keeping me hidden.

'Nate gets to light this then?' It was barely a question. 'What's so special about Nathan Ditchfield?'

'Goddess.' Aiden stepped close to her and brushed the hair from her forehead. 'Why does no one see how special you are?'

'Me?' She swallowed her startled question.

'Jade.' He caressed her shoulder. 'A gem of healing and hope and love. For strength and endurance. Did you know that?'

She shook her head, mouth half open.

'Did your mother know when she named you? No, I don't suppose she did,' Aiden mused, 'but it's the name you were meant to have. True names have true power.'

'Like you?' She looked at him, desperate for something.

'Power from an age when the land still knew its people and they still knew its magic.' He took hold of both her shoulders. 'You've had such trials to endure. The Fates must have known that when they named you.' His gaze slipped past her to stare unfocused across the lake. 'There was a moon child, born of water, but she was lost to you—'

Jade stepped back, shaking herself free of him. 'Who's been telling?' Angry tears glistened on her cheeks.

'No one's betrayed you,' Aiden promised, all concern. 'Please believe me, the Sight's always been strong in my family. We catch glimpses of the unseen world, of the worlds that might have been, given different chances and different choices.'

He looked away over the lake again. 'In these places between air and earth, wood and water, the spirits often make their wisdom known to those who truly open their minds.'

'To anyone?' she asked, with that same fearful longing.

'Those truly committed to the fivefold path.' He looked back at her, unblinking. 'All our journeys along that path begin with purification. That's why we're here tonight. To free ourselves from everything that's coming between us and the truth.'

I had no idea whether he was peddling utter bollocks to nail down this poor little bitch's devotion, or if he was actually going to offer some tangible demonstration of his link to the nix's power. Either way, I saw a conniving bastard taking every possible advantage of a girl who'd had the odds stacked against her since before her birth. I wondered briefly if it would be possible to feed Aiden to the sodding nix, or if that would only make the monster stronger.

They both turned away from me as everyone heard muffled voices coming through the woods. I realised someone had taken Martha's path to the lake and made their way around the edge through the trees.

Sophie, Leanne and the girl I now knew was Courtney abandoned their fire-building efforts as two boys emerged from the darkness. It was Tyler and Nathan Ditchfield. Tyler looked as sharp-eyed as ever, but Nathan already looked stoned. He wore his leather jacket loose over a T-shirt and jeans.

'Blessed be the goddess,' Courtney said quickly, stepping forward to offer a graceful curtsey to them both.

'Blessed be.' Aiden's greeting prompted an echo from the other two girls.

They were wearing layers of floaty dresses, and I sincerely hoped that none of them would get too close to a flame when they were too pissed to be careful. If a spark took hold on a skirt or sleeve, they risked serious burns. The boys were bare-chested beneath their khaki jackets, wearing their usual army-surplus trousers.

Aiden was all in black under his greatcoat. He left Jade to stroll down the slope to the newcomers. 'Nathan, you're very welcome.'

'Right.' Nathan rubbed the back of his neck. 'Cheers. No sign of Rufus Stanlake then?' He looked warily around.

'He's fucked off somewhere for the evening,' Tyler growled. 'I checked. But that new bloke's still in the house.'

You're wrong about that, you little shit, I thought, but that was bad news for me about Rufus.

Aiden waved that away. 'We have more important business tonight.'

Courtney stepped forward, her arms theatrically outstretched. The cool night and the thin cloth of her dress made it very clear she wasn't wearing a bra. Her smile was smug, and possibly drunk, though her words were clear enough. 'When we honour the goddess.'

'So—' Nathan looked from Oliver to Aiden and then back at Courtney's taut nipples.

'We're here to take pleasure with each other in all that we are,' Aiden said solemnly, 'and to connect with the wonders of the natural world.'

I wondered how he'd like my fist to connect with his face.

'And it's a party,' Tyler interjected. 'Like we said, Nate.'

'Yeah?' Nathan looked around, unconvinced.

Tyler grinned. 'There's drink and smokes as well.' He nodded towards a supermarket carrier bag lying on the grass beyond the unlit fire.

'Right.' Nathan looked relieved.

'You didn't bring Tiffany?' Aiden asked casually.

'Tiff?' Nathan was startled. 'Fuck, no.'

'Not hardly,' Courtney mocked. 'Wouldn't want to be late tomorrow morning for her precious college course.'

Nathan scowled. 'I dint ask her, all right?'

Aiden raised placatory hands. 'You're the one we invited, and we're very glad to see you here. Just know that Tiffany's always welcome, when you think she's ready to understand such mysteries.'

He spoke more loudly, to drown out some snide remark from Sophie. 'Tonight we remember the death of the dragon.'

'What the fuck?' Nathan stared at him.

'The Mercians had a dragon on their banner when the Saxons defeated them near here. The Saxon king's standard bearer stuck his own flag's pole right through the Mercian who carried it. As the banner fell to the ground, they said that he'd killed the dragon itself, by slaying its warrior.'

'Who the fuck were the Mercians?' Nathan was utterly bemused.

'Brummies,' Tyler explained, to my considerable surprise.

The lad wasn't as thick as he looked. I should remember that.

'Yeah?' Nathan grinned. 'When was this then?'

'The battle was more than twelve hundred years ago. Three hundred years before the Normans came, when true warriors walked these woods with swords and shields and axes. The land remembers. Your bones remember.' Aiden spared the girls a smile. 'While their wise women knew the secrets of the woods and the waters. Such blood calls to blood across the ages, and you share in this inheritance.'

'Yeah?' Nathan angled his head. 'The Normans still fucking won, dint they?'

'That was then. This is now. Things change,' Aiden assured him with a secretive smile.

'We can make a lot of things change if we want to.' Tyler shoved Nathan's shoulder. 'Once we reconnect with the old power of the land.'

In other circumstances, I reckoned the boy would be a budding neo-nazi recruit. Here and now, I was more concerned to hear Aiden talking about dragons. Eleanor Beauchene's Norman ancestors had allied themselves with dryads to rid these islands of wyrms and worse, but last year we had learned the hard way that such creatures were stirring again. Climate change is doing more than melting the ice caps.

'So let's get this party started.' Oliver snapped his thumb across his cigarette lighter, sparking an orange flame. 'I'll light the fire, yeah?'

'Not yet. We need to swim to purify ourselves.' Aiden shed his greatcoat and began to unbutton his shirt.

'If we're going to follow the path, we have to wash away all the bollocks from the telly and the web, all the bullshit they want us to swallow.' Tyler readily stripped off his own clothes. 'Keep your head down, do your homework and spend the rest of your life stacking fucking supermarket shelves.'

'Big fat fucking deal,' Oliver agreed.

Leanne and Sophie wriggled out of their dresses and were soon gingerly advancing into the water, still wearing their bras and knickers. Courtney was bolder in a black thong, her hands hovering beside her bare breasts as she waded into the shallows

Oliver had stripped to his boxers and was staring at the half-naked girls. Nathan had only shed his jacket and shirt, painfully indecisive. Whooping and bare-arsed, Tyler ran into the lake. As he disappeared in a noisy splash, water surged up the turf. He surfaced, laughing, and swam out further with a noisy backstroke.

If the nix was waiting out there in the dark lake, it had its pick of victims now. There was no way I could rescue all of them, even if I risked going into the water myself. I felt sick.

Chapter Nineteen

Nathan's laugh echoed across the lake, somewhere between embarrassment and incredulity. He still stood by the unlit bonfire, his leather jacket dangling from one hand.

Aiden had got no further than unbuttoning his shirt. He turned and scowled at Jade, who flinched and wrenched her lacy dress off over her head so fast I heard snapping stitches. She wasn't wearing anything under it. Pale and slender, naked, she hurried to Nathan's side.

Caught unawares, he recoiled. 'Fucking hell, Jade! What are you doing?'

For an instant, she looked as if he'd slapped her. Seeing the jerk of Aiden's head, she persevered, reaching for Nathan's hand. 'Come with me. You don't need to swim if you don't want to. We can wash each other clean.'

I saw Aiden watching them intently. If he was so focused on getting Nathan in particular out into the water, maybe I could still do something about that. I took my phone out of my pocket and walked out from the cover of the birch saplings.

'You lot won't be told, will you?' I raised my voice to a shout, lifting my phone as if I were taking pictures. I wasn't, not and risk being caught with what would look like amateur porn. Then I went over to the supermarket carrier bag and stood with it between my feet. 'You're trespassing, and I bet the police will be very interested in whatever's in this.'

Putting my phone away, I stared at Aiden. I silently dared the manipulative bastard to come and try getting the bag back. I would welcome the excuse to beat the living shit out of him.

He looked furious, but he didn't move. Jade snatched her dress off the grass and clutched it to her as she ran for his protection. He used one hand to push her behind him, still standing motionless and staring at me.

I met his gaze and watched for any sign that he was about to move. Since he'd shed his greatcoat, I could see that he was wearing that long knife on his belt. I wished I'd brought a crowbar with me, and moved a few paces away from the carrier bag. If he rushed me, I didn't want to trip over anything.

Between us, Nathan pulled on his leather jacket and legged it. Disappearing into the trees, he headed back the way he'd come. Out of the corner of my eye, I saw Oliver race after him, his own clothes in his arms.

Seeing me distracted, Aiden moved. I saw his hand going to the hilt of his knife. Before he could take more than a couple of steps, he was surrounded by Sophie, Leanne and Courtney. They came running up the slope from the water, splashed with mud from the shallows. They were wailing and begging him or me to do – or not to do – something, incoherent with panic and humiliation.

Where was Tyler? I snatched a glance at the lake. He was swimming back towards us with a fast, effective overarm stroke. If he'd been at my school, the PE teachers would have had him in training for county competitions.

Then I saw that something else was swimming behind him. Something man-sized that shone sickly pale in the moonlight when it breached the dark surface of the water. The thing that I had seen trying to snatch Fin as she flew over the lake as a swan. It was the nix.

Somehow, I knew for a certainty that if the creature couldn't have the victim it had been promised, it would take its revenge on Aiden by taking his most dedicated follower. That would satisfy its appetites.

The girls' shrieks rose to a new pitch of confusion and despair. Looking over to see what was happening, I saw Aiden's back. He hurried away along the footpath leading towards the light. Jade and the others were still struggling into their clothes, fabric sticking to wet skin. The four of them looked at me, fearful. Sophie was grizzling like a small child, any pretence at adult sophistication lost.

I didn't have time for them. Watching the lake, I could see that Tyler was still some distance ahead of the nix. He really was a very good swimmer. It didn't matter. The nix was faster. The monster was going to catch him before he reached the shore.

Not far from the shore though. He was going to be close. Close enough for me to help him? Fuck it. I had to try. I sat down to wrench my laces loose and drag off my boots. I could do that without thinking, so I racked my brains for some idea of something I could use for a weapon.

Lunging across the grass, I grabbed the carrier bag's handles and dragged it towards me. Glass clinked. There were four bottles inside it, as well as a bag of weed. I took out a bottle, ran to the spring and picked up a stone. Holding the bottle by the base, I used the stone to smash off the top and the neck.

You should always hold a bottle by the base if you're breaking it. That's what an electrician with a very dubious past had once told me. I'd thanked him because that seemed safest at the time, not because I had any intention of ever glassing someone in a pub. Now I was grateful I'd listened. I'd cut the nix to shreds without hesitation with the vicious edges on this broken bottle.

One of the girls screamed. I didn't blame her. We'd all seen Tyler throw up his hands and thrash frantically at the water. Then he was dragged under. He was about six or seven metres from safety. Far enough out that I was going to have to swim. Fuck. I emptied my pockets as fast as I could, dropping keys, phone, everything else onto the grass.

'I'd better find my stuff here when I get back!' I was yelling at the Green Man as much as the sobbing girls.

It took all the courage I could summon to step into the dark water. Mud oozed between my toes, soft and treacherous. I could feel water weeds or something in the shallows trying to twine round my ankles. But I had to go on. Tyler was fighting for his life now, rolling and kicking in a surge of dirty foam. I caught glimpses of the nix as it clawed and grabbed at him. It was man-shaped and man-sized, but there was something subtly wrong about its proportions.

I tried to wade in deeper, to get closer to Tyler. I stood on something sharp. As I instinctively pulled my foot away, my other foot slipped out from under me. I lost my balance, fell backwards, and the lake water closed over my face.

I managed to take a deep breath before I went right under. Jack-knifing, I kicked out hard. Spreading my arms, I pulled myself through the water in what I hoped was the right direction. I bumped into something and swam upwards.

Tyler was fighting the nix. He was losing. As I blinked water out of my eyes, I saw the creature rearing up out of the water. It had both black-clawed, webbed hands pressing down on the boy's shoulders. Its weight forced him under the surface. Tyler's arms flailed one last time. Then he went limp.

The monster's skin shone pallid, bluish and faintly scaly in the moonlight. It had no hair, and as its dark eyes fixed on me, it hissed to show me a mouth full of vicious, spiky teeth.

I still had hold of the broken bottle. I shoved it straight into the nix's face. Since I was frantically treading water to keep myself afloat, the blow didn't have much force behind it. I still managed to make contact. A gash on the creature's face bled black in the moonlight.

The sheer surprise of being attacked was more effective than me wounding it. Leaving Tyler to sink into the depths between us, it lunged forward and lashed at me. I floundered backwards, swinging the broken bottle wildly. More by luck than judgement, I hit the creature. The jagged glass ripped a deep gouge along its forearm.

The nix hissed, outraged, and recoiled. It clutched its wounded arm to its chest. Black blood flowed through its fingers. Much good that would do me. The gash on its face had already vanished. It was completely healed. Bastard.

For a moment we stared at each other. Then the creature flung itself backwards to dive beneath the water. As its webbed feet disappeared, a lingering trail of foam on the lake's surface was the only sign it had ever been there.

Where was Tyler? My guts twisted, hollow with apprehension. Had he already drowned? Still watching fearfully for the nix's return, I swept my free hand through the water, back and forth. I let my legs lengthen in hopes of touching bottom, even though the thought of the slimy mud revolted me. I didn't find any footing, and I nearly went under again, when I was startled into a shudder as something brushed against my foot.

Weed? Fish? Nix? I didn't want to find out. I might even have swum back to shore, if I wasn't so determined that the nix wasn't going to get its feast. That fucking bastard Aiden wasn't going to undo the work we'd done by burning that awful tree.

My fingers touched something. Human hair. Thank fuck Tyler wasn't a skinhead. I grabbed a fistful and hauled, swimming clumsily backwards. I had to let go of the broken bottle, but there was no helping that. I kicked out as hard as

I could. My feet kept hitting Tyler's limp legs, and that really didn't help.

I fought to force him upwards. His face broke the surface. His eyes were half closed and his jaw was slack. I tried to remember school lessons about life-saving, but couldn't recall a fucking thing. I didn't dare try to get a better hold of him, for fear of losing him completely.

'Dan!' Someone was shouting my name behind me.

My kicking feet touched mud, and I realised I'd reached the shallows. Staggering, I tried to stand up, and nearly fell over.

'I've got you.' Rufus had my back. I felt his steadying hands below my shoulder blades.

'Get him,' I gasped, fighting to free my hand from Tyler's hair.

Rufus let me go, and I slipped to land on my arse where the grass met the lake. I didn't care. Rufus had got hold of Tyler and was dragging him out of the water. Without any clothes to get a grip on, he had both hands hooked under his armpits.

Once he had the boy clear of the lake's edge, he rolled him onto his front, with his head facing down the slope. Using all his body weight, Rufus pressed down hard on Tyler's back, below his ribs. The boy spewed up a bellyful of water. Rufus quickly got him onto his back again and began mouth-to-mouth resuscitation. After he'd forced a couple of deep breaths into the boy's lungs, Tyler began coughing. Rufus rolled him onto his side, dragging his knee up to keep him in a recovery position.

I'd just about got my own breath back. Getting to my feet, I turned on the huddle of wailing girls. They were clinging to each other, and about thirty seconds from hysterical meltdown. Now that whatever games they'd been playing had turned into this horror show, their noise was indescribable.

'SHUT UP!'

That bellow won me a minute of shocked silence. Then one or another of them started whimpering.

'Stop that!' I clapped my hands, as loudly as I could. 'None of you are hurt, so start making yourselves sodding useful!' I pointed to Aiden's greatcoat, abandoned on the grass. 'That can keep Tyler warm until—'

I turned to Rufus, about to ask where he'd parked the Defender. I realised for the first time that he was wearing motorbike leathers.

Still kneeling beside Tyler, checking his neck for a pulse, Rufus looked up at me with a grimace. 'Can't get him to hospital on the back of the Harley.'

'Do we carry him to my Landy, or can we get an ambulance out here?'

One of the girls, Sophie, interrupted us. 'It's no good. I tried. I can't get 999.'

Rufus took the greatcoat off Courtney and quickly checked the pockets before laying it over Tyler. 'Getting a paramedic out here would be best, I reckon. I can get a phone signal out on the main road.'

'Do it.' I nodded.

As Rufus got to his feet, I saw that he'd ridden his bike down the path from the light. I hadn't even heard the engine approaching as I fought to save Tyler from the nix.

As he passed the huddle of girls, I realised they were looking at me with the hopeless dread of kids who knew they were in deeper shit than they could possibly get out of. At least, these three of them were. Jade had disappeared.

I couldn't care about that now. I was soaking wet and getting colder with each passing minute. The idiot girls looked likely to go down with hypothermia too. I walked over to pick up my keys, wallet and phone, and realised I'd still had Bill Delly's matches with me when I'd emptied my pockets.

'Let's get this fire lit.' I went and picked up the carrier bag, to use it for my own stuff rather than put everything into wet pockets. As I emptied one of the bottles over the firewood, Leanne let slip a murmur of protest. I rounded on her. 'What? You want to explain what you're doing with this booze and these drugs? Don't you think you're in enough trouble?'

Given the choice, I would have saved the full bottles as evidence against Aiden, but getting this fire lit was more important. Once I'd emptied out the liquid, I stood back and chucked three lit matches at the firewood in approved Hollywood fashion. Either the Hunter lent me a hand or whatever was in those bottles was a lot more than just vodka. A blaze erupted.

'Mister?' Courtney was still kneeling on the grass over by Tyler. 'Is he waking up?'

I went to see. The boy was stirring, but his face was slack and his eyes were glazed. He was still away with the faeries, though that's not a phrase I use around my mum. I laid my hand on his bare shoulder. His skin was pale, clammy and as cold as cod from a supermarket fish counter.

'Hold this.' As I handed the greatcoat to Courtney, I stuffed the bag of weed into one of the pockets. She looked up at me, but she didn't say anything. I dragged Tyler across the grass to lay him down a lot closer to the fire. Putting him back in the recovery position, I draped the heavy coat over his back, so the rest of him got some warmth. The girls sat as close to the flames as they could. They looked utterly wretched.

I retrieved my boots and checked the sole of my foot. Thankfully, whatever I'd trodden on had only left a small scratch, even though it had felt so sharp. I put my boots back on. Rather than sitting down and getting chilled, I kept walking around the fire, alert for any sign of movement among the trees or out on the water. To my intense relief, nothing stirred.

As I worked out what I was going to say when help arrived, I wondered exactly what the girls had seen. I decided not to ask. Until they said something aloud, they could still tell themselves they'd imagined it. With any luck they'd keep quiet about anything uncanny, for fear of being called liars or worse.

Sooner than I expected, I heard motorbike engines. Engines, plural.

Courtney looked at me. 'Is that Oliver?'

'And Nathan?' Sophie looked hopefully at the path.

If it was, the teenagers would be sorry. I wasn't sure how I'd manage to make them regret coming back, but one way or another, I'd do it. Then I realised I could see a blue flashing light coming through the trees. Rufus appeared on his Harley, followed by a paramedic in hi-vis gear on a liveried bike.

She took off her helmet, grabbed a bag from her bulky panniers and went straight to Tyler.

'Mister?' Leanne looked at me. 'I got his clothes. They're dry.'

'Let her work.'

The paramedic was already checking Tyler over with various bit of kit. She hadn't finished before more people arrived. Two paramedics in green overalls appeared with a carrying chair and red blankets. They were bundling Tyler up for transport when another ambulance crew arrived. The new arrivals went to see what the girls needed. Overcome with relief, all three started crying, a lot more quietly this time. I was profoundly grateful for that. By now I had a splitting headache.

Rufus came to stand beside me as I watched two uniformed policemen come through the birch trees. They headed straight for us. One handed me one of those crinkly foil blankets, and I wrapped it around my shoulders.

'Well, well, well, what's all this then?' The burly sergeant, who was about Ed Franklin's age, smiled to let everyone know he had a sense of humour.

'Daniel Mackmain.' I explained who I was, what I was doing at Brightwell and who he could contact to verify that. 'We've had some trouble with prowlers lately, so I was having a last walk around outside the house before I went to bed. I saw this lot out in the lane, and suspected they were up to no good, so I followed them here.'

At least I'd had time to come up with a fairly convincing story. Now I had to hope the cops took my word over whatever the girls had to say. There was nothing I could do about that.

'You know that squatter in the caravan, at the corner of the lane by the river?' Rufus interjected. 'We thought he'd been buying them booze. Looks like we were right.' He nodded at the bottles on the grass.

'Sorry, I used that to get the fire lit before we all went down with exposure. The squatter was with them, but he bolted when the lad who went swimming got into trouble. That's his coat though, and I found something dodgy in the pockets.'

I nodded at Aiden's greatcoat, abandoned on the turf a second time. The sergeant nodded at his constable, who went to pick it up.

The sergeant looked at me, thoughtful. 'You could do with a hot bath and a hot drink, I reckon, Mr Mackmain. How about we take your statement tomorrow?'

'I'd appreciate it.' I let him see I was grateful.

'You're okay to drive?' The sergeant gestured at his constable. 'Rich here can handle a Land Rover, and I can follow on behind.'

I'd never had cops so concerned for my welfare. I guessed dragging a drowning kid out of a lake put me on the side of the good guys for once. I was also shivering so hard I couldn't stop now, despite the foil blanket.

'Thanks.' I tossed the constable my keys.

'I'll make sure this is put out.' Rufus headed for the fire.

Tyler and the paramedics were long gone, and the ambulance crew were leading the girls away. I followed the coppers out to the light and let Constable Richard drive me back to the house. He didn't say a word, which suited me fine.

As we both got out of the Land Rover, the sergeant pulled up behind us. He lowered the Škoda estate's window to speak to his underling. 'Let's go and take a look at this caravan, while we're here.'

I left them to it. Good though it would be to see Aiden in handcuffs, I didn't imagine they'd find him there.

I took a long, hot shower, made a mug of tea and threw my sodden clothes into the washer-dryer. I drank my tea, made another mugful and decided I was buying a proper teapot the next time I went to the supermarket. Now that I was finally warm again, I set the alarm on my phone, went to bed and dreamed about hearing footsteps all night.

I was still completely knackered when the alarm went off, but I had to get up for another working day. As I ate my toast, I wondered what Gaffer Kemble would make of all this.

Chapter Twenty

Geoff Kemble wasn't impressed. The heating engineers arrived as scheduled, and we began work. We'd barely done an hour when the cops arrived and asked to see me. It was the pair I'd met last night. I fetched another chair from the housekeeper's sitting room, and we went into the oak parlour.

A couple of Coateses were setting up some scaffolding in the great hall to inspect the cracked plaster above the panelling. Work on the floor above seemed to have made the cracks worse, and the gaffer wanted to know exactly what he'd be dealing with when the redecorating started.

I closed the office door on their curious glances and gave a formal statement to the two cops. I kept my account short and to the point, and kept my fingers firmly crossed that what I said wasn't too far at odds with whatever those girls might be saying.

The sergeant, whose name genuinely turned out to be John Smith, didn't offer any update about Aiden, and I didn't ask. I did have a different question.

'How's the boy doing?'

'He's in a bad way, but he's stable. They'll be keeping him in for a while, mind.' Sergeant Smith didn't sound too concerned.

'It'll be a miracle if he doesn't get pneumonia,' Constable Richard commented. 'My wife's a nurse,' he explained.

'They've got antibiotics for that.' Sergeant Smith stood up and settled his stab vest more comfortably. 'Thank you, Mr Mackmain. We'll be in touch if we need anything else.'

I saw them out to their car and went back to work with the heating guys. I'd barely got up to the old servants' dormitories and picked up my claw hammer when Nicki and Ed Franklin arrived. Rufus was in the Range Rover with them. I fetched the second dining table chair from the housekeeper's sitting room, and we sat around the desk in the office.

'Rufus told us what happened last night.'

Nicki looked so unhappy that I wondered exactly what he had told her. Unfortunately, I could hardly ask him with the two of them sitting right there.

'And he told us about the prowlers.' Ed looked nearly as miserable. 'We know Josh has been hanging around with that gang, when they've been loitering under the market hall.'

I decided they needed to hear something good about their son.

'Josh is the one who really saved Tyler's life. One of the girls texted him to say what they were planning. He's got too much sense to get involved, and he rang me to tell me what they were up to. If he hadn't done that, Tyler would have drowned. Though I told the police that I'd seen the kids out on the lane,' I added, 'and I'd followed them up to the lake. I didn't see any need to drag Josh into this mess.'

'I suppose you can hardly change your statement.' Nicki looked torn between disapproval of me lying to the police and relief that her son need not be involved.

Ed had no such qualms. 'Thanks, we really appreciate that. So what exactly happened?'

I ran through it all again. As I finished, Ed shook his head, scowling.

'I'll get on to Dave. He needs to chase up that consultant who's looking into the Lamp Acre. We've got to get rid of that arsehole.'

'With any luck, the police will catch up with him pretty soon,' Rufus remarked. 'If we see any sign of him, we'll let them know at once.'

'They've got a lot of questions for him, and probably a good few charges planned.' I was about to explain about the bag of weed when someone knocked on the door.

Ed answered automatically. 'Come in.'

Geoff Kemble looked in, totally failing to hide his curiosity. 'Were you looking for a progress report, Mr Franklin?'

Ed got up. 'No, but you may as well give me one while I'm here.'

Nicki looked at me as they left. 'How's Jude getting on with the books? Did she find any of the ones she was looking for?'

I spread my hands. 'Honestly, I'm not sure.'

'I'll go and have a look.'

As she left, Rufus grinned. 'You don't look too bad for a man who must have got fuck all sleep.'

'You too.'

He shook his head. 'I picked a hell of a night to go clubbing. Don't worry, I'll be out in the woods today, regardless. If I see any of those bastards, I'll come straight back and ring the cops.'

Before he could say anything else, we both heard a vehicle arrive outside on the gravel. I stood up and saw Petra Oxway's Mini pulling up. 'Sod it.'

Rufus came to see who it was. 'Like Bess with a bone, that one is. She won't leave until she gets what she wants.'

From his tone, their paths had crossed before now.

'I need coffee. Keep her talking, will you?' I went through to the little kitchen and put the kettle on.

Davey Coates and Jack Kemble were in there, both drinking Coke and eating crisps. They looked at me with keen interest.

Jack was bolder than Davey. 'We heard what you did last night. That was well wicked.'

They grinned at me with clear invitation. They desperately wanted to know more, though neither quite dared to ask me outright.

As apprentices, they must have only been a year or so out of school, I realised. They would both still be plugged into whatever networks or apps spread information around the local teenagers. Their phones must have been buzzing with messages non-stop when their friends realised that working here meant they could get the story first-hand from me. Until they'd lost their signal on the way here, of course.

I gave them a stripped-down version of the account I'd given the police. With any luck that would help quell any wilder rumours.

'I guess Tyler must have got a cramp or something. That water was bloody cold. He was an idiot to go in, especially at night. That's what showing off to impress girls gets you.'

I made myself a coffee, before glancing at the lads with an apparent afterthought. 'Do either of you know Jade Taysel?'

Davey made a dismissive noise. 'I wouldn't touch her with yours—' He broke off and went red as he saw my expression.

'She got herself pregnant,' Jack said, defensive. 'Left school to have an abortion, or had a miscarriage or something.'

I gave him the same hard stare. 'Got herself pregnant, did she? That's quite an achievement. It usually takes two. How about you see if anyone knows where she might have gone? That bastard drug dealer who left Tyler to drown has got his hooks into her good and proper. She needs serious help, not snide little bitches gossiping about her.'

'Who needs help?' Petra Oxway appeared in the kitchen doorway. Jack and Davey seized their chance to flee.

'Jade Taysel. Ask your niece.' I drank some coffee.

'Any chance of one of those?' Petra looked at me, bright-eyed. 'I've got Rufus's account. How about you tell me your side of the story?'

I shook my head. 'I'm not interested in being in the papers again.'

'Tough,' she said crisply. 'You know we'll be covering this, whatever you say, or don't say, to me. Don't be an idiot. This is your chance to make sure that "Hero saves local teenager from drowning" is the first thing that comes up about you online from now on. That's got to be better than half a dozen stories skirting the libel laws to say "probably a murder suspect, even if the police can't find any evidence to arrest him".'

I got a mug out of the cupboard. 'I don't know if the police will want me talking to the press about this.'

'Leave me to worry about that.' She cocked her head. 'And I heard you talking to those two boys. Who do you think is a more reliable source to have in your corner on Twitter? Me or them?'

'Okay.' I made her a coffee. She'd drunk it black with one sugar after we'd had dinner, I remembered. 'Come on through.'

Sitting in the oak parlour, I told my story for the fourth time that morning. Petra made notes using what looked like shorthand as well as recording me. I spoke slowly and chose every word with great care.

When I'd finished, I waited for Petra to stop writing. She looked up.

'Do you know anything more about this Aiden? Did one of those kids have anything to say?'

'Sorry, no.' But I saw something in her eyes. 'What have you found out?'

Petra bit her lip, considering her reply. Then she leaned forward to reach for her phone. She'd laid it on the desk between us, to pick up my voice. She made sure to turn off the recording, and spoke quietly.

'Strictly between ourselves? Seriously, if you say a word to the wrong person, you could screw up a police investigation, as well as lose me a good story. When you showed me that photo, I thought I recognised him. When I got your email and took a closer look, I was sure. He was cleaned up, and dressed like a normal person, though, not in the gear he wears for doing that fortune-teller crap by the market hall. It took me a while, then I remembered. I saw him at an auction last month. I was doing a piece on a firm who've been accused of ripping people off over house clearances, after their relatives have died and no one's thinking straight. You know the sort of thing I mean? Telling someone Auntie Ethel's favourite chair is a reproduction worth a fiver, and then selling it for a fortune because it's really a genuine Chippendale.'

I nodded, and Petra leaned forward again, conspiratorial.

'So I started asking around, discreetly, obviously. I got a visit from the local CID, asking me to back off. They've got their eye on that auction house themselves. The police think they're handling stolen property from these recent burglaries, so they were very interested to hear about our friend. If you do see him anywhere around, ring the cops as well as me.'

She got to her feet. 'Where shall we take your photo then?'

I was about to protest, when I remembered the pictures that had been taken of me unshaven, bruised and scowling when I was being hounded by the papers in Derbyshire. Those were still on the Internet, making me look like I ate raw babies for breakfast. 'Outside.'

I stood by the steps, and Petra used the camera on her phone. She kept asking me to relax and to smile. I did my best, and after a few attempts, she shrugged and lowered the phone.

'We should have something usable. Don't give up the day job to start a modelling career.' She walked over to the Mini. 'Call me if anything – or anyone – turns up.'

She smiled, waved, and left. I went back into the house to find Geoff Kemble in the hallway, looking sour. I decided to get my retaliation in first.

'Who knew that dragging a kid out of a lake would make such a mess of a working day?' I smiled as I said it, but he could see that I was challenging him to make something of it.

Before he could decide if he was going to do that, the office phone rang. I smiled at Geoff again and went to answer it.

'How are you?' It was Fin, and from the concern in her voice, she'd already heard about last night.

'Knackered,' I said ruefully. 'We need to talk.'

'We do. Are you free for lunch?'

I hesitated. 'I'd probably better work through. I've already lost a stupid amount of time this morning.'

Fin took a moment before answering. When she spoke, she sounded tense. 'Okay, but can you get away prompt at six? Come and pick me up?'

'I'll be there as soon as I can,' I assured her.

'See you later then. Bye.'

'Bye.' I put the phone down. I could see the gaffer watching me through the half-open door. 'Is there anything you need from me, or shall I get on?'

'Best get on, I reckon,' he said curtly, and headed into the great hall.

I went to find the central heating guys. They were down in the basement boiler room, discussing the best way of getting the ancient cast-iron cylinder and pipework out of there. Apparently the new system was going to be fuelled by wood pellets supplied by Ashgrove Farm.

Since they weren't locals, they hadn't heard much of the gossip about last night. Since they wanted to get this job done and get paid, they were far more focused on the task in hand than asking me anything. That suited me fine, and we worked steadily for the rest of the day. After spending those hours setting everything else aside to concentrate on my normal job, I felt far less stressed by the time six o'clock came around.

After everyone had gone home, I made myself a quick sandwich, braced myself and drove over to the Whittle and Dub. The sooner we got rid of the nix, the sooner I could go back to Blithehurst, and get back to my normal life there. I hoped Finele had found some way to do that.

This time I took the route along the lane, and I slowed right down as I went past the Lamp Acre. I wanted to see if there was any sign of life at the caravan. We didn't only need to get rid of the nix. There was Aiden to deal with too. Still, it occurred to me that taking the nix out of the equation might screw with whatever that bastard was doing to stay ahead of the police, if he was drawing on its power somehow. I'd have to ask Fin and Sineya if they thought that was possible.

Since there was nothing to see at the caravan, I accelerated and drove on. When I got to the Whittle and Dub, Fin was already waiting for me outside, in the car park.

'Where to?' I asked as she got into the passenger seat.

'Anywhere. Somewhere quiet. We need to talk.' She looked straight ahead through the windscreen. 'Not in the woods.'

'Okay.' I drove away and continued along the road that would take us away from Bourton, Brightwell and the pub.

We soon found ourselves in farmland, and we hadn't gone very far when Fin pointed at a field entrance.

'That'll do. Pull in there.'

I did as I was told, and undid my seatbelt. 'So, about last night.'

I told my story yet again. For the first time today, I told the whole truth, not leaving out any detail. Fin listened, still looking through the windscreen.

'So there's no sign of Aiden, but the police are looking for him,' I concluded.

'We need to get rid of the nix before he turns up again.' Fin looked grim.

'Divide and conquer.' I wondered what was bothering her. 'Have you seen Sineya today?'

I knew how thoroughly talking to a dryad could get under my skin, and Fin had specifically wanted to get away from the woods.

'I have.' Fin fell silent.

I sat and waited. After a few minutes, she undid her seatbelt and turned to face me.

'Sineya has come up with a plan.'

'Let me guess. It's risking your neck and mine, not hers?'

'Got it in one.' Fin stared at me. 'How much do you know about my kind?'

'Just what I've read,' I said cautiously.

Fin smiled without much humour. 'So you know those stories about swan maidens who get trapped in their human form because some mortal man gets hold of their feathered shift, or whatever token makes them vulnerable. Because men seem to lose their minds around us, when they realise what we are and they see they can get their hands on something to control us.'

'So they say.'

'They're right.' Fin sighed. 'Don't ask me why. I don't make the rules. Believe me, explaining why you're wearing a feather vest isn't easy, if you ever get caught out. I keep mine in a lockbox as much as I can, because the thought of losing it is bloody terrifying.'

'I can imagine.'

'No, you can't,' Fin said bluntly, 'any more than I can imagine getting a kick in the balls. Sineya's got some idea, though, and that's given her an idea. Those stories? You know how they go on about the trapped swan maidens weeping and crying and generally wasting away from sorrow? That's right as well. So, what do we know that laps up misery?'

'The nix.' I wasn't sure where this was heading, but I was pretty sure I wasn't going to like it.

Fin nodded. 'Which brings us to Sineya's plan. We need to lure the nix out of the lake, and keep it out of the water, because you've seen how it heals itself. It can't do that on dry land. Sineya wants me to give my feathers to you and go to the lake to act as bait, because believe me, just the thought of anyone having that sort of hold over me means I won't have to fake being scared sick.'

'We can lock up your – whatever you give me – at Brightwell,' I assured her. 'No one will get in there.'

'No, I don't think we can,' Fin sighed, 'because me being more scared than you can imagine will get the nix's attention, but that won't get it out of the water, or close enough to you, for you to kill it. You'll need to have my feathers with you so the nix thinks it can get them off you, and then it's got me enslaved for itself.'

'Shit.' I knew dryads could be ruthless, but this was taking things to a whole new level. 'There has to be another way.'

'If there is, I can't think of it,' Fin said grimly, 'and I was up all night trying. If you've got some bright idea, let's have it, because I don't think we can wait. That boy nearly died last night, and if Aiden's in this much trouble right now, he's going to need whatever power the nix can give him. That means giving it whatever it wants, and I reckon that's going to be a life, and soon.'

After last night, I couldn't argue with that. 'Are you seriously prepared to do this?'

'That depends.' She looked me in the eye. 'Can I trust you to give my feathers back as soon as we've done what needs to be done? Do you think you can kill the nix, now that you've seen what it is?'

I noted her priorities. 'You can trust me. I'll swear to that on whatever you want, and Sineya can set every dryad and naiad she knows on me if I get some rush of shit to the head. Or she can tell my mum.' I realised that was an even scarier prospect.

'As for the nix...' I considered the question from all possible angles. 'I know that I can wound it, and it's no bigger than me. If we can get it out of the lake, it can't heal itself, and, well, it'll be a fish out of water, won't it? As long as we can stop it getting back into the lake. If that happens, or if anything else goes wrong, you take your feathers and get out of there. Deal?'

'Deal.' Fin didn't look happy, but at least she looked resolute.

'What do I need to kill it?' I didn't imagine a broken bottle would do the trick.

'The usual. Iron.' Fin managed a more genuine smile. 'Or silver, apparently.'

'Some local antique shop can probably sell us a silver fruit knife, but I think I'd rather use a bill hook.'

That actually made Fin laugh. I smiled back, briefly.

'So when are we going to do this? Because with the best will in the world, I'm fit for nothing tonight.'

Fin nodded. 'We should wait for Sineya to get back. She's gone to get some help. No, she didn't say what sort of help,' she added before I could ask.

'Hardly surprising.' Still, that was the best news I'd had all day. Blithehurst's dryads had been a formidable trio when Eleanor and I had gone up against the wyrm.

'I need to talk to my family,' Fin said, staring out of the windscreen again. 'Can you give me a lift to the station tomorrow morning?'

'Of course.'

We sat in silence for another long moment.

'So what shall we do now?' Fin sighed. 'That sounds so ridiculously normal, doesn't it?'

'How about we have a normal meal?' I suggested. 'And talk about normal things? We can go back to the pub or find somewhere in Bourton?'

'That sounds like a plan.' Fin put on her seatbelt. 'I saw a decent-looking Italian place while I was shopping the other day.'

I turned the Land Rover around. We found the Italian restaurant, and it was as good as it looked. Fin had fish, and told the waiter she was pescatarian, which answered one question at least.

I took her back to the pub and went for another look around the caravan. It was still deserted, so I went back to the house and rang Rufus. He confirmed that he'd been out and about in the woods all day. He hadn't seen anyone apart from Bess.

I went to bed, slept well, and dreamed of distant clocks chiming.

Chapter Twenty-One

It was a week before Sineya reappeared. I took Fin to catch her train on Saturday morning and spent the rest of the day doing the usual weekend stuff, like laundry and checking over my tools. Thankfully I could spend Sunday resting, after Rufus called round to tell me he and Bess had scoured the woods and there was no sign of Aiden anywhere. He said the police had searched and secured the caravan.

Monday morning came around, and we got on with the renovations. Rufus rang to let me know that Martha was back home, and apparently doing well. On Tuesday Constable Rich rang to say that Tyler was out of immediate danger, though from his tone, it didn't sound as if 'doing well' was something any doctor was going to say any time soon. I hoped the hospital was far enough away that the nix wasn't getting any benefit from the boy's suffering.

The North Cotswold Mercury came out on Thursday. True to her word, Petra had made me a hero. Mark and the others spent the day taking the piss, in a good-humoured way that told me they were impressed. There was less sympathy for Tyler than I expected. I learned he had an older cousin and an uncle who were both in prison, for car theft and handling stolen property respectively.

Petra rang to make sure I'd seen the paper. She suggested we had dinner to celebrate my redemption on the Internet. I could tell she was suggesting more than that. I said I was really sorry, but I had too much work I really wanted to catch up on. That was true, and I don't go to bed with women when I know I'll be thinking about someone else while we're having sex.

Jude Oxway put in a good few hours through the week, sorting through the books in the drawing room. She still hadn't found the ones that we suspected Aiden was after. She did begin stacking different categories of books in boxes, so Davey and Jack could out take those cheap shelf units and chuck them into the latest skip. I was able to give the panelling a thorough check. There were no secret cupboards that I could find.

I was filing a couple of delivery notes after lunch on Friday when one of the Kembles who'd gone outside to use his vape stuck his head around the oak parlour door.

'There's some bird to see you, out the front.'

For a ridiculous instant, I thought he meant Finele. But how would Nige know who a swan wanted to see? Then my common sense caught up with my ears. I looked up and nodded. 'Cheers.'

Nigel went back to whatever the gaffer had him doing, and I went to see who the visitor was. Stepping out of the porch, I saw Sineya gazing up at the house's elegant, ancient frontage. She wasn't alone. Anyone else, apart from Fin, would think this unremarkable young student had an amiable black Labrador sitting patiently at her side. A loyal old family pet, no doubt.

I glimpsed the true, terrifying, shaggy hulk of a black shuck whenever I blinked. It was enough to make me seriously consider letting my eyeballs dry out, and I knew the shuck wouldn't hurt me. At least, I was fairly sure it wouldn't if it was the same fearsome beast I'd grown used to seeing around Blithehurst's woods. If it was, I wondered how Sineya had brought it here. If it wasn't, where had she found it?

'We need to talk,' the dryad said briskly.

'Let's walk around the gardens,' I suggested.

Sineya looked amused. 'I can cross a threshold, you know.'

'Obviously.' How did she think my parents had managed to build a life together? 'But I can barely hear myself think in there.'

Even outside, we could both hear non-stop hammering from the basement. I led the way past the steps down to the kitchen door, and we went on to the back of the house.

Sineya looked around the well-kept flowerbeds and neatly pruned shrubs, very appreciative. 'This is lovely.'

'Isn't it?' I watched the shuck race across the lawn with its tail wagging. Then it pulled up short of the iron fence and began to pace from side to side. Its head and tail were down, and its hackles were raised.

Sineya looked along the length of the boundary. 'Can you open that gate for us, please?'

'Of course.' We walked over, and as soon as I pushed the gate open, the shuck ran away into the trees. I saw Sineya watch the beast go. It was clear that she wanted to follow it.

'Go on,' I prompted. 'As long as you're quick. I can't be out here for long without people wondering what I'm doing.'

'I understand.' The dryad strode swiftly to the closest oak tree. She rested her forehead against it, laying her hands on the bark to either side.

I glanced back towards the house. To my relief, I couldn't see any faces at windows wondering what the good-looking ecology student was doing. I decided that if anyone asked, I'd just say it was tree-hugger stuff. That was perfectly true, after all.

Sineya came back a few minutes later. She might be over a century old, but she understood a lot more about dealing with ordinary people than her grandmother did. 'The trees are relieved that the charnel thorn has gone, but they're still afraid of the nix.'

'Have they got any idea where Aiden might be?' I had no idea if them telling us this was even possible.

Sineya shook her head regardless. 'We must deal with him ourselves. After we've rid the lake of the nix.'

'Fin said you were fetching help. What can the shuck do for us?'

'As long as you keep the foul thing out of the water, it can help tear the nix to pieces.' Sineya looked at me, her eyes vivid green. 'It's not here for that though. I take it Finele told you our plan?'

'She did.' Though I wouldn't have called it *their* plan, exactly.

'The shuck is here for her.' Sineya stared at me, unblinking. 'If you prove false to your word, it will take Finele's feathers from you. It will not let you keep such a hold over her. Do you understand?'

'Absolutely.' I was starting to wonder how strong the lure of power over a swan maiden could be, if the dryad was taking the possibility so seriously. I was still confident I was immune.

Now I sure as hell hoped I was right about that. I wanted the shuck biting lumps out of the nix, not me.

'When are we going to do this?'

'Tonight. Why wait?' Sineya demanded.

'Okay.' It was Friday, so I'd have the weekend to recover. Previous encounters with ethereal creatures doing their very best to kill me told me that I'd need all the rest I could get afterwards, assuming I survived.

The next question was exactly when we were going to do this. 'Get Fin to check on the moon tonight. We'll want as much light as possible. Get her to ring me, so we can agree the best time to meet.'

Sineya was about to say something when the shuck came back. It was trotting rather than bounding through the woods, with its tail held high and head casting from side to side. At least, that's what its Labrador guise was doing. As it flopped onto the grass by Sineya's feet, it heaved a sigh, and

I glimpsed its long, blood-red tongue lolling through ferocious teeth.

The dryad looked down and pursed her lips. 'It hasn't found any scent of Aiden.'

'That's a shame.' Though that cut both ways. I'd certainly like to see the bastard savaged by the shuck, but as long as he was nowhere around here, he couldn't do anything to help the nix.

I was uneasily aware that we still had no idea exactly what Aiden might be able to do. I really don't like trying to account for unknown factors when I'm making any sort of plan. That's how things end up broken and people get hurt.

Sineya nodded. 'We'll be in touch.'

She started walking back towards the house. I went with her, and the shuck heaved itself up from the grass, grumbling as it followed.

I went back to the drawing room, where I was inspecting the panelling now that I could get to it. There was some work to be done, but not a great deal.

When the gaffer blew his whistle to call it quits for the day, Jack hung back for a moment as Davey headed out to the garage yard to wash his hands.

'We did, you know, ask around about Jade. See if anyone seen her. If anyone's got any ideas. We ent come up with anything yet, but people want to help. Maybe someone will see her over the weekend.'

'Let me know if you do. I'll call the cops and keep anyone else out of it.' I followed him out of the drawing room, and was heading for the kitchen sink when the phone in the oak parlour rang.

It was Fin. She got straight to the point. 'I reckon you should pick me up around eleven tonight, if we're going to get the best of the moonlight.'

'What's the weather forecast?' I realised that I should have asked Sineya if a nix could heal itself in the rain. That would keep its skin wet, after all. Folk tales really don't tell you everything that you need to know.

'Clear and dry,' Fin said. 'Wrap up warm. We'll meet Sineya at the entrance to Brightwell Light.'

'Have you met her dog?' I asked cautiously.

'I have.' Even in those two words, I heard Fin's astonishment.

'How do you feel about that?'

'I can see she's trying to help.' Fin hesitated. 'It's not that I don't trust you—'

I interrupted before this conversation got any more awkward. 'I understand. Where are we going to do this? By the spring?'

'I don't think so.' Fin was as relieved as me to change the subject. 'We have a better chance of getting it away from the water down at the other end of the lake.'

I pictured my walk with Martha. 'Yes, I can see that.'

Fin took a deep breath. 'See you later then.'

She ended the call. I had been about to suggest we got some food together. On second thoughts, I realised that was a stupid idea. This was hardly the evening for discussing the latest movies over a pizza.

I locked up and went into Bourton for a burger at The Boar's Head. As I ate, I looked at my phone and thought about ringing my dad. Telling him how I'd risked my neck when it was far too late for him to talk me out of it had caused quite a bit of strain between us last year. I'd promised not to do it again.

Though he already knew I was trying to find a way to get rid of the nix. This wasn't like me and Eleanor fighting the wyrm, when he had no idea what was going on. Telling him exactly what we had planned now would just mean he'd stay awake all night worrying. I'd have to remember to phone him after it was all over. Added to that, I'd have to explain about Fin. That really wasn't my secret to share. I left my phone alone.

Once I'd eaten, I went back to Brightwell. I opened up the back of the Land Rover to dig out an old combat jacket and my worst pair of jeans. I also had a battered pair of work boots that I was prepared to sacrifice if I really must. I kept them in there in case I found myself facing an unexpectedly mucky job.

As I got changed, I reckoned that killing a nix would probably qualify. I also hoped this jacket was thick enough to save me from the monster's grip if it got too close. I'd seen the nix's claws dig deep into Tyler's shoulders. What the hospital's nurses made of those marks was anyone's guess.

Not that I intended to let the sodding thing get within grabbing range if I could possibly help it. I fetched the bill hook that I'd spotted from Bill Delly's gardener's store. It wasn't one of the hand-held type, but a long-handled tool with a blade as heavy and as sturdy as I had hoped. It had also been sharpened to a razor edge. I put it in the back of the Landy.

That still left me with several hours to kill. I got a pad and a pen and went up to the long gallery. Going from room to room, I made notes on the work that had been done so far, and what was still outstanding. The Franklins were paying me to manage this whole project, even if Gaffer Kemble thought he was in charge. I resolutely ignored the sounds the old house was making around me. There was no one else in here, the doors were locked and the alarm was set. The old floorboards and joists had just been stirred out of their slumbers by all the comings and goings and the work in hand.

I got so absorbed in what I was doing that my phone alarm took me by surprise. Switching it off, I put the pad and pen on the oak parlour desk. If I disappeared into the lake's depths tonight, the Franklins would know exactly how this job stood, even if they had no idea what had happened to me. Not that I had any intention of letting the bastard thing drown me. The plan was getting it out of the water and keeping it on dry land.

I drove to the Whittle and Dub, taking the lane to join the main road. There was no hint of lights inside the caravan. Good.

Finele was waiting in the car park again. She got into the passenger seat without a word. She was wearing old clothes as well. I guessed a freshwater ecologist had plenty of experience getting muddy and wet.

I saw she had a calico bag in her hands, the sort of thing that's given away at craft fairs and living history days with a logo on the side. I knew Eleanor was thinking of trying them out at Blithehurst. She reckoned people would happily carry around free advertising in return for the feel-good factor of avoiding plastic carrier bags.

We drove back in silence, both looking at the road ahead. About halfway there, I couldn't stand it any longer.

'Do you know the most irritating pub sign I've ever passed?' I didn't wait for her to answer. 'The pub was called The Turnpike, but they had a polearm on the sign. It wasn't even a pike. It was a bloody halberd.'

Fin made a valiant effort to meet me halfway. 'Maybe they know that. Maybe they make a fortune from people stopping to tell them that a turnpike is actually a sort of road. Maybe the pub owners suggest that since they've already stopped, why not have a drink or a meal?'

'Good point.' I genuinely hadn't thought of that possibility.

We drove on in silence, but the atmosphere between us was less tense.

I turned into the light and pulled up with the engine still running. Sineya and the shuck were waiting by the finger-post. I lowered my window but made no move to get out. 'I'm going to park further up, by the path. If the cops drive past here, or Rufus, we don't want them seeing my Landy and getting curious.'

'Very well.' Sineya nodded and stepped back. I wasn't sure if she disappeared entirely or simply moved beyond the headlights' reach.

It didn't matter. I drove on up the broad track, leaning forward to peer through the darkness to pick out the narrow entrance for the path to the lake. As soon as I saw the gap in the trees, I pulled up. 'Let's do this.'

I got out and went around to the back of the Landy to get the bill hook. Fin got out of the passenger door. She offered me the calico bag.

'Thank you.' I didn't look inside. Carefully folding the cloth around the soft contents, I put it in my coat's right-hand pocket and made sure that the zip was secure.

Fin didn't say a word. She walked around the Landy and headed down the path. I gave her some distance before I followed. We wanted the nix to think she was on her own when she reached the lake. The path was narrow but clear enough, so there was no danger of her losing her way.

I walked slowly, holding the bill hook upright and close to avoid it catching on passing branches. I was taking care to make as little noise as possible. Not only to avoid alerting the nix, but to listen out for any sounds of someone else in the woods. We still didn't know where Aiden and anyone still loyal to him might be.

All I could hear was the usual night noises. Until I drew closer to the lake, that is. Then I heard Finele crying. No, she wasn't crying. She was weeping. That was a better word for the soft keen of inconsolable misery that raised the hairs on the back of my head.

I stopped short of the open, soggy ground at this end of the lake. Stepping into the shadows of an alder thicket, I laid a hand on the ridged bark and silently asked the Green Man for whatever he might do to hide me. Then I gripped the bill hook's solid ash helve with both hands.

With her head in her hands, Fin was kneeling a few metres back from the edge of the water, as far as the shore could be identified. The full moon overhead struck silvery glints from water among the grassy tussocks and plants around her.

I tried to calculate how fast I could get to her if the nix attacked. If the sodding thing turned up. Time passed. I had to shift my feet to avoid getting stiff, as quietly as I could. Fin changed her position from kneeling to sitting and hugging her thighs, still hunched over in palpable despair. The moonlight shone down on the untroubled surface of the lake. A fox trotted down the path, saw me and trotted off again, unconcerned.

Then I saw a ripple that had nothing to do with the gentle night breeze ruffling the water. This was steady, purposeful movement, and it was coming ever closer. Fin still had her face pressed against her knees. There was no way she could see it. I had no idea if she could sense it. I wanted to shout and warn her, but that would only warn the nix.

Our plan was succeeding, this far at least. The nix appeared out in the lake, breaching the surface like a swimmer. It swam back and forth, surging upwards after every few strokes to get a better look at Fin. In the moonlight its back shone like silvery fish skin against the dark water.

Finally temptation overcame its caution. It stopped swimming and began wading out of the water. To my intense relief, its body was as sexless as the creature from the black lagoon, or any other movie monster played by a man in a wetsuit. If it had come out of the water with a hard-on for Fin, I'm not sure if I could have held back.

Because I needed to hold back. The nix was still knee-deep in the water when it halted, looking warily around. I hadn't heard anything, and the breeze was coming towards me, so I didn't think it could have caught my scent. I stood as still as I possibly could, even holding my breath.

After a long moment, the nix advanced on Fin. Now that it was out of the water, it was walking with its black-clawed hands held a little way out from its sides. It looked like someone trying to keep their balance on an icy path. I wasn't smiling though. Those claws looked lethal.

It got closer to her, still cautiously glancing from side to side. As it drew nearer though, it became more and more intent. Its dark eyes fixed on her, and its lipless mouth opened to show a long tongue licking those scarily pointed teeth. It reached for her shoulder, slowly rather than grabbing at her, which surprised me. As it spread its swollen-knuckled hands, the moonlight turned the webbing between its fingers translucent.

Fin moved. However she knew it was coming, she was ready. She rolled forward, diving under its arm. She sprawled on the ground for an instant, but the nix was too startled to react. By the time it had turned around, Fin was on her feet. Now she had her back to the lake, and the nix had its back to me. She was between it and the water. Now she was the one with her arms outspread, shifting her weight from foot to foot. Whichever way the nix went to get past her, she was ready to block its path.

I hefted the bill hook in my hand. I'd been a pretty decent competitor with the javelin at school, but this garden tool wasn't balanced for throwing, or designed for piercing. If I did hit the nix, the best I could hope for would be a glancing blow. I couldn't see that crippling the monster, not sufficiently to stop it reaching the water. It was still close enough to the lake to escape me if I ran at it, ready to take its head off with the bill hook.

I left the long-handled tool propped against the alder tree. Taking the calico bag out of my pocket, I stepped out of the shadows and held it up. 'Hey! Isn't this what you want?'

The nix spun around. Its long tongue tasted the air as it stared at me. It took a step towards me, then wavered. It wasn't convinced it should come any closer. Don't ask me how I knew, I just did.

I took a deep breath and reached into the cloth bag. My fingers touched indescribable softness, silkiness, a sensation that there simply are no words for. I was terrified that my clumsy hands would crush something wonderful. At the same time I was desperate to seize hold of this precious gift so hard that I would never let it go. I gritted my teeth and held the feathery thing between my fingers and thumb, lifting it out of the bag far enough for the nix to see what I had.

Fin screamed. The raw agony in her voice hit me like a physical blow. I felt her pain like salt rubbed into an open wound. The nix shivered with obscene delight. It didn't hesitate now. It was coming towards me with long strides. Its clawed feet dug into the soggy turf to steady it as its hands sought the bag.

Now I had to judge my moment exactly. I needed the nix to be close enough, but not too close, or too far away. I had to have time to grab the bill hook and swing it, without giving the nix time to escape when it saw the danger. I dared not let it get close enough to have any chance to snatching the calico bag out of my hands.

I felt the shuck growl rather than heard it. There was an ominous sensation in the pit of my stomach and at the back of my throat. My balls shrivelled and my mouth dried. Out of the corner of my eye, I caught the menacing red glint of the black beast's eyes.

So did the nix. It whirled around and ran for the lake. I grabbed the bill hook and ran after it, trying to stuff the calico bag back into my pocket. I couldn't do it, not if I was going to stop the nix escaping. I had to settle for getting my forearm though the cloth bag's handles as I took a firm hold on the bill hook.

I had longer legs than the nix, and even on this treacherous ground, I had a firmer footing, thanks to my boots. I swung at the monster, and the hooked tip of the bill scored a black line across its back. It shrieked as it turned to face me. It crouched low with its hands spread wide, as if it was about to spring into attack.

I swung again, with a blow that should have taken its sodding head off. It wasn't there. Not its head, not the entire nix. The fucking thing had disappeared. For an instant I froze, dumbfounded. Then I saw a long, sinuous shape wriggling across the ground. I remembered those stories saying that a nix could turn itself into a snake. Only this wasn't a snake. It was an eel, even if it was as thick as my thigh, and it was writhing swiftly towards its refuge in the lake.

'Fin!' I tried to hack at the eel but only got the tip of the bill stuck in the soft ground. As I wrenched it free, I looked up to see where she was.

Fin was standing by the water. She wasn't alone. Swans flanked her, three to either side. They had their wings spread, their hisses vicious, as they pecked at the eel's eyes. No matter which way the creature twisted, its head met their murderous beaks.

The nix shifted back to its man-shape. It was up on its feet in an instant, clawed hands lashing out. White feathers flew, some spotted with what could only be blood. The nix was bleeding as well though. That wound on its back was a smear of black foulness.

The monster was determined to get back to the lake. The swans were still attacking it, some now airborne, and more agile than any waterfowl I'd ever seen. That left Fin standing alone, empty-handed, between the monster and the water. Even with its back to me, I saw the nix fix its attention on her.

I looked back over my shoulder. 'Shuck!'

The terrifying beast bounded towards me. The great black shadow was an irrevocable promise of death and pain given physical form. I wanted to throw the bill hook away, to run away, to be anywhere but here. Instead, I fought and conquered every instinct to flee and turned my back on the murderous hound.

I swung the long ash handle as I ran forward. This time, I aimed for the nix's legs. Not to hamstring it, since I had no idea if it had sodding hamstrings. I hacked at the side of its thigh. As the sharpened steel bit deep, I hooked the tip of the bill into the front on its leg. I dug my heavy boots deep into the soft ground and hauled, using all my body weight.

The nix lost its footing to fall hard, and landed face down on the ground. The shuck was at my side, snarling, ready to pounce on the monster's back, to rip it to shreds.

'No!' I tore the dangling calico bag free of my arm and held it out to the shuck. 'Go to Fin!'

The hulking beast snatched the bag out of my hand. The briefest touch of its breath felt like plunging my arm to the shoulder into ice-cold water. My fingers were so numb that I couldn't grip the bill hook's handle again. All I could do was swing the heavy blade one-handed as the nix writhed on the ground.

It changed shape again. This time, it looked like a pike, which is to say the fish, not the polearm. A pike around six feet long and as thick as a man's torso. As it snapped at me,

I saw the pale inside of its mouth, but its back was dark, mottled green against the ragged grass. For a moment, even in the bright moonlight, I lost track of exactly where the monster ended and the ground began.

That instant was all the nix needed. As a fish, it was solid muscle, or as good as, whatever it was made of. It thrashed its tail around to knock my feet clean out from under me. I fell hard, twisting awkwardly to avoid stabbing myself with the bill hook. The nix came straight at me. Its jaws were agape and heading for my face. I got my hand up just in time, and its vicious bite fastened on my forearm.

My old coat was thick, but not that thick, and this wasn't the arm numbed by the shuck's breath. I felt the tips of its teeth break my skin. Then something dragged the giant fish backwards. I couldn't pull my arm free of its hold, so I was dragged along with it. I had to let go of the bill hook before I took my own eye out.

Then whatever was happening sent a spasm through the nix from tail to head. It bit deeper into my arm for a moment, and then its jaws relaxed a fraction. That was enough for me to tear myself free with a sound of ripping cloth and the searing sting of torn flesh.

I rolled away and scrambled to my feet. I saw three things in what felt like the single blink of an eye. The shuck had hold of the great fish's tail and was shaking it like any mortal dog intent on killing a rat. The nix couldn't escape, because the grass was weaving itself into a tangling net to hold it down.

Fin was standing by the lake, surrounded by the swans. She can't have been wearing anything under that coat, because she was naked to the waist. She had her arms above her head, and as her feather shift slid down to cover her breasts, I remembered just in time to close my eyes and avoid being dazzled as she transformed herself into a swan.

At least I had some feeling in my numb hand now. I saw the bill hook on the ground and snatched it up. The grass net was doing its best, but the nix had turned back into its man-shape, so it had room to manoeuvre. Its black talons were slashing through the grass as fast as Sineya could weave her snares.

I had no idea where the dryad was, and I didn't waste time looking. I planted my feet wide and raised the bill hook over my head. Taking a breath to judge my aim, I brought the heavy blade down. I put all my weight behind the two-handed blow, as if I was chopping wood, or breaking concrete with a pickaxe. More by luck than judgement, I took the monster's head off.

Black blood flowed across the ground, reeking like the slime from a stagnant pond. The grass unravelled. Undeterred by the stink, the shuck sprang forward to seize the nix's corpse by one arm. Its muffled snarl was triumphant as it dragged its prize towards the lake's edge. I realised that the swans were out on the water now. They were paddling in a loose circle, looking in this direction.

I stepped towards the shuck. 'Wait—'

The shuck's growl warned me not to come closer.

'It's all right.' Sineya appeared at my side, ethereal and beautiful, and in a simple green tunic rather than her grandmother's draperies. 'The nix is of the water, so the water will reclaim it.'

'It won't pollute the lake?'

'Not once the flow from the spring to the river is restored.' Sineya smiled sweetly at me.

'That's my job?' But I was talking to empty air. The dryad had vanished.

As the shuck splashed into the shallows, dragging the dead nix with it, the swans took to the air. I watched them go, and wondered where they were headed. When I looked down again, the shuck was gone. The dead nix was drifting away across the lake. A moment later, it sank without leaving a trace on the calm surface of the water.

Since there was nothing else for me to do, I picked up Fin's discarded coat and rinsed the black muck off the bill hook as best I could. I'd have to wait for daylight to clean it properly.

Then I went back to Brightwell, considering what we should do next as I drove. We'd got rid of the nix, but that was only half our problem. More than that, while killing the nix hadn't been easy, we knew where to find the monster. We still had no idea where Aiden had gone.

Chapter Twenty-Two

I got my first aid kit out of the Landy when I got back to the house. Once I'd locked the dirty bill hook and Fin's coat in the housekeeper's sitting room, I went into the little kitchen. The light was better there, and I needed to see how much damage the nix had done to my arm. Peeling off my sleeve started the gouges oozing red again, but once I'd washed the clotted blood away, it wasn't as bad as I'd thought. The fresh bleeding soon stopped, and the thick fabric seemed to have kept muck out of the bite.

What I couldn't come up with was any explanation for the injury that wouldn't cause complications. Saying I'd hurt myself at work here over the weekend would mean an accident book entry and awkward questions from the gaffer. Saying I'd been bitten by a stray dog in the woods would probably get the police out, as well as wasting Rufus's time with a wild goose chase. Worse, some innocent dog might be accused, if I gave some made-up description that happened to fit a local pet with a bad reputation.

It would have to be long sleeves for me until I healed. Luckily my mother's blood means that happens fast. I stuck the largest plasters I had over the worst of it and wrapped a bandage around my whole forearm. It wasn't a neat job, since I was doing it with my wrong hand. With luck, though, I wouldn't wake up with the plasters stuck to the sheets instead of to me.

I set an alarm and went to bed. I wanted to be up early enough to get that bill hook cleaned and put back in the gardener's store well before there was any chance of Bill Delly turning up. As it turned out, I needn't have worried about oversleeping. I kept waking up, convinced I could hear clocks chiming.

Just after six, I gave up, got up and showered. There was no sign of redness around the bite marks on my arm, and no itching or anything else that might suggest trouble to come. As I ate my toast I decided I could leave off the plasters and wear an old sweatshirt, to let the air get to the worst of the wounds.

In the daylight, the bill hook wasn't too filthy. A bucket of hot water and a scrubbing brush did the job, as I sat on the steps outside. I poured the dirty water away down the drain by the kitchen steps, and was looking in the back of the Landy for a rag to dry it off when I heard footsteps on the gravel.

I turned around to see Finele. 'You're up early.'

She shrugged. 'I couldn't sleep.'

'Me neither.' I carried on with what I was doing.

'How's your arm? I did see it bite you, didn't I?'

'Yes, but it's not too bad.' I pulled my sleeve up a little to prove that.

'Good.'

I waited for her to say something else, but she didn't, and an awkward silence lengthened.

'I've got your coat in the house.'

'Thanks,' she said with relief. 'It was all... a bit hectic last night.'

Since she clearly didn't know what else to say, I decided to ask one of the many questions I'd pondered in the darkness overnight. 'Those other swans. I'm guessing you didn't round them up on the river to lend a hand?'

'No.' She managed a smile. 'That was my mum, two of my aunts, a cousin and my sisters.'

'It's a family thing,' I commented as I walked back to the steps with a rag and my spray can of WD-40 to oil the bill hook's steel.

Fin looked momentarily taken aback, then laughed. 'They're staying on the other side of Bourton. A weekend rental in a holiday cottage. That's where I stayed last night.' She hesitated again. 'It's not that I didn't trust you. It's just when I talked to my mum, she insisted on being here too. She brought the others.'

'I'm very glad they came,' I assured her. 'Even with the shuck, we needed all the help we could get.'

Fin nodded, bit her lip, looked away and then looked back at me. 'Can I ask you something?'

'If you like.' I concentrated on inspecting the bill hook.

'Were you tempted?'

'To hold on to your feathers?' I walked over to put everything back in the Land Rover. 'No, but I won't lie. I could feel the lure, and it's a strong one. Maybe I was able to shake it off because my mum's a dryad. Maybe it's because I've already had a naiad try to make me think with my balls, not my brain. I can certainly see why a man who didn't know what he was dealing with wouldn't be able to cope.'

I guessed greenwood blood only offered some protection, and that weakened over the generations. Robert Beauchene hadn't been able to resist an ethereal lure. I glanced over to see how Fin took my answer.

She was looking thoughtful. 'Thanks.'

'Can I ask you something?' I closed the back of the Landy.

'Okay,' Fin said apprehensively.

I was going to ask if I'd hurt her when I touched those feathers. Or had that fearful scream been an act for the nix? Seeing her face, I realised she guessed that's what I wanted to know, and that she really didn't want to discuss it. I grinned and asked a different question.

'When did you realise you'd left your coat behind?' I won't lie. That brief glimpse of her half naked was something else

I'd thought about more than once as I lay in my bed overnight.

Her expression lightened. 'About halfway back to the holiday let. We found a discreet field to land in, and my sister lent me her sweatshirt.'

I held up the bill hook. 'Let me put this away, and then how about I make some tea? Or coffee?'

'Coffee, please.' Fin went to sit on the steps while I went through to the garage yard.

When I came back, she was looking thoughtful again.

'So what do we do now?' she asked as I approached. 'Getting rid of the nix is only half the job.'

'I've been asking myself the same thing.' I grimaced. 'With any luck, the cops will catch up with Aiden, and he won't be our problem anymore.'

'And if they don't?' Fin was clearly no more inclined to comfortable optimism than me.

'I don't know,' I admitted as we walked up the steps. 'He's surely done enough to get locked up, but if he has some way to stay ahead of the law, how do we get him into their hands? We need to ask Sineya if there's anything she can do. Maybe if we got into that caravan, the shuck could get his scent and track him down?'

The idea of the monstrous black hound pursuing Aiden had definitely appealed as I stared at the ceiling in the darkness.

'Maybe now that the nix is gone—' Fin broke off as I opened the door. She checked her watch. 'That needs adjusting.'

'You heard it?' I stared at her. 'I thought I was imagining it.'

'Why would you imagine a clock chiming?' She looked at me, puzzled.

'I kept dreaming about that last night.' Not for the first time, either. I realised I had been too focused on the nix to remember to pay attention to my dreams.

Fin glanced away towards St Diuma's. 'Maybe it's the church?'

'There's no clock over there, or in the house, come to that.' I closed the door and led the way to the great hall, where the old grandfather clock was waiting for the horologist. It was hidden under a dust sheet now. 'Apart from this one, and I don't think it's been going for decades.'

'You're sure?' Fin pulled aside the cloth to see the motionless pendulum. 'Maybe someone tried winding it up, and it's stopping and starting.'

Before I could stop her, she opened the glass door that protected the face and ornate hands at the top. 'There's a key in here. Two keys.'

'We'd better leave it alone.' But I took a look at the keys.

The first thing I noticed was that they weren't the same. One was clearly a clock key with that typical butterfly top. The other had an oval loop at the end. It was for an old-fashioned lock. A small lock. I picked it up.

'Come with me.' I headed straight for the walnut parlour and opened up the sewing room.

Fin followed me into the hidden room, looking around. 'This place is full of surprises.'

'You have no idea.' I went over to the roll-top desk.

'Good grief!' Fin saw the picture over the mantelpiece. 'What's that?'

'My guess is the Hunter.' I tried the key in the lock. It fitted. It turned and clicked.

'And a swan maiden?' Fin stepped forward to take a closer look.

'Let's see what's in here first.' I pushed the roll-top upwards. It slid back with a soft rattle.

'More books.' Fin gave the picture a last glance and came over to join me.

'These are the books Jude Oxway's been looking for.' I checked the titles against the list I'd memorised in case I came across them in the long gallery library.

The Book of Black Magic and Pacts. The Long Secreted Friend. The Grand Grimoire.

Le Petit Albert. Agrippa Le Noir. Cyprien Mago ante Conversionem.

They were all here, lying on their sides and stacked neatly in size order. They looked old, far older than the ones in Aiden's caravan. I could see a piece of paper tucked inside *The Grand Grimoire*. I slid the book out and opened it up, to find a neatly pre-printed document headed *Bill of Sale*.

I deciphered the handwritten details that had been added to the form. 'Well, these books definitely belong to the Franklins. Constance Sutton bought them off Mungo Peploe.'

Fin stood close beside me, reading the column of figures. 'I'm not sure about adjusting for inflation, but it looks like she paid a fortune for them, even back then.'

'Jude Oxway thinks they could be worth a fortune now. There's an old glove in here as well. Looks like there's something in it.'

I put the book back and reached for the glove. It was definitely packed tight, though not particularly heavy. The ragged cuff was tied off with a leather thong, and I couldn't see me unpicking that knot. It was well worn, with the fine leather deeply creased. I turned it over, and dropped it.

'Shit!'

'What?'

'Finger nails.'

We both stared at the vile thing lying on the floor. Now it was horribly obvious it wasn't a glove at all, but an actual human hand. It wasn't mummified, exactly, but it had been dried out to preserve it somehow.

Fin and I looked at each other.

'A Hand of Glory?'

I'm not sure which of us said it first. Evidently Fin had read some of the same folklore as me.

She frowned. 'What does it do, exactly?'

Evidently she also skipped a lot of the occult stuff in favour of looking for things that were more directly relevant to people like us.

'I'm not sure, but I bet there's a book here that can tell us. One of the ones Jude Oxway has already sorted through.' I didn't want to touch the books in the desk again, any more than I wanted to touch the revolting thing on the floor.

But I couldn't leave it lying there. I stared at the grisly hand. Looking around, I saw the planchette and the candlesticks. I used one of them to edge the hand onto the planchette, and used that to lift the horrid thing up. I tipped it back into the desk and rolled the slats down to hide everything from view. As I turned the key in the lock again, I couldn't help a shudder.

'Coffee,' Fin said firmly.

'Let's get the kettle on,' I agreed.

I showed Fin where the sitting room was, then went to wash my hands as thoroughly as I knew how. I was tempted to get a tub of degreaser out of the Land Rover and use that as well, but I settled for using half a bottle of liquid soap and water as hot as I could stand.

While the kettle was boiling, I went through to the drawing room and found a modern paperback book about the occult in one of Jude Oxway's stacks. As I came back through the door into the corridor, Fin called out from the little kitchen.

'How do you want your coffee?'

'White, two sugars, thanks.' This was definitely a two sugars kind of day.

She appeared with a mug in each hand. I led the way into the sitting room and let Fin take the sofa. I sat at the table with what claimed to be a guide to practical witchcraft. It might not have the black leather binding and mysterious antique smell of those grimoires in the sewing room, but it did have a decent index.

'Okay, this is what it says about a Hand of Glory.' I read the entry aloud. 'According to legend, this amulet was eagerly sought after by burglars and thieves throughout the Middle Ages, as it would ensure everyone in a house would continue sleeping, undisturbed by intruders. The challenge of crafting such an item was reflected in its high price. The hand itself had to be cut from a murderer who had been hanged at a crossroads. It was then placed in an earthenware vessel with salt, saltpetre and peppercorns, and left from the waxing to the waning moon. The hand must then be dried by the sun and the wind during the dog days of summer.'

'What do you do with it then?' Fin asked as I took a sip of coffee.

'There are a whole lot of theories.' I skimmed the page. 'You either set light to the fingers, or if you want to use it more than once, you put a candle in the palm and attach candles to the fingers and light those. That's not quite as powerful though. If you set light to the hand itself, any of the flames going out means that someone has woken up.'

There was a whole lot more about traditions of hands of power going back to antiquity, and still featuring in the iconography of assorted religions. None of that looked particularly relevant. I closed the book and drank more coffee.

Fin looked at me. 'So is Aiden after the hand or the books?'

'I'm going to assume he wants both.' I told Fin about his possible links to local break-ins, according to Petra.

'Is there any way it could possibly work? The hand, I mean.'

Fin's expression reflected my own uncertainty. After all, both our lives included things that other people would swear were impossible.

I tried to recall if there'd been any trace of wax on the dark fingers, but I couldn't be sure either way. I sure as hell wasn't going to take a second look now.

'If it works, I guess he wants it to use the magic. If it doesn't, I bet he could sell it for a fortune, like those books. Either way, we need to decide what we're doing.' I finished my coffee. 'Is there any way we can use these things as bait? Get him caught in the act, trying to steal them?'

Fin considered that. 'He'd have to know that we'd found them. How do we manage that?'

'Get a story in the local paper?' I rejected that idea as soon as I thought it. 'That means telling the Franklins. As soon as they know how valuable those books are, they'll take them away to be auctioned, or kept locked away until they're sold. Aiden might still go after them, but we've no hope of knowing when or where.'

Added to that, I didn't think my employers would be particularly pleased to have their new hotel project associated with that old scandal and those gruesome deaths.

'What are we telling the Franklins?' Fin had other concerns. 'If we've found human remains, we should be contacting the police, and the local coroner. It doesn't matter how old they are.' She grimaced. 'Work with rivers long enough, and you'll have a day when you come across bones, or worse.'

I nodded. 'I worked on a new-build site once that turned out to be an Anglo-Saxon cemetery.'

That had been straightforward enough, once the county archaeologists turned up. Though the building project had lost valuable work days, and I couldn't see the gaffer taking kindly to that. I saw another problem as well.

'I'm guessing the cops would take the hand away and send it to a lab somewhere. Then we've got the same issue as we have with the books. There'll be nothing to lure Aiden here.'

'Is there any way to let him know without telling the Franklins?' Fin was thinking aloud, not necessarily suggesting that.

'Through the local teenagers?' I shook my head. 'There's no way that would stay a secret for long, and then I'd have to explain myself. I'd be sacked by the end of the day.'

More than my job here would be at risk. I could tell Eleanor what had happened, but there was no way I could justify myself to Ben Beauchene. He had an interest in Blithehurst, and so did the rest of the family, and Eleanor would have to listen if I was accused of dishonesty.

'I have got Aiden's mobile number.' I'd remembered memorising it off Jade Taysel's phone.

'Won't he have ditched that, if the police are looking for him?'

'And why should he trust any message from someone he doesn't know, or from an unknown number?' I shook my head. 'Let's look at this another way. We know he's been trying to get into the house. As long as there's no reason for him to think that what he's after has been found, we can hope he'll carry on trying. There are no plans to do anything with that room until the last stages of the renovation, so that gives us some time. We can still hope to catch him trying to break in.'

I took the little key out of my pocket and studied it. 'As long as that desk stays locked, no one knows what's in there, apart from you and me. If we keep quiet, and act surprised when the Franklins get someone in to open it up, no one will be any the wiser.'

'You're going to put that back in the clock?' Fin sounded dubious.

'No. There's some expert coming to look at that any day now. If a key turns up, someone's bound to start looking for a lock.' I looked around the sitting room. 'So I need a believable place to hide this, where I can just happen to find it if we need it to turn up.'

'About that.' Fin put her empty mug on the coffee table. 'The "we" business, I mean. That's what I came to tell you. I've got to go home this weekend. I have to get back to work.'

'Oh.' I hadn't expected that. Then I realised I'd been a fool not to.

'Can you give me a lift to the Whittle and Dub? I need to check out and pay my bill.'

'Of course.' I told myself it was stupid to feel this disappointed. 'And a lift to the station?'

Fin shook her head. 'My sister's coming to pick me up. She drove here from Bristol, so we'll go home together tomorrow. I'll stay at the holiday let tonight, because everyone wants to hear about the nix, and Sineya, and everything else that's been going on.'

'Okay,' I said briskly.

She gave me an unfathomable look. 'It's not as if there's much more I can do here, except keep my mouth shut about what's in that desk.'

I couldn't help myself. 'You could tell me the best way to sort out the drainage between the lake and the river. Sineya said that needs doing, to clear the nix's presence from the water.'

'Not without a contract for my consultancy services,' Fin said with what sounded like genuine regret. 'My sister Blanche and I work together. She'd wring my neck if I committed the company to doing something like that for free.'

'We all have to make a living,' I agreed.

'But I will get in touch with the Franklins.' Fin stood up and took her coat off the back of the sofa. 'See if I can talk them into getting the work done properly. It does need sorting out, regardless.'

'Let's hope so.' I hoped that would happen before my contract here was up.

'Let's hope the police catch Aiden, and quickly, before there's any more trouble,' Fin said fervently as we headed for the door.

I took the route along the lane towards the pub, and we both looked at the caravan as we passed it.

'That's new,' Fin remarked.

There was a bright yellow sign in the end window saying 'POLICE AWARE' in bold black letters.

'Let's hope that means they're serious about finding the bastard.' I wondered what the police had made of Aiden's collection of grimoires. That was assuming the books had still been there when they'd searched the place.

There wasn't much traffic, so we soon reached the pub. I was expecting to find the car park empty, but it was full of cars. Not only cars. I was astonished to see Rufus Stanlake there, looking more cheerful than I could recall seeing him. He was with around ten other men. They were all holding solid-looking sticks, deep in conversation.

'Morris dancing,' Fin said with delight. 'Rehearsing for May Day, I suppose. It's the bank holiday next weekend, isn't it? Okay, thanks for the lift. I'll be in touch.'

She got out of the Landy before I could reply. I watched the morris dancers for a little while and decided anyone telling Rufus that was a camp hobby was taking his life in his hands. The smack of those sticks was loud enough through the Landy's closed window. Then I drove back to Brightwell.

I went to The Boar's Head for lunch, and rang my dad to tell him how we'd dealt with the nix. Then I did some shopping. After that, I spent the day looking around the house for the best place to hide the roll-top desk key.

I kept hearing sounds like soft footsteps following me. Finally I turned round and called out, even though I couldn't see anything, 'Everard Sutton? I found the key in the clock. Thank you for that.'

The house stayed still and silent. I thought I sensed some satisfaction though. Of course, that could have been my imagination.

I definitely sensed contentment when I went for a walk through the woods on Sunday. I didn't see Sineya or the Green Man, but I didn't need them to tell me the blight here was fading.

I did meet Martha Delly. She was walking back down the light from the lake. For an old woman not long out of hospital, she was looking extremely well.

She greeted me with a broad smile. 'Feel that, my duck? Tis the season turning, and Brightwell's luck with it.'

'I'll take your word for that.' I grinned.

We walked back to the lane together. As we passed St Diuma's, we saw that the church door was open.

'Ah, now you come along with me, lad.' Martha was through the lych-gate and heading up the path before I could answer.

The ladies who'd come to dust and polish for next weekend's May Day service were perfectly happy for us to have a look around while they worked. I wished there was a mobile signal here, because I'd have rung Fin at once.

The medieval wall paintings were impressive. A gruesomely wounded Christ was supervising the Last Judgement on the arch above the altar. The blue-robed figure weeping at his right hand could only be the Virgin Mary, and even I could spot St Peter with his keys on the other side. Beyond that, I couldn't guess which faded saints were shepherding the naked blessed away towards some heaven where the paint had peeled and flaked. Comic-book devils on the other side were still vividly red as they used little tridents to shove sinners into what looked like a whale's mouth.

'We got Saint Michael weighing souls back here.' Martha stood by the font.

I contemplated the stern-faced saint, standing more than life-size on the west wall. He brandished a mighty sword over his head and held a set of tilted scales in the other. He wasn't wearing armour though, at least it didn't look like it to me. As far as I was concerned, he was covered in feathers, and his angel's wings looked pretty swan-like. I got my phone out of my pocket.

'No photos, if you don't mind,' one of the church ladies said, with the sort of politeness you don't argue with.

'There are postcards,' another one said helpfully.

'Right, thanks.' I took a couple, and dropped a two-pound coin into the honesty box.

I'd send one to Dad, and we'd see what Mum made of it. I'd send the other one to Fin. That would give me an excuse to ring and ask for her address.

I got an early night. Monday was another working day. Catching that bastard Aiden wasn't the only unfinished business around here.

Chapter Twenty-Three

We put in a solid week's work without any distractions, the Kembles and the Coateses and me. The en-suite bathroom fittings arrived and I lent a hand wherever I could be useful plumbing in toilets, basins and shower trays. The central heating engineers were making good progress, and the basement kitchen and cellars would soon be ready for the specialist fitters to come in. Everything was well on schedule. Even the gaffer was smiling as he told everyone they had earned the bank holiday weekend off.

'You around tomorrow?' Mark Coates paused as we met outside the oak parlour. 'Coming into town?'

'Definitely.' I had been planning on going back to Blithehurst, but when I'd rung Eleanor she had said that wasn't a good idea. Sineya hadn't come back yet, and the old dryad, Frai, was furious with me. I could have gone home, but Dad and I had agreed we should give Mum a little bit longer to get over her irritation at the news that I had taken on the nix after everything she'd said.

Mark grinned. 'Should be a good day.'

'Should be,' I agreed.

For the past week, posters had appeared everywhere in and around Bourton advertising the May Fair. Jude Oxway had one on the bookshop window, and there was even one pasted onto the bus shelter in the Broad.

'I'd walk in, if I were you,' Mark warned. 'The parking's always insane.'

He wasn't wrong. After a lie-in on Saturday morning and a leisurely fry-up, I locked up the house and the garage yard gate and walked down the lane to the Broad to find the grass there was already packed tight with cars. More were parked along the verge that ran alongside the neglected allotments.

When I reached the junction, there was a hell of a queue at the traffic lights. The fair seemed to be drawing everyone from miles around. As I walked across the bridge, I found that Market Hill was closed to traffic and the cars coming into Bourton over the river were being diverted along Church Lane, past the bookshop. Yellow signs directed people to the supermarkets and other car parks at the top of the hill. Police officers in hi-vis vests were making sure no opportunists tried to ignore the no-parking cones and leave their cars somewhere closer.

On the opposite side of the road, beyond the bridge, the meadow was full of massive fairground rides surrounded by sideshows. All the showmen's lorries and trailers were lined up beyond them. The generators and loudspeakers were silent for now, as nothing was open for business as yet.

As I looked up the hill, past the war memorial, I saw that the market hall itself and the area around it were packed with stalls. This wasn't the usual farmers' market crowd and the other weekly traders. There were food stalls and craft stalls and local charities eager to attract passers-by.

I'd walked about halfway up the hill when the people ahead started drawing back against the curb stones. Checking the time on my phone, I realised the May Queen's Parade must be approaching. The day's schedule was on all the posters.

As the crowd parted and I retreated with everyone else, I saw the morris dancers leading the procession. This wasn't white-clad hanky-waving. They brandished the sticks I'd seen them with in the Whittle and Dub car park, clashing them together to cheers from the crowd.

The dancers wore low-crowned black hats that bristled with pheasant feathers glittering in the sunshine. What might once have been ordinary black suit jackets had long streamers of black and green cloth dangling from the shoulders. I tried to see if Rufus was one of them, but they wore green and black face paint in stripes and squares, so it was impossible to see who was who.

Then I did see someone I recognised. Someone wholly unexpected. As one of the dancers on the far side spun around, I saw the Green Man looking at me. I blinked, startled, and as the line of stick-wielding men turned again, the Green Man was gone. In the next breath though, I saw that the Hunter was with them as well. He was dressed like all the rest, but bare-headed apart from his antlers. Like the Green Man, he looked straight at me. In the next instant he had vanished, as the morris dancers went on their way down the hill, followed by their band. One woman was playing a fiddle and another had a flute to accompany the grey-bearded bloke with the accordion.

Children followed in primary school contingents wearing red, blue and bottle green sweatshirts. They carried garlands made from PE hoops decorated with tissue paper flowers. Cubs and Brownies, Scouts and Guides followed on with more rustic offerings of woven twigs thick with green leaves and bright with flowers culled from their parents' gardens.

Cheerful teachers and Scout leaders patrolled the gap between the kids and the crowds, rattling collecting tins. I dug into my pocket for a handful of change as a brass band arrived. They were all ages, from teens to retirees. Flag-bearers followed with the colours of the scouting troops, the British Legion, the Rotary Club and others that I didn't recognise.

Cheers greeted the May Queen's arrival. She was a pretty blonde girl looking almost bridal in a long white dress. Her lace veil was held on by a circlet of spring flowers. Six girls in green dresses walked proudly behind her, smiling and waving their woodland posies at family and friends. I recognised Izzy Oxway and Tasha Franklin.

The Queen's escort was a tall lad who was scarlet-faced with either terminal embarrassment or incipient heatstroke. It was now nearly noon on an unseasonably hot day, and he was wearing a high-collared shirt and a black tail coat crossed with a sash of bright green silk. His hat was similar to the ones the morris dancers wore, though it was ringed with sprays of fresh green leaves instead of feathers. Hopefully he wouldn't get too much teasing from his mates. Probably not as long as he was carrying that rough cudgel of age-darkened wood. I wondered where that had come from.

Looking down the hill, I saw the town band heading for music stands and chairs set up just beyond the market hall, in the space before the war memorial. What must be the secondary school choir drew up in tidily rehearsed lines.

Someone plucked at my elbow. I looked around to see Petra Oxway smiling at me. 'You're an easy man to spot in a crowd. Having fun?'

I grinned back at her. 'Where's the maypole?'

'Fallen victim to Health and Safety,' Petra said with what looked like genuine regret. 'We always used to have one. Half the people in this crowd probably took their turn dancing around it when they were still at school.'

I guessed she had been one of them. 'The morris dancers weren't what I expected,' I remarked.

'It's a sweeps' morris. That's far more of a tradition towards the Welsh borders or further north into the Midlands. No one knows why Bourton doesn't have a Cotswold morris side. You know, the ones that dress in white.' She shrugged. 'But there have always been chimney sweeps involved in morris dancing, and given the name of the town, maybe that's the answer.'

'Let me guess, you did a feature on it once?' I smiled to take any sting out of my words.

She nodded, good-humoured. 'When they decided to change their make-up. It used to be plain black, but that's problematic to say the very least these days. Of course, the usual suspects were outraged by political correctness gone mad, so I got some good quotes to put up against the people saying folk traditions have always been a living art form, changing with the times.'

I realised the crowd was shifting around us. About half were heading down the hill to hear the choir sing. The others were heading for the market stalls or towards the pubs and tea shops.

'Do you fancy a sandwich or some chips?' Petra asked. 'I've been up since sparrow fart, getting everyone's names and ages to go with the photos for the paper. I'm starving.'

'I could do with a drink.' It really was a hot day, and I was wearing a rugby shirt as I still needed to cover the nix's bite marks on my arms.

'The Sundial?' She pointed at an ancient pub on the corner where a side road joined Market Hill.

'Lead on.' I hadn't been in there before, but that didn't matter.

As we crossed the road, I saw that the black-and-green-faced morris dancers had already claimed the outside benches, laying their feathered hats and sticks on the tables. I looked for Rufus but none of them had red hair. I stepped aside to let the accordion player negotiate the steps down from the door with a tray full of pints of beer.

'Dan!' I looked around to see Rufus hurrying towards me, still wearing his jacket and that ferocious make-up. 'Thank fuck I've found you. He's here.'

'Who?' Petra had realised I wasn't following her and turned back to see what was going on.

'Aiden Whoever-he-is.' Rufus barely spared her a glance. 'He was just here, heading down the hill. He's got that kid Oliver with him, and Nathan Ditchfield.'

'You see if you can find them,' Petra said at once. 'I'll go up to the police command caravan and let the officer in charge know what's up. I'll tell them to look out for you two while they're looking for Aiden.'

She had already got her phone out of her pocket. The prospect of an arrest and the story she could write about it clearly interested her far more than lunch.

'Okay.' I nodded to Rufus. 'You take that side of the street, and I'll take this one.'

We made our way through the crowd, searching for those unwelcome, familiar faces. There are times when my height's inconvenient, but this wasn't one of them. I could get a good look at the people around me, as well as being able to pick out Rufus on the other pavement. He was certainly distinctive in his black jacket and with his red hair.

A few moments later, my phone buzzed in my pocket. It was Rufus. 'By the cookware shop.'

It wasn't easy to hear him with loud conversations all around me, but sending texts would mean looking away from our quarry.

'I see them.'

Aiden was wearing that greatcoat despite the warmth, and the boys were both in army-surplus jackets. They were threading their way between families and other groups of people. There was something odd about the way they moved though. It took me a moment to realise no one was looking at them, and that was strange considering what they were wearing. Everyone else was enjoying the spring sunshine in T-shirts and light cotton tops. As I watched them, I saw something else. People weren't making any eye contact with them, like they were doing with everyone else to avoid getting in each other's way. It really looked as if no one could even see Aiden and his minions.

No one except me and Rufus. If this was some magician's spell, I guessed the Green Man and the Hunter weren't putting up with that. They were still moving more easily through the dense crowd than we were though. With all the people we had to get around, we barely kept pace.

We followed them towards the river, down as far as the market hall. Then our quarry ducked into the shadows under the ancient building. I phoned Rufus.

'I can't see them.'

'Me neither. Fuck.'

'What do we do?'

'Keep going.' Rufus's voice was tight with frustration. 'Maybe they're heading for the fair.'

'I'll take a look. Maybe you can see them if you go up into the churchyard?' That was high enough to give him a decent vantage point.

'Okay.'

Now that the parade and the singing were over, the fair had started up. I could hear the dull thud of generators beneath raucous pop music and energetic announcements blaring from loudspeakers. Among the tantalising scents of fried onions and hotdogs coming from the catering wagons, I tasted sickly diesel exhaust in the back of my throat.

I took a moment to buy a bottle of Coke, and drank it in a couple of swallows as I started a systematic search of the fairground. It wasn't easy with so many people queueing for the big rides or throwing hoops or wooden balls to win a box of sweets or a giant teddy. I persevered, and worked my way down to the far end and back again. I had just about decided that the bastards weren't here when I heard someone call my name.

'Daniel!'

Nicki and Ed Franklin were over by a candyfloss stall. Nicki was waving to me as she handed Hannah a sticky pink clump on a stick. Ed was giving Tasha and Josh a couple of notes each. As I went over, the older kids were making plans.

'Fun house or the dodgems?' Tasha was still wearing her long green dress, but that clearly wasn't going to slow her down.

Josh scorned such tame suggestions. 'The Twister.'

He looked more cheerful than I could recall seeing him, though I supposed that was hardly surprising. I certainly didn't want to ruin his day by telling him Aiden was back.

'Mummy, can we go on the gallopers?' Hannah asked through a mouthful of candyfloss.

'What about you?' Ed looked at me. 'Fancy a quick pint while everyone else spends my money?'

I hesitated, searching for an excuse. Then I realised if I got Ed alone, I could warn him to keep his eyes open. He wouldn't want any of the three we were after getting anywhere near his family. If he saw them, he could ring the police as well.

'The Boar's Head?' I suggested. I'd explain what was going on before we got there. With any luck, Rufus would call me with a sighting.

As we headed for the road, two things happened. I saw the Hunter standing on the churchyard wall, glaring down at me. Then the din from the fairground momentarily yielded to sirens. A police car came down Church Lane as fast as it could make its way through the wandering crowds. It didn't even wait for the red lights as it crossed the river, pausing on the crest of the bridge until whatever traffic was coming the other way hastily reversed.

'What's going on?' Ed wondered, concerned.

'No clue.' That was true, though I felt a chill of certainty that Aiden was responsible for whatever it was.

Rufus appeared, forcing his way towards us through the avidly gawking crowd. 'Something's kicking off in the Broad.'

'Looks like it.' If Ed said anything else, his words were lost beneath another siren.

'That's a fire engine.' Rufus turned to look as the big red vehicle came into view by Shayler's.

'What the hell's happening?' Ed's voice tightened with apprehension.

'We should get back to Brightwell.' Rufus looked at me.

I nodded. 'Come on.'

We were all being jostled as more people left the fair to see what there was to see.

'I need to find Nicki and the kids.' Ed wasn't going to be argued with.

I wasn't about to try. 'You go on. We'll ring you as soon as we know what's going on.'

He headed for the carousel with its painted horses. Rufus and I went with the crowd of people moving towards the bridge. Everyone leaving the fair met those who'd come sauntering down the hill to see what was going on. An influx of uniformed coppers were shifting the barricades that had previously closed off the road.

A man trying to slip past an officer was swiftly deterred. His arm-waving protests broke off when the policewoman pointed to a second fire engine now coming straight down the hill towards the bridge. Everyone hastily got out of its way.

'Smoke.' Rufus pointed.

There were ancient willow trees along this bank of the river and more on the far side, screening the Broad's unkempt allotments. A black cloud was rising above their fresh green withies.

Plenty of people were still enjoying the fair, and the May Day Market on the hill, but disquiet was spreading. Over by the market hall, some jostling had escalated into a shoving and shouting match. Two coppers hurried to separate the combatants.

'We have to get back.' I wondered how the hell we were going to do that.

No cars were being allowed to cross the bridge. Instead they were being directed to circle around the war memorial and head back up Church Lane.

'Right.' Rufus clearly had a plan. He was scanning the police who were now making a firm cordon along the barriers. 'There's Andy Lybrook. Come on.'

I followed him through the crowd, using my size to get through without apology. I could taste smoke on the air.

'Andy!' Rufus reached the barricade a couple of strides ahead of me. I couldn't hear what he was saying to the copper he knew, but the constable soon nodded and beckoned to a colleague. Stepping away from the barrier once his position was filled, the cop spoke into the radio clipped to his shoulder.

He paused and spoke again, nodding. 'Yes, the key holder.'

I caught that much of his reply. I tapped Rufus on the shoulder. 'What's he talking about? Have the alarms at the house gone off?'

'No, but I told him there's only Bill and Martha over there, and he knows that bastard Aiden is somewhere around.'

I guessed we had Petra Oxway to thank for that. Then I wondered what the cops were going to do about it, when they had their hands full with crowd control. My conviction that Aiden was somehow behind this grew even stronger.

A moment later, Andy Lybrook beckoned to Rufus. 'Okay, come on through, both of you.'

Two other cops in hi-vis helped separate the barricade while still preventing anyone else from getting into the road. Andy clapped Rufus on the shoulder. 'You're clear to go.'

'Hang on,' one of the other constables said sharply.

A siren yelped beyond the market hall. An ambulance was making its way down the hill. Andy's radio crackled and he ducked aside to answer it.

'Churchyard.' Rufus pointed, and sprinted to get across the road before the ambulance arrived.

I ran after him, not wasting time on questions. Rufus headed up the steps to St Michael's. I caught up, and we hurried along the path between the headstones. His Harley Davidson was chained to the railings beside a narrow gate at the far end of the churchyard.

Rufus unclipped his helmet from however it was secured by the seat and handed me a second one. 'Good thing I gave Neil a lift this morning.'

I was just glad to find the helmet fitted. 'I'm not used to bikes,' I warned.

It's not that I don't like motorbikes in theory, but I like the idea of solid steel panels and airbags between me and the wankers on the road a whole lot more.

'Hang on, and lean into the corners with me.' Rufus unlocked the chain, got on the bike and started the engine.

I got on behind him and took a firm hold of his waist. I wasn't at all keen on this idea, but I didn't see we had much choice. At least I was tall enough to see over Rufus's shoulder as he expertly manoeuvred the bike down the sloping path from the gate to Church Lane.

As we hit the tarmac, he sped up. When we reached the junction, Andy Lybrook waved us on and across the river. As we reached the crest of the bridge, I saw two police cars parked a good way further up the road. The officers were turning cars back, and there was a lengthy line of stationary traffic stretching back around Brightwell's woods.

If the tailback started any closer to the lights, it would block the emergency vehicles going down the lane to the Broad. As Rufus took the turn, I saw that the end house of the terrace curving round the green was well alight. One of the cars parked by the bus shelter was also being consumed by flames. Firefighters were using hoses and foam to contain both blazes while police were holding the residents back on the far side of the grass. Drunk, stupid or both, plenty of the Broad's inhabitants seemed to want to argue the point.

Rufus accelerated. We rounded the bend and left the uproar behind.

'Wait!'

But Rufus couldn't hear me. He didn't stop until we reached Brightwell's entrance.

I got off the bike and pulled off the helmet as fast as I could. 'I saw him – Aiden. He had that girl with him, Jade.' He'd been dragging her towards the woods by one arm. I'd only caught a glimpse of her face, but she looked as if she was crying.

'Shit. Where?' Rufus demanded.

'That rough pasture on the slope below the trees, just before we got to your house.'

'Was there any sign of the boys?'

'Not that I could see.'

'Where have those little shits got to?' Rufus thought for a moment. 'You check on things here. I'll go and tell Bill and

Martha to lock their doors, and I'll ring the cops and let them know we've seen him.'

I nodded. 'Then ring me.'

'Will do.' He spun the Harley around and headed back up the lane.

I stood between the holly trees and felt the Green Man's presence as their branches rattled on either side of me. Ahead, the house looked as peaceful as ever.

I took the keys out of my pocket, alert for any hint of movement from either side as I approached the steps. If the bastards were going to try to rush me, they could come from the garage yard or up from the basement steps, or around the corner, under the walnut parlour windows. Three to one wasn't good odds if they trapped me on the steps.

Nothing happened. I got to the porch, opened up, got inside and relocked the door. By the time I switched off the alarm, my pulse was racing and I was breathing hard.

I forced myself to walk slowly as I made a circuit of the ground floor. I checked every window. All was secure, and the silent house was serene. When I returned to the oak parlour, I was breathing more evenly again.

I didn't have long to wait before Rufus rang. I could hear him scowling.

'No sign of the bastards anywhere, but Bill and Martha are fine. They've been watching some old musical. I told them to lock up, stay in and ring 999 if they see or hear anything.'

'That sounds good to me.'

'I'm going to ring the cops and see what they want us to do.'

'Call me back and let me know. I'll ring Ed Franklin and tell him everything's okay here.

I put the handset down and went to find Nicki's phone list to get Ed's mobile number. Once I had it, I picked up the phone and began hitting buttons. I was halfway through the number when the confident dial tone went silent.

I looked at the phone. I hit the bar on the old-fashioned cradle as I put the handset to my ear. Nothing. I hit the bar again. Still nothing.

The phone line was completely dead.

Chapter Twenty-Four

The long case clock in the great hall chimed a single, lingering stroke. I didn't bother going to see if the pendulum had started swinging. Everard Sutton was warning me of trouble to come. To be honest, I could have worked that out for myself.

I thumped the panel to open the hidden cupboard and checked the alarm control box. That was dead too. Okay, there had to be some fail-safe system that would let the security company know that had happened. The bank holiday weekend shouldn't make any difference. So the first thing the security company would do was ring the house. When they got no answer, they would ring the Franklins. But David was in London, and Nicki and Ed weren't at Ashgrove today.

Somebody was sure to have their mobile numbers, but who knew how soon a call would reach them? Then Ed would have to negotiate the police road block as well as the chaos in the Broad. Either that, or he'd have to take the long way round, which would be clogged with backed-up traffic. Meantime, if someone was breaking in here, there'd be no loud alarms to alert Rufus or the Dellys that something was up.

Scratch that. When somebody broke in. As I closed the alarm cupboard, movement outside on the steps caught my eye. Before I could see who was there, they were gone. I heard footsteps on the gravel. At exactly the same time, there was a rattle at the basement kitchen door. That couldn't be the same person. They were testing both ways into the house.

I backed away down the corridor, into the shadows beyond the servants' stair. If they did get in through the basement, I didn't want anyone coming up behind me. Then I wondered if they knew I was in here. If so, did they know

I was on my own? Had Aiden been out there, somewhere, watching and waiting, until I got back?

If he had been, what difference did that make? He must know someone was coming. Like me, he had no way to know how soon they might arrive. So whatever he was going to do, he was going to do it fast.

I thought about going around the house to close the ground-floor shutters. Doing that risked showing anyone watching from outside what room I was in. They could redouble their efforts to break into a room where I wasn't. Besides, how much good would breaking a window do them? They could smash the leaded glass, but the stone mullions were narrow and awkwardly high up, compared to the ground level outside.

Of course, there were ladders and tools in Bill Delly's store, if they broke into that. The skip in the garage yard was half full as well, and probably offered stuff they could use. I could hope for the best, but I'd better plan for the worst.

Their best bet was getting in through one of the two doors. If I couldn't stop them doing that, I could certainly slow them down once they were in the house. I locked the housekeeper's sitting room and the door to the drawing room. Moving quickly, I secured the kitchenette and the oak parlour. I crossed the great hall, staying close to the inner wall, and locked the walnut parlour door. Even if they knew about the sewing room, if they knew about the desk with its gruesome secrets, they'd have to break down two doors to get to it.

I was about to head past the grand staircase to lock the great parlour door when I heard the unmistakable ring of steel on stone. Not close though. I took a few steps back towards the great hall and paused to listen as the sound rang out again. It wasn't coming from outside, on the steps to the porch. It took me a moment to realise the noise was coming up the servants' stair. Whether they'd come equipped or broken in to steal something from Bill Delly's storeroom, someone was using a crowbar, or something like it, on the basement entrance.

I went and locked the great parlour door anyway. Once I'd done that, I thought about heading up the grand staircase. There wasn't much point in me hiding in one of the bedrooms, but the bastards breaking in wouldn't know that. Searching every room for me would take up more time, and that could only help me. If I went straight to the top floor, I could lock the long gallery to protect the books in there. Then I could hide in the lumber room, where the access to the roof space was. That door was very well hidden in the panelling. Easily overlooked, if you didn't know it was there.

Right, and there was no knowing how much damage these bastards would do while I was cowering in a cupboard like some useless shithead. I remembered the power tools that the Coateses and the Kembles would have left in the old servants' hall. The tossers could use those on more than the interior doors or the ancient wooden panelling. I didn't fancy being caught like a rat in a trap facing three pricks holding cordless drills.

As I came back to the great hall, I froze. I could see someone in the corridor, beyond the carved oak screen. How the fuck had they got in? Then I realised the sounds of hammering were still coming up from the basement.

I felt gooseflesh rise on my forearms, despite my rugby shirt. It was cool inside the old stone house compared to the hot day outside, but this was different. Now I really was freezing, as if I'd stepped outside in midwinter. I also realised that the figure in the corridor was dressed like some actor in a TV Dickens adaptation. I could see straight through him as he stepped into a shaft of sun sparkling with dust motes where the light fell through a window on the stairs.

The ghost headed down to the basement. I had no idea what he could possibly do if the bastards down there got in, but I was going to have to leave him to it. Something had smashed the glass in the bay window at the end of the dais.

Before I could react, Jade Taysel scrambled through the ragged shards and torn leading. The stone mullions might be narrow, but she was skinny enough to get through them in jeans and a T-shirt. She jumped down from the window seat and smiled spitefully at me. Blood was trickling from deep scratches on her scrawny arms. She didn't care, triumphant.

I seriously thought about picking her up and shoving her straight back out through the broken window. She was in no fit state to fight back, gaunt and hollow-eyed with lack of sleep or something worse. Wherever these wankers had been hiding out for the past week and a half, she was as filthy as someone who'd been sleeping rough.

I took a step forward. So did Jade, and she produced a knife. Not the long, wicked thing that Aiden carried, but a chunky DIY utility knife with a retractable blade. It looked new. I had a couple of those in my toolboxes and I knew exactly how sharp they were, fresh out of the packet.

That electrician who'd told me about breaking bottles reckoned it was easy enough to get a blade off someone if you knew what you were doing. I reckoned Jade didn't need to know anything much to do me some serious damage if I got too close. Besides, what did that tosser know? He had ragged scars at both corners of his mouth. One of the bricklayers told me that 'Glasgow smile' meant he'd come off very second best in a knife fight.

I backed off a step. Jade stayed where she was.

Aiden shouted from somewhere outside the broken window. 'Daniel!'

I said nothing.

'Daniel!' he called again.

'He's here!' Jade yelled, gloating. 'He's got the keys in his hand.'

Unfortunately that was true. I wished I'd shoved them into a pocket, so I could deny I had them on me. That would have helped spin things out a bit longer.

'Give the keys to Jade, Daniel,' Aiden ordered, 'so she can unlock the door.'

Fuck that noise, I didn't say. As long as I didn't reply, the better the chances were that he'd be drawn into making more and more threats and demands. He was welcome to spend all the time he wanted doing that. Every minute he wasted brought me a minute closer to the Franklins or Rufus arriving.

'Let us in.' Now he sounded annoyed.

No, he wasn't only annoyed. I realised Aiden was expecting to be obeyed. I wondered if he thought he was using some sort of magic, or if he thought the nix was still here to help him. Either way, I didn't care. Whether it was thanks to my mother's blood or the fact that the nix was dead, his voice had no effect on me.

Of course, his so-called magic might just be so much bollocks, but I couldn't help remembering the way he and those lads had slid through the crowd. I'd be a fool to underestimate him.

'Jade!'

She flinched at his anger. 'He's just standing here.'

'Let us in, Daniel,' Aiden demanded again. 'You know we'll get in there sooner or later.'

Later was absolutely fine with me. Though I could hear splintering sounds coming up from the basement. Whoever was working on that door was making progress.

'Those books and everything with them belong to me. Let us in, let us take what's mine, and we'll go.' Now he was angry with me. 'Or do you want us to trash the place as well as beating the shit out of you?'

I didn't answer. I reckoned that was a bluff. At least the threat about trashing the house was. As soon as they had what they wanted, they'd be gone as fast as they could. Of course, if they still didn't know where the old books and the Hand of Glory were, they could make a hell of a mess while they were looking.

As far as beating the shit out of me, Aiden was welcome to try. I outweighed him by a fair margin, and I had a longer reach. Though I reminded myself that whoever was trying to break in through the basement would surely back him up. Most likely by trying to stab me in the back with whatever they were using on the kitchen door.

'Jade!' Aiden's voice cracked. He was losing his temper. 'Get those keys off him.'

Whatever hold the bastard had over the girl was as strong as ever. She began walking towards me, swiping the knife from side to side in front of her.

Now I had a problem. I had no doubt that I could deck her with one punch. I wasn't at all sure how much damage I could end up doing to her. I was a foot taller than Jade and probably weighed twice as much.

People getting knocked out and waking up again perfectly fine is another of those Hollywood fantasies. There are horribly good reasons why tabloid headlines and documentaries about 'One-Punch Killers' keep coming back around. I didn't want the next one to be me.

I backed off and shoved the keys deep into my pocket, so that I had both hands free. One for her throat and one for her knife hand, if she really did try to rush me.

Jade kept coming. Her grin widened. She really thought I was scared of her. Poor little cow. She was utterly pathetic, in the truest sense of the word. Aiden needed to answer for what he'd done to her.

I kept moving backwards, towards the grand staircase. I didn't look at the walnut parlour door, and neither did Jade. If Aiden knew where his treasures were hidden, I guessed he hadn't told her.

Maybe the time had come for me to leg it up the stairs. I could take them two or three at a time, and I was physically fit. Jade was skin and bone, and she looked wrecked by drink and drugs. I'd soon outpace her.

I could easily get to the hidden storeroom. When the others got in, they would have no idea where I'd gone. Though if we started playing hide and seek, I would have no way to know if Aiden had gone straight after the things he'd come for. I really didn't want him to have them, and not just because I like to win. Quite apart from the fact that those valuable books belonged to the Franklins, I was sure the thieving bastard had some plan to use the Hand of Glory for no good.

I heard the basement door break open with a tearing sound of splintering wood. Whoever had done that cheered at their own success. Two voices, as far as I could make out. Footsteps thudded on the servants' stair. A breath later, yells of shock echoed through the house. Someone, or maybe both of them, fell back down the stairs with a tumbling crash. A shriek of agony was followed by muffled sobbing.

'Jade! What the fuck's going on?'

She was standing still and looking towards the oak screen, distracted by whatever calamity was going on over there. Aiden's voice snapped her out of that. She ran at me, waving the stubby knife wildly. I braced myself to try and grab her arms without breaking too many bones or getting cut too badly. But I wouldn't lose any sleep if it took me breaking her wrist to get that knife off her.

Before she reached me, we both heard barking outside. Jade skidded to a halt on the floorboards. I don't know what she felt, but I could sense a deeper, darker note beneath Bess's furious barking.

Rufus was out there. I heard him shouting something, mostly obscenities. We both heard running feet on the gravel. Jade caught me by surprise, turning and running to the bay window.

'Aiden!' she screamed.

I moved as fast as I could, but I wasn't quick enough. She scrambled up onto the window seat, climbed out through the mullions and jumped.

I ran up to the window to see what had happened. I hoped she'd broken an ankle, or even a leg. That would keep her out of that bastard's clutches. With any luck, ending up in hospital would get her into the hands of people who could help sort out her dreadful life.

No such luck. Being skinny and lightweight has its advantages. I saw she had landed on her hands and feet. She sprang up and ran away around the side of the house, under the walnut parlour windows. I had no idea which way Aiden had gone.

'Dan!' Rufus was running down from the entrance. Bess was at his side. They weren't alone. I could see blue lights coming down the lane.

'Basement!' I yelled, sticking my head out through the broken window.

Rufus headed straight for the kitchen door. I ran the length of the great hall and then slowed, to go more cautiously down the servants' stair.

I found Nathan and the scrawny lad, Oliver, in a heap at the bottom of the wooden steps. Nathan was panting with pain, ashen-faced and hugging a broken arm. Oliver was unconscious with a bleeding gash splitting one eyebrow. I guessed he had fallen and hit his head.

Rufus came in through the old kitchen and took in the scene. He'd shed his morris jacket and wiped off some of his face paint, but not all. He looked as if he was wearing camouflage to go with his olive-green T-shirt. He looked like a hunter.

'Two down, two to go,' he said with satisfaction.

'Did you see which way they went?'

'Around the back. Bess will find them.' He had no doubt of that.

Two coppers came in through the kitchen. It was the pair I'd met before.

'Dearie me.' Sergeant Smith nodded at his constable. 'Get on to Control, Rich, and let them know we need an ambulance.'

I heard the shuck baying outside. No one else reacted, so I guessed I was the only one. Apart from Bess, that is. The Retriever looked towards the door, her ears pricked, and made an impatient noise.

Rufus glanced at the sergeant, as the other cop was busy on his radio. 'If we get after him, the dog can track him.'

'It was the man you've been looking for,' I said urgently. 'The one who calls himself Aiden. The one who left Tyler to drown.'

'He's got that girl with him, Jade Taysel.' Rufus turned to go.

'I think we had better wait,' the sergeant said firmly. 'We can get the dog unit here, and enough manpower for a proper search.'

Rufus glared, frustrated. 'He'll get away.'

The copper was unmoved. 'We've already got this pair heading for hospital. Let's not make any more work for the nurses today. They've already got enough to deal with.'

Movement on the stairs snagged my attention. I looked up and felt an arctic shiver run down my spine like ice water. Mary Anne Sutton was standing there. It could only be her, wearing a pale gown stiff with embroidery, and with a tall collar of linen and lace framing her face.

She stared straight at me, and I didn't need Constance Sutton's planchette or a ouija board to get the ghost's message. If I didn't rescue that abused girl, Mary Anne would haunt me to the end of my days.

Nathan whimpered, still hugging his broken arm. I glanced at him, along with everyone else. Only I realised from his fixed look of terror that he could see the ghost as well. His eyes flicked to me with desperate appeal. I answered with the slightest of shrugs. He'd made his choices, and that meant facing whatever consequences Mary Anne and Everard had planned for him.

I looked back, held Mary Anne's gaze and hoped she understood that I planned to do whatever I could for Jade. The ghost nodded, turned and went up the stairs. As she did, she looked back to make sure I was following. The chill around me was making my teeth ache, while Sergeant Smith took his hat off to wipe sweat from his forehead.

'I should unlock the main door.' I took the keys out of my pocket. 'Mr Franklin must be on his way.

Sergeant Smith nodded. 'Good idea.'

I caught Rufus's eye. 'Let's see how much damage they did to the bay window.'

He nodded and whistled to Bess. 'Come on, girl.'

They followed me up the servants' stair. I headed straight for the front door, unlocked it and left the keys in the lock as

I opened it. The house would be secure enough while it was full of coppers. If needs be, I'd apologise to Ed Franklin later.

Rufus followed me out onto the steps. He crouched down, resting his hand on Bess's head.

'Seek!'

The dog shot off, heading for the gardens at the back of the house. We had to run to keep up. She went straight across the lawn and jumped the iron fence. Rufus vaulted it like a gymnast, and I got over it quickly enough.

The woods cleared a path for us, I was sure of it. I also caught glimpses of another running figure away towards the river. Taller than me, broader in the shoulder and crowned with antlers. The Hunter had joined this pursuit. I could hear the shuck as well, in the trees between us and the road.

'Watch your step,' Rufus called out to me. 'The broken culverts.'

'Right,' I shouted back.

We still ran on as fast as we dared. I decided to trust that the trees would save me from a broken ankle. With my longer stride, I soon got ahead of Rufus.

The shuck's barking reached a new pitch of ferocity. I reached the clearing where the blackthorn had stood and skidded to a halt. The monstrous black hound was standing over a slumped figure. Bess was a few feet away, with her belly and muzzle pressed against the dead leaves. The Retriever was submissive rather than afraid, with her attention fixed on the shuck.

The slumped figure had bare, bloodied arms, and was so skinny that the fearsome beast could probably bite her in half with one snap of its drooling jaws. It was Jade, lying half on her side and half on her front. I wondered what the shuck was going to do to her.

Rufus appeared at my side. The shuck sprang away from the girl, twisting to bound deeper into the woods. Bess leaped to her feet. She wanted to follow, but Rufus was here, and he held the dog's allegiance.

'Shit.' Rufus was looking at Jade. There was no sign he had even seen the shuck.

We hurried over. I saw far more blood than those scratches on her arms could account for.

Rufus knelt down and gently pushed at her shoulder. As he rolled her slowly backwards, we both saw the ragged gash across her throat, oozing scarlet.

'Fuck,' Rufus said softly. 'Is she still breathing?'

I cupped a hand over her mouth and nose. 'Yes. Barely.'

He stripped off his T-shirt and looked at me. 'Can you—?'

'You carry her back. Let me get the fucker.'

I could see the Hunter standing where the path to the Lamp Acre came through the trees. He had his hands on his hips and was glaring at the pair of us. In the shadows beneath the trees, I could see that his eyes were blazing gold below ferocious brows. Somewhere close, the shuck was howling with blood-curdling menace.

Rufus looked down at Jade for a moment, then nodded. 'Help me get some pressure on that. Lift her up.'

I scooped up the girl's limp body, cradling her head like a baby's to avoid opening up that awful wound. Rufus twisted his shirt into a thick rope of cloth and wrapped it carefully around her neck.

'He can't have hit an artery,' he observed, 'or she'd already be dead.'

I still wondered if she'd survive, however fast Rufus got her to help. As I stood up, she seemed to weigh nothing at all.

He got to his feet and held out his arms to take her from me. 'Don't do anything stupid. Give it up if Bess loses his scent.'

'If I can't find him, I'll head back to the house.'

Rufus looked over at the Retriever. 'Bess! Seek!'

The dog bolted down the path and I sprinted after her. The Hunter was running ahead of me, and the shuck's howling grew louder.

We reached the edge of the trees. I couldn't see where the Hunter had gone, but Bess had stopped dead on the rutted track, halfway to the battered caravan. She was growling, with her hackles raised and her dark lips drawn back from long white teeth.

The shuck was growling too, and that was a thousand times more terrifying. Even in the daylight, its eyes glowed ominous red. Its body was a black shadow dense enough to defy the sun. It stalked slowly towards the caravan, stiff-legged and hunch-backed.

Whatever locks the police had used must have been ripped off earlier in the day. Aiden was standing in the open doorway. He had one hand braced on the door frame and his long knife held out in the other, as if that would ward off the shuck. I wished him the best of luck. The thing would probably use the blade as a toothpick.

As I walked closer, the breeze carried a waft of incense towards me. No, that wasn't incense drifting out of the caravan. It was something rank with dark intent. Something that had no place here.

Aiden's gaze cut to me. His eyes widened when he realised I could see the shuck. 'Call it off!'

That was so ridiculous that I laughed out loud. 'It doesn't answer to me.'

Of course, as soon as I said that, the shuck immediately stopped growling. It dropped to the ground and crouched, waiting obediently just like Bess.

'Who are you?' Aiden rasped.

I shrugged. 'The Green Man sent me to stop you, and to get rid of the nix.'

'Where has it gone? What did you do to it?'

Furious, he looked ready to use that knife on me. The steel was clotted with blood.

'That doesn't matter. It's gone for good, forever. You tried to murder Jade for no reason.'

I'd realised that had been his last desperate attempt to give the monster what it wanted, in return for whatever power it could give him.

'Who are you?' Now he was raging. If the shuck hadn't been there, he'd have attacked me.

Even with the beast so close, I could see he was weighing up his chances.

'Give it up,' I said sharply. 'Who do you want to answer to? The cops and the courts, or the powers you have profaned? Who do you think will be more merciful?'

Actually, I was convinced that the arcane and unseen would make him pay regardless. I just wanted him safely locked in a cell while he waited for their judgement.

'Fuck you!' he spat.

For a second, I thought he was coming for me. Instead, he grabbed at the door handle. As he fumbled for it, he dropped his knife onto the tussocky grass. He might have jumped down to get it back, but the shuck sprang forward. In the doorway, Aiden recoiled, falling backwards into the caravan. The door slammed shut.

The Hunter appeared beside me. He raised a hand and a wind sprang up at our backs. The blast was so strong that it made me stagger. The gale kept coming. It was hard enough to make the caravan rock so violently that I thought the whole thing was going to topple over.

It didn't, but there was a thud inside. I heard that ominous soft cough of something igniting, and an awful scream. Fists hammered on the inside of the door, but the Hunter kept his hand raised. The relentless wind held the door closed tight. The hammering slowed and stopped.

The blankets that covered the windows were burning now. The plastic frames were melting and the dirty paint was blistering. The whole caravan was alight within minutes, and the greedy roar of the flames drowned out any other possible sounds.

The heat was so intense that I couldn't have got close enough to attempt any sort of rescue even if I'd wanted to. I didn't want to. Aiden could have chosen to face human justice. He'd rejected that, and judgement had come for him.

The Hunter lowered his hand and the wind fell away. A thick column of black smoke rose into the clear spring sky. The Hunter vanished, and so did the shuck.

I walked over to Bess and sat on the grass beside her. I put an arm around the cowering dog's shoulders and hugged her close to reassure her. It wasn't long before we heard sirens. It wasn't as if the fire engines had far to come. Aiden had seen to that.

Chapter Twenty-Five

Brightwell House Hotel opened on schedule. I got the work I was contracted for done to spec, and Kemble and Coates finished off the rest, together with the specialist firms brought in for things like fitting the cold stores and cleaning the plasterwork ceilings and marble fireplaces.

One of those firms was Fin and her sister's consultancy. They got the job of sorting out the drainage between the lake and the river. We met up a couple of times, when I had to come down to Gloucester. I had to give evidence into the inquest into Aiden's death, and at the first hearings in the court cases that followed. It turned out that the bastard had indeed been involved with those local burglaries, along with some of Tyler Campden's relatives.

If there ever was any honour among thieves, that had gone out of the window once they realised Aiden had left Tyler to drown. They'd been looking for him to deliver their own justice, too irate to be discreet. That had given the police their opportunity to get the evidence they needed to unravel the gang. Of course, with Aiden dead, the thieves were blaming him for everything they could.

His fiery death prompted some lurid newspaper stories. Initially, I braced myself for another shower of shit from the tabloids, and wondered grimly how to stop nosy journalists bothering Martha and Bill, or Rufus. I needn't have worried. *The North Cotswold Mercury* had the story on their website the very next day, and set the tone by reminding everyone I'd dragged Tyler out of the lake before explaining how I'd foiled the attempted break-in at Brightwell. Beyond that, I barely got a mention as Petra detailed the dramatic sequence of arson and attempted murder. This story only needed one villain and that was most definitely Aiden.

So it was the Taysels, Asthalls, Hawlings, Foxhills, Campdens and Summerhills who ended up with journalists and news crews on their doorsteps. That kept the reporters fully occupied. All we saw was a photographer getting a few shots of the house from the lane, before heading in the direction of the burned-out caravan, presumably to get some pictures of that. The one optimistic junior reporter who did knock on Brightwell's door was sent briskly on his way by Geoff Kemble, clutching the name and number of David Franklin's solicitors in London, if he wanted a copy of the family's statement.

Once they heard what the kids' families had to say, the national papers were much more interested in wild speculation about witchcraft at work in the depths of the countryside. Squashing all that was probably one reason why the coroner sought an expert witness's opinion on exactly what had been going on. At the inquest, I thought the no-nonsense-looking woman with a mass of dark hair was someone's solicitor until she listed her qualifications and gave evidence. Dr Williams had an impressive academic CV and apparently ran a major annual conference on the occult.

Having reviewed the statements and the evidence, it was Dr Williams's considered opinion that Aiden had drawn vulnerable teenagers into following him by offering them a mishmash of Wicca, grimoire-based occultism, a bit of goddess worship and whatever quick talking he felt would impress them most at any given moment. Since they knew nothing about any of it, they would lap up whatever he told them.

She would not call Aiden an actual pagan, or a real occultist, since there was no evidence that he knew what he was doing, and good reason to think he didn't care. Though Dr Williams did allow that the dead man could be classed as a hereditary occultist, whatever that meant, if his descent from Mungo Peploe could be proved.

That question remained stubbornly unanswered, as far as the official record went. Even with his DNA from the knife that proved he'd attacked Jade, the police couldn't make a firm ID. No one knew his full name for certain. He'd given different people at least three surnames, and the passports and driving licences in the rented flat the cops traced were all forgeries.

Fin and I were convinced regardless. It turned out she knew Dr Williams, though she didn't say how, and I didn't ask. We went for a drink in a pub called The Fountain after the inquest, and Fin told her that Aiden had known there were grimoires and a Hand of Glory hidden at Brightwell. She also told her about the nix. Since Dr Williams clearly had no problem with any of that, I told her I'd seen Mungo Peploe's books in the caravan.

Dr Williams looked thoughtful, taking a moment to drink her wine. 'I don't think he knew what he was doing. He's obviously done some shit, met a supernatural being, was arrogant enough to think he could work with it, and then thought he could control it. What could possibly go wrong?'

We all knew the answer to that. Dr Williams clearly wasn't going to lose any sleep over the bastard's fate, and neither were we. Though it did occur to me as I drove back up the motorway that things could have turned out very differently if Aiden *had* known what he was doing.

The next time I saw Fin was when David and Ed Franklin invited me down to Brightwell for what they called a trial-run weekend. That was in mid-September, a fortnight before the hotel officially opened. I booked a long weekend off from work at Blithehurst and arrived early Friday afternoon. As I passed St Diuma's, a sign directed me past the holly trees to the guest parking in the garage yard. I walked through to the house with my bag and saw Petra and a shaven-headed photographer peering at the back of a camera. I guessed they were assessing some pictures he had taken of the frontage.

Petra waved and walked over to greet me with a reassuringly impersonal kiss on the cheek. Whatever she might have felt for me, she'd clearly got over it. From the thoughtful way the photographer was looking at me, I reckoned he was currently enjoying her company in bed.

'How are things with you?'

'Excellent.' Petra smiled with satisfaction. 'I'm moving to Leeds next month. Getting my by-line in the nationals with this has been my ticket out of here.' Her gesture took in Brightwell House and the spring's dramatic events.

'Congratulations.'

'I'll still see the court cases through for the *Mercury*,' she assured me. 'It looks like they'll go pretty easy on the boys, now it's apparent how deliberately Aiden groomed them. Social services are taking the lead with Courtney, Sophie and Leanne. They hadn't actually done much that could be classed as criminal.'

'What about Jade?' I asked, apprehensive.

Petra looked more serious. 'Apparently the reports on her are heart-breaking. I've heard she's being sent to a specialist juvenile offenders unit, where she should get the support she needs.'

'Let's hope so.' I meant it.

'Dan!' Ed Franklin appeared on the steps.

'I'll let you get on.' Petra went back to her photographer.

I went to shake Ed's hand. 'Good to see you.'

'Glad you could make it. Come in, come in. Leave your bag with reception and let me give you the tour.'

Reception turned out to be the oak parlour, where some furniture restorer had worked wonders with the kneehole desk, and with the oak gate-leg table. That was now displaying brochures for local tourist attractions.

Josh Franklin sat behind the desk with a laptop. He was wearing a white shirt and a green tie. 'Good afternoon, Mr Mackmain,' he said with a cheeky grin. 'Welcome to Brightwell House. I'll just need a few details to check you in.'

We went through the usual routine, and I signed the register while Ed waited by the door.

'Thank you, sir, and here's your key.' Josh took it from the drawer. 'You're in the Hazel Room, overlooking the gardens. I'll have your bag taken up.'

'Thank you.' I pocketed the key.

'You should give him a job,' I commented as I joined Ed in the corridor.

'Already done,' he said as we walked through the great hall. That had been transformed with cosy clusters of armchairs, sofas and low tables. 'For an early gap year, at least. It was Dave's idea. See how he gets on. He can always go to the FE College to do his A Levels.'

'Right.' I thought it was a very good idea, though it wasn't my business to say so.

'Quiet lounge in here.' Ed led the way into the walnut parlour. 'Nicki reckons some guests will prefer a bit more privacy.'

The sewing room door was wide open, so I walked through to see what was in there now. The table and chairs had gone, replaced by two sofas. The roll-top desk was still in the corner. The top was open, and pens and postcards lay ready for any guest who fancied writing something so retro.

Ed looked around. 'Josh says anyone who wants to use a computer will have their own laptop or tablet. No one prints things much these days, he says, and if they want to, the printer in reception is wireless. We'll see.'

I gestured towards the mantelpiece. 'I see you kept the picture.'

Ed laughed. 'It's certainly a conversation piece. Those books fetched even more than Jude imagined. We sent that ghastly hand to a forensics institute though.' He shuddered at the memory.

'Good thing we found the key to that desk.' I kept my eyes on the picture, in case Ed saw anything to arouse his suspicions in my face.

The day after the fire, I'd suggested we search the house for whatever supposed inheritance Aiden had been after. Nathan Ditchfield had confessed that much, once his broken arm had been set and painkillers were making him talkative. Sergeant Smith had rung Ed to let him know. Ed had called me to ask if I had any ideas what this mysterious treasure could be.

When we reached the sewing room, I had wondered aloud if the painting might be what Aiden wanted. Perhaps it was valuable. Ed had been dubious, since it wasn't even signed. So I suggested seeing if there was a label or any useful information on the back.

As soon as we'd got it off the wall, with each of us taking a side, Ed had seen the key hanging on the picture hook. He'd remembered that the desk right there in the corner was still locked, without any prompting from me.

I looked at the picture. I was glad it was still here in the house. I was also having second thoughts about the story it told. Maybe the Hunter had come to the swan maiden's rescue.

Ed's mobile phone chimed. I hadn't even thought to check mine. Now that I did, I saw that I had a good, strong signal.

'David got the phones sorted out then.'

Ed looked up from reading his message. 'The landlines and the broadband. The mobile reception sorted itself out somehow. Excuse me, can I leave you to it? You know your way around. Some of the London guests are nearly here.'

'I'll be fine,' I assured him. 'I'll see you at dinner.'

Ed ran a hand through his hair. 'Nicki says you're bringing a plus-one. Anyone we know?'

I guessed Nicki must have asked him to ask me. 'Fin Wicken.'

'Right. Is she...?'

'Staying at the Whittle and Dub,' I said, before he could embarrass us both.

'Right.' He held up his phone. 'Better see to this.'

'Right.' I let him leave, took another look at the picture and went upstairs to find my room.

The corridor running around the first floor was deserted. My footsteps sounded loud even with the runner carpeting the floorboards. I paused at the corner to see if I could hear any other steps, or maybe catch a glimpse of Everard or Mary Anne.

Nothing happened, so I carried on walking. Named rather than numbered, the Hazel Room was certainly luxurious, with crisp white sheets and soft towels, and solid wood furniture made by a craftsman who knew his trade. The Franklins' windfall from the occult books had been put to good use.

Since I had a phone signal, I called Fin's mobile number. She'd said she'd get here around the same time as me.

She answered at once. 'Hi, where are you? I'm already here.'

'At Brightwell. I was thinking, I'd like to have a look at the lake. We've got plenty of time before dinner, if I come over and pick you up.'

'Okay. See you soon.'

I headed straight out and took the fastest route to the pub. That took me past the Lamp Acre, where the burned wreckage had been cleared away. At the inquest, the fire investigator had referred to the earlier police search report noting the number of candles in the caravan. Apparently chemical analysis of the debris showed traces of the same accelerant that had been used to commit arson in the Broad. The working theory was that Aiden had somehow got some of that onto his clothes. He hadn't realised until he got too close to a naked flame when he came back to the caravan. Though no one had any idea why he had done that.

I still wondered where Mungo Peploe's books had got to. No one had ever mentioned them, and I couldn't find a reason to ask. After all, after searching the woods for Aiden, I'd arrived at the Lamp Acre to find the caravan was already an inferno. That's what my statement said.

Rufus was going to plant trees between the lane and the river. Fin had told me that David Franklin's consultant had finally established that Brightwell had owned the land all along. Constance Sutton's husband had bought it from the Diocese of Gloucester the day before he had broken his neck falling off his horse. No one here knew what he'd done, so no one had realised that the paperwork confirming the sale had somehow gone astray.

Fin was waiting for me in the car park again. We drove down the main road, turned off onto the grassy light and parked by the path to the spring. As we walked through the silver birches towards the water, I could feel the contentment in the trees.

'Good afternoon, Daniel. Fin.' Sineya appeared beside us, in her ethereal form. It looked as if she'd abandoned draperies in favour of that short tunic for good. 'How are you both?'

'I'm very well,' Fin assured her.

'I'm okay,' I said severely, 'considering your grandmother's still furious with me.'

Initially Frai had made my life a sodding misery when Sineya announced she was going to stay at Brightwell. The Landy wouldn't start six mornings out of seven, my tools blunted or broke, and every piece of woodwork I put my hand to ended up a disaster. I got so pissed off that I seriously considered leaving Blithehurst.

Eventually I asked for Eleanor's help instead. I don't know what she said to the old dryad, but Frai stopped tormenting me. Now I just had to put up with her scowling whenever I met her walking through the woods. Asca simply looked dreadfully disappointed in me, on the rare occasions I saw her these days.

'She'll get over it, in time,' Sineya said, unconcerned, as we reached the grassy slope and the spring.

'Dryad time or human time?' My mother could hold grudges for centuries.

Sineya didn't answer. She pointed out over the lake. 'Look.'

I saw ducks, and some swans that I hoped weren't related to Fin. I also saw someone swimming, far out in the deepest part of the lake. Someone, or something? Whatever that was, it wasn't human, not with silvery-blue skin.

Before I could ask Sineya what was going on, the naiad I'd first met in Derbyshire appeared. She looked wholly human, in a guise I'd seen before: a lithe woman around my own age, with long brown hair, wearing jeans and a T-shirt. She looked totally harmless, unless you'd met a naiad before.

'Good afternoon, Daniel.'

'Hello, Kalei.' I think I managed to hide my surprise. 'It's been a while.'

'So it has.' She waved at whoever was swimming in the lake. 'Finele, I am very pleased to meet you.'

'The pleasure is all mine.' Fin was better at faking calmness than me.

Kalei slid me a sideways turquoise glance. 'Your friend has a real feeling for water. Whereas I gather you can still barely not-drown whenever you're not on dry land.'

I could see Fin wanted to ask what the naiad knew about her, and what she knew about what had happened to the nix. Clearly, she also knew the risks of asking questions. The naiad would ask for favours in return for any information.

I pointed across the water. 'Who's your friend?'

Kalei looked a little irritated that I wasn't playing her game, but she answered readily enough. 'That's Tireis. You would call her my niece. These waters are hers now.'

Her confident declaration surprised me into an incautious question. 'What does the Hunter think about that?'

'These woods are not his home.' Sineya's laugh suggested a child should know this. 'He comes and goes as his presence is needed, when and wherever he sees fit.'

'Thanks to you, he knows these woods are once again in good hands.' Kalei smiled at me with what looked like genuine approval. Her gaze took in Fin as well. 'So are these waters, now that the flow of life and luck is restored.'

'That's very good to know.' And I reckoned we should quit while we were ahead. I held out my hand to Fin. 'Now that we know all's well here, we'll leave you in peace.'

'Come back any time,' Sineya said warmly.

Kalei didn't say anything, but as we walked back to the Land Rover, I heard the naiad's silvery laughter through the trees. Fin didn't say anything until we got into the vehicle.

'That was unexpected,' she said with feeling as she closed her door. 'Do you suppose they've been watching me and

Blanche, when we've been here supervising the work putting in the new culverts and soakaways?'

'It's probably safest to assume so.' I started the engine. 'Still, they seem to like you.'

'Right.' Fin clearly knew how that could cut both ways.

We drove back to the main road in thoughtful silence. At the junction, I paused and looked at her. 'What are we going to do now?'

'Take me back to the pub,' she said with sudden decision. 'I'm going to ring my mum. She'll want to hear about this new naiad turning up.'

'Fair enough.' I couldn't help feeling a bit disappointed. 'When shall I pick you up for dinner?'

'I've already booked a taxi, so we can both have a few glasses of wine.' Fin smiled at me. 'Then we can plan what we're doing tomorrow. It'll be fun being here as a tourist instead of for work.'

'That sounds good to me.'

After I left her at the pub, I went back to Brightwell and found a whole load of guests had arrived to fill up the great hall. Since I don't particularly enjoy having the same superficial conversations over and over with people I don't know, I was ready to escape to my room until it was dinner time.

Only Nicki Franklin saw me and insisted we sit down so she could tell me about the Bourton Abroad Residents Association that had been set up after the May Day fire. All sorts of improvements were planned.

By the time she had given me every last detail, David Franklin had arrived, so at least he was someone familiar I could talk to. Given his car and his watch, I half expected him to arrive with some trophy wife on his arm. I was wrong. Lydia was a no-nonsense South Londoner dressed with understated class. She was clearly his equal and partner in every sense.

Ben Beauchene was the next person I found to talk to, until waiters and waitresses began circulating with trays of glasses and canapés. I realised I had better go and put on something smarter for dinner. As far as I'm concerned, that meant the formal trousers I wear about twice a year, a new shirt with the packet creases ironed out and the tie I don't wear to court or to funerals. As always, I found the sensation of wearing a collar and buttoned cuffs as welcome as wearing a straitjacket.

When I came back downstairs, I found that more people I knew had arrived, including Geoff Kemble with his wife, as well as Bill and Martha. Both the Dellys looked very well indeed, and Martha was soon telling tales of the house in its heyday, without mentioning any murders. Rufus looked surprisingly relaxed in a suit. He was sitting talking to Jude Oxway, who was holding hands with the amiable bearded man beside her.

Ben Beauchene was talking to Fin. She looked absolutely gorgeous in a lacy lavender dress and dangly silver earrings. Ben was doing his very best to charm her. While she was being perfectly nice to him, I could see he was getting nowhere fast. That was fine with me.

The dinner was three superb courses, and even better wine. David and Ed made short, gracious speeches, thanking the people who'd turned their dream for Brightwell's future into a reality. They proposed a toast to Great-Uncle Cecil, to celebrate the fact that his legacy was now secure. I felt a breeze on the back of my neck and turned to catch a glimpse of the Green Man's reflection in the window. That was enough to tell me that he agreed.

Port and petit-fours were served, followed by coffee in the great hall. People who were staying in the hotel began to drift off to bed. Josh Franklin started calling taxis for the locals who were going home.

I walked Finele outside to get her taxi back to the pub. I'd much rather have taken her up to my room, but we were spending the weekend together and I could look forward to that. As far as doing more than talking and walking and sharing jokes and meals went, I could be patient.

Things that are worthwhile are worth waiting for. Dryads take the long view, and I am a dryad's son.

Acknowledgements

Once again, producing this book is a joint enterprise. As ever, I am tremendously grateful to Cheryl Morgan, for all that she does as the driving force and technical expert behind Wizard's Tower Press.

My thanks go to Toby Selwyn who has scrutinised the text as my editor once again, bringing his keen eye and impeccable skills to flag up and smooth out any awkwardnesses that might mar your enjoyment.

Ben Baldwin had a very different challenge with the artwork this time round. Instead of bringing his skills and imagination to an iconic image, he has created this new vision of an ancient myth, and I am more thrilled with it than words can convey.

I am indebted to Liz Williams, talented SF author and expert on Wicca and the occult, for reading the final draft at my request, to check that those particular aspects of this story are plausible, and to offer me a perspective on the book from the pagan community. Any errors or infelicities that remain are my responsibility. Incidentally, I highly recommend Liz's fiction, and also the two volumes (so far) of Diary of a Witchcraft Shop from Newcon Press.

Lastly, I want to acknowledge the part that my first literary agent, Maggie Noach, played in this story. As well as representing my epic fantasy fiction, Maggie encouraged me to take my writing in other directions. She knew and loved the Cotswolds, where I live, and we discussed the sense of history and folklore that's so embedded in the local woods and villages. I wrote a draft of a novel about a country house being turned into a hotel, and a visitor from London who gets drawn into its secrets, that may or may not include the supernatural. We were discussing how to improve on that when all of us who knew and admired Maggie were devastated by her untimely death on 2006. Over the next few years, I looked at the novel a few times, and tried a couple of different approaches, but somehow, whatever I ended up with was never quite right. Looking at the dates on the files on the hard drive, I see I last revised it in 2010 before setting it aside.

The success of The Green Man's Heir meant a great many people were asking hopefully about a sequel. Frankly, I was at a loss until quite suddenly one day, I remembered those drafts were still tucked away in my computer archive. I found I had a detailed setting, background characters and a framework of events that I could use for a whole new story, where Daniel has no doubt about the supernatural threat to this hotel project. Once I stared writing, everything came together in a way that my attempts to rework that early draft novel never had. I only wish that Maggie was still here to see the end result. I have no doubt what she would say. This story goes to show that no writing is ever wasted.

About the Author

Juliet E McKenna is a British fantasy author, living in the Cotswolds. She has always been fascinated by myth and history, other worlds and other peoples. After studying Greek and Roman history and literature at Oxford University, she worked in personnel management before a career change to combine motherhood and book-selling. Her debut novel, *The Thief's Gamble*, first of *The Tales of Einarinn* was published in 1999, followed by *The Aldabreshin Compass* sequence and *The Chronicles of the Lescari Revolution*. Her fifteenth epic fantasy novel, *Defiant Peaks*, concluded *The Hadrumal Crisis* trilogy.

She reviews for the web and print magazines notably *Interzone*, and promotes SF&Fantasy by blogging on book trade issues. She also teaches creative writing from time to time, and writes diverse shorter fiction, from epic fantasy to forays into dark fantasy, steampunk and science fiction. Recent stories include contributions to the themed anthologies *Alternate Peace*, *Soot and Steel*, and *The Scent of Tears (Tales of the Apt)*. *The Green Man's Heir* was her first modern fantasy, and *The Green Man's Foe* is the sequel. Who's to say what will come next?

www.julietemckenna.com

The Tales of Einarinn

1. The Thief's Gamble (1998)
2. The Swordsman's Oath (1999)
3. The Gambler's Fortune (2000)
4. The Warrior's Bond (2001)
5. The Assassin's Edge (2002)

The Aldabreshin Compass

1. The Southern Fire (2003)
2. Northern Storm (2004)
3. Western Shore (2005)
4. Eastern Tide (2006)

Turns & Chances (2004)

The Chronicles of the Lescari Revolution

1. Irons in the Fire (2009)
2. Blood in the Water (2010)
3. Banners in The Wind (2010)

The Wizard's Coming (2011)

The Hadrumal Crisis

1. Dangerous Waters (2011)
2. Darkening Skies (2012)
3. Defiant Peaks (2012)

A Few Further Tales of Einarinn (2012) (ebook from Wizards Tower Press)

Challoner, Murray & Balfour: Monster Hunters at Law (2014) (ebook from Wizards Tower Press)

Shadow Histories of the River Kingdom (2016) (Wizards Tower Press)

The Green Man's Heir (2018) (Wizards Tower Press)

CPSIA information can be obtained
at www.ICGtesting.com
Printed in the USA
LVHW031736200120
644174LV00002B/449